Maria Edgeworth, Richard Lovell Edgeworth, William Croome

Popular Tales

Maria Edgeworth, Richard Lovell Edgeworth, William Croome

Popular Tales

ISBN/EAN: 9783337344290

Printed in Europe, USA, Canada, Australia, Japan

Cover: Foto ©Andreas Hilbeck / pixelio.de

More available books at **www.hansebooks.com**

POPULAR TALES

By

THE GRATEFUL NEGRO

MARIA EDGEWORTH

BY

MARIA EDGEWORTH

WITH ORIGINAL DESIGNS BY CROOME

A New Edition.

PHILADELPHIA
DUFFIELD ASHMEAD
No. 724 CHESTNUT STREET
1867

PREFACE.

Some author says that a good book needs no apology; and as a preface is usually an apology, a book enters into the world with a better grace without one. I, however, appeal to those readers who are not gluttons, but epicures, in literature, whether they do not wish to see the bill of fare. I appeal to monthly critics whether a preface that gives a view of the pretensions of the writer is not a good thing. The author may overvalue his subject, and very naturally may overrate the manner in which it is treated; but still he will explain his views, and facilitate the useful and necessary art which the French call *reading with the thumb*. We call this *hunting a book*,—a term certainly invented by a sportsman. I leave the reader to choose which he pleases, while I lay before him the contents and design of these volumes.

Burke supposes that there are eighty thousand readers in Great Britain,—nearly one-hundredth part of its inhabitants! Out of these we may calculate that ten thousand are nobility, clergy, or gentlemen of the learned professions. Of seventy thousand readers which remain, there are many who might be amused and instructed by books which were not

professedly adapted to the classes that have been
enumerated.   With this view the following volumes
have been composed.   The title of POPULAR TALES
has been chosen, not as a presumptuous and prema-
ture claim to popularity, but from the wish that they
may be current beyond circles which are sometimes
exclusively considered as polite.

The art of printing has opened to all classes of
people various new channels of entertainment and
information.   Among the ancients wisdom required
austere manners and a length of beard to command
attention; but in our days, instruction in the dress of
innocent amusement is not denied admittance among
the wise and good of all ranks.   It is therefore hoped
that a succession of stories adapted to different ages,
sexes, and situations in life will not be rejected by
the public unless they offend against morality, tire
by their sameness, or disgust by their imitation of
other writers.

RICHARD LOVELL EDGEWORTH.

Edgeworth's Town Feb. 1804.

CONTENTS

MURAD THE UNLUCKY.

CHAPTER I.

It is well known that the grand seignior amuses himself by going at night, in disguise, through the streets of Constantinople; as the caliph Haroun Alraschid used formerly to do in Bagdad.

One moonlight night, accompanied by his grand vizier, he traversed several of the principal streets of the city, without seeing any thing remarkable. At length, as they were passing a rope-maker's, the sultan recollected the Arabian story of Cogia-Hassan Alhabal, the rope-maker, and his two friends Saad and Saadi, who differed so much in their opinion concerning the influence of fortune over human affairs.

"What is your opinion on this subject?" said the grand seignior to his vizier.

"I am inclined, please your majesty," replied the vizier, "to think that success in the world de-

pends more upon prudence than upon what is called
luck, or fortune."

" And I," said the sultan, " am persuaded that
fortune does more for men than prudence.   Do
you not every day hear of persons who are said to
be fortunate or unfortunate?   How comes it that
this opinion should prevail among men, if it be not
justified by experience ?"

" It is not for me to dispute with your majesty,"
replied the prudent vizier.

" Speak your mind freely ; I desire and command it," said the sultan.

" Then I am of opinion," answered the vizier,
" that people are often led to believe others fortunate, or unfortunate, merely because they only
know the general outline of their histories ; and are
ignorant of the incidents and events in which they
have shown prudence or imprudence. I have heard,
for instance, that there are at present in this city
two men, who are remarkable for their good and
bad fortune : one is called *Murad the Unlucky*,
and the other *Saladin the Lucky*.   Now I am inclined to think, if we could hear their stories, we
should find that one is a prudent and the other an
imprudent character."

" Where do these men live ?" interrupted the sultan. "I will hear their histories, from their own lips, before I sleep."

"Murad the Unlucky lives in the next square," said the vizier.

The sultan desired to go thither instantly. Scarcely had they entered the square, when they heard the cry of loud lamentations. They followed the sound till they came to a house of which the door was open ; and where there was a man tearing his turban, and weeping bitterly. They asked the cause of his distress, and he pointed to the fragments of a china vase, which lay on the pavement at his door.

"This seems undoubtedly to be beautiful china," said the sultan, taking up one of the broken pieces ; "but can the loss of a china vase be the cause of such violent grief and despair ?"

"Ah, gentlemen," said the owner of the vase, suspending his lamentations, and looking at the dress of the pretended merchants, "I see that you are strangers : you do not know how much cause I have for grief and despair! You do not know that you are speaking to Murad the Unlucky! Were you to hear all the unfortunate accidents that have happened to me, from the time I was born till this instant, you would perhaps pity me, and acknowledge I have just cause for despair."

Curiosity was strongly expressed by the sultan ;
and the hope of obtaining sympathy inclined Murad
to gratify it, by the recital of his adventures.
" Gentlemen," said he, " I scarcely dare invite you
into the house of such an unlucky being as I am ;
but, if you will venture to take a night's lodging
under my roof, you shall hear at your leisure the
story of my misfortunes."

The sultan and the vizier excused themselves
from spending the night with Murad ; saying that
they were obliged to proceed to their khan, where
they should be expected by their companions ; but
they begged permission to repose themselves for
half an hour in his house, and besought him to relate the history of his life, if it would not renew his
grief too much to recollect his misfortunes.

Few men are so miserable as not to like to talk
of their misfortunes, where they have, or where
they think they have, any chance of obtaining compassion.   As soon as the pretended merchants were
seated, Murad began his story in the following manner :

" My father was a mercham of this city.   The
night before I was born, he dreamed that I came
into the world with the head of a dog and the tail
of a dragon ; and that, in haste to conceal my de-

formity, he rolled me up in a piece of linen, which unluckily proved to be the grand seignior's turban; who, enraged at his insolence in touching his turban, commanded that his head should be struck off.

" My father awaked before he lost his head; but not before he had half lost his wits from the terror of his dream. He considered it as a warning sent from above, and consequently determined to avoid the sight of me. He would not stay to see whether I should really be born with the head of a dog and the tail of a dragon; but he set out the next morning on a voyage to Aleppo.

" He was absent for upwards of seven years; and during that time my education was totally neglected. One day, I inquired from my mother why I had been named Murad the Unlucky? She told me that this name was given to me in consequence of my father's dream; but she added, that perhaps it might be forgotten, if I proved fortunate in my future life. My nurse, a very old woman, who was present, shook her head, with a look which I shall never forget, and whispered to my mother, loud enough for me to hear, ' Unlucky he was, and is, and ever will be. Those that are born to ill luck cannot help themselves: nor can any but the great prophet Mahomet himself do any

thing for them. It is a folly for an unlucky per
son to stri ve with their fate; it is better to yield to
it at once.'

" This speech made a terrible impression upon
me, young as I then was ; and every accident that
happened to me afterward confirmed my belief in
my nurse's prognostic. I was in my eighth year
when my father returned from abroad. The year
after he came home my brother Saladin was born,
who was named Saladin the Lucky, because the
day he was born a vessel freighted with rich merchandise for my father arrived safely in port.

" I will not weary you with a relation of all the
little instances of good fortune by which my brother
Saladin was distinguished, even during his childhood. As he grew up, his success in every thing
he undertook was as remarkable as my ill luck in
all that I attempted. From the time the rich vessel arrived, we lived in splendour : and the supposed prosperous state of my father's affairs was of
course attributed to the influence of my brother
Saladin's happy destiny.

" When Saladin was about twenty my father
was taken dangerously ill ; and as he felt that he
should not recover, he sent for my brother to the
side of his bed, and, to his great surprise, informed

him that the magnificence in which we had lived
had exhausted all his wealth ; that his affairs were
in the greatest disorder; for, having trusted to the
hope of continual success, he had embarked in projects beyond his powers.

" The sequel was, he had nothing remaining to
leave to his children but two large china vases, remarkable for their beauty, but still more valuable
on account of certain verses inscribed upon them
in an unknown character, which were supposed to
operate as a talisman or charm in favour of their
possessors.

" Both these vases my father bequeathed to my
brother Saladin ; declaring he could not venture to
leave either of them to me, because I was so unlucky that I should inevitably break it. After his
death, however, my brother Saladin, who was blest
with a generous temper, gave me my choice of the
two vases ; and endeavoured to raise my spirits,
by repeating frequently that he had no faith either
in good fortune or ill fortune.

" I could not be of this opinion ; though I felt
and acknowledged his kindness in trying to persuade me out of my settled melancholy. I knew
it was in vain for me to exert myself, because I
was sure that, do what I would, I should still be

2

Murad the Unlucky.   My brother, on the contrary, was nowise cast down, even by the poverty in which my father left us : he said he was sure he should find some means of maintaining himself, and so he did.

" On examining our china vases he found in them a powder of a bright scarlet colour ; and it occurred to him that it would make a fine dye.   He tried it, and after some trouble it succeeded to admiration.

" During my father's lifetime, my mother had been supplied with rich dresses by one of the merchants who was employed by the ladies of the grand seignior's seraglio.   My brother had done this merchant some trifling favours ; and, upon application to him, he readily engaged to recommend the new scarlet dye.   Indeed it was so beautiful that the moment it was seen it was preferred to every other colour.   Saladin's shop was soon crowded with customers ; and his winning manners and pleasant conversation were almost as advantageous to him as his scarlet dye.   On the contrary, I observed that the first glance at my melancholy countenance was sufficient to disgust every one who saw me.   I perceived this plainly ; and it only confirmed me the more in my belief in my own evil destiny.

" It happened one day that a lady, richly appa-
relled, and attended by two female slaves, came to
my brother's house to make some purchases. He
was out, and I alone was left to attend to the shop.
After she had looked over some goods, she chanced
to see my china vase, which was in the room.   She
took a prodigious fancy to it, and offered me any
price if I would part with it; but this I declined
doing, because I believed that I should draw down
upon my head some dreadful calamity if I volun-
tarily relinquished the talisman.   Irritated by my
refusal, the lady, according to the custom of her
sex, became more resolute in her purpose; but
neither entreaties nor money could change my determination.   Provoked beyond measure at my obstinacy, as she called it, she left the house.

" On my brother's return I related to him what
had happened, and expected that he would have
praised me for my prudence : but, on the contrary,
he blamed me for the superstitious value I set upon
the verses on my vase; and observed that it would
be the height of folly to lose a certain means of advancing my fortune, for the uncertain hope of magical protection   I could not bring myself to be of
his opinion · I had not the courage to follow the
advice he gave.   The next day the lady returned,

and my brother sold his vase to her for ten thousand pieces of gold. This money he laid out in the most advantageous manner, by purchasing a new stock of merchandise. I repented when it was too late ; but I believe it is part of the fatality attending certain persons, that they cannot decide rightly at the proper moment. When the opportunity has been lost, I have always regretted that I did not do exactly the contrary to what I had previously determined upon. Often, while I was hesitating, the favourable moment passed.* Now this is what I call being unlucky. But to proceed with my story.

" The lady who bought my brother Saladin's vase was the favourite of the sultan, and all-powerful in the seraglio. Her dislike to me, in consequence of my opposition to her wishes, was so violent, that she refused to return to my brother's house while I remained there. He was unwilling to part with me ; but I could not bear to be the ruin of so good a brother. Without telling him my design, I left his house, careless of what should become of me. Hunger, however, soon compelled me to think of some immediate mode of obtaining relief. I sat

---

* " Whom the gods wish to destroy they first deprive of understanding."

down upon a stone before the door of a baker's shop: the smell of hot bread tempted me in, and with a feeble voice I demanded charity.

" The master baker gave me as much bread as I could eat, upon condition that I should change dresses with him, and carry the rolls for him through the city this day. To this I readily consented; but I had soon reason to repent of my compliance. Indeed, if my ill luck had not, as usual, deprived me at the critical moment of memory and judgment, I should never have complied with the baker's treacherous proposal. For some time before the people of Constantinople had been much dissatisfied with the weight and quality of the bread furnished by the bakers. This species of discontent has often been the sure forerunner of an insurrection; and in these disturbances the master bakers frequently lose their lives. All these circumstances I knew; but they did not occur to my memory when they might have been useful.

" I changed dresses with the baker; but scarcely had I proceeded through the adjoining street with my rolls, before the mob began to gather round me, with reproaches and execrations. The crowd pursued me even to the gates of the grand seignior's palace; and the grand vizier, alarmed at their vio-

2 *

lence, sent out an order to have my head struck off; the usual remedy in such cases being to strike off the baker's head.

" I now fell upon my knees, and protested I was not the baker for whom they took me; that I had no connexion with him; and that I had never furnished the people of Constantinople with bread that was not weight. I declared I had merely changed clothes with a master baker for this day; and that I should not have done so, but for the evil destiny which governs all my actions. Some of the mob exclaimed that I deserved to lose my head for my folly; but others took pity on me, and while the officer who was sent to execute the vizier's order turned to speak to some of the noisy rioters, those who were touched by my misfortune opened a passage for me through the crowd, and thus favoured I effected my escape.

" I quitted Constantinople : my vase I had left in the care of my brother. At some miles' distance from the city I overtook a party of soldiers. I joined them; and learning that they were going to embark with the rest of the grand seignior's army for Egypt, I resolved to accompany them. If it be, thought I, the will of Mahomet that I should perish, the sooner I meet my fate the better. The despondency into which I was sunk was attended by so great a degree of indolence that I scarcely would take the necessary means to preserve my existence. During our passage to Egypt, I sat all day long upon the deck of the vessel, smoking my pipe ; and I am convinced that if a storm had risen, as I expected, I should not have taken my pipe from my mouth : nor should I have handled a rope to save myself from destruction. Such is the effect of that species of resignation or torpor, whichever you please to call it, to which my strong belief in *fatality* had reduced my mind.

" We landed, however, safely, contrary to my melancholy forebodings. By a trifling accident, not worth relating, I was detained longer than any of my companions in the vessel when we disembarked ; and I did not arrive at the camp at El Arish till late at night. It was moonlight, and I could see the whole scene distinctly. There was a vast number of small tents scattered over a desert of white sand ; a few date-trees were visible at a distance ; all was gloomy, and all still ; no sound was to be heard but that of the camels feeding near the tents ; and as I walked on I met with no human creature.

" My pipe was now out, and I quickened my

pace a little towards a fire, which I saw near one of the tents.   As I proceeded, my eye was caught by something sparkling in the sand : it was a ring. I picked it up, and put it on my finger, resolving to give it to the public crier the next morning, who might find out its rightful owner : but by ill luck I put it on my little finger, for which it was much too large ; and as I hastened towards the fire to light my pipe, I dropped the ring.   I stooped to search for it among the provender on which a mule was feeding ; and the cursed animal gave me so violent a kick on the head that I could not help roaring aloud.

" My cries awakened those who slept in the tent near which the mule was feeding.   Provoked at being disturbed, the soldiers were ready enough to think ill of me ; and they took it for granted that I was a thief, who had stolen the ring I pretended to have just found.   The ring was taken from me by force ; and the next day I was bastinadoed for having found it : the officer persisting in the belief that stripes would make me confess where I had concealed certain other articles of value, which had lately been missed in the camp.   All this was the consequence of my being in a hurry to light my pipe, and of my having put the ring on a finger that was too little for it; which no one but Murad the Unlucky would have done.

"When I was able to walk again after my wounds were healed, I went into one of the tents distinguished by a red flag, having been told that these were coffee-houses. While I was drinking coffee I heard a stranger near me complaining that he had not been able to recover a valuable ring he had lost; although he had caused his loss to be published for three days by the public crier, offering a reward of two hundred sequins to whoever should restore it. I guessed that this was the very ring which I had unfortunately found. I addressed myself to the stranger, and promised to point out to him the person who had forced it from me. The stranger recovered his ring; and being convinced that I had acted honestly, he made me a present of two hundred sequins as some amends for the punishment which I had unjustly suffered on his account.

"Now you would imagine that this purse of gold was advantageous to me: far the contrary; it was the cause of new misfortunes.

"One night, when I thought that the soldiers who were in the same tent with me were all fast asleep, I indulged myself in the pleasure of counting

my treasure. The next day I was invited by my
companions to drink sherbet with them. What
they mixed with the sherbet which I drank I know
not : but I could not resist the drowsiness it brought
on. I fell into a profound slumber ; and, when I
awoke, I found myself lying under a date-tree, at
some distance from the camp.

" The first thing I thought of, when I came to
my recollection, was my purse of sequins. The
purse I found still safe in my girdle ; but on opening it, I perceived that it was filled with pebbles,
and not a single sequin was left. I had no doubt that
I had been robbed by the soldiers with whom I had
drunk sherbet ; and I am certain that some of them
must have been awake the night I counted my money : otherwise, as I had never trusted the secret
of my riches to any one, they could not have suspected me of possessing any property ; for, ever
since I kept company with them, I had appeared to
be in great indigence.

" I applied in vain to the superior officers for re-
dress : the soldiers protested they were innocent ;
no positive proof appeared against them, and I
gained nothing by my complaint but ridicule and
ill-will. I called myself, in the first transport of
my grief, by that name which, since my arrival in

Egypt, I had avoided to pronounce : I called my-self Murad the Unlucky ! The name and the story ran through the camp ; and I was accosted after-ward, very frequently, by this appellation. Some indeed varied their wit, by calling me Murad with the purse of pebbles.

" All that I had yet suffered is nothing compared to my succeeding misfortunes.

" It was the custom at this time in the Turkish camp for the soldiers to amuse themselves with firing at a mark. The superior officers remon-strated against this dangerous practice,* but inef-fectually. Sometimes a party of soldiers would stop firing for a few minutes, after a message was brought them from their commanders ; and then they would begin again, in defiance of all orders. Such was the want of discipline in our army, that this disobedience went unpunished. In the mean time, the frequency of the danger made most men totally regardless of it. I have seen tents pierced with bullets, in which parties were quietly seated smoking their pipes ; while those without were pre-paring to take fresh aim at the red flag on the top.

" This apathy proceeded, in some, from the un-

* Antis's Observations on the Manners and Customs of the Egyptians.

conquerable indolence of body ; in others, from the
intoxication produced by the fumes of tobacco and
opium ; but in most of my brother Turks it arose
from the confidence the belief in predestination inspired.   When a bullet killed one of their companions, they only observed, scarcely taking the
pipes from their mouths, ' Our hour is not yet
come ; it is not the will of Mahomet that we should
fall.'

"I own that this rash security appeared to me,
at first, surprising ; but it soon ceased to strike me
with wonder ; and it even tended to confirm my
favourite opinion, that some were born to good and
some to evil fortune.   I became almost as careless
as my companions, from following the same course
of reasoning.   It is not, thought I, in the power of
human prudence to avert the stroke of destiny.   I
shall perhaps die to-morrow ; let me therefore
enjoy to-day.

"I now made it my study, every day, to procure
as much amusement as possible.   My poverty, as
you will imagine, restricted me from indulgence
and excess ; but I soon found means to spend what
did not actually belong to me.   There were certain
Jews, who were followers of the camp, and who,
calculating on the probability of victory for our

troops, advanced money to the soldiers ; for which they engaged to pay these usurers exorbitant interest. The Jew to whom I applied traded with me also upon the belief that my brother Saladin, with whose character and circumstances he was acquainted, would pay my debts, if I should fall. With the money I raised from the Jew I continually bought coffee and opium, of which I grew immoderately fond. In the delirium it created, I forgot all my misfortunes, all fear of the future.

" One day, when I had raised my spirits by an unusual quantity of opium, I was strolling through the camp, sometimes singing, sometimes dancing, like a madman, and repeating that I was not now Murad the Unlucky. While these words were on my lips, a friendly spectator, who was in possession of his sober senses, caught me by the arm, and attempted to drag me from the place where I was exposing myself. ' Do you not see,' said he, ' those soldiers, who are firing at a mark ? I saw one of them, just now, deliberately taking aim at your turban ; and, observe, he is now reloading his piece.' My ill luck prevailed even at this instant, the only instant in my life when I defied its power. I struggled with my adviser, repeating, ' I am not the wretch you take me for ; I am not Murad the

3

Unlucky.' He fled from the danger himself: I remained, and in a few seconds afterward a ball
reached me, and I fell senseless on the sand.

" The ball was cut out of my body by an awkward surgeon, who gave me ten times more pain
than was necessary. He was particularly hurried
at this time, because the army had just received orders to march in a few hours, and all was confusion
in the camp. My wound was excessively painful,
and the fear of being left behind with those who
were deemed incurable added to my torments. Perhaps, if I had kept myself quiet, I might have escaped some of the evils I afterward endured; but,
as I have repeatedly told you, gentlemen, it was
my ill fortune never to be able to judge what was
best to be done till the time for prudence was past.

" During that day, when my fever was at the
height, and when my orders were to keep my bed,
contrary to my natural habits of indolence, I rose a
hundred times and went out of my tent, in the very
heat of the day, to satisfy my curiosity as to the
number of tents which had not been struck, and of
the soldiers who had not yet marched. The orders
to march were tardily obeyed; and many hours
elapsed before our encampment was raised. Had
I submitted to my surgeon's orders, I might have

been in a state to accompany the most dilatory of the stragglers; I could have borne, perhaps, the slow motion of a litter, on which some of the sick were transported; but in the evening, when the surgeon came to dress my wounds, he found me in such a situation that it was scarcely possible to remove me.

" He desired a party of soldiers, who were left to bring up the rear, to call for me the next morning. They did so; but they wanted to put me upon the mule which I recollected, by a white streak on its back, to be the cursed animal that had kicked me while I was looking for the ring. I could not be prevailed upon to go upon this unlucky animal. I tried to persuade the soldiers to carry me, and they took me a little way; but, soon growing weary of their burden, they laid me down on the sand, pretending that they were going to fill a skin with water at a spring they had discovered, and bade me lie still, and wait for their return.

" I waited and waited, longing for the water to moisten my parched lips; but no water came—no soldiers returned; and there I lay, for several hours, expecting every moment to breathe my last. I made no effort to move, for I was now convinced my hour was come; and that it was the will of Mahomet that I should perish in this miserable man-

ner, and lie unburied like a dog; a death, thought
I, worthy of Murad the Unlucky.

" My forebodings were not this time just ; a de-
tachment of English soldiers passed near the place
where I lay ; my groans were heard by them, and
they humanely came to my assistance. They carried me with them, dressed my wound, and treated
me with the utmost tenderness. Christians though
they were, I must acknowledge that I had reason
to love them better than any of the followers of Mahomet, my good brother only excepted.

" Under their care I recovered ; but scarcely
had I regained my strength before I fell into new
disasters. It was hot weather, and my thirst was
excessive. I went out, with a party, in hopes of
finding a spring of water. The English soldiers
began to dig for a well, in a place pointed out to
them by one of their men of science. I was not inclined to such hard labour, but preferred sauntering
on in search of a spring. I saw at a distance something that looked like a pool of water ; and I pointed
it out to my companions. Their man of science
warned me, by his interpreter, not to trust to this
deceitful appearance ; for that such were common
in this country, and that, when I came close to the
spot, I should find no water there. He added, that

it was at a greater distance than I imagined; and that I should, in all probability, be lost in the desert, if I attempted to follow this phantom.

" I was so unfortunate as not to attend to his advice: I set out in pursuit of this accursed delusion, which assuredly was the work of evil spirits, who clouded my reason, and allured me into their dominion. I went on, hour after hour, in expectation continually of reaching the object of my wishes; but it fled faster than I pursued, and I discovered at last that the Englishman, who had doubtless gained his information from the people of the country, was right; and that the shining appearance which I had taken for water was a mere deception.

" I was now exhausted with fatigue: I looked back in vain after the companions I had left; I could see neither men, animals, nor any trace of vegetation in the sandy desert. I had no resource but, weary as I was, to measure back my footsteps, which were imprinted in the sand.

" I slowly and sorrowfully traced them as my guides in this unknown land. Instead of yielding to my indolent inclinations, I ought, however, to have made the best of my way back before the evening breeze sprang up. I felt the breeze rising, and, unconscious of my danger, I rejoiced, and opened

3 *

my boson to meet it; bu. what was my dismay
when I saw that the wind swept before it all trace
of my footsteps in the sand! I knew not which
way to proceed; I was struck with despair, tore my
garments, threw off my turban, and cried aloud;
but neither human voice nor echo answered me.
The silence was dreadful. I had tasted no food for
many hours, and I now became sick and faint. I
recollected that I had put a supply of opium into the
folds of my turban; but, alas! when I took my turban up, I found that the opium had fallen out. I
searched for it in vain on the sand where I had
thrown the turban.

"I stretched myself out upon the ground, and
yielded without further struggle to my evil destiny.
What I suffered from thirst, hunger, and heat cannot be described. At las' I fell into a sort of trance,
during which images of various kinds seemed to flit
before my eyes. How long I remained in this state
I know not; but I remember that I was brought to
my senses by a loud shout, which came from persons belonging to a caravan returning from Mecca.
This was a shout of joy for their safe arrival at a
certain spring, well known to them, in this part of
the desert.

" The spring was not a hundred yards from the

spot where I lay; yet, such had been the fate of Murad the Unlucky, that he missed the reality, while he had been hours in pursuit of the phantom. Feeble and spiritless as I was, I sent forth as loud a cry as I could, in hopes of obtaining assistance; and I endeavoured to crawl to the place from which the voices appeared to come. The caravan rested for a considerable time, while the slaves filled the skins with water, and while the camels took in their supply. I worked myself on towards them; yet, notwithstanding my efforts, I was persuaded that, according to my usual ill-fortune, I should never be able to make them hear my voice. I saw them mount their camels! I took off my turban, unrolled it, and waved it in the air. My signal was seen! the caravan came towards me!

" I had scarcely strength to speak; a slave gave me some water; and, after I had drunk, I explained to them who I was, and how I came into this situation.

" While I was speaking, one of the travellers observed the purse which hung to my girdle: it was the same the merchant for whom I recovered the ring had given to me; I had carefully preserved it, because the initials of my benefactor's name and a passage from the Koran were worked upon it.

When he gave it to me, he said that perhaps we should meet again in some other part of the world, and he should recognise me by this token. The person who now took notice of the purse was his brother; and, when I related to him how I had obtained it, he had the goodness to take me under his protection. He was a merchant, who was now going with the caravan to Grand Cairo: he offered to take me with him, and I willingly accepted the proposal, promising to serve him as faithfully as any of his slaves. The caravan proceeded, and I was carried with it.

CHAPTER II.

" The merchant who was become my master treated me with great kindness; but, on hearing me relate the whole series of my unfortunate adventures, he exacted a promise from me that I would do nothing without first consulting him. ' Since you are so unlucky, Murad,' said he, ' that you always choose for the worst when you choose for yourself, you should trust entirely to the judgment of a wiser or a more fortunate friend.'

" I fared well in the service of this merchant, who

was a man of a mild disposition, and who was so
rich that he could afford to be generous to all his de-
pendents. It was my business to see his camels
loaded and unloaded at proper places, to count his
bales of merchandise, and to take care that they
were not mixed with those of his companions.
This I carefully did till the day we arrived at Alex-
andria; when, unluckily, I neglected to count the
bales, taking it for granted that they were all right,
as I had found them so the preceding day. However, when we were to go on board the vessel that
was to take us to Cairo, I perceived that three bales
of cotton were missing.

"I ran to inform my master, who, though a good
deal provoked at my negligence, did not reproach
me as I deserved. The public crier was immediately sent round the city, to offer a reward for the
recovery of the merchandise; and it was restored
by one of the merchants' slaves with whom we had
travelled. The vessel was now under sail; my
master and I and the bales of cotton were obliged
to follow in a boat; and when we were taken on
board, the captain declared he was so loaded that he
could not tell where to stow the bales of cotton.
After much difficulty, he consented to let them remain upon deck; and I promised my master to
watch them night and day.

" We had a prosperous voyage, and were actually in sight of shore, which the captain said we
could not fail to reach early the next morning. I
staid, as usual, this night upon deck ; and solaced
myself by smoking my pipe. Ever since I had indulged in this practice at the camp at El Arish, I
could not exist without opium and tobacco. I suppose that my reason was this night a little clouded
with the dose I took ; but towards midnight, I was
sobered by terror. I started up from the deck on
which I had stretched myself ; my turban was in
flames ; the bale of cotton on which I had rested was
on fire. I awakened two sailors, who were fast
asleep on deck. The consternation became general,
and the confusion increased the danger. The captain and my master were the most active, and suffered the most in extinguishing the flames : my
master was terribly scorched.

" For my part, I was not suffered to do anything :
the captain ordered that I should be bound to the
mast ; and when at last the flames were extinguished, the passengers, with one accord, besought him
to keep me bound hand and foot, lest I should be
the cause of some new disaster. All that had happened was, indeed, occasioned by my ill-luck. I
hal laid my pipe down, when I was falling asleep,

upon the bale of cotton that was beside me. The
fire from my pipe fell out, and set the cotton in
flames. Such was the mixture of rage and terror
with which I had inspired the whole crew, that I
am sure they would have set me ashore on a desert island, rather than have had me on board for a
week longer. Even my humane master, I could
perceive, was secretly impatient to get rid of Murad
the Unlucky and his evil fortune.

" You may believe I was heartily glad when we
landed, and when I was unbound. My master put
a purse containing fifty sequins into my hand, and
bade me farewell. ' Use this money prudently,
Murad, if you can,' said he, ' and perhaps your fortune may change.' Of this I had little hopes ; but
determined to lay out my money as prudently as
possible.

" As I was walking through the streets of Grand
Cairo, considering how I should lay out my fifty
sequins to the greatest advantage, I was stopped by
one who called me by name, and asked me if I
could pretend to have forgotten his face. I looked
steadily at him, and recollected, to my sorrow, that
he was the Jew Rachub, from whom I had borrowed certain sums of money at the camp at E. Arish.
What brought him to Grand Cairo, except it was

my evil destiny, I cannot tell.   He would not quit
me ; he would take no excuses ; he said he knew
that I had deserted twice, once from the Turkish
and once from the English army ; that I was not
entitled to any pay ; and that he could not imagine
it possible that my brother Saladin would own me,
or pay my debts.

"I replied, for I was vexed by the insolence of
this Jewish dog, that I was not, as he imagined, a
beggar ; that I had the means of paying him my
just debt, but that I hoped he would not extort from
me all that exorbitant interest which none but a Jew
could exact.   He smiled, and answered that, if a
Turk loved opium better than money, this was no
fault of his ; that he had supplied me with what I
loved best in the world ; and that I ought not to complain when he expected I should return the favour.

"I will not weary you, gentlemen, with all the
arguments that passed between me and Rachub.
At last we compromised matters ; he would take nothing less than the whole debt : but he let me have
at a very cheap rate a chest of second-hand clothes,
by which he assured me I might make my fortune.
He brought them to Grand Cairo, he said, for the
purpose of selling them to slave-merchants ; who,
at this time of the year, were in want of them to

supply their slaves: but he was in haste to get home to his wife and family at Constantinople, and therefore he was willing to make over to a friend the profits of this speculation. I should have distrusted Rachub's professions of friendship, and especially of disinterestedness; but he took me with him to the khan, where his goods were, and unlocked the chest of clothes to show them to me. They were of the richest and finest materials, and had been but little worn. I could not doubt the evidence of my senses; the bargain was concluded, and the Jew sent porters to my inn with the chest.

" The next day I repaired to the public market-place; and, when my business was known, I had choice of customers before night: my chest was empty—and my purse was full. The profit I made upon the sale of these clothes was so considerable, that I could not help feeling astonishment at Rachub's having brought himself so readily to relinquish them.

" A few days after I had disposed of the contents of my chest, a Damascene merchant, who had bought two suits of apparel from me, told me, with a very melancholy face, that both the female slaves who had put on these clothes were sick. I could not conceive that the clothes were the cause of their

4

sickness; but, soon afterward, as I was crossing the
market, I was attacked by at least a dozen merchants, who made similar complaints. They insisted upon knowing how I came by the garments,
and demanded whether I had worn any of them myself. This day I had for the first time indulged
myself with wearing a pair of yellow slippers, the
only finery I had reserved for myself out of all the
tempting goods. Convinced by my wearing these
slippers that I could have no insidious designs, since
I shared the danger, whatever it might be, the merchants were a little pacified; but what was my terror and remorse, the next day, when one of them
came to inform me that plague-boils had broken out
under the arms of all the slaves who had worn this
pestilential apparel. On looking carefully into the
chest, we found the word Smyrna written, and half-
effaced, upon the lid. Now the plague had for
some time raged at Smyrna; and, as the merchants
suspected, these clothes had certainly belonged to
persons who had died of that distemper. This was
the reason why the Jew was willing to sell them to
me so cheap; and it was for this reason that he
would not stay at Grand Cairo himself, to reap *the
profits of his speculation.* Indeed, if I had paid attention to it at the proper time, a slight circumstance

might have revealed the truth to me.   While I was
bargaining with the Jew, before he opened the chest,
he swallowed a large dram of brandy, and stuffed
his nostrils with sponge dipped in vinegar : this he
told me he did to prevent his perceiving the smell
of musk, which always threw him into convulsions.

"The horror I felt, when I discovered that I had
spread the infection of the plague, and that I had
probably caught it myself, overpowered my senses;
a cold dew spread over all my limbs, and I fell upon the lid of the fatal chest in a swoon.   It is said
that fear disposes people to take the infection : however this may be, I sickened that evening, and soon
was in a raging fever.   It was worse for me whenever the delirium left me, and I could reflect upon
the miseries my ill fortune had occasioned.   In my
first lucid interval, I looked round and saw that I
had been removed from the khan to a wretched hut.
An old woman, who was smoking her pipe in the
farthest corner of my room, informed me that I had
been sent out of the town of Grand Cairo by order
of the cadi, to whom the merchants had made their
complaint.   The fatal chest was burnt, and the
house in which I had lodged razed to the ground.
'And, if it had not been for me,' continued the
old woman, ' you would have been dead, pro-

bably, at this instant; but I have made a vow to
our great prophet, that I would never neglect an opportunity of doing a good action : therefore, when
you were deserted by all the world, I took care of
you.   Here too is your purse, which I saved from
the rabble, and, what is more difficult, from the officers of justice.   I will account to you for every
para that I have expended ; and will moreover tell
you the reason of my making such an extraordinary vow.'

" As I perceived that this benevolent old woman
took great pleasure in talking, I made an inclination
of my head to thank her for her promised history,
and she proceeded ; but I must confess I did not listen with all the attention her narrative doubtless deserved.   Even curiosity, the strongest passion of
us Turks, was dead within me.   I have no recollection of the old woman's story.   It is as much as
I can do to finish my own.

" The weather became excessively hot : it was
affirmed by some of the physicians, that this heat
would prove fatal to their patients ;* but, contrary
to the prognostics of the physicans, it stopped the
progress of the plague.   I recovered, and found my

* Antis's Observations on the Manners and Customs of
the Egyptians.

purse much lightened by my illness. I divided the remainder of my money with my humane nurse, and sent her out into the city, to inquire how matters were going on.

" She brought me word that the fury of the plague had much abated; but that she had met several funerals, and that she had heard many of the merchants cursing the folly of Murad the Unlucky, who, as they said, had brought all this calamity upon the inhabitants of Cairo. Even fools, they say, learn by experience. I took care to burn the bed on which I had lain, and the clothes I had worn : I concealed my real name, which I knew would inspire detestation, and gained admittance, with a crowd of other poor wretches, into a lazaretto, where I performed quarantine, and offered up prayers daily for the sick.

" When I thought it was impossible I could spread the infection, I took my passage home. I was eager to get away from Grand Cairo, where I knew I was an object of execration. I had a strange fancy haunting my mind ; I imagined that all my misfortunes, since I left Constantinople, had arisen from my neglect of the talisman upon the beautiful china vase. I dreamed three times, when I was recovering from the plague, that a genius appeared to me,

4 *

and said, in a reproachful tone, ' Murad, where is
the vase that was intrusted to thy care ?'

" This dream operated strongly upon my imagination.   As soon as we arrived at Constantinople,
which we did, to my great surprise, without meeting
with any untoward accidents, I went in search of
my brother Saladin, to inquire for my vase.   He
no longer lived in the house in which I left him, and
I began to be apprehensive that he was dead ; but a
porter, hearing my inquiries, exclaimed, ' Who is
there in Constantinople that is ignorant of the dwelling of Saladin the Lucky ?   Come with me, and I
will show it to you.'

" The mansion to which he conducted me looked
so magnificent, that I was almost afraid to enter lest
there should be some mistake.   But, while I was
hesitating, the doors opened, and I heard my brother Saladin's voice. He saw me almost at the same
instant that I fixed my eyes upon him, and immediately sprang forward to embrace me.   He was
the same good brother as ever, and I rejoiced in his
prosperity with all my heart.   ' Brother Saladin,'
said I, 'can you now doubt that some men are born
to be fortunate, and others to be unfortunate ?   How
often you used to dispute this point with me ?'

" 'Let us not dispute it now in the public street,'

said he, smiling ; ' but come in and refresh yourself, and we will consider the question afterward at leisure.'

" ' No, my dear brother,' said I, drawing back, ' you are too good : Murad the Unlucky shall not enter your house, lest he should draw down misfortunes upon you and yours. I come only to ask for my vase.'

" ' It is safe,' cried he ; ' come in, and you shall see it, but I will not give it up till I have you in my house. I have none of these superstitious fears : pardon me the expression, but I have none of these superstitious fears.'

" I yielded, entered his house, and was astonished at all I saw ! My brother did not triumph in his prosperity ; but, on the contrary, seemed intent only upon making me forget my misfortunes : he listened to the account of them with kindness, and obliged me by the recital of his history ; which was, I must acknowledge, far less wonderful than my own. He seemed, by his own account, to have grown rich in the common course of things ; or rather, by his own prudence. I allowed for his prejudices, and, unwilling to dispute further with him, said, ' You must remain of your opinion, brother ; and I of mine ; you are Saladin the Lucky, and I Murad the Unlucky ; and so we shall remain to the end of our lives.'

"I had not been in his house four days when an accident happened, which showed how much I was in the right. The favourite of the sultan, to whom he had formerly sold his china vase, though her charms were now somewhat faded by time, still retained her power, and her taste for magnificence. She commissioned my brother to bespeak for her, at Venice, the most splendid looking-glass that money could purchase. The mirror, after many delays and disappointments, at length arrived at my brother's house. He unpacked it, and sent to let the lady know it was in perfect safety. It was late in the evening, and she ordered it should remain where it was that night ; and that it should be brought to the seraglio the next morning. It stood in a sort of antechamber to the room in which I slept ; and with it were left some packages, containing glass chandeliers for an unfinished saloon in my brother's house. Saladin charged all his domestics to be vigilant this night ; because he had money to a great amount by him, and there had been frequent robberies in our neighbourhood. Hearing these orders, I resolved to be in readiness at a moment's warning. I laid my scimitar beside

MURAD THE UNLUCKY

me upon a cushion; and left my door half-open,
that I might hear the slightest noise in the antechamber, or the great staircase. About midnight
I was suddenly awakened by a noise in the antechamber. I started up, seized my scimitar, and the
instant I got to the door, saw, by the light of the
lamp which was burning in the room, a man standing opposite to me, with a drawn sword in his hand.
I rushed forward, demanding what he wanted, and
received no answer; but, seeing him aim at me with
his scimitar, I gave him, as I thought, a deadly
blow. At this instant I heard a great crash; and
the fragments of the looking-glass, which I had
shivered, fell at my feet. At the same moment
something black brushed by my shoulder: I pursued it, stumbled over the packages of glass, and
rolled over them down the stairs.

"My brother came out of his room, to inquire
the cause of all this disturbance; and when he saw
the fine mirror broken, and me lying among the
glass chandeliers at the bottom of the stairs, he could
not forbear exclaiming, ' Well, brother! you are
indeed Murad the Unlucky.'

"When the first emotion was over, he could not,
however, forbear laughing at my situation. With
a degree of goodness which made me a thousand

times more sorry for the accident, he came down
stairs to help me up, gave me his hand, and said,
' Forgive me, if I was angry with you at first. I
am sure you did not mean to do me any injury;
but tell me how all this has happened ?'

" While Saladin was speaking, I heard the same
kind of noise which had alarmed me in the antechamber; but, on looking back, I saw only a black
pigeon, which flew swiftly by me, unconscious of
the mischief he had occasioned. This pigeon I had
unluckily brought into the house the preceding day ;
and had been feeding and trying to tame it for my
young nephews. I little thought it would be the
cause of such disasters. My brother, though he
endeavoured to conceal his anxiety from me, was
much disturbed at the idea of meeting the favourite's
displeasure, who would certainly be grievously disappointed by the loss of her splendid looking-glass.
I saw that I should inevitably be his ruin, if I continued in his house; and no persuasions could prevail upon me to prolong my stay. My generous
brother, seeing me determined to go, said to me,
' A factor, whom I have employed for some years
to sell merchandise for me, died a few days ago.
Will you take his place ? I am rich enough to bear
any little mistakes you may fall into, from ignorance

of business ; and you will have a partner who is able and willing to assist you. '

" I was touched to the heart by this kindness; especially at such a time as this. He sent one of his slaves with me to the shop in which you now see me, gentlemen. The slave, by my brother's directions, brought with us my china vase, and delivered it safely to me, with this message : ' The scarlet dye that was found in this vase, and its fellow, was the first cause of Saladin's making the fortune he now enjoys ; he therefore does no more than justice in sharing that fortune with his brother Murad.'

" I was now placed in as advantageous a situation as possible ; but my mind was ill at ease, when I reflected that the broken mirror might be my brother's ruin. The lady by whom it had been bespoken was, I well knew, of a violent temper ; and this disappointment was sufficient to provoke her to vengeance. My brother sent me word this morning, however, that though her displeasure was excessive, it was in my power to prevent any ill consequences that might ensue. ' In my power !' I exclaimed ; ' then, indeed, I am happy ! Tell my brother there is nothing I will not do to show him my gratitude, and to save him from the consequences of my folly.' ,

" The slave who was sent by my brother seemed
unwilling to name what was required of me, saying
that his master was afraid I should not like to grant
the request.   I urged him to speak freely, and he
then told me the favourite declared nothing would
make her amends for the loss of the mirror but the
fellow vase to that which she had bought from Saladin.   It was impossible for me to hesitate ; gratitude for my brother's generous kindness overcame
my superstitious obstinacy : and I sent him word
I would carry the vase to him myself.

" I took it down this evening, from the shelf on
which it stood : it was covered with dust, and I
washed it ; but, unluckily, in endeavouring to clean
the inside from the remains of the scarlet powder,
I poured hot water into it, and immediately I heard
a simmering noise, and my vase, in a few instants,
burst asunder with a loud explosion.   These fragments, alas ! are all that remain.   The measure
of my misfortunes is now completed ! Can you
wonder, gentlemen, that I bewail my evil destiny ?
Am I not justly called Murad the Unlucky ? Here
end all my hopes in this world !   Better would it
have been if I had died long ago !   Better that I
had never been born !   Nothing I ever have done,
or attempted, has prospered.   Murad the Unlucky is
my name, and ill-fate has marked me for her own."

CHAPTER III.

THE lamentations of Murad were interrupted by the entrance of Saladin. Having waited in vain for some hours, he now came to see if any disaster had happened to his brother Murad. He was surprised at the sight of the two pretended merchants; and could not refrain from exclamations on beholding the broken vase. However, with his usual equanimity and good-nature, he began to console Murad; and taking up the fragments, examined them carefully one by one, joined them together again, found that none of the edges of the china were damaged, and declared he could have it mended so as to look as well as ever.

Murad recovered his spirits upon this. "Brother," said he, "I comfort myself for being Murad the Unlucky, when I reflect that you are Saladin the Lucky. See, gentlemen," continued he, turning to the pretended merchants, "scarcely has this most fortunate of men been five minutes in company before he gives a happy turn to affairs. His presence inspires joy: I observe your countenances, which had been saddened by my dismal history, have

5

brightened up since he has made his appear n.,
Brother, I wish you would make these gentlemen
some amends for the time they have wasted in
listening to my catalogue of misfortunes, by relating your history, which I am sure, they will find
rather more exhilarating."

Saladin consented, on condition that the strangers
would accompany him home, and partake of a so-
cial banquet. They at first repeated the former
excuse of their being obliged to return to their inn :
but at length the sultan's curiosity prevailed, and he
and his vizier went home with Saladin the Lucky,
who, after supper, related his history in the following manner.

"My being called Saladin the Lucky first inspired me with confidence in myself : though I own
that I cannot remember any extraordinary instances
of good luck in my childhood. An old nurse of
my mother's, indeed, repeated to me twenty times
a day, that nothing I undertook could fail to succeed ; because I was Saladin the Lucky. I became
presumptuous and rash ; and my nurse's prognostics might have effectually prevented their accomplishment, had I not, when I was about fifteen, been
roused to reflection during a long confinement,
which was the consequence of my youthful conceit
and imprudence.

" At this time there was at the Porte a Frenchman, an ingenious engineer, who was employed and
favoured by the sultan, to the great astonishment
of many of my prejudiced countrymen. On the
grand seignior's birthday, he exhibited some extra-
ordinarily fine fireworks, and I, with numbers of
the inhabitants of Constantinople, crowded to see
them. I happened to stand near the place where
the Frenchman was stationed; the crowd pressed
upon him, and I among the rest; he begged we
would, for our own sakes, keep at a greater distance;
and warned us that we might be much hurt by the
combustibles which he was using. I, relying upon
my good fortune, disregarded all these cautions;
and the consequence was, that, as I touched some
of the materials prepared for the fireworks, they
exploded, dashed me upon the ground with great
violence, and I was terribly burnt.

" This accident, gentlemen, I consider as one of
the most fortunate circumstances of my life; for it
checked and corrected the presumption of my temper. During the time I was confined to my bed,
the French gentleman came frequently to see me.
He was a very sensible man; and the conversations
he had with me enlarged my mind, and cured me
of many foolish prejudices: especially of that

which I had been taught to entertain, concerning
the predominance of what is called luck, or fortune,
in human affairs. 'Though you are called Saladin the Lucky,' said he, ' you find that your neglect of prudence has nearly brought you to the
grave, even in the bloom of youth. Take my advice, and henceforward trust more to prudence than
to fortune. Let the multitude, if they will, call
you Saladin the Lucky : but call yourself, and
make yourself, Saladin the Prudent.'

" These words left an indelible impression on
my mind, and gave a new turn to my thoughts and
character. My brother Murad has doubtless told
you that our difference of opinion on the subject of
predestination produced between us frequent arguments ; but we could never convince one another,
and we each have acted, through life, in consequence of our different beliefs. To this I attribute
my success and his misfortunes.

" The first rise of my fortune, as you have probably heard from Murad, was owing to the scarlet
dye, which I brought to perfection with infinite difficulty. The powder, it is true, was accidentally
found by me in our china vases ; but there it might
have remained to this instant, useless, if I had not
taken the pains to make it useful. I grant that we

can only partially foresee and command events : yet on the use we make of our own powers, I think depends our destiny. But, gentlemen, you would rather hear my adventures, perhaps, than my reflections ; and I am truly concerned, for your sakes, that I have no wonderful events to relate. I am sorry I cannot tell you of my having been lost in a sandy desert. I have never had the plague, nor even been shipwrecked : I have been all my life an inhabitant of Constantinople, and have passed my time in a very quiet and uniform manner.

" The money I received from the sultan's favourite for my china vase, as my brother may have told you, enabled me to trade on a more extensive scale. I went on steadily with my business ; and made it my whole study to please my employers, by all fair and honourable means. This industry and civility succeeded beyond my expectations ; in a few years I was rich for a man in my way of business.

" I will not proceed to trouble you with the journal of a petty merchant's life ; I pass on to the incident which made a considerable change in my affairs.

" A terrible fire broke out near the walls of the
5 *

grand seignior's seraglio :* as you are strangers,
gentlemen, you may not have heard of this event,
though it produced so great a sensation in Constantinople. The vizier's superb palace was utterly
consumed; and the melted lead poured down from
the roof of the mosque of St. Sophia. Various were
the opinions formed by my neighbours respecting
the cause of the conflagration. Some supposed it
to be a punishment for the sultan's having neglected, one Friday, to appear at the mosque of St.
Sophia; others considered it as a warning sent by
Mahomet to dissuade the Porte from persisting in a
war in which we were just engaged. The generality, however, of the coffee-house politicians contented themselves with observing that it was the
will of Mahomet that the palace should be consumed. Satisfied by this supposition, they took no
precaution to prevent similar accidents in their own
houses. Never were fires so common in the city
as at this period; scarcely a night passed without
our being wakened by the cry of fire.

"These frequent fires were rendered still more
dreadful by villains, who were continually on the
watch to increase the confusion by which they pro-
fited, and to pillage the houses of the sufferers. It

---

* *Vide* Baron de Tott's Memoirs.

was discovered that these incendiaries frequently skulked, towards evening, in the neighbourhood of the bezestein where the richest merchants store their goods ; some of these wretches were detected in throwing *coundaks*,* or matches, into the windows ; and, if these combustibles remained a sufficient time, they could not fail to set the house on fire.

"Notwithstanding all these circumstances, many even of those who had property to preserve continued to repeat, 'It is the will of Mahomet ;' and consequently to neglect all means of preservation. I, on the contrary, recollecting the lesson I had learned from the sensible foreigner, neither suffered

---

* "A *coundak* is a sort of combustible that consists only of a piece of tinder wrapped in brimstone matches, in the midst of a small bundle of pine shavings. This is the method usually employed by incendiaries. They lay this match by stealth behind a door, which they find open, or in a window ; and, after setting it on fire, they make their escape. This is sufficient often to produce the most terrible ravages in a town where the houses built with wood and painted with oil of spike, afford the easiest opportunity to the miscreant who is disposed to reduce them to ashes. This method, employed by the incendiaries, and which often escapes the vigilance of the masters of the houses, added to the common causes of fires, gave for some time very frequent causes of alarm."—*Translation of Memoirs of Baron de Tott*, vol. i.

my spirits to sink with superstitious fears of ill luck,
nor did I trust presumptously to my good fortune.
I took every possible means to secure myself. I
never went to bed without having seen that all the
lights and fires in the house were extinguished ; and
that I had a supply of water in the cistern. I had
likewise learned from my Frenchman that wet mortar was the most effectual thing for stopping the
progress of flames : I therefore had a quantity of
mortar made up, in one of my outhouses, which
I could use at a moment's warning. These precautions were all useful to me ; my own house, indeed, was never actually on fire : but the houses of
my next door neighbours were no less than five
times in flames in the course of one winter. By my
exertions, or rather by my precautions, they suffered
but little damage ; and all my neighbours looked
upon me as their deliverer and friend : they loaded
me with presents, and offered more indeed than I
would accept. All repeated that I was Saladin the
Lucky. This compliment I disclaimed ; feeling
more ambitious of being called Saladin the Prudent.
It is thus that what we call modesty is often only
a more refined species of pride. But to proceed
with my story.

"One night I had been later than usua at supper, at a friend's house : none but the *passevans*, or watch, were in the streets ; and even they, I believe, were asleep.

" As I passed one of the conduits which convey water to the city, I heard a trickling noise; and, upon examination, I found that the cock of the water-spout was half-turned, so that the water was running out. I turned it back to its proper place, thought it had been left unturned by accident, and walked on ; but I had not proceeded far before I came to another spout, and another, which were in the same condition. I was convinced that this could not be the effect merely of accident, and suspected that some ill-intentioned persons designed to let out and waste the water of the city, that there might be none to extinguish any fire that should break out in the course of the night.

" I stood still for a few moments, to consider how it would be most prudent to act. It would be impossible for me to run to all parts of the city, that I might stop the pipes that were running to waste. I first thought of wakening the watch, and the firemen, who were most of them slumbering at their stations ; but I reflected that they were perhaps not to be trusted, and that they were in a confederacy with the incendiaries ; otherwise, they would

certainly, before this hour, have observed and
stopped the running of the sewers in their neighbourhood.   I determined to waken a rich merchant,
called Damat Zade, who lived near me, and who
had a number of slaves, whom he could send to
different parts of the city, to prevent mischief, and
give notice to the inhabitants of their danger.

" He was a very sensible, active man, and one
that could easily be wakened : he was not, like some
Turks, an hour in recovering their lethargic senses.
He was quick in decision and action ; and his slaves
resembled their master.   He despatched a messenger immediately to the grand vizier, that the sultan's safety might be secured ; and sent others to
the magistrates, in each quarter of Constantinople.
The large drums in the janizary aga's tower beat
to rouse the inhabitants ; and scarcely had this been
heard to beat half an hour before the fire broke out
in the lower apartments of Damat Zade's house,
owing to a *coundak*, which had been left behind
one of the doors.

" The wretches who had prepared the mischief
came to enjoy it, and to pillage : but they were disappointed.   Astonished to find themselves taken
into custody, they could not comprehend how their
designs had been frustrated.   By timely exertions,

the fire in my friend's house was extinguished; and
though **fires** broke out, during the night, in many
parts of the city, but little damage was sustained,
because there **was time for** precautions; and, by
the stopping of the spouts, sufficient water was **pre-**
served. **People were** awakened, and warned of the
danger; **and they consequently** escaped unhurt.

" The **next day, as** soon as I made my appearance at the bezetstein, **the merchants** crowded round,
called me their benefactor, and the **preserver of their**
lives and **fortunes.** Damat Zade, the merchant
whom I had awakened **the** preceding night, presented to me a heavy purse of gold; and put upon
my finger a diamond ring of considerable value :
each of the merchants followed his example, in making me rich presents ; the magistrates also sent
me tokens of their approbation ; and the grand
vizier sent me a diamond of the first water, with a
line written by his own hand—' To the man who
has saved Constantinople.' Excuse me, gentlemen,
for the vanity I seem to show in mentioning these
circumstances. You desired to hear my history,
and I cannot therefore omit the principal circumstance of my life. In the course of four-and-twenty
hours, I found myself raised, by the munificent
gratitude of the inhabitants of this city, to a state of

affluence far beyond what I had ever dreamed of
attaining.

" I now took a house suited to my circumstances,
and bought a few slaves. As I was carrying my
slaves home, I was met by a Jew, who stopped me,
saying, in his language, ' My lord, I see, has been
purchasing slaves ; I could clothe them cheaply.'
There was something mysterious in the manner of
this Jew, and I did not like his countenance ; but I
considered that I ought not to be governed by caprice in my dealings, and that, if this man could really clothe my slaves more cheaply than another, I
ought not to neglect his offer merely because I took
a dislike to the cut of his beard, the turn of his eye,
or the tone of his voice. I therefore bade the Jew
follow me home, saying that I would consider of his
proposal.

" When we came to talk over the matter, I was
surprised to find him so reasonable in his demands.
On one point, indeed, he appeared unwilling to com-
ply. I required, not only to see the clothes I was
offered, but also to know how they came into his
possession. On this subject he equivocated ; I therefore suspected there must be something wrong. I
reflected what it could be, and judged that the goods
had been stolen, or that they had been the apparel

of persons who had died of some contagious distemper. The Jew showed me a chest, from which he said I might choose whatever suited me best. I observed, that as he was going to unlock the chest, he stuffed his nose with some aromatic herbs. He told me that he did so to prevent his smelling the musk with which the chest was perfumed; musk, he said, had an extraordinary effect upon his nerves. I begged to have some of the herbs which he used himself; declaring that musk was likewise offensive to me.

" The Jew, either struck by his own conscience, or observing my suspicions, turned as pale as death. He pretended he had not the right key, and could not unlock the chest; said he must go in search of it, and that he would call on me again.

" After he had left me, I examined some writing upon the lid of the chest that had been nearly effaced. I made out the word Smyrna, and this was sufficient to confirm all my suspicions. The Jew returned no more: he sent some porters to carry away the chest, and I heard nothing of him for some time, till one day, when I was at the house of Damat Zade, I saw a glimpse of the Jew passing hastily through one of the courts, as if he wished to avoid me. ' My friend,' said I to Damat Zade, ' do not

6

attribute my question to impertinent curiosity, or to
a desire to intermeddle with your affairs, if I venture
to ask the nature of your business with the Jew who
has just now crossed your court?'

"'He has engaged to supply me with clothing
for my slaves,' replied my friend, 'cheaper than I
can purchase it elsewhere. I have a design to surprise my daughter Fatima, on her birthday, with
an entertainment in the pavilion in the garden; and
all her female slaves shall appear in new dresses
on the occasion.'

"I interrupted my friend, to tell him what I suspected relative to this Jew and his chest of clothes.
It is certain that the infection of the plague can be
communicated by clothes, not only after months but
after years have elapsed. The merchant resolved
to have nothing more to do with this wretch, who
could thus hazard the lives of thousands of his fellow-creatures for a few pieces of gold: we sent notice of the circumstance to the cadi, but the cadi was
slow in his operations; and before he could take
the Jew into custody, the cunning fellow had effected his escape. When his house was searched, he
and his chest had disappeared: we discovered that
he sailed for Egypt, and rejoiced that we had driven
him from Constantinople.

" My friend Damat Zade expressed the warmest gratitude to me. ' You formerly saved my fortune; you have now saved my life; and a life yet dearer than my own, that of my daughter Fatima.'

" At the sound of that name I could not, I believe, avoid showing some emotion. I had accidentally seen this lady; and I had been captivated by her beauty, and by the sweetness of her countenance; but, as I knew she was destined to be the wife of another, I suppressed my feeling, and determined to banish the recollection of the fair Fatima for ever from my imagination. Her father, however, at this instant, threw into my way a temptation which it required all my fortitude to resist. ' Saladin,' continued he, ' it is but just that you, who have saved our lives, should share our festivity. Come here on the birthday of my Fatima : I will place you in a balcony, which overlooks the garden, and you shall see the whole spectacle. We shall have *a feast of tulips ;* in imitation of that which, as you know, is held in the grand seignor's gardens. I assure you, the sight will be worth seeing ; and besides, you will have a chance of beholding my Fatima, for a moment, without her veil.'

" ' That,' interrupted I, ' is the thing I most wish to avoid. I dare not indulge myself in a pleasure which might cost me the happiness of my life. I will conceal nothing from you, who treat me with so much confidence. I have already beheld the charming countenance of your Fatima; but I know that she is destined to be the wife of a happier man.'

"Damat Zade seemed much pleased by the frankness with which I explained myself; but he would not give up the idea of my sitting with him, in the balcony, on the day of the feast of tulips : and I, on my part, could not consent to expose myself to another view of the charming Fatima. My friend used every argument, or rather every sort of persuasion, he could imagine to prevail upon me: he then tried to laugh me out of my resolution; and when all failed, he said, in a voice of anger, 'Go then, Saladin; I am sure you are deceiving me : you have a passion for some other woman, and you would conceal it from me, and persuade me you refuse the favour I offer you from prudence, when, in fact, it is from indifference and contempt. Why could you not speak the truth of your heart to me with that frankness with which one friend should treat another ?'

"Astonished at this unexpected charge, and at the anger which flashed from the eyes of Damat Zade, who, till this moment, had always appeared

to me a man of a mild and reasonable temper, I was
for an instant tempted to fly into a passion and leave
him : but friends once lost are not easily regained.
This consideration had power sufficient to make me
command my temper.   ' My friend,' replied I, ' we
will talk over this affair to-morrow : you are now
angry, and cannot do me justice ; but to-morrow
you will be cool : you will then be convinced that
I have not deceived you ; and that I have no design
but to secure my own happiness by the most prudent means in my power, by avoiding the sight of
the dangerous Fatima.   I have no passion for any
other woman.'

   " ' Then,' said my friend, embracing me, and
quitting the tone of anger which he had assumed
only to try my resolution to the utmost, ' then, Saladin, Fatima is yours.'

   " I scarcely dared to believe my senses !   I could
not express my joy !   ' Yes, my friend !' continued
the merchant, ' I have tried your prudence to the
utmost ; it has been victorious, and I resign my
Fatima to you, certain that you will make her
happy.   It is true, I had a greater alliance in view
for her : the Pacha of Maksoud has demanded her
from me ; but I have found, upon private inquiry,
he is addicted to the intemperate use of opium : and

6 *

my daughter shall never be the wife of one who is a violent madman one-half the day, and a melancholy idiot during the remainder. I have nothing to apprehend from the pacha's resentment, because I have powerful friends with the grand vizier, who will oblige him to listen to reason, and to submit quietly to a disappointment he so justly merits. And now, Saladin, have you any objection to seeing the feast of tulips?'

" I replied only by falling at the merchant's feet, and embracing his knees. The feast of tulips came and on that day I was married to the charming Fatima! The charming Fatima I continue still to think her, though she has now been my wife some years. She is the joy and pride of my heart; and, from our mutual affection, I have experienced more felicity than from all the other circumstances of my life, which are called so fortunate. Her father gave me the house in which I now live, and joined his possessions to ours; so that I have more wealth even than I desire. My riches, however, give me continually the means of relieving the wants of others; and therefore I cannot affect to despise them. I must persuade my brother Murad to share them with me, and to forget his misfortunes: I shall then think myself completely happy. As to the sultana's

looking-glass, and your broken vase, my dear brother," continued Saladin, " we must think of some
means—"

" Think no more of the sultana's looking-glass,
or of the broken vase," exclaimed the sultan,
throwing aside his merchant's habit, and shoWing
beneath it his own imperial vest. " Saladin, I re-
joice to have heard from your own lips, the history
of your life. I acknowledge, vizier, I have been
in the wrong in our argument," continued the sultan, turning to his vizier. " I acknowledge that
the histories of Saladin the Lucky and Murad the
Unlucky favour your opinion, that prudence has
more influence than chance in human affairs. The
success and happiness of Saladin seem to me to have
arisen from his prudence : by that prudence Constantinople has been saved from flames, and from
the plague. Had Murad possessed his brother's
discretion he would not have been on the point of
losing his head for selling rolls which he did not
bake : he would not have been kicked by a mule,
or bastinadoed for finding a ring : he would not
have been robbed by one party of soldiers, or shot
by another : he would not have been lost in a desert, or cheated by a Jew : he would not have set
a ship on fire : nor would he have caught the plague,

and spread it through Grand Cairo: he would not
have run my sultana's looking-glass through the
body, instead of a robber: he would not have believed that the fate of his life depended on certain
verses on a china vase: nor would he, at last, have
broken this precious talisman by washing it with
hot water.   Henceforward, let Murad the Unlucky
be named Murad the Imprudent: let Saladin preserve the surname he merits, and be henceforth
called Saladin the Prudent."

So spake the sultan, who, unlike the generality
of monarchs, could bear to find himself in the
wrong: and could discover his vizier to be in the
right without cutting off his head.   History further
informs us that the sultan offered to make Saladin
a pacha, and to commit to him the government of
a province; but Saladin the Prudent declined this
honour; saying he had no ambition, was perfectly
happy in his present situation, and that when this
was the case it would be folly to change, because
no one can be more than happy.   What further
adventures befell Murad the Imprudent are not re-
corded; it is known only that he became a daily
visiter to the *Teriaky;* and that he died a martyr
to the immoderate use of opium.*

---

* Those among the Turks who give themselves up to an
immoderate use of opium are easily to be distinguished by

a sort of rickety complaint, which this poison produces in course of time. Destined to live agreeably only when in a sort of drunkenness, these men present a curious spectacle when they are assembled in a part of Constantinople called Teriak, or Tcharkissy; the market of opium-eaters. It is there that towards the evening you may see the lovers of opium arrive by the different streets which terminate at the Solymania (the greatest mosque in Constantinople): their pale and melancholy countenances would inspire only compassion, did not their stretched necks, their heads twisted to the right or left, their backbones crooked, one shoulder up to their ears, and a number of other whimsical attitudes which are the consequences of the disorder, present the most ludicrous and the most laughable picture.--*Vide* De Tott's Memoirs.

January 1802.

THE MANUFACTURERS.

By patient, persevering attention to business, **Mr.** John Darford succeeded in establishing a considerable cotton manufactory, by means of which he secured to himself in his old age what is called, or what he called, a competent fortune. His ideas of a competent fortune were, indeed, rather unfashionable; for they included, as he confessed, only, the comforts and conveniences, without any of the vanities of life. He went further still in his unfashionable singularities of opinion, for he was often heard to declare that he thought a busy manufacturer might be as happy as an idle gentleman.

Mr. Darford had taken his two nephews, Charles , and William, into partnership with him. William, who had been educated by him, resembled him in character, habits, and opinions. Always active and cheerful, he seemed to take pride and pleasure

in the daily exertions and care which his situation
and the trust reposed in him required. Far from
being ashamed of his occupations, he gloried in
them : and the sense of duty was associated in his
mind with the idea of happiness. His cousin
Charles, on the contrary, felt his duty and his ideas
of happiness continually at variance : he had been
brought up in an extravagant family, who considered tradesmen and manufacturers as a *caste* dis-
graceful to polite society. Nothing but the utter
ruin of his father's fortune could have determined
him to go into business.

He never applied to the affairs of the manufactory ; he affected to think his understanding above
such vulgar concerns, and spent his days in regretting that his brilliant merit was buried in obscurity.

He was sensible that he hazarded the loss of his
uncle's favour by the avowal of his prejudices ; yet
such was his habitual conceit, that he could not
suppress frequent expressions of contempt for Mr.
Darford's liberal notions. Whenever his uncle's
opinion differed from his own, he settled the argument, as he fancied, by saying to himself, or to his
clerk, " My uncle Darford knows nothing of the
world : how should he, poor man ! shut up as he
has been all his life in a counting-house ?"

Nearly sixty years' experience, which his uncle sometimes pleaded as an apology for trusting to his own judgment, availed nothing in the opinion of our prejudiced youth.

Prejudiced youth, did we presume to say! Charles would have thought this a very improper expression; for he had no idea that any but old men could be prejudiced. Uncles, and fathers, and grandfathers were, as he thought, the race of beings peculiarly subject to this mental malady; from which all young men, especially those who have their boots made by a fashionable boot-maker, are of course exempt.

At length the time came when Charles was at liberty to follow his own opinions: Mr. Darford died, and his fortune and manufactory were equally divided between his two nephews. "Now," said Charles, " I am no longer chained to the oar. I will leave you, William, to do as you please, and drudge on, day after day, in the manufactory, since that is your taste : for my part, I have no genius for business. I shall take my pleasure; and all I have to do is to pay some poor devil for doing my business for me."

" I am afraid the poor devil will not do your business as well as you would do it yourself," said

7

William : " you know the proverb of the master's eye."

" True ! true !   Very likely," cried Charles, going to the window to look at a regiment of dra- goons galloping through the town ; " but I have other employment for my eyes.   Do look at those fine fellows who are galloping by !   Did you ever see a handsomer uniform than the colonel's ?   And what a fine horse !   'Gad ! I wish I had a commis- sion in the army : I should so like to be in his place this minute."

" This minute ?   Yes, perhaps you would ; be- cause he has, as you say, a handsome uniform and a fine horse ; but all his minutes may not be like this minute."

" Faith, William, that is almost as soberly said as my old uncle himself could have spoken. See what it is to live shut up with old folks ! You catch all their ways, and grow old and wise before your time."

" The danger of growing wise before my time does not alarm me much : but perhaps, cousin, you feel that danger more than I do ?"

" Not I," said Charles, stretching himself still farther out of the window, to watch the dragoons, as they were forming on the parade in the market-

place. " I can only say, as I said before, that I
wish I had been put into the army instead of into
this cursed cotton manufactory. Now the army is
a genteel profession, and I own I have spirit enough
to make it my first object to look and live like a
gentleman."

"And I have spirit enough," replied William,
" to make it my first object to look and live like an
independent man ; and I think a manufacturer,
whom you despise so much, may be perfectly independent. I am sure, for my part, I am heartily
obliged to my uncle for breeding me up to business ; for now I am at no man's orders ; no one
can say to me, ' Go to the east, or go to the west ;
march here, or march there ; fire upon this man,
or run your bayonet into that.' I do not think the
honour and pleasure of wearing a red coat, or of
having what is called a genteel profession, would
make me amends for all that a soldier must suffer
if he does his duty. Unless it were for the defence
of my country, for which I hope and believe I should
fight as well as another, I cannot say that I should
like to be hurried away from my wife and children
to fight a battle against a people with whom I have
no quarrel, and in a cause which perhaps I might
not approve."

" Well, as you say, William, you that have a
wife and children are quite in a different situation
from me.   You cannot leave them, of course.
Thank my stars, I am still at liberty ; and I shall
take care and keep myself so ; my plan is to live
for myself, and to have as much pleasure as I possibly can."

Whether this plan of living for himself was com-
patible with the hopes of having as much pleasure
as possible, we leave it to the heads and hearts of
our readers to decide.   In the mean time we must
proceed with his history.

Soon after this conversation had passed between
the two partners, another opportunity occurred of
showing their characters still more distinctly.

A party of ladies and gentlemen travellers came
to the town, and wished to see the manufactories
there.   They had letters of recommendation to the
Mr. Darfords; and William, with great good-nature,
took them to see their works.   He pointed out to
them with honest pride the healthy countenances
of the children whom they employed.

" You see," said he, " that we cannot be reproached with sacrificing the health and happiness
of our fellow-creatures to our own selfish and mer-
cenary views.   My good uncle took all the means

in his power to make every person concerned in this manufactory as happy as possible; and I hope we shall follow his example. I am sure the riches of both the Indies could not satisfy me, if my conscience reproached me with having gained wealth by unjustifiable means. If these children were overworked, or if they had not fresh air and wholesome food, it would be the greatest misery to me to come into this room and look at them. I could not do it. But, on the contrary, knowing, as I do, that they are well treated and well provided for in every respect, I feel joy and pride in coming among them, and in bringing my friends here."

William's eyes sparkled as he thus spoke the generous sentiments of his heart; but Charles, who had thought himself obliged to attend the ladies of the party to see the manufactory, evidently showed he was ashamed of being considered as a partner. William, with perfect simplicity, went on to explain every part of the machinery, and the whole process of the manufacture; while his cousin Charles, who thought he should that way show his superior liberality and politeness, every now and then interposed with, " Cousin, I'm afraid we are keeping the ladies too long standing. Cousin, this noise must certainly annoy the ladies horridly. Cousin, all

7 *

this sort of thing cannot be very interesting, I apprehend, to the ladies.   Besides, they won't have
time at this rate to see the china works ; which is
a style of thing more to their taste, I presume."

The fidgeting impatience of our hero was extreme; till at last he gained his point, and hurried
the ladies away to the china works.   Among these
ladies there was one who claimed particular attention, Miss Maude Germaine, an *elderly young
lady*, who, being descended from a high family,
thought herself entitled to be proud.   She was yet
more vain than proud, and found her vanity in some
degree gratified by the officious attention of her
new acquaintance, though she affected to ridicule
him to her companions when she could do so unob-
served.   She asked them in a whisper, how they
liked her new cicerone ; and whether he did not
show the lions very prettily, considering who and
what he was ?

It has been well observed that " people are never
ridiculous by what they are, but by what they pretend to be."*   These ladies, with the best dispositions
imaginable for sarcasm, could find nothing to laugh
at in Mr. William Darford's plain unassuming man-

* Rochefoucault.

ners : as he did not pretend to be a fine gentleman, there was no absurd contrast between his circumstances and his conversation ; while almost every word, look, or motion of his cousin was an object of ridicule, because it was affected. His being utterly unconscious of his foibles, and perfectly secure in the belief of his own gentility, increased the amusement of the company. Miss Maude Germaine undertook to play him off, but she took sufficient care to prevent his suspecting her design. As they were examining the beautiful china, she continually appealed to Mr. Charles Darford as a man of taste ; and he, with awkward gallantry, and still more awkward modesty, always began his answers by protesting he was sure Miss Maude Germaine was infinitely better qualified to decide in such matters than he was ; he had not the smallest pretensions to taste ; but that, in his humble opinion, the articles she pitched upon were evidently the most superior in elegance, and certainly of the newest fashion. " Fashion, you know, ladies, is all in all in these things, as in every thing else."

Miss Germaine, with a degree of address which afforded much amusement to herself and her companions, led him to extol or reprobate whatever she pleased ; and she made him pronounce an absurd

eulogium on the ugliest thing in the room, by observing it was vastly like what her friend Lady
Mary Crawley had just bought for her chimney-
piece.

Not content with showing she could make our
man of taste decide as she thought proper, she was
determined to prove that she could make him reverse his own decisions, and contradict himself as
often as she pleased. They were at this instant
standing opposite to two vases of beautiful work-
manship. " Now," whispered she to one of her
companions, " I will lay you any wager I first make
him say that both those vases are frightful ; and that
they are charming ; afterward that he does not know
which he likes best ; next, that no person of any
taste can hesitate between them ; and at last when
he has pronounced his decided humble opinion, he
shall reverse his judgment, and protest he meant to
say quite the contrary."

All this the lady accomplished much to her satisfaction and to that of her friends ; and, so blind and
deaf is self-love, our hero neither heard nor saw
that he was the object of derision. William, however, was rather more clear-sighted ; and as he
could not bear to see his cousin make himself the
butt of the company, he interrupted the conversation,

by begging the ladies would come into another room
to look at the manner in which the china was
painted. Charles, with a contemptuous smile, observed that the ladies would probably find the odour
of the paint rather too much for their nerves. Full
of the sense of his own superior politeness, he followed; since it was determined that they must go,
as he said, *nolens volens.* He did not hear Miss
Germaine whisper to her companions as they passed,
" Can any thing in nature be much more ridiculous
than a vulgar manufacturer who sets up for a fine
gentleman ?"

Among the persons who were occupied in painting a set of china with flowers, there was one who
attracted particular attention, by the ease and quickness with which she worked. An iris of her painting was produced, which won the admiration of all
the spectators; and while Charles was falling into
ecstasies about the merit of the painting, and the
perfection to which the arts are now carried in England, William was observing the flushed and un-
healthy countenance of the young artist. He
stopped to advise her not to overwork herself, to
beg she would not sit in a draught of wind where
she was placed, and to ask her with much humanity
several questions concerning her health and her
circumstances. •

While he was speaking to her, he did not perceive that he had set his foot by accident on Miss Germaine's gown; and, as she walked hastily on, it was torn in a deplorable manner. Charles apologized for his cousin's extreme absence of mind and rudeness: and with a candid condescension added, "Ladies, you must not think ill of my cousin William, because he is not quite so much your humble servant as I am: notwithstanding his little rusticities, want of polish, gallantry, and so forth,—things that are not in every man's power,—I can assure you there is not a better man in the world; except that he is so entirely given up to business, which indeed ruins a man for every thing else."

The apologist little imagined he was at this moment infinitely more awkward and ill-bred than the person whom he affected to pity and to honour with his protection. Our hero continued to be upon the best terms possible with himself and with Miss Maude Germaine during the remainder of this day. He discovered that his lady intended to pass a fortnight with a relation of hers in the town of ——. He waited upon her the next day, to give her an account of the manner in which he had executed some commissions about the choice of china with which she had honoured him.

One visit led to another; and Charles Darford was delighted to find himself admitted into the society of such very genteel persons. At first, he was merely proud of being acquainted with a lady of Miss Maude Germaine's importance; and contented himself with boasting of it to all his acquaintance; by degrees, he became more audacious; he began to fancy himself in love with her, and to flatter himself she would not prove inexorable. The raillery of some of his companions piqued him to make good his boast; and he determined to pay his addresses to a lady who, they all agreed, could never think of a man in business.

Our hero was not entirely deluded by his vanity the lady's coquetry contributed to encourage his hopes. Though she always spoke of him to her friends as a person whom it was impossible she could ever think of for a moment, yet as soon as he made a declaration of his love to her, she began to consider that a manufacturer might have common sense, and even some judgment and taste. Her horror of people in business continued in full force; but she began to allow there was no general rule that did not admit of an exception. When her female friends laughed, following the example she had set them, at Charles Darford, her laughter became fainter than theirs; and she was one evening heard to ask a stranger, who saw him for the first time, whether that young gentleman looked as if he was in business?

Sundry matters began to operate in our hero's favour; precedents, opportunely produced by her waiting-maid, of ladies of the first families in England, ladies even of the first fashion, who had married into mercantile houses; a present too, from her admirer of the beautiful china vase of which she had so often made him change his opinion, had its due effect; but the preponderating motive was the dread of dying an old maid, if she did not accept of this offer.

After various airs, and graces, and doubts, and disdains, this fair lady consented to make her lover happy, on the express conditions that he should change his name from Darford to Germaine, that he should give up all share in the odious cotton manufactory, and that he should purchase the estate of Germaine-park, in Northamptonshire, to part with which, as it luckily happened, some of her great relations were compelled.

In the folly of his joy at the prospect of an alliance with the great Germaine family, he promised every thing that was required of him; notwithstanding the remonstrances of his friend William, who represented to him, in the forcible language of common sense, the inconveniences of marrying into a family that would despise him ; and of uniting himself to such an old coquette as Miss Germaine, who would make him not only a disagreeable but a most extravagant wife.

"Do you not see," said he, "that she has not the least affection for you? she marries you only because she despairs of getting any other match ; and because you are rich, and she is poor. She is seven years older than you, by her own confession, and consequently will be an old woman while you are a young man. She is, as you see—I mean as I see—vain and proud in the extreme ; and if she honours you with her hand, she will think you can never do enough to make her amends for having married beneath her pretensions. Instead of finding in her, as I find in my wife, the best and most affectionate of friends, you will find her your torment through life ; and consider, this is a torment likely to last these thirty or forty years. Is it not worth while to pause—to reflect for as many minutes, or even days ?"

Charles paused double the number of seconds, perhaps, and then replied, "You have married to

8

please yourself, cousin William, and I shall marry
to please myself. As I don't mean to spend my
days in the same style in which you do, the same
sort of wife that makes you happy could never content me. I mean to make some figure in the world;
I know no other use of fortune; and an alliance
with the Germaines brings me at once into fashionable society. Miss Maude Germaine is very proud,
I confess; but she has some reason to be proud of
her family; and then, you see, her love for me
conquers her pride, great as it is."

William sighed, when he saw the extent of his
cousin's folly. The partnership between the two
Darfords was dissolved.

It cost our hero much money, but no great trouble, to get his name changed from Darford to Germaine, and it was certainly very disadvantageous
to his pecuniary interest to purchase Germaine-
park, which was sold to him for at least three years'
purchase more than its value; but in the height of
his impatience to get into the fashionable world, all
prudential motives appeared beneath his consideration. It was, as he fancied, part of the character of
a man of spirit, the character he was now to assume
and support for life, to treat pecuniary matters as
below his notice. He bought Germaine-park, mar-

ried Miss Germaine, and determined no mortal should **ever** find out, by his equipages or style of life, that **he** had not been born the possessor of this **estate.**

In this laudable resolution it cannot possibly be doubted but that his bride encouraged him to the ut-most of her power. **She was** eager to leave the country where his former friends and acquaintance resided ; for they were people with whom, of course, it could not be expected that she should keep up any manner of intercourse. Charles, in whose mind vanity at this moment smothered every better feel-ing, was in reality glad of **a** pretext for breaking off all connexion with those whom he had formerly **loved.** He went to take leave of William in a fine **chariot, on which** the Germaine arms were osten-tatiously blazoned. That real dignity which arises from a sense of independence of mind appeared in William's manners ; **and** quite overawed and abashed our hero, **in the** midst of all his finery and airs. " I **hope, cousin** William," said Charles, " when you can spare time—though, to be sure, that is a thing hardly to be expected, as you are si-tuated,—but, in case you should be able any ways to make it convenient, I hope you will come and take **a** look at what we are doing at Germaine-park."

There was much awkward embarrassment in the
enunciation of this feeble invitation; for Charles
was conscious he did not desire it should be accepted, and that it was made in direct opposition to the
wishes of his bride.   He was at once relieved from
his perplexity, and at the same time mortified, by
the calm' simplicity with which William replied, " I
thank you, cousin, for this invitation : but you know
I should be an encumbrance to you at Germaine-
park ; and I make it a rule neither to go into any
company that would be ashamed of me, or of which
I should be ashamed."

   " Ashamed of you !   But—What an idea, my
dear William !   Surely you don't think—you can't
imagine—I should ever consider you as any sort of
encumbrance ?—I protest—"

   " Save yourself the trouble of protesting, my dear
Charles," cried William, smiling with much good-
nature : " I know why you are so much embarrassed at this instant ; and I do not attribute this to
any want of affection for me.   We are going to lead
quite different lives.   I wish you all manner of satisfaction.   Perhaps the time may come when I shall
be able to contribute to your happiness more than
I can at present."

   Charles uttered some unmeaning phrases, and

hurried to his carriage. At the sight of its varnished panels he recovered his self-complacency and courage; and began to talk fluently about chariots and horses, while the children of the family followed to take leave of him, saying, " Are you going quite away, Charles? Will you never come back to play with us, as you used to do?"

Charles stepped into his carriage with as much dignity as he could assume; which, indeed, was very little. William, who judged of his friends always with the most benevolent indulgence, excused the want of feeling which Charles betrayed during this visit. " My dear," said he to his wife, who expressed some indignation at the slight shown to their children, " we must forgive him; for, you know, a man cannot well think of more than one thing at a time; and the one thing that he is thinking of is his fine chariot. The day will come when he will think more of fine children; at least I hope so, for his own sake."

And now, behold our hero in all his glory; shining upon the Northamptonshire world in the splendour of his new situation! The dress, the equipage, the entertainments, and, above all, the airs of the bride and bridegroom, were the general subject of conversation in the county for ten days.

8 *

Our hero, not precisely knowing what degree of importance Mr. Germaine of Germaine-park was entitled to assume, out-Germained Germaine.

The country gentlemen first stared, then laughed, and at last unanimously agreed, over their bottle, that this new neighbour of theirs was an upstart, who ought to be kept down; and that a vulgar manufacturer should not be allowed to give himself airs merely because he had married a proud lady of good family. It was obvious, they said, he was not born for the situation in which he now appeared. They remarked and ridiculed the ostentation with which he displayed every luxury in his house; his habit of naming the price of every thing, to enforce its claim to admiration; his affected contempt for economy; his anxiety to connect himself with persons of rank; joined to his ignorance of the genealogy of nobility, and the strange mistakes he made between old and new titles.

Certain little defects in his manners, and some habitual vulgarisms in his conversation, exposed him also to the derision of his well-bred neighbours. Mr. Germaine saw that the gentlemen of the county were leagued against him; but he had neither temper nor knowledge of the world sufficient to wage this unequal war. The meanness with which he alternately attempted to court and to bully his adversaries showed them, at once, the full extent of their power, and of his weakness.

Things were in this position when our hero unluckily affronted Mr. Cole, one of the proudest gentlemen in the county, by mistaking him for a merchant of the same name; and, under this mistake, neglecting to return his visit. A few days afterward, at a public dinner, Mr. Cole and Mr. Germaine had some high words, which were repeated by the persons present in various manners; and this dispute became the subject of conversation in the county, particularly among the ladies. Each related, according to her fancy, what her husband had told her: and, as these husbands had drunk a good deal, they had not a perfectly clear recollection of what had passed; so that the whole and every part of the conversation was exaggerated. The fair judges, averse as they avowed their feelings were to duelling, were clearly of opinion, among themselves, that a rea' gentleman would certainly have called·Mr. Cole to account for the words he uttered; though none of them could agree what those words were.

Mrs. Germaine's female friends, in their coteries,

were the first to deplore, with becoming sensibility, that she should be married to a man who had so little the spirit as well as the manners of a man of birth.　Their pity became progressively vehement the more they thought of, or at least the more they talked of, the business; till at last one old lady, the declared and intimate friend of Mrs. Germaine, unintentionally, and in the heat of tattle, made use of one phrase that led to another, and another, till she betrayed, in conversation with that lady, the gossiping scandal of these female circles.

Mrs. Germaine, piqued as her pride was, and though she had little affection for her husband, would have shuddered with horror to have imagined him in the act of fighting a duel; and especially at her instigation: yet of this very act she became the cause.　In their domestic quarrels, her tongue was ungovernable: and at such moments the malice of husbands and wives often appears to exceed the hatred of the worst of foes; and, in the ebullition of her vengeance, when his reproaches had stung her beyond the power of her temper to support, unable to stop her tongue, she vehemently told him he was a coward, who durst not so talk to a man!　He had proved himself a coward; and was become the by-word and contempt of the whole county.　Even women despised his cowardice.

THE MANUFACTURERS

However astonishing it may appear to those who are unacquainted with the nature of quarrels between man and wife, it is but too certain that such quarrels have frequently led to the most fatal consequences. The agitation of mind which Mrs. Germaine suffered the moment she could recollect what she had so rashly said, her vain endeavours to prove to herself that, so provoked, she could not say less, and the sudden effect which she plainly saw her words had produced upon her husband, were but a part of the punishment that always follows conduct and contentions so odious.

Mr. Germaine gazed at her a few moments, with wildness in his eyes : his countenance expressed the stupefaction of rage : he spoke not a word ; but started at length, and snatched up his hat. She was struck with panic terror, gave a scream, sprang after him, caught him by the coat, and, with the most violent protestations, denied the truth of all she had said. The look he gave her cannot be described ; he rudely plucked the skirt from her grasp, and rushed out of the house.

All day and all night she neither saw nor heard of him : in the morning he was brought home, accompanied by a surgeon, in the carriage of a gentleman who had been his second, dangerously wounded.

He was six weeks confined to his bed; and, in the first moment of doubt expressed by the surgeon for his life, she expressed contrition which was really sincere: but, as he recovered, former bickerings were renewed; and the terms on which they lived, gradually became what they had been.

Neither did his duel regain that absurd reputation for which he fought; it was malignantly said he had neither the courage to face a man nor the understanding to govern a wife.

Still, however, Mrs. Germaine consoled herself with the belief that the most shocking circumstance of his having been partner in a manufactory was a profound secret. Alas! the fatal moment arrived when she was to be undeceived in this her last hope. Soon after Mr. Germaine recovered from his wounds, she gave a splendid ball; to which the neighbouring nobility and gentry were invited. She made it a point, with all her acquaintance, to come on this grand night.

The more importance the Germaines set upon success, and the more anxiety they betrayed, the more their enemies enjoyed the prospect of their mortification. All the young belles who had detested Miss Maude Germaine for the airs she used to give herself at country assemblies, now leagued to prevent their admirers from accepting her invitation. All the married ladies whom she had outshone in dress and equipage protested they were not equal to keep up an acquaintance with such prodigiously fine people; and that, for their part, they must make a rule not to accept of such expensive entertainments, as it was not in their power to return them.

Some persons of consequence in the county kept their determination in doubt, suffered themselves to be besieged daily with notes and messages, and hopes that their imaginary coughs, headaches, and influenzas were better, and that they would find themselves able to venture out on the 15th. When the coughs, headaches, and influenzas could hold out no longer, these ingenious tormentors devised new pretexts for supposing it would be impossible to do themselves the honour of accepting Mr. and Mrs. Germaine's obliging invitation on the 15th. Some had recourse to the roads, and others to the moon.

Mrs. Germaine, whose pride was now compelled to make all manner of concessions, changed her night from the 15th to the 20th; to ensure a full moon to those timorous damsels whom she had known to go home nine miles from a ball the dark-

est night imaginable, **without** scruple or complaint.
Mr. Germaine, at his own expense, mended some
spots in the roads, which were obstacles to the delicacy of other travellers; and, when all this was
accomplished, the haughty leaders of the county
fashions condescended to promise they would do
themselves the pleasure to wait upon Mr. and Mrs.
Germaine on the 20th.

Their cards of acceptation were shown with triumph by the Germaines; but it was a triumph of
short duration. With all the refinement of cruelty,
they gave hopes which they never meant to fulfil.
On the morning, noon, and night of the 20th, notes
poured in with apologies, or rather with excuses,
for not keeping their engagements. Scarcely one
was burnt before another arrived. Mrs. Germaine
could not command her temper; and she did not
spare her husband in this trying moment.

The arrival of some company for the ball interrupted a warm dispute between the happy pair.
The ball was very thinly attended; the guests
looked as if they were more inclined to yawn than
to dance. The supper-table was not half-filled;
and the profusion with which it was laid out was
forlorn and melancholy: every thing was on too
grand a scale for the occasion; wreaths of flowers,

and pyramids, and triumphal arches, sufficient for ten times as many guests! Even the most inconsiderate could not help comparing the trouble and expense incurred by the entertainment with the small quantity of pleasure it produced. Most of the guests rose from the table, whispering to one another, as they looked at the scarcely-tasted dishes, " What a waste! What a pity! Poor Mrs. Germaine! What a melancholy sight this must be to her !"

The next day, a mock heroic epistle, in verse, in the character of Mrs. Germaine, to one of her noble relations, giving an account of her ball and disappointment, was handed about, and innumerable copies were taken. It was written with some humour and great ill-nature. The good old lady who occasioned the duel thought it but friendly to show Mrs. Germaine a copy of it; and to beg she would keep it out of her husband's way : it might be the cause of another duel! Mrs. Germaine, in spite of all her endeavours to conceal her vexation, was obviously so much hurt by this mock heroic epistle, that the laughers were encouraged to proceed ; and the next week a ballad, entitled THE MANUFACTURER TURNED GENTLEMAN, was circulated with the same injunctions to secrecy, and the same success. Mr.

9

and Mrs. Germaine, perceiving themselves to be the objects of continual enmity and derision, determined to leave the county. Germaine-park was forsaken; a house in London was bought; and, for a season or two, our hero was amused with the gayeties of the town, and gratified by finding himself actually moving in that sphere of life to which he had always aspired. But he soon perceived that the persons whom, at a distance, he had regarded as objects of admiration and envy, upon a nearer view were capable of exciting only contempt or pity. Even in the company of honourable and right honourable men he was frequently overpowered with *ennui ;* and, among all the fine acquaintances with which his fine wife crowded his fine house, he looked in vain for a friend : he looked in vain for a William Darford.

One evening, at Ranelagh, Charles happened to hear the name of Mr. William Darford pronounced by a lady who was walking behind him : he turned eagerly to look at her; but, though he had a confused recollection of having seen her face before, he could not remember when or where he had met with her. He felt a wish to speak to her, that he might hear something of those friends whom he had neglected, but not forgotten. He was not, however, acquainted with any of the persons with whom she was walking, and was obliged to give up his purpose. When she left the room, he followed her, in hopes of learning from her servants who she was; but she had no servants—no carriage !

Mrs. Germaine, who clearly inferred she was a person of no consequence, besought her husband not to make any further inquiries. " I beg, Mr. Germaine, you will not gratify your curiosity about the Darfords at my expense. I shall have a whole tribe of vulgar people upon my hands, if you do not take care. The Darfords, you know, are quite out of our line of life, especially in town."

This remonstrance had a momentary effect upon Mr. Germaine's vanity; but a few days afterward he met the same lady in the park, attended by Mr. William Darford's old servant. Regardless of his lady's representations, he followed the suggestions of his own heart, and eagerly stopped the man to inquire after his friends in the most affectionate manner. The servant, who was pleased to see that Charles was not grown quite so much a fine gentleman as to forget all his friends in the country, became very communicative; he told Mr. Germaine that the lady whom he was attending was a Miss Locke, governess to Mr. William Darford's children ; and that she was now come to town to spend a few days with a relation, who had been very anxious to see her. This relation was not either rich or genteel ; and though our hero used every persuasion to prevail upon his lady to show Miss Locke some civility while she was in town, he could not succeed. Mrs. Germaine repeated her former phrase, again and again, " The Darfords are quite out of our line of life ;" and this was the only rea-son she would give.

Charles was disgusted by the obstinacy of his wife's pride, and indulged his better feelings by go-ing frequently to visit Miss Locke. She stayed, how-ever, but a fortnight in town ; and the idea of his friends, which had been strongly recalled by his conversations with her, gradually faded away. He continued the course of life into which he had been forced, rather from inability to stop than from in-clination to proceed. Their winters were spent in dissipation in town ; their summers wasted at wa-tering-places, or in visits to fine relations, who were tired of their company, and who took but little pains to conceal this sentiment. Those who do not live happily at home can seldom contrive to live respect-ably abroad. Mr. and Mrs. Germaine could not purchase esteem, and never earned it from the world

or from one another. Their mutual contempt increased every day. Only those who have lived
with bosom friends whom they despise can fully
comprehend the extent and intensity of the evil.

We spare our readers the painful detail of domestic grievances and the petty mortifications of
vanity: from the specimens we have already given
they may form some idea, but certainly not a competent one, of the manner in which this ill-matched
pair continued to live together for twelve long years.
Twelve long years! The imagination cannot distinctly represent such a period of domestic suffering;
though, to the fancy of lovers, the eternal felicity
to be ensured by their union is an idea perfectly
familiar and intelligible. Perhaps, if we could
bring our minds to dwell more upon the hours, and
less upon the years of existence, we should make
fewer erroneous judgments. Our hero and heroine
would never have chained themselves together for
life, if they could have formed an adequate picture
of the hours contained in the everlasting period of
twelve years of wrangling. During this time,
scarcely an hour, certainly not a day, passed in
which they did not, directly or indirectly, reproach
one another; and tacitly form, or explicitly express,

9 *

the wish that they had never been joined in holy
wedlock.

They, however, had a family. Children are
either the surest bonds of union between parents,
or the most dangerous causes of discord. If parents
agree in opinion as to the management of their children, they must be a continually increasing source
of pleasure : but where the father counteracts the
mother, and the mother the father—where the children cannot obey or caress either of their parents
without displeasing the other, what can they become
but wretched little hypocrites, or detestable little
tyrants ?

Mr. and Mrs. Germaine had two children, a boy
and a girl. From the moment of their birth they
became subjects of altercation and jealousy. The
nurses were obliged to decide whether the infants
were most like the father or the mother : two nurses
lost their places by giving what was in Mr. Germaine's opinion an erroneous decision upon this important question. Every stranger who came to
pay a visit was obliged to submit to a course of in-
terrogations on this subject ; and afterward, to their
utter confusion, saw biting of lips and tossing of
heads, either on the paternal or maternal side. At
last it was established that Miss Maude was the most

like her mamma, and Master Charles the most like his papa. Miss Maude, of course, became the fault-less darling of her mother ; and Master Charles the mutinous favourite of his father. A comparison between their features, gestures, and manners was daily instituted, and always ended in words of scorn from one party or the other. Even while they were pampering these children with sweetmeats, or inflaming them with wine, the parents had al-ways the same mean and selfish views. The mo-ther, before she would let her Maude taste the sweet-meats, insisted upon the child's lisping out that she loved mamma best ; and before the little Charles was permitted to carry the bumper of wine to his lips, he was compelled to say he loved papa best. In all their childish quarrels, Maude ran roaring to her mamma, and Charles sneaked up to his papa.

As the interests of the children were so deeply concerned in the question, it was quickly discovered who ruled in the house with the strongest hand. Mr. Germaine's influence over his son diminished as soon as the boy was clearly convinced that his sis-ter, by adhering to her mamma, enjoyed a larger share of the good things. He was wearied out by the incessant rebuffs of the nursery-maids, who were all in their lady's interests ; and he endeavoured to find grace in their sight by recanting all the declarations he had made in his father's favour. "I don't like papa best now: I love mamma best to-day."

"Yes, master, but you must love mamma best every day, or it won't do, I promise you."

By such a course of nursery precepts, these unfortunate children were taught equivocation, falsehood, envy, jealousy, and every fault of temper which could render them insupportable to themselves and odious to others. Those who have lived in the house with spoiled children must have a lively recollection of the degree of torment they can inflict upon all who are within sight or hearing. These domestic plagues became more and more obnoxious; and Mrs. Germaine, in the bitterness of her heart, was heard to protest she wished she had never had a child! Children were pretty things at three years old; but began to be great plagues at six, and were quite intolerable at ten.

Schools, and tutors, and governesses were tried without number; but those capricious changes served only to render the pupils still more unmanageable. At length Mr. and Mrs. Germaine's children became so notoriously troublesome that everybody dreaded the sight of them.

One summer, when Mrs. Germaine was just setting out on a visit to my Lady Mary Crawley, when the carriage was actually at the door, and the trunks tied on, an express arrived from her ladyship with a letter, stipulating that neither Miss Maude nor Master Charles should be of the party.   Lady Mary declared she had suffered so much from their noise, quarrelling, and refractory tempers when they were with her the preceding summer, that she could not undergo such a trial again ; that their mother's nerves might support such things, but that hers really could not : besides, she could not, in justice and politeness to the other friends who were to be in her house, suffer them to be exposed to such torments.   Lady Mary Crawley did not give herself any trouble to soften her expressions, because she would have been really glad if they had given offence, and if Mrs. Germaine had resented her conduct, by declining to pay that annual visit which was now become, in the worst sense of the word, visitation.   To what meanness proud people are often forced to submit!   Rather than break her resolution never to spend another summer at her own country-seat, Mrs. Germaine submitted to all the haughtiness of her Leicestershire relations ; and continued absolutely to force upon them visits which she knew to be unwelcome.

But what was to be done about her children? The first thing, of course, was to reproach her husband. " You see, Mr. Germaine, the effect of the pretty education you have given that boy of yours. I am sure, if he had not gone with us last summer into Leicestershire, my Maude would not have been in the least troublesome to Lady Mary."

" On the contrary, my dear, I have heard Lady Mary herself say, twenty times, that Charles was the best of the two; and I am persuaded, if Maude had been away, the boy would have become quite a favourite."

" There you are utterly mistaken, I can assure you, my dear; for you know you are no great favourite of Lady Mary's yourself; and I have often heard her say that Charles is your image."

" It is very extraordinary that all your great relations show us so little civility, my dear. They do not seem to have much regard for you."

" They have regard enough for me, and showed it formerly; but of late, to be sure, I confess, things are altered. They never have been so cordial since my marriage; and, all things considered, I scarcely know how to blame them."

Mr. Germaine bowed, by way of thanking his lady for this compliment. She besought him not to bow so like a man behind a counter, if he could possibly help it. He replied, it became him to submit to be schooled by a wife who was often taken for his mother. At length, when every species of reproach, mental and personal, which conjugal antipathy could suggest, had been exhausted, the orators recurred to the business of the day, and to the question, "What is to be done with the children while we are at Lady Mary Crawley's?"

CHAPTER II.

In this embarrassment we must leave the Germaines for the present, and refresh ourselves with a look at a happy circle—the family of Mr. Darford, where there is no discordance of opinions, of tastes, or of tempers; none of those evils which arise sometimes from the disappointment, and sometimes from the gratification of vanity and pride.

Mr. Darford succeeded beyond his most sanguine expectations in the management of his business. Wealth poured in upon him; but he considered wealth, like a true philosopher, only as one of the means of happiness; he did not become prodigal

or avaricious; neither did he ever feel the slightest
ambition to quit his own station in society. He
never attempted to purchase from people of superior rank admission into their circles, by giving
luxurious and ostentatious entertainments. He possessed a sturdy sense of his own value, and commanded a species of respect very different from
that which is paid to the laced livery or the varnished equipage.

The firmness of his character was, however,
free from all severity: he knew how to pardon in
others the weakness and follies from which he was
himself exempt. Though his cousin was of such
a different character, and though, since his marriage, Mr. Germaine had neglected his old friends,
William felt more compassion for his unhappiness
than resentment for his faults. In the midst of
his own family, William would often say, " I wish
poor Charles may ever be as happy as we are!"
Frequently, in his letters to London correspondents,
he desired them to inquire privately how Mr. Germaine went on.

For some time he heard of nothing but his extravagance, and of the entertainments given to the
fine world by Mrs. Germaine; but in the course
of a few years his correspondents hinted that Mr.

Germaine began to be distressed for money, and that this was a secret which had been scrupulously kept from his lady, as scrupulously as she concealed from him her losses at play. Mr. Darford also learned from a correspondent who was intimately acquainted with one of Mrs. Germaine's friends, that this lady lived upon very bad terms with her husband; and that her children were terribly spoiled by the wretched education they received.

These accounts gave William sincere concern: far from triumphing in the accomplishment of his prophecies, he never once recalled them to the memory even of his own family; all his thoughts were intent upon saving his friend from future pain.

One day as he was sitting with his family round their cheerful tea-table, his youngest boy, who had climbed upon his knees, exclaimed, " Papa! what makes you so very grave to-night? You are not at all like yourself! What can make you sorry?"

" My dear little boy," said his father, " I was thinking of a letter I received to-day from London."

" I wish those letters would never come, for they always make you look sad, and make you sigh! Mamma, why do you not desire the ser-

10

vants not to bring papa any more such letters?
What did this letter say to you, papa, to make you
so grave?"

"My dear," said his father, smiling, at the
child's simplicity, "this letter told me that your
little cousin Charles is not quite so good a boy as
you are."

"Then, papa, I will tell you what to do: send
our Miss Locke to cousin Charles, and she will
soon make him very good."

"I dare say she would," replied the father,
laughing, "but, my dear boy, I cannot send Miss
Locke; and I am afraid she would not like to go:
besides, we should be rather sorry to part with
her."

"Then, papa, suppose you were to send for my
cousin, and Miss Locke could take care of him
here, without leaving us."

"Could take care of him—true; but would she?
If you can prevail upon her to do so, I will send
for your cousin."

The proposal, though playfully made, was seriously accepted by Miss Locke: and the more
willingly, as she remembered, with gratitude, the
attention Mr. Germaine had paid to her some years
before, when with poor relations in London.

Mr. Darford wrote immediately to invite his cousin's children to his house: the invitation was most gladly accepted, for it was received the very day when Mr. and Mrs. Germaine were so much embarrassed by Lady Mary Crawley's absolute refusal to admit these children into her house. Mrs. Germaine was not too proud to accept of favours from those whom she had treated as beneath her acquaintance, " quite out of her line of life !" She despatched her children directly to Mr. Darford's; and Miss Locke undertook the care of them. It was not an easy or agreeable task; but she had great obligations to Mrs. Darford, and was rejoiced at finding an opportunity of showing her gratitude.

Miss Locke was the young woman whose painting of an iris had been admired by Charles and by Miss Maude Germaine when they visited the china works, thirteen or fourteen years before this time. She was at that period very ill, and in great distress: her father had been a bankrupt, and to earn bread for herself and her sisters she was obliged to work harder than her health and strength allowed. Probably she would have fallen a sacrifice to her exertions if she had not been saved by the humanity of Mr. Darford; and, fortunately for him, he was married to a woman who sympathized in all his generous feelings, and who assisted him in every benevolent action.

Mrs. Darford, after making sufficient inquiries as to the truth of the story and the character of the girl, was so much pleased with all she heard of her merit, and so much touched by her misfortunes, that she took Miss Locke into her family to teach her daughters to draw. She well knew that a sense of dependence is one of the greatest evils; and she was careful to relieve the person whom she obliged, from this painful feeling, by giving her an opportunity of being daily useful to her benefactress. Miss Locke soon recovered her health; she perceived she might be serviceable in teaching the children of the family many things besides drawing; and with unremitting perseverance she informed her own mind, that she might be able to instruct her pupils. Year after year she pursued this plan, and was rewarded by the esteem and affection of the happy family in which she lived.

But though Miss Locke was a woman of great abilities, she had not the magical powers attributed to some characters in romance; she could not instantaneously produce a total reformation of manners. The habits of spoiled children are not to be

changed by the most skilful preceptress without
the aid of time. Miss Maude Germaine and her
brother had tempers which tried Miss Locke's patience to the utmost; but gradually she acquired
some influence over these wayward spirits. She
endeavoured with her utmost skill to eradicate the
jealousy which had been implanted in the minds
of the brother and sister. They found that they
were now treated with strict impartiality, and they
began to live together more peaceably.

Time was willingly allowed to Miss Locke by
their parents, who were glad to be disencumbered
of their children. Eighteen months passed away,
and no news was heard of Mr. and Mrs. Germaine,
except that they continued the same extravagant,
dissipated course of life, and that they began to be
much embarrassed in their circumstances. At
last Mr. Darford received a letter which informed
him that an execution was laid on Mr. Germaine's
fine house in town, and that he and his family
were all in the greatest distress and affliction.

William hastened immediately to London. He
was denied admittance at Mr. Germaine's: the
porter, with an air of mystery, said that his master
was ill, and did not choose to see anybody. William, however, forced his way up stairs.

10 *

Charles at the sight of him stepped back, exclaiming, "May I believe my eyes! William!
Is it you?"

"Yes, it is William; your old friend William,"
said Mr. Darford, embracing him affectionately.
Pride and shame struggled in the mind of Charles;
and turning aside to repress the tears which in the
first instance of emotion had started into his eyes,
he went to the farthest end of the room for an
arm-chair for his cousin, placed it with awkward
ceremony, and said, "Won't you be seated, cousin
Darford? I am sure Mrs. Germaine and I are
much indebted to you and Mrs. Darford for your
goodness to our children. I was just thinking of
writing to you about them; but we are in sad confusion here, just at this moment. I am quite
ashamed—I did not expect—Why did you never
honour us with a visit before? I am sure you
could not possibly have hit upon a more unlucky
moment for a visit—for yourself, I mean."

"If it proves lucky to you, my dear Charles,"
replied William mildly, "I shall think it the most
fortunate moment I could possibly have chosen."

Vanquished by the tone of this reply, our hero
burst into tears: he squeezed his friend's hand,
but could not speak. Recovering himself after a

few moments, he said, " You are too good, cousin William, and always were! I thought you called in by accident; I had no supposition that you came on purpose to assist me in this moment of distress—embarrassment I ought to say! for in fact it is only a mere temporary embarrassment."

" I am heartily glad to hear it. But speak to me freely, Charles; do not conceal the real state of your affairs from your best friend. What tendency could this have but to plunge you into irretrievable ruin?"

Charles paused for a minute. " The truth of the matter is, my dear William," continued he, " that there are circumstances in this business which I should be sorry reached Mrs. Germaine's ear, or any of her cursed proud relations; for if once they heard of it, I should have no peace for the rest of my life. Indeed, as to peace, I cannot boast of much as it is; but it might be worse, much worse, if the whole truth came out. To you, however, I can trust it, though in your line of life it would be counted a shocking thing: but still you are so indulgent—"

William listened, without being able to guess where this preamble would end.

" In the first place," continued Charles, " you

know—Mrs. Germaine is almost ten years older than I am."

"Six years, I thought you formerly told me?"

"I beg your pardon, ten—ten—within a few months. If I said six it was before our marriage, when I knew no better. She owns to seven; her own relations say eight; her nurse said nine; and I say ten."

"Well, ten let it be, since you will have it so."

"I should be very glad to have it otherwise, I promise you, if I could: for it is not very pleasant to a man like me to be *quizzed* by half the young men of fashion in town for having married a woman old enough to be my mother."

"Not quite old enough to be your mother," said his cousin, in a conciliatory tone; "these young men of fashion are not the best calculators. Mrs. Germaine could not well have been your mother, since, at the worst, by your own account, there is only ten years' difference between you."

"Oh, but that is not all; for, what is still worse, Mrs. Germaine, thanks to the raking hours she keeps, and gaming and fretting, looks full ten years older than she is: so that you see, in fact, there are twenty years between us."

"I do not see it indeed," replied William, smiling; "but I am bound to believe what you assert. Let

me ask you to what does this discussion concerning
poor Mrs. Germaine's age tend?"

"To justify, or at least to excuse, poor Mr. Germaine for keeping a mistress, who is something
younger, something prettier, and, above all, something more good-humoured than his wife."

"Perhaps the wife would be as good-humoured
as the mistress, if she were as happy in possessing
her husband's affections."

"Affections! Oh Lord! Affections are out of the
question. Mrs. Germaine does not care a straw
about my affections."

"And yet you dread that she should have the
least hint of your having a mistress?"

"Of course. You don't see my jet. You don't
consider what a devil of a handle that would give
her against me. She has no more love for me than
this table; but she is jealous beyond all credibility,
and she knows right well how to turn her jealousy
to account. She would go caballing among her
tribes of relations, and get all the women and all
the world on her side, with this hue and cry of a
mistress; and then I should be branded as the worst
husband upon earth. That indeed I should laugh
at, because all the young men in town would keep
me in countenance; but Mrs. Germaine would rum-

mage out the history of the sums of money I have
given this girl, and then would set those against her
play-debts, and I should have no more hold over
her; for, you know, if I should begin to reproach
her with the one, she would recriminate. She is
a devil of a hand at that work! Neither you nor
any man on earth, except myself, can form any
idea of the temper of Mrs. Germaine! She is—to
you, my dear friend, I may have the relief of saying
so—she is, without exception, the most proud, peevish, selfish, unreasonable, extravagant, tyrannical,
unfeeling woman in Christendom!"

"In Christendom! Oh, you exaggerate, Charles!"

"Exaggerate! Upon my soul, I do not: she is
all I have said, and more."

"More! Impossible. Come, I see how it is
she has been unlucky at the card-table; you are
angry, and therefore you speak, as angry people
always do, worse than you think."*

"No, not at all, I promise you. I am as perfectly cool as you are. You do not know Mrs.
Germaine as well as I do."

"But I know that she is much to be pitied, if her
husband has a worse opinion of her than anybody
else expresses."

* Swift.

" That is precisely because I am her husband—
and know her better than other people do. Will
not you give me leave to be the best judge in what
relates to my own wife? I never, indeed, expected
to hear you, of all people upon earth, cousin
William, undertake her defence. I think I remember that she was no great favourite of yours
before I married, and you dissuaded me as much
as possible from the match: yet now you are quite
become her advocate, and take her part to my face
against me."

" It is not taking her part against you, my dear
Charles," replied his cousin, " to endeavour to
make you better satisfied with your wife. I am
not so obstinate in self-opinion as to wish, at the
expense of your domestic happiness, to prove that
I was right in dissuading you from the match ; on
the contrary, I would do all in my power to make
the best of it ; and so should you."

" Ah, cousin William, it is easy for you to talk
of making the best of a bad match ; you who are
married to one of the best-tempered women alive !
I wish you were to live with Mrs. Germaine for
one month."

William smiled ; as much as to say, " I cannot
join in that wish."

"Besides," continued Charles, "if I were to open my whole heart to you, you would pity me on another account. My wife is not my only plague; my mistress is almost as great a torment as my wife."

"What! this mistress of whom you are so fond?"

"Ay! there is the curse! I cannot help being fond of her: and that she knows, and plays me off as she pleases. But I believe the little jilt loves me all the time: because she has offers enough, and from men of the first fashion, if she would leave me. She is certainly a good girl; but then so passionate!"

"I thought you told me she was good-humoured," interrupted his cousin.

"Well, so she is at times, the best-humoured creature in nature; and then she is charming: but when she falls into a passion, she is a little fury! absolutely a little devil! There is nothing she would not do. Now, do you know, all this terrible business, this execution against me, is her doing?"

"A singular proof of love!" said Mr. William Darford.

"Oh, the fool loves me, notwithstanding; I must do her that justice: but she is quite a child.

I put her into a passion by going down to Leicestershire when she wanted me to stay with her in town.   She told me she would be revenged; but I could not believe she would go such lengths.   She gave a note of mine, for two hundred guineas, to her uncle; and he got a writ.   Now she is in despair about it.   I saw her two hours ago all in tears, and tearing her hair, because her uncle won't consent to withdraw the execution.   I am sure she is really and truly sorry; and would give her eyes to get me out of this scrape."

"Whether she would give her eyes or not, I will not pretend to determine; but it is plain she would not pay two hundred guineas 'to get you out of this scrape.'   Now, where do you intend to get the money?"

"Ah, there's the rub! I have not a farthing till our next rents come in and you see these heaps of bills.   Then the agent, who manages every thing, Heaven knows how! at Germaine-park, says tenants are breaking; that we are I do not know how much in his debt, and that we must sell: but that, if we sell in a hurry, and if our distress be talked of, we shall get nothing for the land, and so shall be ruined, outright.   Now this all originates in Mrs. Germaine's pride and posi-

11

tiveness : she never could be prevailed upon to go
down to Germaine-park, these ten years past, because some of the Northamptonshire people affronted her: so our affairs have gone on just as the
agent pleases ; and he is a rascal, I am convinced,
for he is always writing to say we are in his debt.
But indeed, my dear William, you are too good to
take any interest in this history of my affairs : I
am conscious that I have not treated you well."

"Do not talk of that now ; do not think of it,
Charles," interrupted Mr. Darford. " I am come
to town on purpose to be of all the service to you
I can. I will discharge this writ upon one, and
only upon one, condition."

" Upon any condition you please," cried Charles.
" I will give you my bond. I will give you security upon the Germaine estate, if you require
it."

" I require no security; I require no bond,
Charles ; I require only a condition which I believe
to be absolutely necessary for your happiness.
Promise me you will break off all connexion with
this treacherous mistress of yours."

•" Treacherous ! No, no ! I assure you, you mistake the girl."

" Mistake her or not, Charles, without arguing

the matter further, on this one point I must be peremptory; and, positively, the only condition on which I will pay this money is your promise never to see her again."

Charles hesitated. "Upon my soul," cried he, "I believe the girl will break her heart. But then she is so cursedly extravagant, she ruins me! I would have broken with her long ago, if I could have summoned up courage enough. After all, I believe it was more habit, idleness, and fashion, than any thing else, that made me go to see her so often. When I did not know what to do with myself, or when I was put out of humour at home, I went to this girl. Well, let us say no more about it : she is not worth thinking of; I give her up. You may depend upon it, my dear William, I will have nothing more to do with her. I will, since you make that your ultimatum, never see her again."

"Will you write to her then immediately, to let her know your determination ?"

"Certainly; immediately."

Charles wrote, to bid adieu to this mistress; to whom, by his own account, habit, idleness, fashion, and the want of a happy home had attached him ; and William gave him a draft for the amount of his debt, by which the execution was taken off.

Mr. Darford seized the moment when his cousin's mind was warmed with gratitude to say a few words, as little in the form of advice as possible, in praise of economy.

"You know, my dear Charles," said he, "that I am, and always was, a very plain man, in my way of living, and I dare say my ideas will appear quite absurd to you, who are used to live with men of taste and fashion; but really these rooms, this furniture, and this house appear to me fitter for a nobleman than for a man of your fortune."

"It is so. Mrs. Germaine would insist upon my taking it. But I will part with it before next winter. I will advertise it immediately. I will begin a course of economy."

Mr. Germaine's projects of economy were at this moment interrupted by the sudden entrance of his wife. Her eyes flashing with anger, she walked with the proud air of an enraged tragedy queen across the room, seated herself upon a sofa, and in a voice which trembled with ill-suppressed rage, said, "I am to thank you, Mr. Germaine, for the many obliging things you have said of me this last hour! I have heard them all! You are under a mistake, sir, if you imagine I have been hitherto your dupe. You have never imposed upon me for a moment. I have suspected, this twelvemonth, that you kept a mistress; and now I am happy to have the truth confirmed from your own lips. But I deserve all that has happened! I am justly treated! Weak woman, to marry as I did! No gentleman, sir, would have behaved or would have spoken as you have done! Could not you have been content with ruining yourself and your family, Mr. Germaine, by your profligate low tastes, without insulting me by base reflections upon my temper, and downright falsehoods about my age? No gentleman, sir, would have treated me as you have done. I am the most miserable of women!"

Passion choked her utterance, and she fell back in a violent fit of hysterics. Mr. William Darford was much shocked at this matrimonial scene. The lady had caught hold of his arm, in one of her convulsive motions; and she held it so fast that he could not withdraw. Charles stood in silent dismay. His conscience smote him; and though he could not love his wife, he blamed himself for having rendered her " the most miserable of women." " Leave her to me, Charles," said Mr. Darford, " and I will endeavour to set matters to rights."

Charles shook his head, and left the room. Mrs.

11 *

Germaine by degrees recovered herself; for an hysteric fit cannot last for ever. She cast her eyes round the room, and exclaimed, " He has done well to leave me! Oh, that it were for ever! Oh, that we had never met! But may I ask why Mr. William Darford is here? My own servant—my own maid should have been summoned to attend me. We have servants still, sir; and, humbled as I am, I see no necessity for submitting to have cool spectators of our family distresses and family quarrels."

" Believe me, madam," said Mr. Darford, " I am not a cool spectator of either. I do not wish to recall disagreeable things, but to obtain the right of speaking to you of your affairs as a friend. Permit me to remind you that, when I could not guess you heard me, I defended your interests."

" Really, sir, you spoke so low that I did not distinctly hear what you said; and my feelings were so much hurt by all I heard from Mr. Germaine, who spoke loud enough, that I attended to nothing else. Upon recollection, I do however remember you made some offer to get Mr. Germaine out of his present embarrassments, upon condition that he would break off all connexion with this girl, whom nobody knows; or rather whom everybody knows *too* well."

" And was not this offer of mine some proof, Mrs. Germaine, that I wish your happiness ?"

" Why, really, Mr. Darford, having lived in the world as I have done from my childhood, I am not apt to expect much friendship from any one, especially from people in the habits of calculation ; and I have been so much deceived where I have unguardedly trusted to the friendship and love of a man brought up in that sort of way, that you must forgive me if I could not bring my mind to think you had any concern for my happiness in the offer you made. I did indeed suppose it would be a mortifying circumstance to you, to see your cousin quite ruined by this infamous creature. I say, I did imagine you would be shocked at seeing your cousin sent to jail. That, you know, is a thing discreditable to a whole family, let it be of what sort it may. From your kindness to our children, I see you consider us as relations. Every human being, I do suppose, has some family pride in their own way."

" I own I have a great deal of family pride, in my own way, madam," replied Mr. Darford, with a calm smile; " I am proud, for instance, of having, and of being able to maintain in perfect independence, a number of good and affectionate children,

and a wife whose good sense and sweetness of temper constitute the happiness of my existence!"

Mrs. Germaine coloured, threw back her head,
and strove to conceal the anguish of her conscience.
William was sorry he had inflicted pain, but he saw
that the only way to make himself understood, in
this conversation, was to assert that real superiority
of character to which, in certain situations, the
factitious pretensions of rank or fashion never fail
to yield.

"You are at liberty, Mrs. Germaine," continued
William, "to interpret my offers and my actions
as you think proper; but you will, when you are
cool, observe that neither I nor any of my family
have any thing to gain from you or yours; not
even a curtsy or a bow in public places; for we
do not frequent them. We live retired, and have
no connexion with fine people; we preserve our
own independence by confining ourselves to our
own station in life; and by never desiring to quit
it, nor to ape those who are called our betters.
From what I have just heard you say, I think it
possible you may have formed the idea that we invited your children to our house with the selfish
supposition that the *connexion*, I believe that is the
fashionable phrase, might be advantageous to our

own? But this is quite a mistake. Our children will live as we do: they have no idea of forming high connexions, because they have been taught not to think them necessary to happiness. I assure you it is not my habit to talk so much of myself, and of mine; but I thought it best to explain the truth to you at once, as this was the only way to gain your confidence, and as we have neither of us time to spare."

"Very true," said Mrs. Germaine.

"And now, madam, I have a proposal to make to you, which I hope you will take as it is meant. I understand, from Mr. Germaine, you have some play-debts."

"Mr. Germaine does not know their amount," said Mrs. Germaine; lowering her voice, as if she apprehended she might be overheard.

"If you will trust me with that secret, I will not make a bad use of it."

Mrs. Germaine in a whisper named the sum. It was certainly considerable, for the naming of it made Mr. Darford step back with surprise. After a few minutes' thought, he recovered himself, and said, "This is a larger debt than I was aware of, but we will see what can be done. From the time that Charles and I dissolved our partnership, I have never remitted my attention to business; and that very circumstance, for which you must despise me, puts it now in my power to assist you without injuring my own family. I am a man who speak my mind freely, perhaps bluntly. You must solemnly promise me you will never again play at any game of hazard. Upon this condition, I will pay your present debts immediately."

With all the eagerness of a person who wishes to seize an offer which appears too generous to be repeated, Mrs. Germaine promised all that was required. Her debts were paid.

And now her benefactor had hopes that she and her husband would live more prudently; and that they might still enjoy some portion of domestic happiness. Vain hopes! Charles really wished to retrench his expenses; but Mrs. Germaine's pride was an insuperable obstacle to all his plans of economy. She had always been accustomed to such and such things. There was no possibility of living without them. Her relations would be perfectly astonished if she did not appear in the style in which she had always lived before her marriage. Provoked by the insolent absurdity of such arguments, Mr. Germaine insisted with the authoritative voice of a husband who was conscious that he had both reason and power on his side. Hence arose daily altercations, more bitter even than those which jealousy had formerly occasioned. Some wives acknowledge they can more easily forgive a husband's infidelity than his interference in the regulation of their household expenses. Of this class of amiable females was Mrs. Germaine. Though her husband strictly adhered to his promise never to have any further connexion with his mistress, yet he was not rewarded by any increase of affection or kindness from his wife; on the contrary, she seemed to be rather vexed that she was deprived of this legitimate subject of complaint. She could not, with so much tragic effect, bewail that her husband would ruin himself and her by his follies.

To loud altercations silent hatred succeeded. Mrs. Germaine grew sullen, low-spirited, nervous, and hysterical. Among fashionable and medical dowagers, she became an interesting personage: but this species of consequence was by no means sufficient to support her self-complacency, and, as she declared, she felt herself incapable of supporting the intolerable burden of *ennui*.

In various situations, the conduct of many individuals may be predicted with certainty by those who are acquainted with their previous habits.

Habit is, to weak minds, a species of moral predestination, from which they have no power to escape.   Their common language expresses their
sense of their own inability to struggle against that
destiny which their previous folly has prepared.
They usually say, " For my part, I cannot help
doing so and so.   I know it is very wrong.   I know
it is my ruin ; but I own I cannot resist.   It is in
vain to argue with me : it is my way ; it is my fate."

Mrs. Germaine found herself led, " by an irre-
sistible impulse," to the card-table, notwithstanding
her solemn promise never more to play at any game
of hazard.   It was in vain to argue with her.   " It
was her way ; it was her fate : she knew it was
very wrong ; she knew it was her ruin ; but she
could not resist !"

In the course of a few months she was again in-
volved in debt ; and she had the meanness and the
assurance again to apply to the generosity of Mr.
William Darford.   Her letter was written in the
most abject strain, and was full of all the flattering
expressions which she imagined must, from a woman of her birth and consequence in the world,
have a magical effect upon one in Mr. William
Darford's station.   She was surprised when she
received a decided refusal.   He declined all further

interference, as he perceived it was impossible that
he could be of any real utility. He forbore to
reproach the lady with her breach of promise:
" She will," said he to himself, " be sufficiently
punished by the consequences of her own conduct:
I would not increase her distress."

A separation from her husband was the immediate consequence. Perhaps it may be thought that,
to Mrs. Germaine, this would be no punishment:
but the loss of all the pride, pomp, and circumstance of married life was deeply felt. She was
thrown absolutely upon the charity of relations;
who had very little charity in any sense of the
word. She was disregarded by all her fine acquaintance; she had no friend upon earth to pity
her; even her favourite maid gave warning, because she was tired of her mistress's temper, and
of receiving no wages.

The detail of poor Mrs. Germaine's mortifications and sufferings cannot be interesting. She
was a prey to low spirits, or, in other words, to
mortified vanity, for some time; and at last died
of a nervous fever.

Her husband wrote the following letter to Mr.
William Darford, soon after her death:

" My Dear William,

" You have heard of poor Mrs. Germaine's death, and of the manner of it; no more need be said upon that subject. Whatever were her faults, she has suffered for them; and so have I for mine. Believe me, I am effectually cured of all desire to be a fine gentleman. I shall quit the name of Germaine immediately, and resume that of Darford. You know the state of my affairs. There is yet hope I may set things to rights by my own industry; and I am determined to go into business, and to apply to it in good earnest, for my own sake, and for the sake of my children, whom I have hitherto shamefully neglected. But I had it not always in my power, after my marriage, to do as I wished. No more of that. The blame be upon me for the past; for the future I shall, I hope, be a different man. I dare not ask you to trust so far to these good resolutions as to take me into partnership with you in your manufactory; but perhaps your good-nature can direct me to some employment suited to my views and capacity. I ask only a fair trial; I think I shall not do as I used to do, and leave all the letters to be written by my partner.

' Give my love to my dear little boy and girl.

How can I thank you and Mrs. Darford enough
for all you have done for them! There is another
person whom I should wish to thank, but scarcely
dare to name; feeling, as I do, so unworthy of her
goodness.   Adieu, yours sincerely,

> "CHARLES DARFORD, again,
> thank God."

It is scarcely necessary to inform our readers
that Mr. William Darford received his penitent
friend with open arms, took him into partnership,
and assisted him in the most kind and judicious
manner to re-establish his fortune and his credit.
He became remarkable for his steady attention to
business; to the great astonishment of those who
had seen him only in the character of a dissipated
fine gentleman. Few have sufficient strength of
mind thus to stop short in the career of folly, and
few have the resolution to bear the ridicule thrown
upon them even by those whom they despise.
Our hero was ridiculed most unmercifully by all his
former companions,—by all the Bond-street loun-
gers. But of what consequence was this to him?
He did not live among them; he did not hear their
witticisms, and well knew that, in less than a twelvemonth, they would forget that such a person as

Charles Germaine had ever existed. His knowledge of what is called high life had sufficiently
convinced him that happiness is not in the gift or
in the possession of those who are often, to ignorant mortals, objects of supreme admiration and
envy.

Charles Darford looked for happiness, and found
it in domestic life.

Belief, founded upon our own experience, is more
firm than that which we grant to the hearsay evidence of moralists; but happy those who, according
to the ancient proverb, can profit by the experience
of their predecessors.

Feb. 1803.

THE CONTRAST.

CHAPTER I.

"WHAT a blessing it is to be the father of such a family of children!" said Farmer Frankland, as he looked round at the honest affectionate faces of his sons and daughters, who were dining with him on his birthday. "What a blessing it is to have a large family of children!"

"A blessing you may call it, if you will, neighbour," said Farmer Bettesworth; "but if I was to speak my mind, I should be apt to call it a curse."

"Why, as to that, we may both be right and both be wrong," replied Frankland; "for children are either a blessing or a curse, according as they turn out; and they turn out according as they are brought up. 'Bring up a child in the way it should go;' that has ever been my maxim: show me a better, show me a happier, family than my own, and show me a happier father than myself,"

12 *

continued the good old man, with pleasure sparkling in his eyes. Observing, however, that his
neighbour Bettsworth looked blank and sighed
deeply, he checked himself, and said, in a more
humble tone, " To be sure, it is not so mannerly
for a man to be praising his own ; except it just
come from the heart unawares, among friends, who
will excuse it ; especially upon such a day as this.
This day I am seventy years of age, and never
was heartier or happier! So, Fanny, love, fill
neighbour Bettesworth a glass of your sister's cider.
'T is my Patty's making, sir ; and better never
was drunk. Nay, nay, sit ye still, neighbour ; as
you happened to call in just as we were all dining,
and making merry together, why you cannot do
better than to stay and make one of us, seeing
that you are heartily welcome."

Mr. Bettesworth excused himself, by saying that
he was in haste home.

No happy home had he, no affectionate children
to welcome his return. Yet he had as numerous
a family as Mr. Frankland's ; three sons and two
daughters,—Idle Isaac, Wild Will, Bullying Bob,
Saucy Sally, and Jilting Jessy. Such were the
names by which they were called by all who
knew them in the town of Monmouth, where they

lived. Alliteration had "lent its artful aid" in giving these nicknames; but they were not mis-applied.

Mr. Bettesworth was an indolent man, fond of his pipe, and fonder of building castles in the air by his fireside. Mrs. Bettesworth was a vain, foolish vixen; fond of dress, and fonder of her own will. Neither of them took the least care to breed up their children well. While they were young, the mother humoured them: when they grew up, she contradicted them in every thing, and then wondered how they could be so ungrateful as not to love her.

The father was also surprised to find that his boys and girls were not as well-mannered, nor as well-tempered, nor as clever, nor as steady, nor as dutiful and affectionate, as his neighbour Frank-land's; and he said to himself, " Some folks have the luck of having good children. To be sure, some children are born better than others."

He should rather have said, " To be sure, some children are bred better than others."

Mr. Frankland's wife was a prudent sensible woman, and had united with him in constant endeavours to educate their family. While they were yet infants, prattling at their mother's knee, she taught them to love and help one another, to conquer their little froward humours, and to be obedient and tractable. This saved both them and herself a great deal of trouble afterward; and their father often said, both to the boys and girls, " You may thank your mother, and so may I, for the good tempers you have."

The girls had the misfortune to lose this ex- cellent mother, when one was about seventeen, and the other eighteen; but she was always alive in their memory. Patty, the eldest sister, was homely in her person; but she was so neat in her dress, and she had such a cheerful agreeable temper, that people forgot she was not handsome ; particularly as it was observed that she was very fond of her sister Fanny, who was remarkably pretty.

Fanny was neither prudish nor censorious; neither a romp nor a flirt: she was so unaffected and unassuming that most of her neighbours loved her; and this is saying a great deal in favour of one who had so much the power to excite envy.

Mr. Frankland's eldest son, George, was bred to be a farmer; and he understood country business uncommonly well for a young man of his age. He constantly assisted his father in the manage- ment of the farm; and by this means acquired much experience with little waste of time or money. His father had always treated him so much as his friend, and had talked to him so openly of his affairs, that he ever looked upon his father's business as his own ; and he had no idea of having any separate interest.

James, the second son, was bred to trade. He had been taught whatever was necessary and useful for a man in business ; he had habits of punctuality, civil manners, and a thorough love of fair dealing.

Frank, the youngest son, was of a more lively disposition than his brothers: and his father used often to tell him, when he was a boy, that, if he did not take care, his hasty temper would get him into scrapes ; and that the brightest parts, as they are called, will be of little use to a man, unless he has also steadiness to go through with whatever he begins. These hints, from a father whom he heartily loved, made so strong an impression upon Frank, that he took great pains to correct the natural violence of his temper, and to learn patience and industry. The three brothers were attached to one another ; and their friendship was a source of improvement, as well as of pleasure.

The evening of Mr. Frankland's birthday the

whole family retired to an arbour in their garden,
and began to talk over their affairs with open
hearts.

" Well, Frank, my boy," said the happy father,
who was the confidant of his children, " I am sure
if your heart is set upon this match with Jessy
Bettesworth, I will do my best to like the girl ; and
her not being rich shall be no objection to me : we
can made that up among us, some way or other.
But, Frank, it is fair to tell you my opinion of the
girl, plainly and fully, beforehand, as I have done.
She that has jilted others, I think would be apt to
jilt you, if she met with a better offer."

" Why, then, father, I 'll not be in a hurry : I 'll
take time to consider, before I speak to her any
more ; and I thank you for being so kind, which I
hope I shall not forget."

The morning after this conversation passed,
Jilting Jessy, accompanied by her sister, Saucy
Sally, came to pay Patty and Fanny Frankland a
visit. They were full of some piece of news,
which they were eager to tell.

" Well, to be sure, I dreamed I had a diamond
ring put on my finger by a great lord, not a week
ago," cried Jessy ; " and who knows but it may

come true? You have not heard the news, Fanny Frankland? Hey, Patty?"

"Not they: they never hear any news!" said Sally.

"Well, then, I'll tell you," cried Jessy. "Rich Captain Bettesworth, our relation, who made the great *fortin* abroad, over seas, has just broken his neck out a hunting, and the *fortin* all comes to us."

"We shall now see whether Mrs. Craddock shall push by me again, as she did yesterday in the street! We'll see whether I sha'n't make as good a fine lady as herself, I warrant it, that's all. It's my turn to push by folk now," said Saucy Sally.

Fanny and Patty Frankland, with sincere good-nature, congratulated their neighbours on this increase of fortune; but they did not think that pushing by Mrs. Craddock could be one of the most useful or agreeable consequences of an increase in fortune.

"Lord, Patty! how you sit moping yourself there at your work" continued Sally; "but some people must work, to be sure, that can't afford to be idle. How you must envy us, Patty!"

Patty assured her she did not in the least envy those who were idle.

"Fine talking! Fine airs, truly, Miss Patty! This is by way of calling me over the coals for being idle, I suppose!" said Sally; "but I 've no notion of being taken to task this way. You think you 've had a fine *edication*, I suppose, and so are to set a pattern for all Monmouthshire, indeed : but you 'll find some people will be as much thought of now as other people ; and may hold their heads as high. *Edication's* a fine thing, no doubt ; but *fortin's* a better, as the world goes, I 've a notion : so you may go moping on here as long as you please, being a good child all the days of your life !

'Come when you 're called;
And do as you 're bid;
Shut the door after you;
And you 'll never be chid.'

I 'm sure I would not let my nose be kept to the grindstone, as yours is, for any one living. I 've too much spirit, for my part, to be made a fool of, as some people are ; and all for the sake of being called a vastly good daughter, or a vastly good sister, forsooth !"

Nothing but the absolute want of breath could have suspended the remainder of this speech ; for she was so provoked to see Patty did not envy her, that she was determined to say every thing she could invent, to try her. Patty's temper, however, was proof against the trial; and Saucy Sally, despairing of success against one sister, turned to the other.

" Miss Fanny, I presume," said she, " won't give herself such high and mighty airs as she used to do, to one of her sweethearts, who shall be nameless."

Fanny blushed; for she knew this speech alluded to Wild Will, who was an admirer of hers, but whom she had never encouraged.

" I hope," said she, " I never gave myself airs to anybody: but if you mean to speak of your brother William, I assure you that my opinion of him will not be changed by his becoming richer; nor will my father's."

Here the conversation was interrupted by the entrance of Frank, who had just heard from one of the Bettesworths of their good fortune. He was impatient to see how Jessy would behave in prosperity. " Now," said he to himself, " I shall judge whether my father's opinion of her or mine is right."

Jilting Jessy had certainly given Frank reason to believe she was very fond of him; but the sudden change in her fortune quite altered her views and opinions. As soon as Frank came in, she pre-

13

tended to be in great haste to be gone; and by various petty manœuvres, avoided giving him an opportunity of speaking to her; though she plainly
saw he was anxious to say something to her in
private.   At length, when she was looking out of
the window, to see whether a shower was over, he
went behind her and whispered, " Why are you in
such haste?   Cannot you stay a few minutes with
us?   You are not always in such a hurry to run
away!"

    " Lord, nonsense! Mr. Frank.   Why will you
always plague me with nonsense, Mr. Frank?"

    She opened the lattice window as she spoke, put
out her beautiful neck as far as possible, and looked
up eagerly to the clouds.

    " How sweet this jasmine smells!" said Frank,
pulling a bit of it which hung over the casement.
" This is the jasmine you used to like so much.
See, I 've nailed it up, and it 's finer than ever it
was.   Won't you have a sprig of it?" offering to
put some in her hat, as he had done before; but
she now drew back disdainfully, saying,

    " Lord! Mr. Frank, it 's all wet; and will spoil
my new lilac ribands.   How awkward and disagreeable you are always!"

THE CONTRAST

" Always ! you did not always think so ; at least, you did not say so."

" Well, I think so, and say so now ; and that's enough." .

" And too much, if you are in earnest ; but that I can hardly believe."

" That's your business, and not mine. If you don't choose to believe what I say, how can I help it ? But this you'll remember, if you please, sir."

" Sir !!! Oh, Jessy ! is it come to this ?"

" To what, sir ? For I vow and declare I don't understand you !"

" I have never understood you till now, I am afraid."

" Perhaps not : it's well we understand one another at last. Better late than never."

The scornful lady walked off to a looking-glass, to wipe away the insult which her new lilac ribands had received from Frank's sprig of jasmine.

" One word more, and I have done," said Frank, hastily following her. " Have I done anything to displease you ? Or does this change in you proceed from the change in your fortune, Jessy ?"

" I'm not obliged, sir, to account for my proceedings to anybody ; and don't know what right you have to question me, as if you were my lord and judge . which you are not, nor never will be, thank God !"

Frank's passion struggled with his reason for a few instants. He stood motionless ; then, in an altered voice, repeated, " Thank God !" and turned from her with proud composure. From this time forward he paid no more court to Jessy.

" Ah, father !" said he, " you knew her better than I did. I am glad I did not marry her last year, when she would have accepted of me, and when she seemed to love me. I thought you were rather hard upon her then. But you were not in love with her as I was, and now I find you were right."

" My dear Frank," said the good old man, " I hope you will not think me hard another time, when I do not think just the same as you do. I would, as I told you, have done everything in my power to settle you well in the world, if you had married this girl. I should never have been angry with you ; but I should have been bitterly grieved if you had, for the whim of the minute, made your-self unhappy for life. And was it not best to put you upon your guard? What better use can an old man make of his experience than to give it to his children ?"

Frank was touched by the kind manner in which his father spoke to him; and Fanny, who was present, immediately put a letter into her father's hand, saying, " I have just received this from Will Bettesworth: what answer do you think I had best give him ?"

Now Fanny, though she did not quite approve of Wild Will's character, felt a little partiality for him, for he seemed to be of a generous temper, and his manners were engaging. She hoped his wildness was only the effect of good spirits, and that he would soon settle to some business. However, she had kept these hopes and this partiality a secret from all but her father, and she had never given Will Bettesworth any encouragement. Her father had not a good opinion of this young man; and she had followed his advice in keeping him at a distance. His letter was written in so vile a hand that it was not easy to decipher the meaning.

" MY SWEET PRETTY FANNY,

" Notwithstanding your cruilty, I ham more in love with you than hever; and now I ham come in for a share in a great fortin; and shall ask no questions from father nor mother, if you will marry me, having no reason to love or care for either.

13 *

Mother's as cross as hever, and will never, I am
shure, agre to my doing any thing I like myself;
which makes me more set upon having my own
whay, and I ham more and more in love with you
than hever, and would go through fire and water to
get you.   Your true love (in haste)

"WILL BETTESWORTH."

At first reading the letter, Fanny was pleased to
find that her lover did not, like Jilting Jessy, change
his mind the moment that his situation was altered :
but upon looking over it again, she could not help
considering that such an undutiful son was not likely
to make a very good husband ; and she thought
even that Wild Will seemed to be more and more
in love with her than ever, from the spirit of opposition ; for he had not been much attached to her,
till his mother, as he said, set herself against the
match.   At the end of this letter were the words
turn over ; but they were so scrawled and blotted,
that Fanny thought they were only one of the
strange flourishes which he usually made at the end
of his name ; and consequently she had never
turned over, or read the postscript, when she put
the epistle into her father's hands.   He deciphered
the flourish, and read the following addition :

" I know your feather does not like me; but never mind his not being agreeuble. As shure as my name 's Will, I 'd carry you hoff, night or day ; and Bob would fight your brothers along with me, if they said a word : for Bob loves fun. I will be at your windor this night, if you are agreuble, like a gurl of spirit."

Fanny was shocked so much that she turned quite pale, and would have sunk to the ground, if she had not been supported by her father. As soon as she recovered herself sufficiently to be able to think, she declared that all the liking she had ever felt for William Bettesworth was completely conquered ; and she thanked her father for having early warned her of his character. " Ah ! father," said she, " what a happiness it has been to me that you never made me afraid of you ! Else, I never should have dared to tell you my mind ; and in what a sad snare might I have been at this instant ! If it had not been for you, I should perhaps have encouraged this man ; I might not then, maybe, have been able to draw back ; and what would have become of me !"

It is scarcely necessary to say that Fanny wrote a decided refusal to Wild Will. All connexion be-

tween the Bettesworths and Franklands was now
broken off.

Will was enraged at being rejected by Fanny ;
and Jessy was equally incensed at finding she
was no longer admired by Frank. They, however, affected to despise the Franklands, and to
treat them as people beneath their notice. The
fortune left by Captain Bettesworth to his relations
was said to be about twenty thousand pounds : with
this sum they thought, to use their own expression,
they were entitled to live in as great style, and cut
as grand a dash, as any of the first families in
Monmouthshire. For the present we shall leave
them to the enjoyment of their new grandeur, and
continue the humble history of Farmer Frankland
and his family.

By many years of persevering industry, Mr.
Frankland had so improved the farm upon which
he lived, that he was now affluent, for a man in
his station of life. His house, garden, farm-yard,
every thing about him, were so neat and comfortable, that travellers, as they passed by, never
failed to ask, " Who lives there !" Travellers,
however, only saw the outside ; and that was not,
in this instance, the best part. They would have
seen happiness, if they had looked within these

farm-house walls : happiness which may be enjoyed as well in the cottage as in the palace,—that which arises from family union.

Mr. Frankland was now anxious to settle his sons in the world. George had business enough at home, in taking care of the farm : and James proposed to set up a haberdasher's shop in Monmouth ; accordingly, the goods were ordered, and the shop was taken.

There was a part in the roof of the house which let in the wet, and James would not go into it till this was completely repaired : so his packages of goods were sent from London to his father's house, which was only a mile distant from Monmouth. His sisters unpacked them by his desire, to set shop-marks upon each article. Late at night, after all the rest of the family were asleep, Patty was sitting up to finish setting the marks on a box full of ribands : the only thing that remained to be done. Her candle was just burnt out ; and, as she was going for another, she went by a passage window that faced the farm-yard, and suddenly saw a great light without. She looked out, and beheld the large hay-rick all in flames. She ran immediately to awaken her brothers and her father. They used every possible exertion to extinguish the fire, and to prevent it from communicating to the dwelling-house; but the wind was high; it blew directly towards the house. George poured buckets of water over the thatch, to prevent its catching fire; but all was in vain : thick flakes of fire fell upon it faster than they could be extinguished, and in an hour's time the dwelling-house was in a blaze.

The first care of the sons had been to get their father and sisters out of danger ; then, with great presence of mind, they collected every thing that was most valuable and portable, and laboured hard to save poor James's stock of haberdashery. They were all night hard at work : towards three o'clock the fire was got under, and darkness and silence succeeded. There was one roof of the house saved, under which the whole family rested for a few hours, till the return of daylight renewed the melancholy spectacle of their ruin. Hay, oats, straw, corn-ricks, barn, every thing that the farm-yard contained, was utterly consumed : the walls and some half-burnt beams remained of the dwelling-house, but it was no longer habitable. It was calculated that six hundred pounds would not repair the loss occasioned by this unfortunate accident. How the hay-rick had caught fire nobody knew.

George, who had made up the hay-stack, was most inclined to think that the hay had not been sufficiently dried; and that the rick had heated from this cause. He blamed himself extremely; but his father declared he had seen, felt, and smelt the hay when the rick was making, and that it was as well saved hay as ever was brought into a farm-yard. This, in some measure, quieted poor George's conscience: and he was yet more comforted by Patty's good-nature, who showed him a bucket of ashes which had been left very near the spot where the hay-rick stood. The servant-girl, who, though careless, was honest, confessed she recollected having accidentally left this bucket in that dangerous place the preceding evening; that she was going with it across the yard to the ash-hole, but she heard her lover whistle to her from the lane, and she set down the bucket in a hurry, ran to meet him, and forgot the ashes. All she could say in her own defence was that she did not think there was any fire in the bucket.

Her good master forgave her carelessness: he said he was sure she reproached herself enough for it, as indeed she did; and the more so when her master spoke to her so kindly: she cried as if her heart would break, and all that could be done

to comfort her was to set her to work as hard **as**
possible for the family.

They did not, any of them, spend their time in
vain lamentations : ready money was wanting to
rebuild the house and barns, and James sold to a
haberdasher in Monmouth all of his stock which
had been saved out of the fire, and brought the
money to his father.

" Father," said he, " you gave this to me when
you were able to afford it ; you want it now, and I
can do very well without it. I will go and be
shopman in some good shop in Monmouth; and
by degrees I shall get on, and do very well in the
world. It would be strange if I did not, after the
education you have given me."

The father took the money from his son with
tears of pleasure. " It is odd enough," said he,
" that I should feel pleasure at such a time ; but
this is the blessing of having good children. As
long as we all are ready to help one another in this
manner, we can never be very miserable, happen
what may. Now let us think of rebuilding our
house," continued the active old man. " Frank,
reach me down my hat. I 've a twinge of the rheumatism in this arm : I caught a little cold the night
of the fire, I believe ; but stirring about will do me

good, and I must not be lazy; I should be ashamed to be lazy among so many active young men."

The father and sons were very busy at work, when an ill-looking man rode up to them; and, after asking if their name was Frankland, put a paper into each of their hands. These papers were copies of a notice to quit their farm before the ensuing first of September, under pain of paying double rent for the same.

"This is some mistake, sir," said old Frankland, mildly.

"No mistake, sir," replied the stranger. "You will find the notice is a good notice, and duly served. Your lease I have seen myself within these few days; it expired last May, and you have held over, contrary to law and justice, eleven months, this being April."

"My father never did any thing contrary to law and justice in his whole life," interrupted Frank, whose eyes flashed with indignation.

"Softly, Frank," said his father, putting his hand on his son's shoulder: "softly, my dear boy; let this gentleman and I come to an understanding quietly. Here is some mistake, sir. It is very true that my lease expired last May; but I had a promise of a renewal from my good landlord."

14

" I don't know, sir, anything of that," replied
the stranger, as he looked over a memorandum-
book. "I do not know whom you denominate your
good landlord; that being no way of describing a
man in the eye of the law: but if you refer to the
original grantor, or lessor, Francis Folingsby, of
Folingsby place, Monmouthshire, Esq., I am to inform you that he died at Bath the 17th instant."

" Died! My poor landlord dead! I am very
sorry for it."

" And his nephew, Philip Folingsby, Esq., came
into possession as heir at law," continued the
stranger, in an unvaried tone; " and under his
orders I act, having a power of attorney for that
purpose."

" But, sir, I am sure Mr. Philip Folingsby cannot
know of the promise of renewal which I had from
his uncle."

" Verbal promises, you know, are nothing, sir;
mere air without witnesses; and, if gratuitous on
the part of the deceased, are noways binding, either
in common law or equity, on the survivor or heir.
In case the promise had been in writing, and on a
proper stamp, it would have been something."

" It was not in writing, to be sure, sir," said

Frankland; " but I thought my good landlord's word was as good as his bond; and I said so."

" Yes," cried Frank; " and I remember when you said so to him, I was by; and he answered, ' You shall have my promise in writing. Such things are of little use between honest men; but who knows what may happen, and who may come after me? Every thing about business should be put into writing. I would never let a tenant of mine be at an uncertainty. You have improved your farm, and deserve to enjoy the fruits of your own industry, Mr. Frankland.' Just then company came in, and our landlord put off writing the promise. He next day left the country in a hurry; and, I am sure, thought afterward he had given us the promise in writing."

" Very clear evidence, no doubt, sir; but not at all to the point at present," said the stranger. " As an agent, I am to know nothing but what is my employer's intent. When we see the writing and stamp I shall be a better judge," added he, with a sneer. " In the mean time, gentlemen, I wish you a good morning; and you will please to observe that you have been duly served with notice to quit or pay double rent."

" There can be no doubt, however," said Frank,

"that Mr. Folingsby will believe you, father. He is a gentleman, I suppose, and not like this new agent, who talks like an attorney. I hate all attorneys."

"All dishonest attorneys, I suppose you mean, Frank," said the benevolent old man; who, even when his temper was most tried, never spoke, or even felt, with acrimony.

The new landlord came into the country : and a few days after his arrival old Frankland went to wait upon him. There was little hope of seeing young Mr. Folingsby; he was a man whose head was at this time entirely full of gigs, and tandems, and unicorns : business was his aversion ; pleasure was his business. Money he considered only as the means of pleasure; and tenants only as machines who make money. He was neither avaricious nor cruel ; but thoughtless and extravagant.

While he appeared merely in the character of a young man of fashion, these faults were no offence to his equals, to whom they did no injury : but when he came into possession of a large estate, and when numbers were dependent upon him, they were severely felt by his inferiors.

Mr. Folingsby had just gathered up the reins in hand, and was seated in his unicorn, when Farmer

Frankland, who had been waiting some hours to see him, come to the side of the carriage. As he took off his hat the wind blew his gray hair over his face.

"Put on your hat, pray, my good friend; and don't come near these horses, for I can't answer for them. Have you any commands with me?"

"I have been waiting some hours to speak to you, sir, but if you are not at leisure I will come again to-morrow morning," said old Frankland.

"Ay, do so; call to-morrow morning; for now . have not one moment to spare," said young Folingsby, as he whipped his horses and drove off as if the safety of the nation had depended upon twelve miles an hour.

The next day, and the next, and the next, the old tenant called upon his young landlord, but without obtaining an audience: still he was desired to call to-morrow, and to-morrow, and to-morrow. He wrote several letters to him, but received no answer: at last, after giving half a guinea to his landlord's gentleman, he gained admittance. Mr. Folingsby was drawing on his boots, and his horses were coming to the door. Frankland saw it was necessary to be concise in his story: he slightly touched on the principal circumstances,—the length

14 *

of time he had occupied his farm, the improvements he had made upon the land, and the misfortune which had lately befallen him. The boots
were on by the time that he got to the promise of
renewal and the notice to quit.

"Promise of renewal: I know of no such thing.
Notice to quit; that's my agent's business; speak
to him; he'll do you justice. I really am sorry
for you, Mr. Frankland; very sorry; extremely
sorry,—damn the rascal who made these boots!—
but you see how I'm circumstanced; haven't a
moment to myself; only came to the country for a
few days; set out for Ascot races to-morrow;
really have not a moment to think of any thing.
But speak to Mr. Deal, my agent. He'll do you
justice, I'm sure. I leave all these things to him.
Jack, that bay horse is coming on—"

"I have spoken to your agent, sir," said the old
tenant, following his thoughtless young landlord;
"but he said that verbal promises without a witness present were nothing but air; and I have
nothing to rely on but your justice. I assure you,
sir; I have not been an idle tenant: my land will
show that I have not."

"Tell Mr. Deal so; make him understand it in
this light. I leave every thing of this sort to Mr.

Deal. I really have not time for business, but I'm sure Mr. Deal will do you justice."

This was all that could be obtained from the young landlord. His confidence in his agent's sense of justice was somewhat misplaced. Mr. Deal had received a proposal from another tenant for Frankland's farm; and with this proposal, a bank-note was sent, which spoke more forcibly than all that poor Frankland could urge. The agent took the farm from him; and declared he could not, in justice to his employer, do otherwise; because the new tenant had promised to build upon the land, a lodge fit for any gentleman to inhabit, instead of a farm-house.

The transaction was concluded without Mr. Folingsby's knowing any thing more of the matter except signing the leases, which he did without reading them, and receiving half a years' rent in hand as a fine, which he did with great satisfaction. He was often distressed for ready money, though he had a large estate; and his agent well knew how to humour him in his hatred of business. No interest could have persuaded Mr. Folingsby deliberately to commit so base an action as that of cheating a deserving old tenant out of a promised renewal; but, in fact, long before the leases were

sent to him, he had totally forgotten every syllable
that poor Frankland had said to him on the subject.

CHAPTER II.

THE day on which they left their farm was a
melancholy day to this unfortunate family. Mr.
Frankland's father and grandfather had been tenants, and excellent tenants, to the Folingsby family; all of them had occupied, and not only occupied, but highly improved this farm. All the
neighbours were struck with compassion, and cried
shame upon Mr. Folingsby ! But Mr. Folingsby
was at Ascot, and did not hear them. He was on
the race-ground, betting hundreds upon a favourite
horse; while this old man and his family were
slowly passing in their covered cart down the lane
which led from their farm, taking a last farewell of
the fields they had cultivated, and the harvest they
had sown, but which they were never to reap.

Hannah, the servant-girl, who had reproached
herself so bitterly for leaving the bucket of ashes
near the hay-rick, was extremely active in assisting
her poor master. Upon this occasion she seemed

to be endowed with double strength ; and a degree of cleverness and presence of mind of which she had never shown any symptoms in her former life ; but gratitude awakened all her faculties.

Before she came to this family, she had lived some years with a farmer who, as she now recollected, had a small farm, with a snug cottage upon it, which was to be this very year out of lease. Without saying a word of her intentions, she got up early one morning, walked fifteen miles to her old master's, and offered to pay out of her wages, which she had laid by for six or seven years, the year's rent of this farm beforehand, if the farmer would let it to Mr. Frankland. The farmer would not take the girl's money, for he said he wanted no security from Mr. Frankland or his son George : they bore the best of characters, he observed, and no people in Monmouthshire could understand the management of land better. He willingly agreed to let him the farm ; but it contained only a few acres, and the house was so small that it could scarcely lodge above three people.

Here old Frankland and his eldest son George settled. James went to Monmouth, where he became shopman to Mr. Cleghorn, a haberdasher, who took him in preference to three other young men who applied on the same day. " Shall I tell you the reason why I fixed upon you, James ?" said Mr. Cleghorn. " It was not whim ; I had my reasons."

" I suppose," said James, " you thought I had been honestly and well brought up ; as I believe in former times, sir, you knew something of my mother."

" Yes, sir ; and in former times I knew something of yourself. You may forget, but I do not, that when you were a child not more than nine years old,* you came to this shop to pay a bill of your mother's : the bill was cast up a pound too little : you found out the mistake, and paid me the money. I dare say you are as good an accountant and as honest a fellow still. I have just been terribly tricked by a lad to whom I trusted foolishly ; but this will not make me suspicious towards you, because I know how you have been brought up ; and that is the best security a man can have."

Thus, even in childhood, the foundation of a good character may be laid ; and thus children inherit the good name of their parents. A rich inheritance! of which they cannot be deprived by the utmost malice of fortune.

* This circumstance is a fact.

The good characters of Fanny and Patty Frankland were well known in the neighbourhood; and
when they could no longer afford to live at home,
they found no difficulty in getting places. On the
contrary, several of the best families in Monmouth
were anxious to engage them. Fanny went to live
with Mrs. Hungerford, a lady of an ancient family,
who was proud, but not insolent, and generous, but
not what is commonly called affable. She had
several children, and she hired Fanny Frankland
for the particular purpose of attending them.

" Pray let me see that you exactly obey my orders, young woman, with respect to my children,"
said Mrs. Hungerford, "and you shall have no reason to complain of the manner in which you are
treated in this house. It is my wish to make everybody happy in it, from the highest to the lowest.
You have, I understand, received an education
above your present station in life; and I hope and
trust that you will deserve the high opinion I am,
from that circumstance, inclined to form of you."

Fanny was rather intimidated by the haughtiness of Mrs. Hungerford's manner; yet she felt a
steady though modest confidence in herself, which
was not displeasing to her mistress.

About this time Patty also went into service.

Her mistress was a Mrs. Crumpe, a very old rich lady, who was often sick and peevish, and who confessed that she required an uncommonly good-humoured person to wait upon her. She lived a few miles from Monmouth, where she had many relations; but, on account of her great age and infirmities, she led an extremely retired life.

Frank was now the only person in the family who was not settled in the world. He determined to apply to a Mr. Barlow, an attorney of an excellent character. He had been much pleased with the candour and generosity Frank showed in a quarrel with the Bettesworths; and he had promised to befriend him, if ever it should be in his power. It happened that, at this time, Mr. Barlow was in want of a clerk; and as he knew Frank's abilities, and had reason to feel confidence in his integrity, he determined to employ him in his office. Frank had once a prejudice against attorneys: he thought that they could not be honest men; but he was convinced of his mistake when he became acquainted with Mr. Barlow. This gentleman never practised any mean pettifogging arts; on the contrary, he always dissuaded those who consulted him from commencing vexatious suits. Instead of fomenting quarrels, it was his pleasure and pride to bring about reconciliations. It was said of Mr. Barlow, that he had lost more suits out of the courts, and fewer in them, than any attorney of his standing in England. His reputation was now so great that he was consulted more as a lawyer than as an attorney. With such a master, Frank had a prospect of being extremely happy; and he determined that nothing should be wanting on his part to ensure Mr. Barlow's esteem and regard.

James Frankland, in the mean time, went on happily with Mr. Cleghorn, the haberdasher; whose customers all agreed that his shop had never been so well attended as since this young man had been his foreman. His accounts were kept in the most exact manner; and his bills were made out with unrivalled neatness and expedition. His attendance on the shop was so constant that his master began to fear it might hurt his health; especially as he had never, till of late, been used to so confined a life.

"You shall go abroad, James, these fine evenings," said Mr. Cleghorn. "Take a walk in the country now and then in the fresh air. Don't think I want to nail you always to the counter. Come, this is as fine an evening as you can wish: take your hat, and away; I'll mind the shop myself

15

till you come back. He must be a hard master,
indeed, that does not know when he is well served,
and that never will be my case I hope. Good servants make good masters, and good masters good
servants. Not that I mean to call you, Mr. James,
a servant; that was only a slip of the tongue; and
no matter for the tongue, where the heart means
well, as mine does towards you."   •

Towards all the world Mr. Cleghorn was not
disposed to be indulgent: he was not a selfish man,
but he had a high idea of subordination in life.
Having risen himself by slow degrees, he thought
that every man in trade should have what he called
" the rough as well as the smooth." He saw that
his new foreman bore the rough well; and therefore he was now inclined to give him some of the
smooth.   •

James, who was extremely fond of his brother
Frank, called upon him, and took him to Mrs. Hungerford's, to ask Fanny to accompany them in this
walk. They had seldom seen her since they had
quitted their father's house and lived in Monmouth;
and they were disappointed when they were told
by Mrs. Hungerford's footman that Fanny was not
at home; she was gone to walk out with the children   The man did not know which road they

went, so they had no hopes of meeting her; and they took their way through one of the shady lanes near Monmouth. It was late before they thought of returning: for, after several weeks' confinement in close houses, the fresh air, green fields, and sweet-smelling wild flowers in the hedges were delightful novelties. "Those who see these things every day," said James, "scarcely notice them; I remember I did not when I lived at our farm. So things, as my father used to say, are made equal to people in this world. We who are hard at work in a close room all day long have more relish for an evening walk, a hundred to one, than those who saunter about from morning till night."

The philosophic reflections of James were interrupted by the merry voices of a troop of children, who were getting over a stile into the lane where he and Frank were walking. The children had huge nosegays of honeysuckles, dog-roses, and bluebells in their little hands; and they gave their flowers to a young woman who attended them, begging she would hold them while they got over the stile. James and Frank went to offer their services to help the children; and then they saw that the young woman who held the flowers was their sister Fanny.

"Our own Fanny!" said Frank. "How lucky this is! It seems almost a year since I saw you. We have been all the way to Mrs. Hungerford's, to look for you; and have been forced to take half our walk without you; but the other half will make amends. I've a hundred things to say to you: which is your way home? Take the longest way, I entreat you. Here is my arm. What a delightful fine evening it is! But what's the matter?"

"It is a very fine evening," said Fanny, hesitating a little; "and I hope to-morrow will be as fine. I'll ask my mistress to let me walk out with you to-morrow; but this evening I cannot stay with you, because I have the children under my care; and I have promised her that I will never walk with any one when they are with me."

"But your own brother!" said Frank, a little angry at this refusal.

"I promised I would not walk with any one; and surely you are somebody: so good night; good-by," replied Fanny, endeavouring to turn off his displeasure with a laugh.

"But what harm, I say, can I do the children, by walking with you?" cried Frank, catching hold of her gown.

"I don't know; but I know what the orders of

my mistress are; and you know, dear Frank, that while I live with her I am bound to obey them."

"Oh, Frank, she must obey them," said James.

Frank loosened his hold of Fanny's gown immediately. "You are right, dear Fanny," said he; "you are right, and I was wrong: so good-night; good-by. Only remember to ask leave to walk with us to-morrow evening; for I have had a letter from father and brother George, and I want to show it you. Wait five minutes and I can read it to you now, Fanny."

Fanny, though she was anxious to hear her father's letter, would not wait, but hurried away with the children that were under her care; saying she must keep her promise to her mistress exactly. Frank followed her, and put the letter into her hands. "You are a dear good girl, and deserve all the fine things father says of you in this letter. Take it, child: your mistress does not forbid you receiving a letter from your father, I suppose. I shall wish her hanged, if she does not let you walk with us to-morrow," whispered he.

The children frequently interrupted Fanny as she was reading her father's letter. "Pray pull that high dog-rose for me, Fanny," said one. "Pray hold me up to that large honeysuckle," said

15 *

another. "And do, Fanny," said the youngest boy, "let us go home by the common, that I may see the glowworms. Mamma said I might; and while we are looking for the glowworms, you can sit on a stone, or a bank, and read your letter in peace."

Fanny, who was always very ready to indulge the children in any thing which her mistress had not forbidden, agreed to this proposal; and when they came to the common, little Gustavus, for that was the name of the eldest boy, found a charming seat for her, and she sat down to read the letter while the children ran to hunt for glowworms.

Fanny read her father's letter over three times; and yet few people except those who have the happiness to love a father as well, and to have a father as deserving to be loved, would think it at all worth reading even once.

"My dear Boys and Girls,

"It is a strange thing to me to be without you; but with me or from me, I am sure you are doing well; and that is a great comfort; ay, the best a father can have, especially at my age. I am heartily glad to hear that my Frank has, by his own deserts, got so good a place with that excellent man Mr. Barlow. He does not hate attorneys now,

I am sure. Indeed, it is my belief he could not hate anybody for half an hour together if he was to do his worst. Thank God, none of my children have been brought up to be revengeful or envious, and they are not fighting with one another, as I hear the poor Bettesworths now all are for the fortune. 'Better is a dinner of herbs where love is, than a stalled ox and hatred therewith.' I need not have troubled myself to write this text to any of you; but old men will be talkative. My rheumatism, however, prevents me from being as talkative as I could wish. It has been rather severe or so, owing to the great cold I caught the day that I was obliged to wait so long at Squire Folingsby's in my wet clothes. But I hope soon to be stirring again, and to be able to take a share of the work about our little farm with your dear brother George. Poor fellow! he has so much to do, and does so much, that I fear he will overwork himself. He is at this present time out in the little field opposite my window, digging up the docks, which are very hard to conquer; he has made a brave large heap of them, but I wish to my heart he would not toil so desperately.

"I desire, my dear James and Frank, you will not confine yourselves too much in your shop and at your desk : this is all I have to dread for either of you. Give my love and blessing to my sweet girls. If Fanny was not as prudent as she is pretty, I should be in fear for her; hearing, as I do, that Mrs. Hungerford keeps so much fine company. A waiting-maid in such a house is in a dangerous place : but my Fanny, I am sure, will ever keep in mind her mother's precepts and example. I am told that Mrs. Crumpe, Patty's mistress, is (owing I suppose to her great age and infirmities) difficult in her humour : but my Patty has so even and pleasant a temper that I defy any one living, that knows her, not to love her. My hand is now quite tired of writing, this being penned with my left, as my right arm is not yet free from rheumatism : I have not James with me to write. God bless and preserve you all, my dear children. With such comforts I can have nothing to complain of in this world. This I know, I would not exchange any one of you for all my neighbour Bettesworth's fine fortune. Write soon to

" Your affectionate father,

" B. FRANKLAND."

" Look ! look at the glowworms !" cried the children, gathering round Fanny, just as she had finished reading her letter. There were prodigious numbers of them on this common ; and they shone over the whole ground in clusters, or singly, like little stars.

While the children were looking with admiration and delight at this spectacle, their attention was suddenly diverted from the glowworms by the sound of a French horn. They looked round, and perceived that it came from the balcony of a house which was but a few yards distant from the spot where they were standing.

" Oh ! let us go nearer to the balcony !" said the children, " that we may hear the music better." A violin and a clarionet at this moment began to play.

" Oh ! let us go nearer !" repeated the children, drawing Fanny with all their little force towards the balcony.

" My dears, it is growing late," said she, " and we must make haste home. There is a crowd of company, you see, at the door and at the windows of that house, and if we go near to it some of them will certainly speak to you, and that you know your mamma would not like."

The children paused, and looked at one another, as if inclined to submit ; but at this moment a

kettle-drum was heard, and little Gustavus could
not resist his curiosity to hear and see more of this
instrument : he broke loose from Fanny's hands,
and escaped to the house, exclaiming, " I must and
will hear it, and see it too !"

Fanny was obliged to pursue him into the midst
of the crowd ; he made his way up to a young
gentleman in regimentals, who took him up in his
arms, saying, " By Jove, a fine little fellow !   A
soldier, every inch of him !   By G— he shall see
the drum, and beat it too ; let us see who dares say
to the contrary."

As the gallant ensign spoke, he carried Gustavus up a flight of stairs that led to the balcony.
Fanny, in great anxiety called after him, to beg
that he would not detain the child, who was trusted
to her care : her mistress, she said, would be extremely displeased with her if she disobeyed her
orders.

She was here interrupted in her remonstrance by
the shrill voice of a female who stood on the same
stair with the ensign, and whom, notwithstanding
the great alteration in her dress, Fanny recognised
to be Sally Bettesworth.   Jilting Jessy stood beside
her.

" Fanny Frankland, I protest !   What a pother

she keeps about nothing," cried Saucy Sally. "Know your betters, and keep your distance, young woman. Who cares whether your mistress is displeased or not? She can't turn us away, can she, pray? She can't call Ensign Bloomington to account, can she, hey?"

An insolent laugh closed this speech; a laugh in which several of the crowd joined: but some gentlemen were interested by Fanny's beautiful and modest countenance as she looked up to the balcony, and with tears in her eyes entreated to be heard. "Oh, for shame, Bloomington! Give her back the boy. It is not fair that she should lose her place," cried they.

Bloomington would have yielded; but Saucy Sally stood before him, crying, in a threatening tone, "I'll never speak to you again, I promise you, Bloomington, if you give up. A fine thing indeed for a man and a soldier to give up to a woman and a servant-girl! and an impertinent servant-girl! Who cares for her or her place either?"

"I do! I do!" exclaimed little Gustavus, springing from the ensign's arms. "I care for her! She is not an impertinent girl, and I'll give up

seeing the kettle-drum, and go home with her directly, with all my heart."

In vain Sally attempted to withhold him; the
boy ran down the stairs to Fanny, and marched
off with her in all the conscious pride of a hero,
whose generosity has fairly vanquished his passions.   Little Gustavus was indeed a truly generous child: the first thing he did, when he got
home, was to tell his mother all that had passed
this evening.   Mrs. Hungerford was delighted
with her son, and said to him, "I cannot, I am
sure, reward you better, my dear, than by rewarding this good young woman. The fidelity
with which she has fulfilled my orders, in all that
regards my children, places her, in my opinion,
above the rank in which she was born.   Henceforward she shall hold in my house a station to
which her habits of truth, gentleness, and good
sense entitle her."

From this time forward, Fanny, by Mrs. Hungerford's desire, was always present when the
children took their lessons from their several
masters.   Mrs. Hungerford advised her to apply
herself to learn all those things which were necessary for a governess to young ladies.   "When
you speak, your language in general is good, and

correct; and no pains shall be wanting on my part," said this haughty but benevolent lady, " to form your manners, and to develope your talents. This I partly owe you for your care of my children; and I am happy to reward my son Gustavus in a manner which I am certain will be most agreeable to him."

" And, mamma," said the little boy, " may she walk out sometimes with her brothers? for I do believe she loves them as well as I love my sisters."

Mrs. Hungerford permitted Fanny to walk out for an hour, every morning, during the time that her children were with their dancing-master; and at this hour sometimes her brother James, and sometimes her brother Frank, could be spared; and they had many pleasant walks together. What a happiness it was to them to have been thus bred up, from their earliest years, in friendship with one another! This friendship was now the sweetest pleasure of their lives.

Poor Patty! She regretted that she could not join in these pleasant meetings; but, alas! she was so useful, so agreeable, and so necessary to her infirm mistress, that she could never be spared from home. " Where's Patty? why does not

16

Patty do this?" were Mrs. Crump's constant questions whenever she was absent.   Patty had all the
business of the house upon her hands, because
nobody could do any thing so well as Patty.   Mrs.
Crumpe found that no one could dress her but
Patty; nobody could make her bed so that she
could sleep on it, but Patty ; no one could make
jelly, or broth, or whey that she could taste,·
but Patty ; no one could roast, or boil, or bake, but
Patty.   Of course all these things must be done by
nobody else.   The ironing of Mrs. Crumpe's caps,
which had exquisitely nice plaited borders, at last
fell to Patty's share ; because once, when the
laundry-maid was sick, she plaited one so charmingly, that her lady would never afterward wear
any but of her plaiting.   Now Mrs. Crumpe
changed her cap, or rather had her cap changed,
three times a day ; and never wore the same cap
twice.

The labours of washing, ironing, plaiting, roast-
ing, boiling, baking, making jelly, broth, and whey
were not sufficient: Mrs. Crumpe took it into her
head that she could eat no butter but of Patty's
churning.   But what was worse than all, not a
night passed without Patty's being called up to see
" what could be the matter with the dog that was

barking, or the cat that was mewing?" And when she was just sinking to sleep again, at daybreak, her lady, in whose room she slept, would call out, "Patty! Patty! there's a dreadful noise in the chicken-yard."

"Oh, ma'am, it is only the cocks crowing."

"Well, do step out, and hinder them from crowing at this terrible rate."

"But, ma'am, I cannot hinder them indeed."

"Oh, yes, you could if you were up. Get up and whip 'em, child. Whip 'em all round, or I shall not sleep a wink more this night."*

How little poor Patty slept her lady never considered: not that she was in reality an ill-natured woman, but sickness inclined her to be peevish; and she had so long been used to be humoured and waited upon by relations and servants, who expected she would leave them rich legacies, that she considered herself as a sort of golden idol, to whom all that approached should and would bow as low as she pleased. Perceiving that almost all around her were interested, she became completely selfish. She was from morning till night, from night till morning, nay, from year's end to year's end, so

* Taken from life.

much in the habit of seeing others employed for
her, that she absolutely considered this to be the
natural and necessary course of things ; and she
quite forgot to think of the comforts, or even of the
well-being, of those creatures who were " born for
her use, and live but to oblige her."

From time to time she was so far wakened to
feeling by Patty's exertions and good-humour, that
she would say, to quiet her own conscience,
" Well! well! I'll make it all up to her in my
will!   I'll make it all up to her in my will !"

She took it for granted that Patty, like the rest
of her dependants, was governed entirely by mer-
cenary considerations; and she was persuaded that
the hopes of this legacy would secure Patty her
slave for life.   In this she was mistaken.

One morning Patty came into her room with a
face full of sorrow ; a face so unlike her usual
countenance that even her mistress, unaccustomed
as she was to attend to the feelings of others, could
not help noticing the change.

" Well! What's the matter, child?" said she.

" Oh! sad news, madam!" said Patty, turning
aside to hide her tears.

" But what's the matter, child, I say?   Can't
you speak, whatever it is, hey?   What, have you

burnt my best cap in the ironing, hey? Is that it?"

"Oh! worse, worse, ma'am!"

"Worse! What can be worse?"

"My brother, ma'am, my brother George is ill, very ill of a fever; and they don't think he'll live! Here is my father's letter, ma'am!"

"Lord! how can I read it without spectacles? and why should I read it, when you've told me all that's in it? How the child cries!" continued Mrs. Crumpe, raising herself a little on her pillow, and looking at Patty with a sort of astonished curiosity. "Heigho! But I can't stay in bed this way till dinner-time. Get me my cap, child, and dry your eyes; for crying won't do your brother any good."

Patty dried her eyes. "No: crying will not do him any good," said she, "but—"

"But where is my cap? I don't see it on the dressing-table."

"No, ma'am: Martha will bring it in a minute or two: she is plaiting it."

"I will not have it plaited by Martha. Go and do it yourself."

"But, ma'am," said Patty, who, to her mistress's surprise, stood still, notwithstanding she heard this

16 *

order, " I hope you will be so good as to give me
leave to go to my poor brother to-day. My brothers
and sister are with him, and he wants to see me ;
and they have sent a horse for me."

" No matter what they have sent ; you sha'n't
go ; I can't spare you. If you choose to serve
me, serve me. If you choose to serve your brother,
serve your brother, and leave me."

" Then, madam," said Patty, " I must leave you :
for I cannot but choose to serve my brother at such
a time as this, if I can serve him ; which God
grant I mayn't be late to do !"

" What! You will leave me! Leave me contrary to my orders! Take notice, then : these
doors you shall never enter again, if you leave me
now," cried Mrs. Crumpe, who, by this unexpected
opposition to her orders, was actually worked up
to a state unlike her usual peevishness. She started
up in her bed, and growing quite red in the face,
cried, " Leave me now, and you leave me for ever.
Remember that! Remember that !"

" Then, madam, I must leave you for ever," said
Patty, moving towards the door. " I wish you your
health and happiness ; and am sorry to break so
short."

" The girl's an idiot !" cried Mrs. Crumpe.

• After this you cannot expect that I should re-member you in my will."

" No, indeed, madam ; I expect no such thing," said Patty. Her hand was on the lock of the door as she spoke.

" Then," said Mrs. Crumpe, " perhaps you will think it worth your while to stay with me, when I tell you I have not forgot you in my will. Con-sider that, child, before you turn the handle of the door. Consider that, and don't disoblige me for ever."

" Oh, madam, consider my poor brother. I am sorry to disoblige you for ever ; but I can consider nothing but my poor brother," said Patty. The lock of the door turned quickly in her hand.

" Why! Is your brother rich? What upon earth do you expect from this brother, that can make it worth your while to behave to me in this strange way?" said Mrs. Crumpe.

Patty was silent with astonishment for a few mo-ments, and then answered, " I expect nothing from him, madam ; he is as poor as myself; but that does not make me love him the less."

Before Mrs. Crumpe could understand this last speech Patty had left the room. Her mistress sat up in her bed, in the same attitude, for some minutes

after she was gone, looking fixedly at the place
where Patty had stood: she could scarcely recover
from her surprise; and a multitude of painful
thoughts crowded upon her mind.

"If I was dying, and poor, who would come to
me? Not a relation I have in the world would
come near me! Not a creature on earth loves me
as this poor girl loves her brother, who is as poor
as herself."

Here her reflections were interrupted by hearing
the gallopping of Patty's horse as it passed by the
windows. Mrs. Crumpe tried to compose herself
again to sleep, but she could not; and in half an
hour's time she rang the bell violently, took her
purse out of her pocket, counted out twenty bright
guineas, and desired that a horse should be saddled
immediately, and that her steward should gallop
after Patty, and offer her that *whole sum in hand*,
if she would return. "Begin with one guinea, and
bid on till you come up to her price," said Mrs.
Crumpe. "Have her back again I will, if it was
only to convince myself that she is to be had for
money as well as other people."

The steward, as she counted the gold in his hand,
thought it was a great sum to throw away for such
a whim: he had never seen his lady take the whim

of giving away ready money before ; but it was in vain to remonstrate ; she was peremptory, and he obeyed.

In two hours' time he returned; and Mrs. Crumpe *saw her gold again with extreme astonishment. The steward said he could not prevail upon Patty even to look at the guineas. Mrs. Crumpe now flew into a violent passion, in which none of our readers will probably sympathize: we shall there-fore forbear to describe it.

CHAPTER III

WHEN Patty came within half a mile of the cottage in which her father lived, she met Hannah, the faithful servant, who had never deserted the family in their misfortunes : she had been watch-ing all the morning on the road for the first sight of Patty; but when she saw her, and came quite close up to her, she had no power to speak ; and Patty was so much terrified that she would not ask her a single question. She walked her horse a slow pace, and kept silence.

" Won't you go on, ma'am ?" said Hannah, at

last forcing herself to speak.' "Won't you go on
a bit faster? He's almost wild to see you."

"He is alive then!" cried Patty. The horse
was in full gallop directly, and she was soon at her
father's door. James and Frank were there watch-
ing for her: they lifted her from the horse; and
feeling that she trembled so much as to be scarcely
able to stand, they would have detained her a little
while in the air; but she passed or rather rushed
into the room where her brother lay. He took no
notice of her when she came in; for he was insensible. Fanny was supporting his head; she
held out her nand to Patty, who went on tiptoe to
the side of the bed. "Is he asleep?" whispered
she.

"Not asleep, but—he'll come to himself presently," continued Fanny, "and he will be very,
very glad you are come; and so will my father."

"Where is my father?" said Patty; "I don't see
him."

Fanny pointed to the farthest end of the room,
where he was kneeling at his devotion. The shut-
ters being half-closed, she could but just see the
faint beam which shone upon his gray hairs. He
rose, came to his daughter Patty, with an air of
resigned grief, and taking her hand between both

of his, said, " My love, we must lose him—God's will be done !"

" Oh ! there is hope, there is hope still !" said Patty. " See ! The colour is coming back to his lips again ; his eyes open ! Oh ! George, dear George, dear brother ! It is your own sister Patty : don't you know Patty ?"

" Patty ! Yes. Why does not she come to me ? I would go to her if I could," said the sufferer, without knowing what he talked of. " Is not she come yet ? Send another horse, Frank. Why, it is only six miles. Six miles in three hours, that is—how many miles an hour ? ten miles, is it ? Don't hurry her—don't tell her I'm so bad ; nor my father—don't let him see me, nor James, nor Frank, nor pretty Fanny, nor anybody—they are all too good to me : I only wished to see poor Patty once before I die ; but don't frighten her—I shall be very well, tell her—quite well by the time she comes."

After running on in this manner for some time, his eyes closed again, and he lay in a state of stupor. He continued in this condition for some time : at last his sisters, who were watching beside the bed, heard a knocking at the door. It was Frank and James : they had gone for a clergyman, whom

George, before he became delirious, had desired to see. The clergyman was come, and with him a benevolent physician, who happened to be at his house, and who insisted upon accompanying him. As soon as the physician saw the poor young man, and felt his pulse, he perceived that the ignorant apothecary who had been first employed had entirely mistaken George's disease, and had treated him improperly. His disease was a putrid fever, and the apothecary had bled him repeatedly. The physician thought he could certainly have saved his life, if he had seen him two days sooner; but now it was a hopeless case. All that could be done for him he tried.

Towards evening, the disease seemed to take a favourable turn. George came to his senses, knew his father, his brothers, and Fanny, and spoke to each with his customary kindness, as they stood round his bed: he then asked whether poor Patty was come. When he saw her, he thanked her tenderly for coming to him; but could not recollect he had any thing particular to say to her.

" I only wished to see you all together, to thank you for your good-nature to me ever since I was born, and to take leave of you before I die; for I feel that I am dying. Nay, do not cry so! My father! Oh! my father is most to be pitied; but he will have James and Frank left."

Seeing his father's affliction, which the good old man struggled in vain to subdue, George broke off here; he put his hand to his head, as if fearing it was again growing confused.

"Let me see our good clergyman, now that I am well enough to see him," said he. He then took a hand of each of his brothers and sisters, joined them together, and pressed them to his lips, looking from them to his father, whose back was now turned. "You understand me," whispered George: "he can never come to want while you are left to work and comfort him. If I should not see you again in this world, farewell! Ask my father to give me his blessing!"

"God bless you, my son! God bless you, my dear good son! God will surely bless so good a son!" said the agonized father, laying his hand upon his son's forehead, which even now was cold with the damp of death.

"What a comfort it is to have a father's blessing!" said George. "May you all have it when you are as I am now!"

"I shall be out of this world long, long before that time, I hope," said the poor old man, as he left

17

the room. "But God's will be done! Send the
clergyman to my boy!"

The clergyman remained in the room but a short
time: when he returned to the family, they saw
by his ooks that all was over!

There was a solemn silence.

"Be comforted," said the good clergyman.
"Never man left this world with a clearer conscience, or had happier hope of a life to come. Be
comforted. Alas! at such a time as this you cannot be comforted by any thing that the tongue of
man can say."

All the family attended the funeral. It was on
a Sunday, just before morning prayers; and as
soon as George was interred, his father, brothers,
and sisters left the churchyard, to avoid being seen
by the gay people who were coming to their devotion. As they went home, they passed through
the field in which George used to work: there they
saw his heap of docks, and his spade upright in the
ground beside it, just as he had left it the last time
that he had ever worked.

The whole family stayed for a few days with their
poor father. Late one evening, as they were all
walking out together in the fields, a heavy snow
began to fall; and James urged his father to make

haste home, lest he should catch cold, and should have another fit of the rheumatism. They were then at some distance from their cottage; and Frank, who thought he knew a short way home, took them by a new road, which unluckily led them far out of their way; it brought them unexpectedly within sight of their old farm, and of the new house which Mr. Bettesworth had built upon it.

"Oh! my dear father, I am sorry I brought you this way," cried Frank. "Let us turn back."

"No, my son, why should we turn back?" said his father, mildly; "we can pass by these fields, and this house, I hope, without coveting our neighbour's goods."

As they came near the house, he stopped at the gate to look at it. "It is a good house," said he; "but I have no need to envy any man a good house; I, that have so much better things—good children!"

Just as he uttered these words, Mr. Bettesworth's house door opened, and three or four men appeared on the stone steps, quarrelling and fighting. The loud voices of Fighting Bob and Wild Will were heard too plainly.

"We have no business here," said old Frankland, turning to his children: "let us go."

The combatants pursued each other with such furious rapidity that they were near to the gate in a few instants.

" Lock the gate, you without there, whoever you are! Lock the gate! or I'll knock you down when I come up, whoever you are," cried Fighting Bob, who was hindmost in the race.

Wild Will was foremost; he kicked open the gate, but his foot slipped as he was going through : his brother overtook him, and, seizing him by the collar, cried, " Give me back the bank-notes, you rascal! they are mine, and I'll have 'em in spite of you."

" They are mine, and I'll keep 'em in spite of you," retorted Will, who was much intoxicated.

" Oh! what a sight! brothers fighting! Oh! part them, part them! Hold! hold! for heaven's sake!" cried old Frankland to them.

Frank and James held them asunder, though they continued to abuse one another in the grossest terms.   Their father, by this time, came up : he wrung his hands, and wept bitterly.

" Oh! shame, shame to me in my old age!" cried he : " can't you two let me live the few years I have to live in peace?   Ah, neighbour Frankland, you are better off!   My heart will break soon!   These children of mine will be the ruin and the death of me !"

At these words the sons interrupted their father with loud complaints of the manner in which he had treated them. They had quarrelled with one another, and with their father, about money. The father charged them with profligate extravagance ; and they accused him of sordid avarice. Mr. Frankland, much shocked at this scene, besought them at least to return to their house, and not to expose themselves in this manner ; especially now that they were in *the station of gentlemen.* Their passions were too loud and brutal to listen to this appeal to their pride : their being raised to the rank of gentlemen could not give them principles or manners ; that can only be done by education. Despairing to effect any good, Mr. Frankland retired from this scene, and made the best of his way home to his peaceful cottage.

" My children," said he to his family, as they sat down to their frugal meal, " we are poor, but we are happy in one another. Was not I right to say I need not envy neighbour Bettesworth his fine house ? Whatever misfortunes befall me, I have the blessing of good children. It is a blessing I

17 *

would not exchange for any this world affords.
God preserve them in health!"

He sighed, and soon added, "It is a bitter thing
to think of a good son who is dead; but it is worse,
perhaps, to think of a bad son who is alive. That
is a misfortune I can never know. But, my dear
boys and girls," continued he, changing his tone,
"this idle way of life of ours must not last for ever.
You are too poor to be idle; and so much the better for you. To-morrow you must all away to
your own business."

"But, father," cried they all at once, "which of
us may stay with you."

"None of you, my good children. You are all
going on well in the world; and I will not take
you from your good masters and mistresses."

Patty now urged that she had the strongest right
to remain with her father; because Mrs. Crumpe
would certainly refuse to receive her into her service again, after what had passed at their parting:
but nothing could prevail upon Frankland; he
positively refused to let any of his children stay
with him. At last Frank cried, "How can you
possibly manage this farm without help? You must
let either James or me stay with you, father. Sup-

pose you should be seized with another fit of the rheumatism."

Frankland paused for a moment, and then answered, " Poor Hannah will nurse me if I fall sick. I am able still to pay her just wages. I will not be a burden to my children. As to this farm, I am going to give it up; for, indeed," said the old man, smiling, " I should not be well able to manage it with the rheumatism in my spade-arm. My landlord, Farmer Hewitt, is a good-natured, friendly man; and he will give me my own time for the rent: nay, he tells me he would let me live in this cottage for nothing; but I cannot do that."

" Then what will you do, dear father?" said his sons.

" The clergyman who was here yesterday has made interest for a house for me which will cost me nothing, nor him neither; and I shall be very near you both, boys."

" But, father," interrupted Frank, " I know, by your way of speaking, there is something about this house which you do not like."

" That is true," said old Frankland: " but that is the fault of my pride, and of my old prejudices; which are hard to conquer at my time of life. It is certain I do not much like the thoughts of going into an almshouse."

" An almshouse !" cried all his children at once, in a tone of horror. " Oh ! father, you must not, indeed you must not, go into an almshouse !"

The pride which renders the English yeoman averse to live upon public charity is highly advantageous to the industry and virtue of the nation. Even where it is instilled early into families as a prejudice, it is useful, and ought to be respected.

Frankland's children, shocked at the idea of their father's going into an almshouse, eagerly offered to join together the money they had earned, and to pay the rent of the cottage in which he now lived ; but Frankland knew that, if he took this money, his children would themselves be in distress. He answered, with tears in his eyes,

" My dear children, I thank you all for your goodness ; but I cannot accept of your offer. Since I am no longer able to support myself, I will not, from false pride, be the ruin of my children. I will not be a burden to them ; and I prefer living upon public charity to accepting of the ostentatious liberality of any one rich man. I am come to a resolution, which nothing shall induce me to break.

I am determined to live in the Monmouth alms-house—nay, hear me, my children, patiently—to live in the Monmouth almshouse for one year; and during that time I will not see any of you unless I am sick. I lay my commands upon you, not to attempt to see me till this day twelvemonth. If at that time you are all together able to maintain me, without hurting yourselves, I will most willingly accept of your bounty for the rest of my days."

His children assured him they should be able to earn money sufficient to maintain him, without in-jury to themselves, long before the end of the year; and they besought him to permit them to do so as soon as it was in their power; but he con-tinued firm in his resolution, and made them so-lemnly promise they would obey his commands, and not even attempt to see him during the ensuing year. He then took leave of them in a most af-fectionate manner, saying, "I know, my dearest children, I have now given you the strongest pos-sible motive for industry and good conduct. This day twelvemonth we shall meet again; and I hope it will be as joyful a meeting as this is a sorrowful parting." His children, with some difficulty, ob-tained permission to accompany him to his new abode.

The almshouses at Monmouth are far superior to common institutions of this kind; they are remarkably neat and comfortable little dwellings, and form a row of pretty cottages, behind each of which there is a garden full of gooseberries, currants, and a variety of useful vegetables. These the old men cultivate themselves. The houses are fitted up conveniently; and each individual is provided with every thing that he wants in his own habitation: so that there is no opportunity or temptation for those petty disputes about property which often occur in charitable institutions that are not prudently conducted. Poor people who have their goods in common must necessarily become quarrelsome.

" You see," said old Frankland, pointing to the shining row of pewter on the clean shelf over the fireplace in his little kitchen—" you see I want for nothing here. I am not much to be pitied."

His children stood silent and dejected, while he dressed himself in the uniform belonging to the almshouse. Before they parted, they all agreed to meet at this place that day twelvemonth, and to bring with them the earnings of the year; they had hopes that thus, by their united efforts, a sum might be obtained sufficient to place their father once more in a state of independence.   With these hopes they separated, and returned to their masters and mistresses.

CHAPTER IV.

PATTY went to Mrs. Crumpe's to get her clothes which she had left there, and to receive some months' wages, which were still due for her services.   After what had passed, she had no idea that Mrs. Crumpe would wish she should stay with her; and she had heard of another place in Monmouth, which she believed would suit her in every respect.

The first person she saw when she arrived at the house of her late mistress was Martha, who, with a hypocritical length of face, said to her, " Sad news! sad news, Mrs. Patty!   The passion my lady was thrown into by your going away so sudden was of terrible detriment to her.   That very night she had a stroke of the palsy, and has scarce spoken since."

" Don't take it to heart, it is none of your fault : don't take it to heart, dear Patty," said Betty, the

housemaid, who was fond of Patty. "What could
you do but go to your brother? Here, drink this
water, and don't blame yourself at all about the
matter. Mistress had a stroke sixteen months ago,
afore ever you came into the house; and I dare
say she'd have had this last, whether you had
stayed or gone."

Here they were interrupted by the violent ringing of Mrs. Crumpe's bell. They were in the
room next to her; and as she heard voices louder
than usual, she was impatient to know what was
going on. Patty heard Mrs. Martha answer, as
she opened her lady's door, "'Tis only Patty
Frankland, ma'am, who is come for her clothes
and her wages."

"And she is very sorry to hear you have been
so ill; very sorry," said Betty, following to the
door.

"Bid her come in," said Mrs. Crumpe, in a
voice more distinct than she had ever been heard
to speak in since the day of her illness.

"What! are you sorry for me, child?" said
Mrs. Crumpe, fixing her eyes upon Patty's. Patty
made no answer; but it was plain how much she
was shocked.

"Ay, I see you *are* sorry for me," said her mis-

tress. " And so am I for you," added she, stretching out her hand, and taking hold of Patty's black
gown. " You shall have a finer stuff than this for
mourning for me. But I know that is not what
you are thinking of; and that's the reason I have
more value for you than for all the rest of them
put together. Stay with me, stay with me, to
nurse me; you nurse me to my mind. You cannot leave me, in the way I am in now, when I ask
you to stay."

Patty could not without inhumanity refuse; she
stayed with Mrs. Crumpe, who grew so dotingly
fond of her that she could scarcely bear to have
her a moment out of sight. She would take neither food nor medicines but from Patty's hand;
and she would not speak, except in answer to Patty's
questions. The fatigue and confinement she was
now forced to undergo were enough to hurt the
constitution of any one who had not very strong
health. Patty bore them with the greatest patience
and good-humour; indeed, the consciousness that
she was doing right, supported her in exertions
which would otherwise have been beyond her
power.

She had still more difficult trials to go through :
Mrs. Martha was jealous of her favour with her

18

lady, and often threw out hints that some people had
much more luck, and more cunning too, than other
people; but that some people might perhaps be
disappointed at last in their ends.

Patty went on her own straight way, without
minding these insinuations at first; but she was
soon forced to attend to them.   Mrs. Crumpe's relations received intelligence from Mrs Martha, that
her lady was growing worse and worse every
hour; and that she was quite shut up under the
dominion of an artful servant-girl, who had gained
such power over her that there was no knowing
what the consequence might be.   Mrs. Crumpe's
relations were much alarmed by this story; they
knew she had made a will in their favour some
years before this time, and they dreaded that Patty
should prevail upon her to alter it, and should get
possession herself of the fortune.   They were particularly struck with this idea, because an instance
of undue power acquired by a favourite servant-
maid over her doting mistress happened about this
period to be mentioned in an account of a trial in
the newspapers of the day.   Mrs. Crumpe's nearest
relations were two grandnephews.   The eldest was
Mr. Josiah Crumpe, a merchant who was settled
at Liverpool; the youngest was that Ensign Bloom

.ngton whom we formerly mentioned. He had
been intended for a merchant, but he would never
settle to business : and at last ran away from the
counting-house where he had been placed, and
went into the army. He was an idle, extravagant
young man : his great-aunt was by fits very angry
with him, or very fond of him. Sometimes she
would supply him with money ; at others she would
forbid him her presence, and declare he should
never see another shilling of hers. This had been
her latest determination ; but Ensign Bloomington
thought he could easily get into favour again, and
he resolved to force himself into the house. Mrs.
Crumpe positively refused to see him : the day
after this refusal he returned with a reinforcement,
for which Patty was not in the least prepared : he
was accompanied by Miss Sally Bettesworth in
a regimental riding-habit. Jessy had been the
original object of this gentleman's gallantry ; but
she met with a new and richer lover, and of course
jilted him. Sally, who was in haste to be married,
took undisguised pains to fix the ensign ; and she
thought she was sure of him. But to proceed
with our story.

Patty was told that a lady and gentleman desired to see her in the parlour : she was scarcely

in the room when Sally began, in a voice capable
of intimidating the most courageous of scolds,
" Fine doings! Fine doings, here! You think
you have the game in your own hands, I warrant,
my lady paramount; but I'm not one to be bullied,
you know of old."

" Nor am I one to be bullied, I hope," replied
Patty, in a modest but firm voice. " Will you be
pleased to let me know, in a quiet way, what are
your commands with me, or my lady?"

" This gentleman here must see your lady, as
you call her. To let you into a bit of a secret,
this gentleman and I *is* soon to be one; so no
wonder I stir in this affair, and I never stir for nothing; so it is as well for you to do it with fair
words as foul. Without more preambling, please
to show this gentleman into his aunt's room, which
sure he has the best right to see of any one in this
world; and if you prevent it in any species, I'll
have the law of you; and I take this respectable
woman," looking at Mrs. Martha, who came in
with a salver of cakes and wine, " I take this here
respectable gentlewoman to be my witness, if you
choose to refuse my husband (that is to be) admittance to his true and lawful nearest relation upon
earth. Only say the doors are locked, and that

you won't let him in; that's all we ask of you,
Mrs. Patty Paramount. Only say that afore this
here witness."

"Indeed, I shall say no such thing, ma'am," replied Patty: "for it is not in the least my wish to
prevent the gentleman from seeing my mistress.
It was she herself who refused to let him in; and
I think, if he forces himself into the room, she will
be apt to be very much displeased: but I shall not
hinder him, if he chooses to try. There are the
stairs, and my lady's room is the first on the right-
hand. Only, sir, before you go up, let me caution
you, lest you should startle her so as to be the
death of her. The least surprise or fright might
bring on another stroke in an instant."

Ensign Bloomington and Saucy Sally now looked
at one another, as if at a loss how to proceed:
they retired to a window to consult; and while they
were whispering, a coach drove up to the door.
It was full of Mrs. Crumpe's relations, whc came
post-haste from Monmouth, in consequence of the
alarm given by Mrs. Martha. Mr. Josiah Crumpe
was not in the coach: he had been written for, but
was not yet arrived from Liverpool.

Now, it must be observed, this coachful of relations were all enemies to Ensign Bloomington;

18 *

and the moment they put their heads out of the
carriage-window, and saw him standing in the
parlour, their surprise and indignation were too
great for coherent utterance. With all the rash-
ness of prejudice, they decided that he had bribed
Patty to let him in and to exclude them. Possessed
with this idea, they hurried out of the coach, passed
by poor Patty, who was standing in the hall, and
beckoned to Mrs. Martha, who showed them into
the drawing-room, and remained shut up with them
there for some minutes. " She is playing us false,"
cried Saucy Sally, rushing out of the parlour. " I
told you not to depend on that Martha ; nor on nobody but me : I said I 'd force a way for you up
to the room, and so I have ; and now you have not
the spirit to take your advantage. They 'll get in
all of them before you ; and then where will you
be, and what will you be ?"

Mrs. Crumpe's bell rang violently, and Patty ran
up stairs to her room.

' · I have been ringing for you, Patty, this quarter
of an hour ! What is all the disturbance I hear
below ?"

" Your relations, ma'am, who wish to see you :
I hope you won't refuse to see them, for they are
very anxious."

"Very anxious to have me dead and bur ed. Not one of them cares a groat for me. I have made my will, tell them; and they will see that in time. I will not see one of them."

By this time they were all at the bedchamber-door, struggling which party should enter first. Saucy Sally's loud voice was heard, maintaining her right to be there as wife-elect to Ensign Bloom-ington.

"Tell them the first who enters this room shall never see a shilling of my money," cried Mrs. Crumpe.

Patty opened the door; the disputants were in-stantly silent. "Be pleased, before you come in, to hearken to what my mistress says. Ma'am, will you say whatever you think proper yourself?" said Patty; "for it is too hard for me to be sus-pected of putting words into your mouth, and keep-ing your friends from the sight of you."

"The first of them who comes into this room," cried Mrs. Crumpe raising her feeble voice to the highest pitch she was able, "the first who enters this room shall never see a shilling of my money; and so on to the next, and the next, and the next. I'll see none of you."

No one ventured to enter. Their infinite solici-

tude to see how poor Mrs. Crumpe found herself to-
day suddenly vanished. The two parties adjourned
to the parlour and the drawing-room; and there was
nothing in which they agreed, except in abusing
Patty. They called for pen, ink, and paper, and
each wrote what they wished to say. Their notes
were carried up by Patty herself; for Mrs. Martha
would not run the risk of losing her own legacy to
oblige any of them, though she had been bribed by
all. With much difficulty Mrs. Crumpe was prevailed upon to look at the notes; at last she exclaimed, "Let them all come up; all! this moment
tell them, all!"

They were in the room instantly, all except
Saucy Sally: Ensign Bloomington persuaded her
it was for the best that she should not appear.
Patty was retiring as soon as she had shown them
in; but her mistress called to her, and bade her
take a key, which she held in her hand, and unlock an escritoir that was in the room. She did so.

"Give me that parcel which is tied up with red
tape, and sealed with three seals," said Mrs.
Crumpe.

All eyes were immediately fixed upon it, for it
was her will.

She broke the seals deliberately, untied the red

string, opened the huge sheet of parchment, and without saying one syllable, tore it down the middle; then tore the pieces again, and again, till they were so small that the writing could not be read. The spectators looked upon one another in dismay.

"Ay! you may all look as you please," cried Mrs. Crumpe. "I 'm alive, and in my sound senses still: my money 's my own; my property 's my own; I 'll do what I please with it. You were all handsomely provided for in this will; but you could not wait for your legacies till I was under ground. No! you must come hovering over me, like so many ravens. It is not time yet! It is not time yet! The breath is not yet out of my body; and when it is, you shall none of you be the better for it, I promise you. My money 's my own; my property 's my own; I 'll make a new will to-morrow. Good-by to you all. I 've told you my mind."

Not the most abject humiliations, not the most artful caresses, not the most taunting reproaches, from any of the company, could extort another word from Mrs. Crumpe. Her disappointed and incensed relations were at last obliged to leave the house; though not without venting their rage upon

Patty, whom they believed to be the secret cause of all that had happened. After they had left the house, she went up to a garret, where she thought no one would see her or hear her, sat down on an old bedstead, and burst into tears. She had been much shocked by the scenes that had just passed, and her heart wanted this relief.

" Oh," thought she, " it is plain enough that it is not riches which make people happy. Here is this poor lady, with heaps of money and fine clothes, without any one in this whole world to love or care for her; but all wishing her dead; worried by her own relations, and abused by them, almost in her hearing, upon her death-bed! Oh! my poor brother! how different it was with you!"

Patty's reflections were here interrupted by the entrance of Martha; who came and sat down on the bedstead beside her, and with a great deal of hypocritical kindness in her manner, began to talk of what had passed; blaming Mrs. Crumpe's re- lations for being so hardhearted and inconsiderate as to force business upon her when she was in such a state. " Indeed, they have no one to thank but themselves, for the new turn things have taken. I hear my mistress has torn her will to atoms, and is going to make a new one! To be sure, you,

. Mrs. Patty, will be handsomely provided for in this, as is, I am sure becoming; and I hope, if you have an opportunity, as for certain you will, you won't forget to speak a good word for me!"

Patty, who was disgusted by this interested and deceitful address, answered she had nothing to do with her mistress's will; and that her mistress was the best judge of what should be done with her own money, which she did not covet.

Mrs. Martha was not mistaken in her opinion that Patty would be handsomely remembered in this new will. Mrs. Crumpe the next morning said to Patty, as she was giving her some medicine, "It is for your interest, child, that I should get through this day, at least; for if I live a few hours longer, you will be the richest single woman in Monmouthshire. I'll show them all that my money's my own; and that I can do what I please with my own. Go yourself to Monmouth, child, as soon as you have plaited my cap, and bring me the attorney your brother lives with, to draw my new will. Don't say one word of your errand to any of my relations, I charge you, for your own sake as well as mine. The harpies would tear you to pieces; but I'll show them that I can do what I please with my own. That's the least satisfaction

I can have for my money before I die. God knows, it has been plague enough to me all my life long! But now, before I die—"

"Oh! ma'am," interrupted Patty, "there is no need to talk of your dying now; for I have not heard you speak so strong, or so clear, nor seem so much yourself this long time. You may live yet, and I hope you will, to see many a good day and to make it up, if I may be so bold to say it with all your relations : which, I am sure, would be a great ease to your heart ; and I am sure they are very sorry to have offended you."

"The girl's a fool!" cried Mrs. Crumpe. "Why, child, don't you understand me yet? I tell you as plain as I can speak, I mean to leave the whole fortune to you. Well! what makes you look so blank?"

"Because, ma'am, indeed I have no wish to stand in anybody's way ; and would not for all the world do such an unjust thing as to take advantage of your being a little angry or so with your relations, to get the fortune for myself : for I can do, having done all my life, without fortune well enough ; but I could not do without my own good opinion, and that of my father, and brothers, and sister ; all which I should lose, if I was to be guilty of a mean thing. So, ma'am," said Patty, " I have made bold to speak the whole truth of my mind to you; and I hope you will not do me an injury by way of doing me a favour. I am sure I thank you with all my heart for your goodness to me."

Patty turned away as she finished speaking; for she was greatly moved.

" You are a strange girl!" said Mrs. Crumpe. " I would not have believed this, if any one had sworn it to me. Go for the attorney, as I bid you, this minute; I will have my own way."

When Patty arrived at Mr. Barlow's she asked immediately for her brother Frank, whom she wished to consult: but he was out, and she then desired to speak to Mr. Barlow himself. She was shown into his office, and she told him her business, without any circumlocution, with the plain language and ingenuous countenance of truth.

" Indeed, sir," said she, " I should be glad you would come directly to my mistress and speak to her yourself; for she will mind what you say, and I only hope she may do the just thing by her relations. I don't want her fortune, nor any part of it, but a just recompense for my service. Knowing this in my own heart, I forgive them for all

19

the ill-will they bear me: it being all founded in a mistaken notion."

There was a gentleman in Mr. Barlow's office, who was sitting at a desk writing a letter, when Patty came in: she took him for one of the clerks. While she was speaking, he turned about several times, and looked at her very earnestly. At last he went to a clerk, who was folding up some parchments, and asked who she was. He then sat down again to his writing, without saying a single word. This gentleman was Mr. Josiah Crumpe, the Liverpool merchant, Mrs. Crumpe's eldest nephew; who had come to Monmouth, in consequence of the account he had heard of his aunt's situation. Mr. Barlow had lately amicably settled a suit between him and one of his relations at Monmouth; and Mr. Crumpe had just been signing the deed relative to this affair. He was struck with the disinterestedness of Patty's conduct; but he kept silence that she might not find out who he was, and that he might have full opportunity of doing her justice hereafter. He was not one of the ravens, as Mrs. Crumpe emphatically called those who were hovering over her, impatient for her death: he had, by his own skill and industry, made himself, not only independent, but rich. After Patty was gone, he, with the true spirit of a British merchant, declared that he was as independent in his sentiments as in his fortune; that he would not crouch or fawn to man or woman, peer or prince, in his majesty's dominions; no, not even to his own aunt. He wished his old aunt Crumpe, he said, to live and enjoy all she had as long as she could; and, if she chose to leave it to him after her death, well and good; he should be much obliged to her: if she did not, why well and good; he should not *be obliged* to be obliged to her; and that, to his humour, would perhaps be better still.

With these sentiments Mr. Josiah Crumpe found no difficulty in refraining from going to see, or, as he called it, from paying his court to his aunt. "I have some choice West India sweetmeats here for the poor soul," said he to Mr. Barlow: "she gave me sweetmeats when I was a schoolboy; which I don't forget. I know she has a sweet tooth still in her head; for she wrote to me last year, to desire I would get her some; but I did not relish the style of her letter, and I never complied with the order, however, I was to blame: she is an infirm poor creature, and should be humoured now, let her be ever so cross. Take her the sweetmeats; but mind, do not let her have a taste or a sight of them till she has made her will. I do not want to bribe her to leave me her money-bags; I thank my God and myself, I want them not."

Mr. Barlow immediately went to Mrs. Crumpe's. As she had land to dispose of, three witnesses were necessary to the will. Patty said she had two men-servants who could write; but to make sure of a third, Mr. Barlow desired that one of his clerks should accompany him. Frank was out; so the eldest clerk went in his stead.

This clerk's name was Mason: he was Frank's chief friend, and a young man of excellent character. He had never seen Patty till this day; but he had often heard her brother speak of her with so much affection, that he was prepossessed in her favour, even before he saw her. The manner in which she spoke on the subject of Mrs. Crumpe's fortune quite charmed him; for he was of an open and generous temper, and said to himself, " I would rather have this girl for my wife, without sixpence in the world, than any woman I ever saw in my life—if I could but afford it—and if she was but a little prettier. As it is, however, there is no danger of my falling in love with her; so I may just indulge myself in the pleasure of talking to her : besides, it is but civil to lead my horse and walk a part of the way with Frank's sister."

Accordingly, Mason set off to walk a part of the way to Mrs. Crumpe's with Patty; and they fell into conversation, in which they were both so earnestly engaged that they did not perceive how time passed. Instead, however, of part of the way, Mason walked the whole way: and he and Patty were both rather surprised, when they found themselves within sight of Mrs. Crumpe's house.

"What a fine healthy colour this walking has brought into her face," thought Mason, as he stood looking at her, while they were waiting for some one to open the door. "Though she has not a single beautiful feature, and though nobody could call her handsome, yet there is so much goodnature in her countenance, that, plain as she certainly is, her looks are more pleasing to my fancy than those of many a beauty I have heard admired."

The door was now opened; and Mr. Barlow, who had arrived some time, summoned Mason to business. They went up to Mrs. Crumpe's room to take her instructions for her new will. Patty showed them in.

"Don't go, child. I will not have you stir," said Mrs. Crumpe. "Now stand there at the foot

19 *

of my bed, and, without hypocrisy, tell me truly
child, your mind. This gentleman, who under-
stands the law, can assure you that in spite of all
the relations upon earth, I can leave my fortune to
whom I please : so do not let fear of my relations
prevent you from being happy."

"No, madam," interrupted Patty, "it was not
fear that made me say what I did to you this morning; and it is not fear that keeps me in the same
mind still. I would not do what I thought was
wrong myself if nobody else in the whole world
was to know it. But, since you desire me to say
what I really wish, I have a father, who is in great
distress, and I should wish you would leave fifty
pounds to him."

"With such principles and feelings," cried Mr.
Barlow, " you are happier than ten thousand a year
could make you !"

Mason said nothing, but his looks said a great
deal : and his master forgave him the innumerable
blunders he made, in drawing Mrs. Crumpe's will.
" Come, Mason, give me up the pen," whispered
he, at last; " you are not your own man, I see ;
and I like you the better for being touched with
good and generous conduct. But a truce with sentiment, now ; I must be a mere man of law. Go

you and take a walk, to recover your *legal* senses."

The, contents of Mrs. Crumpe's new will were kept secret: Patty did not in the least know how she had disposed of her fortune; nor did Mason, for he had written only the preamble, when his master compassionately took the pen from his hand. Contrary to expectation, Mrs. Crumpe continued to linger on for some months; and, during this time, Patty attended her with the most patient care and humanity. Though long habits of selfishness had rendered this lady in general indifferent to the feelings of her servants and dependants, yet Patty was an exception: she often said to her, "Child, it goes against my conscience to keep you prisoner here the best days of your life, in a sick room: go out and take a walk with your brothers and sister, I desire, whenever they call for you."

These walks with her brothers and sister were very refreshing to Patty; especially when Mason was of the party, as he almost always contrived to be. Every day he grew more and more attached to Patty; for every day he became more and more convinced of the goodness of her disposition and the sweetness of her temper. The affection which he saw her brothers and sister bore her spoke to his mind most strongly in her favour. " They have known her from her childhood," thought he, " and cannot be deceived in her character. 'T is a good sign that those who know her best love her most; and her loving her pretty sister Fanny, as she does, is a proof that she is incapable of envy and jealousy."

In consequence of these reflections, Mason determined he would apply diligently to his business, that he might in due time be able to marry and support Patty. She ingenuously told him she had never seen the man she could love so well as himself; but that her first object was to earn some money, to release her father from the almshouse, where she could not bear to see him living upon charity. " When, among us all, we have accomplished this," said she, " it will be time enough for me to think of marrying. Duty first, and love afterward."

Mason loved her the better, when he found her so steady in her gratitude to her father; for he was a man of sense, and knew that so good a daughter and sister would, in all probability, make a good wife.

We must now give some acccouut of what Fanny has been doing all this time. Upon her return to Mrs. Hungerford's after the death of her brother, she was received with the greatest kindness by her mistress, and by all the children, who were really fond of her, though she had never indulged them in any thing that was contrary to their mother's wishes.

Mrs. Hungerford had not forgotten the affair of the kettle-drum. One morning she said to her little son, "Gustavus, your curiosity about the kettle-drum and the clarionet shall be satisfied : your cousin Philip will come here in a few days, and he is well acquainted with the colonel of the regiment which is quartered in Monmouth : he shall ask the colonel to let us have the band here, some day. We may have them at the farthest end of the garden ; and you and your brothers and sisters shall dine in the arbour, with Fanny, who upon this occasion particularly deserves to have a share in your amusement."

The cousin Philip of whom Mrs. Hungerford spoke was no other than Frankland's landlord. young Mr. Folingsby. Besides liking fine horses and fine curricles, this gentleman was a great admirer of fine women.

He was struck with Fanny's beauty the first day he came to Mrs. Hungerford's : every succeeding day he thought her handsomer and handsomer; and every day grew fonder and fonder of playing with his little cousins. Upon some pretence or other, he contrived to be constantly in the room with them when Fanny was there; the modest propriety of her manners, however, kept him at that distance at which it was no easy matter for a pretty girl, in her situation, to keep such a gallant gentleman. His intention, when he came to Mrs. Hungerford's, was to stay but a week; but when that week was at an end, he determined to stay another: he found his aunt Hungerford's house uncommonly agreeable. The moment she mentioned to him her wish of having the band of music in the garden, he was charmed with the scheme, and longed to dine out in the arbour with the children; but he dared not press this point, lest he should excite suspicion.

Among other company who dined this day with Mrs. Hungerford was a Mrs. Cheviott, a blind lady, who took the liberty, as she said, to bring with her a young person, who was just come to live with her as a companion. This young person was Jessy Bettesworth, or, as she is henceforward to be called, Miss Jessy Bettesworth. Since her father had " come in for Captain Bettesworth's fortin," her mother had spared no pains to push Jessy forward in the world; having no doubt that " her beauty, when well dressed, would charm some great gentleman; or, maybe, some great lord!" Accordingly, Jessy was dizened out in all sorts of finery: her thoughts were wholly bent on fashions and flirting; and her mother's vanity, joined to her own, nearly turned her brain.

Just as this fermentation of folly was gaining force, she happened to meet with Ensign Bloomington at a ball at Monmouth: he fell, or she thought he fell, desperately in love with her; she, of course, coquetted with him: indeed, she gave him so much encouragement, that everybody concluded they were to be married. She and her sister Sally were continually seen walking arm-in-arm with him in the streets of Monmouth, and morning, noon, and night, she wore the drop-earrings of which he had made her a present. It chanced, however, that Jilting Jessy heard an officer, in her ensign's regiment, swear she was pretty enough to be the captain's lady instead of the ensign's; and, from that moment, she thought no more of the ensign.

He was enraged to find himself jilted thus by a country girl, and determined to have his revenge

consequently he immediately transferred all his at-
tentions to her sister Sally; judiciously calculating
that, from the envy and jealousy he had seen between the sisters, this would be the most effectual
mode of mortifying his perfidious fair. Jilting
Jessy said her sister was welcome to her cast-off
sweethearts: and Saucy Sally replied, her sister
was welcome to be her bridemaid; since, with all
her beauty and all her airs, she was not likely to
be a bride.

Mrs. Bettesworth had always confessed that Jessy
was her favourite: like a wise and kind mother,
she took part in all these disputes; and set these
amiable sisters yet more at variance, by prophesy-
ing that "her Jessy would make the grandest
match."

To put her into fortune's way, Mrs. Bettesworth
determined to get her into some genteel family, as
companion to a lady. Mrs. Cheviot's housekeeper
was nearly related to the Bettesworths, and to her
Mrs. Bettesworth applied. "But I'm afraid Jessy
is something too much of a flirt," said the housekeeper, "for my mistress; who is a very strict,
staid lady. You know, or at least we in Monmouth know, that Jessy was greatly talked of about
a young officer here in town. I used myself to see

her go trailing about, with her muslin and pink, and fine coloured shoes, in the dirt."

"Oh! that's all over now," said Mrs. Bettesworth: "the man was quite beneath her notice—that's all over now: he will do well enough for Sally; but, ma'am, my daughter Jessy has quite laid herself out for goodness now, and only wants to get into some house where she may learn to be a little genteel."

The housekeeper, though she had not the highest possible opinion of the young lady, was in hopes that, since Jessy had now laid herself out for goodness, she might yet turn out well; and, considering that she was her relation, she thought it her duty to speak in favour of Miss Bettesworth. In consequence of her recommendation, Mrs. Cheviott took Jessy into her family; and Jessy was particularly glad to be the companion of a blind lady.

She discovered, the first day she spent with Mrs. Cheviott, that, besides the misfortune of being blind, she had the still greater misfortune of being inordinately fond of flattery. Jessy took advantage of this foible, and imposed so far on the understanding of her patroness, that she persuaded Mrs. Cheviott into a high opinion of her judgment and prudence.

20

Things were in this situation when Jessy, for the
first time, accompanied the blind lady to Mrs.
Hungerford's. Without having the appearance or
manners of a gentlewoman, Miss Jessy Bettesworth was, notwithstanding, such a pretty, showy
girl that she generally contrived to attract notice.
She caught Mr. Folingsby's eye at dinner, as she
was playing off her best airs at the side-table; and
it was with infinite satisfaction that she heard him
ask one of the officers, as they were going out to
walk in the garden, " Who is that girl? She has
fine eyes, and a most beautiful long neck!" Upon
the strength of this whisper, Jessy flattered herself
she had made a conquest of Mr. Folingsby; by
which idea she was so much intoxicated, that she
could scarcely restrain her vanity within decent
bounds.

" Lord! Fanny Frankland, is it you? Who expected to meet you sitting here?" said she, when,
to her great surprise, she saw Fanny in the arbour
with the children. To her yet greater surprise, she
soon perceived that Mr. Folingsby's attention was
entirely fixed upon Fanny; and that he became so
absent he did not know he was walking upon the
flower-borders.

Jessy could scarcely believe her senses when she

saw that her rival, for as such she now considered her, gave her lover no encouragement. "Is it possible that the girl is such a fool as not to see that this here gentleman is in love with her? No; that is out of the nature of things. Oh! it's all artifice; and I will find out her drift, I warrant, before long!"

Having formed this laudable resolution, she took her measures well for carrying it into effect. Mrs. Cheviott, being blind, had few amusements: she was extremely fond of music, and one of Mrs. Hungerford's daughters played remarkably well on the piano-forte. This evening, as Mrs. Cheviott was listening to the young lady's singing, Jessy exclaimed, "Oh! ma'am, how happy it would make you, to hear such singing and music every day."

"If she would come every day, when my sister is practising with the music-master, she might hear enough of it," said little Gustavus. "I'll run and desire mamma to ask her; because," added he, in a low voice, "if I was blind, maybe I should like it myself."

Mrs. Hungerford, who was good-natured as well as polite, pressed Mrs. Cheviott to come whenever it should be agreeable to her. The poor blind lady was delighted with the invitation, and went regu larly every morning to Mrs. Hungerford's at the time the music-master attended. Jessy Bettesworth always accompanied her, for she could not go any-where without a guide.

Jessy had now ample opportunities of gratifying her malicious curiosity; she saw, or thought she saw, that Mr. Folingsby was displeased by the re-serve of Fanny's manners; and she renewed all her own coquettish efforts to engage his attention. He amused himself sometimes with her, in hopes of rousing Fanny's jealousy; but he found that this expedient, though an infallible one in ordinary cases, was here totally unavailing. His passion for Fanny was increased so much by her unaffected modesty, and by the daily proofs he saw of the sweetness of her disposition, that he was no longer master of himself: he plainly told her that he could not live without her.

"That's a pity, sir," said Fanny, laughing, and trying to turn off what he said, as if it were only a jest. "It is a great pity, sir, that you cannot live without me; for you know I cannot serve my mis-tress, do my duty, and live with you."

Mr. Folingsby endeavoured to convince, or ra-ther to persuade her that she was mistaken; and swore that nothing within the power of his fortune should be wanting to make her happy.

"Ah! sir," said she, "your fortune could not make me happy, if I were to do what I know is wrong, what would disgrace me for ever, and what would break my poor father's heart!"

"But your father shall never know any thing of the matter. I will keep your secret from the whole world: trust to my honour "

"Honour! Oh! sir, how can you talk to me of honour? Do you think I do not know what honour is, because I am poor? Or do you think I do not set any value on mine, though you do on yours? Would not you kill any man, if you could, in a duel, for doubting of your honour? And yet you expect me to love you, at the very moment you show me, most plainly, how desirous you are to rob me of mine!"

Mr. Folingsby was silent for some moments; but when he saw that Fanny was leaving him, he hastily stopped her, and said, laughing, " You have made me a most charming speech about honour; and, what is better still, you looked most charmingly when you spoke it; but now take time to consider what I have said to you. Let me have

20 *

your answer to-morrow; and consult this book before you answer me, I conjure you."

Fanny took up the book as soon as Mr. Folingsby had left the room; and, without opening it, determined to return it immediately. She instantly wrote a letter to Mr. Folingsby, which she was just wrapping up with the book in a sheet of paper, when Miss Jessy Bettesworth, the blind lady, and the music-master came into the room. Fanny went to set a chair for the blind lady; and while she was doing so, Miss Jessy Bettesworth, who had observed that Fanny blushed when they came in, slyly peeped into the book, which lay on the table. Between the first pages she opened there was a five-pound bank-note; she turned the leaf, and found another, and another, and another at every leaf! Of these notes she counted one-and-twenty! while Fanny, unsuspicious of what was doing behind her back, was looking for the children's music-books.

"Philip Folingsby! So, so! Did he give you this book, Fanny Frankland!" said Jessy, in a scornful tone: "it seems truly to be a very valuable performance; and, no doubt, he had good reasons for giving it to you."

Fanny coloured deeply at this unexpected

speech; and hesitated, from the fear of betraying Mr. Folingsby. "He did not give me the book: he only lent it to me," said she, "and I am going to return it to him directly."

"Oh! no; pray lend it to me first," replied Jessy in an ironical tone; "Mr. Folingsby, to be sure, would lend it to me as soon as to you. I'm growing as fond of reading as other folks, lately," continued she, holding the book fast.

"I dare say, Mr. Folingsby would—Mr. Folingsby would lend it to you, I suppose," said Fanny, colouring more and more deeply; "but, as it is trusted to me now, I must return it safe. Pray let me have it, Jessy."

"Oh! yes; return it, madam, safe! I make no manner of doubt you will! I make no manner of doubt you will!" replied Jessy, several times, as she shook the book; while the bank-notes fell from between the leaves, and were scattered upon the floor. "It is a thousand pities, Mrs. Cheviott, you can't see what a fine book we have got, full of bank-notes! But Mrs. Hungerford is not blind, at any rate, it is to be hoped," continued she, turning to Mrs. Hungerford, who at this instant opened the door.

She stood in dignified amazement. Jessy had an

air of malignant triumph. Fanny was covered
with blushes; but she looked with all the tranquil-
lity of innocence. The children gathered round
her; and blind Mrs. Cheviott cried, " What is
goir.g on? What is going on? Will nobody tell
me what is going on? Jessy! What is it you are
talking about, Jessy?"

" About a very valuable book, ma'am; containing more than I can easily count, in bank-notes,
ma'am, that Mr. Folingsby has lent, only lent,
ma'am, she says, to Miss Fanny Frankland, ma'am,
who was just going to return them to him, ma'am,
when I unluckily took up the book, and shook them
all out upon the floor, ma'am."

" Pick them up, Gustavus, my dear," said Mrs.
Hungerford, coolly. " From what I know of Fanny
Frankland, I am inclined to believe that whatever
she says is truth. Since she has lived with me, I
have never, in the slightest instance, found her de-
viate from the truth; therefore I must entirely depend upon what she says."

" O! yes, mamma," cried the children, all together, " that I am sure you may."

" Come with me, Fanny," resumed Mrs. Hungerford; " it is not necessary that your explanation

should be public, though I am persuaded it will be satisfactory."

Fanny was glad to escape from the envious eye of Miss Jessy Bettesworth, and felt much gratitude to Mrs. Hungerford for this kindness and confidence; but when she was to make her explanation, Fanny was in great confusion. She dreaded to occasion a quarrel between Mr. Folingsby and his aunt; yet she knew not how to exculpate herself, without accusing him.

" Why these blushes and tears, and why this silence, Fanny?" said Mrs. Hungerford, after she had waited some minutes, in expectation she would begin to speak. "Are not you sure of justice from me; and of protection, both from slander and insult? I am fond of my nephew, it is true; but I think myself obliged to you, for the manner in which you have conducted yourself towards my children, since you have had them under your care. Tell me then, freely, if you have any reason to complain of young Mr. Folingsby."

" Oh! madam," said Fanny, "thank you a thousand times for your goodness to me. I do not, indeed I do not wish to complain of anybody; and I would not for the world make mischief between you and your nephew. I would rather leave your

family at once ; and that," continued the poor girl,
sobbing, " that is what I believe I had best ; nay,
is what I must and will do."

" No, Fanny, do not leave my house without
giving me an explanation of what has passed this
morning ; for, if you do, your reputation is at the
mercy of Miss Jessy Bettesworth's malice "

" Heaven forbid !" said Fanny, with a look of
real terror. " I must beg, madam, that you will
have the kindness to return this book, and these
bank-notes, to Mr. Folingsby ; and that you will
give him this letter, which I was just going to wrap
up in the paper, with the book, when Jessy Bettesworth came in and found the bank-notes, which I
had never seen. These can make no difference in
my answer to Mr. Folingsby : therefore I shall
leave my letter just as it was first written, if you
please, madam."

Fanny's letter was as follows

" SIR,
" I return the book which you left with me, as
nothing it contains can ever alter my opinion on
the subject of which you spoke to me this morning.
I hope you will never speak to me again, sir, in the
same manner. Consider, sir, that I am a poor un-

protected girl. If you go on as you have done lately, I shall be obliged to leave good Mrs. Hungerford, who is my only friend. Oh! where shall I find so good a friend! My poor old father is in the almshouse! and there he must remain till his children can earn money sufficient to support him. Do not fancy, sir, that I say this by way of begging from you; I would not, nor would he, accept of any thing that you could offer him, while in your present way of thinking. Pray, sir, have some compassion, and do not injure those whom you cannot serve.

"I am, sir,

"Your humble servant,

"FANNY FRANKLAND."

Mr. Folingsby was surprised and confounded when this letter and the book containing his bank-notes were put into his hand by his aunt. Mrs. Hungerford told him by what means the book had been seen by Miss Jessy Bettesworth, and to what imputations it must have exposed Fanny. "Fanny is afraid of making mischief between you and me," continued Mrs. Hungerford; "and I cannot prevail upon her to give me an explanation, which, I am persuaded, would be much to her honour."

" Then you have not seen this letter ! Then she has decided without consulting you ! She is a charming girl !" cried Mr. Folingsby ; " and whatever you may think of me, I am bound, in justice to her, to show you what she has written : that will sufficiently explain how much I have been to blame, and how well she deserves the confidence you place in her."

As he spoke, Mr. Folingsby rang the bell to order his horses. " I will return to town immediately," continued he ; " so Fanny need not leave the house of her only friend to avoid me. As to these bank-notes, keep them, dear aunt. She says her father is in great distress. Perhaps, now that I am come ' to a right way of thinking,' she will not disdain my assistance. Give her the money when and how you think proper. ' I am sure I cannot make a better use of a hundred guineas ; and wish I had never thought of making a worse."

Mr. Folingsby returned directly to town ; and his aunt thought he had in some measure atoned for his fault by his candour and generosity.

Miss Jessy Bettesworth waited all this time, with malicious impatience, to hear the result of Fanny's explanation with Mrs. Hungerford. How painfully was she surprised and disappointed, when Mrs.

Hungerford returned to the company, to hear her speak in the highest terms of Fanny! "Oh, mamma," cried little Gustavus, clapping his hands, "I am glad you think her good, because we all think so; and I should be very sorry indeed if she was to go away, especially in disgrace."

"There is no danger of that, my dear!" said Mrs. Hungerford. "She shall never leave my house, as long as she desires to stay in it. I do not give, or withdraw, my protection without good reasons."

Miss Jessy Bettesworth bit her lips. Her face, which nature intended to be beautiful, became almost ugly; envy and malice distorted her features; and when she departed with Mrs. Cheviott, her humiliated appearance was a strong contrast to the air of triumph with which she had entered.

CHAPTER V.

AFTER Jessy and Mrs. Cheviott had left the room, one of the little girls exclaimed, "I don't like that Miss Bettesworth; for she asked me whether I did not wish that Fanny was gone, because she refused to let me have a peach that was not

21

ripe. I am sure I wish Fanny may always stay here."

There was a person in the room who seemed to join most fervently in this wish : this was Mr. Reynolds, the drawing-master. For some time his thoughts had been greatly occupied by Fanny. At first, he was struck with her beauty ; but he had discovered that Mr. Folingsby was in love with her, and had carefully attended to her conduct ; resolving not to offer himself till he was sure on a point so serious. Her modesty and prudence fixed his affections ; and he now became impatient to declare his passion. He was a man of excellent temper and character ; and his activity and talents were such as to ensure independence to a wife and family.

Mrs. Hungerford, though a proud, was not a selfish woman : she was glad that Mr. Reynolds was desirous to obtain Fanny ; though she was sorry to part with one who was so useful in her family. Fanny had now lived with her nearly two years ; and she was much attached to her. A distant relation, about this time, left her five children a small legacy of ten guineas each. Gustavus, though he had some ambition to be master of a watch, was the first to propose that this legacy should be given to Fanny. His brothers and sisers applauded the idea; and Mrs. Hungerford added fifty guineas to their fifty. " I had put by this money," said she, " to purchase a looking-glass for my drawing-room; but it will be much better applied in rewarding one who has been of real service to my children."

Fanny was now mistress of two hundred guineas,—a hundred given to her by Mr. Folingsby, fifty by Mrs. Hungerford, and fifty by the children. Her joy and gratitude were extreme; for with this money she knew she could relieve her father; this was the first wish of her heart; and it was a wish in which her lover so eagerly joined that she smiled on him, and said, " Now, I am sure you really love me."

" Let us go to your father directly," said Mr. Reynolds. " Let me be present when you give him this money."

" You shall," said Fanny; " but first I must consult my sister Patty and my brothers; for we must all go together; that is our agreement. The first day of next month is my father's birthday; and on that day we are all to meet at the alms-house. What a happy day it will be!"

But what has James been about all this time?

How has he gone on with his master, Mr. Cleghorn, the haberdasher?

During the eighteen months that James had
spent in Mr. Cleghorn's shop, he never gave his
master the slightest reason to complain of him,
on the contrary, this young man made his employer's interests his own, and, consequently, completely deserved his confidence. It was not, however, always easy to deal with Mr. Cleghorn; for
he dreaded to be flattered, yet could not bear to be
contradicted. James was very near losing his favour for ever, upon the following occasion.

One evening, when it was nearly dusk, and
James was just shutting up shop, a strange-looking
man, prodigiously corpulent, and with huge pockets
to his coat, came in. He leaned his elbows on the
counter, opposite to James, and stared him full in
the face without speaking. James swept some loose
money off the counter into the till. The stranger
smiled, as if purposely to show him this did not escape his quick eye. There was in his countenance
an expression of roguery and humour: the humour seemed to be affected, the roguery natural.
" What are you pleased to want, sir?" said James.

" A glass of brandy, and your master."

" My master is not at home, sir; and we have

ɔ brandy. You will find brandy, I believe, at the house over the way."

"I believe I know where to find brandy a little better than you do; and better brandy than you ever tasted, or the devil's in it," replied the stranger. "I want none of your brandy. I only asked for it to try what sort of a chap you were. So you don't know who I am?"

"No, sir; not in the least."

"No! Never heard of Admiral Tipsey! Where do you come from? Never heard of Admiral Tipsey! whose noble paunch is worth more than a Laplander could reckon," cried he, striking the huge rotundity he praised. "Let me into this back parlour, I'll wait there till your master comes home."

"Sir, you cannot possibly go into that parlour, there is a young lady, Mr. Cleghorn's daughter, sir, at tea in that room: she must not be disturbed," said James, holding the lock of the parlour door. He thought the stranger was either drunk or pretending to be drunk: and contended, with all his force, to prevent him from getting into the parlour.

While they were struggling, Mr. Cleghorn came home. "Heyday! what's the matter? O, admiral, is it you?" said Mr. Cleghorn, in a voice of

21 *

familiarity that astonished James. "Let us by, James; you don't know the admiral."

Admiral Tipsey was a smuggler: he had the command of two or three smuggling vessels, and thereupon created himself an admiral; a dignity which few dared to dispute with him, while he held his oak stick in his hand. As to the name of Tipsey, no one could be so unjust as to question his claim to it; for he was never known to be perfectly sober, during a whole day, from one year's end to another. To James's great surprise, the admiral, after he had drunk one dish of tea, unbuttoned his waistcoat from top to bottom, and deliberately began to unpack his huge false corpulence! Round him were wound innumerable pieces of lace, and fold after fold of fine cambric. When he was completely unpacked, it was difficult to believe that he was the same person, he looked so thin and shrunk.

He then called for some clean straw, and began to stuff himself out again to what he called a passable size. "Did not I tell you, young man, I carried that under my waistcoat which would make a fool stare? The lace that's on the floor, to say nothing of the cambric, is worth full twice the sum for which you shall have it, Cleghorn. Good night

I 'll all again to-morrow, to settle our affairs; but don'ι let your young man here shut the door, as he did to-day, in the admiral's face. Here is a cravat for you, notwithstanding," continued he, turning to James, and throwing him a piece of very fine cambric "I must 'list you in Admiral Tipsey's service."

James followed him to the door, and returned the cambric in despite of all his entreaties that he would " wear it, or sell it, for the admiral's sake."

" So, James," said Mr. Cleghorn, when the smuggler was gone, " you do not seem to like our admiral."

" I know nothing of him, sir, except that he is a smuggler; and for that reason I do not wish to have any thing to do with him."

" I am sorry for that," said Mr. Cleghorn, with a mixture of shame and anger in his countenance: " my conscience is as nice as other people's; and yet I have a notion I shall have something to do with him, though he is a smuggler; and, if I am not mistaken, shall make a deal of money by him. I have not had any thing to do with smugglers yet · but I see many in Monmouth who are making large fortunes by their assistance. There is our neighbour, Mr. Raikes; what a rich man he

is become! And why should I, or why should
you, be more scrupulous than others? Many gentlemen, ay, gentlemen, in the country are connected with them; and why should a shopkeeper
be more conscientious than they? Speak; I must
have your opinion."

With all the respect due to his master, James
gave it as his opinion that it would be best to have
nothing to do with Admiral Tipsey, or with any
of the smugglers. He observed that men who carried on an illicit trade, and who were in the
daily habits of cheating, or of taking false oaths,
could not be safe partners. Even putting morality
out of the question, he remarked that the smuggling
trade was a sort of gaming, by which one year a
man might make a deal of money, and another
might be ruined.

"Upon my word!" said Mr. Cleghorn, in an
ironical tone, "you talk very wisely, for so young
a man! Pray, where did you learn all this wisdom?"

"From my father, sir; from whom I learned
every thing that I know; every thing that is good,
I mean. I had an uncle once, who was ruined by
his dealings with smugglers; and who would have
died in jail, if it had not been for my father. I

was but a young lad at the time this happened; but I remember my father saying to me, the day my uncle was arrested, when my aunt and all the children were crying, ' Take warning by this, my dear James: you are to be in trade, some day or other, yourself: never forget that honesty is the best policy. The fair trader will always have the advantage, at the long run.'"

" Well, well, no more of this," interrupted Mr. Cleghorn. " Good night to you. You may finish the rest of your sermon against smugglers to my daughter there, whom it seems to suit better than it pleases me."

The next day, when Mr. Cleghorn went into the shop, he scarcely spoke to James, except to find fault with him. This he bore with patience, knowing that he meant well, and that his master would recover his temper in time.

" So the parcels were all sent, and the bills made out, as I desired," said Mr. Cleghorn. " You are not in the wrong there. You know what you are about, James, very well; but why should not you deal openly by me, according to your father's maxim, that ' Honesty is the best policy?' Why should not you fairly tell me what were your secret

views in the advice you gave me about Admiral
Tipsey and the smugglers ?"

"I have no secret views, sir," said James, with
a look of such sincerity that his master could not
help believing him: "nor can I guess what you
mean by *secret views*. If I consulted my own advantage instead of yours, I should certainly use all
my influence with you in favour of this smuggler:
for here is a letter, which I received from him this
morning, ' hoping for my friendship,' and enclosing
a ten-pound note, which I returned to him."

Mr. Cleghorn was pleased by the openness and
simplicity with which James told him all this; and
immediately throwing aside the reserve of his manner, said, " James, I beg your pardon; I see I have
misunderstood you. I am convinced you were not
acting like a double dealer, in the advice you gave
me last night. It was my daughter's colouring so
much that led me astray. i did, to be sure, think
you had an eye to her more than to me, in what
you said; but if you had, I am sure you would tell
me so fairly."

James was at a loss to comprehend how the advice that he gave concerning Admiral Tipsey and
the smugglers could relate to Miss Cleghorn, ex-

cept so far as it related to her father. He waited in silence for a further explanation.

"You don't know, then," continued Mr. Cleghorn, "that Admiral Tipsey, as he calls himself, is able to leave his nephew, young Raikes, more than I can leave my daughter? It is his whim to go about dressed in that strange way in which you saw him yesterday; and it is his diversion to carry on the smuggling trade, by which he has made so much; but he is in reality a rich old fellow, and has proposed that I should marry my daughter to his nephew. Now you begin to understand me, I see. The lad is a smart lad; he is to come here this evening. Don't prejudice my girl against him. Not a word more against smugglers, before her, I beg."

"You shall be obeyed, sir," said James. His voice altered, and he turned pale as he spoke; circumstances which did not escape Mr. Cleghorn's observation.

Young Raikes and his uncle, the rich smuggler, paid their visit. Miss Cleghorn expressed a decided dislike to both uncle and nephew. Her father was extremely provoked: and in the height of his anger, declared he believed she was in love with James Frankland; that he was a treacherous rascal; and that he should leave the house within three days, if his daughter did not, before that time, consent to marry the man he had chosen for her husband. It was in vain that his daughter endeavoured to soften her father's rage, and to exculpate poor James, by protesting he had never, directly or indirectly, attempted to engage her affections; neither had he ever said one syllable that could prejudice her against the man whom her father recommended. Mr. Cleghorn's high notions of subordination applied, on this occasion, equally to his daughter and to his foreman: he considered them both as presumptuous and ungrateful; and said to himself, as he walked up and down the room in a rage, "My foreman to preach to me, indeed! I thought what he was about all the time! But it sha'n't do—it sha'n't do! My daughter shall do as I bid her, or I'll know why! Have not I been all my life making a fortune for her? and now she won't do as I bid her! She would, if this fellow was out of the house; and out he shall go, in three days, if she does not come to her senses. I was cheated by my last shopman out of my money; I won't be duped by this fellow out of my daughter. No! no! Off he shall trudge! A shopman, indeed, to think of his mas-

ter's daughter without his consent! What insolence! What the times are come to! Such
a thing could not have been done in my days!
I never thought of my master's daughter, I'll
take my oath! And then the treachery of the
rascal! To carry it all on so slyly! I could forgive
him any thing but that : for that he shall go out of
this house in three days, as sure as he and I are
alive, if his young lady does not give him up before that time."

Passion so completely deafened Mr. Cleghorn
that he would not listen to James, who assured him
he had never, for a moment, aspired to the honour
of marrying his daughter. " Can you deny that
you love her? Can you deny," cried Mr. Cleghorn, " that you turned pale yesterday, when you
said I should be obeyed ?"

James could not deny either of these charges ;
but he firmly persisted in asserting that he had
been guilty of no treachery ; that he had never
attempted secretly to engage the young lady's
affections ; and that, on the contrary, he was sure
she had no suspicion of his attachment. " It is
easy to prove all this to me by persuading my girl
to do as I bid her. Prevail on her to marry Mr.
Raikes, and all is well."

22

" That is out of my power, sir," replied James
" I have no right to interfere, and will not. Indeed, I am sure I should betray myself, if I were
to attempt to say a word to Miss Cleghorn in favour
of another man ; that is a task I could not undertake, even if I had the highest opinion of this Mr.
Raikes ; but I know nothing concerning him ; and
therefore should do wrong to speak in his favour
merely to please you. I am sorry, very sorry, sir,
that you have not the confidence in me which I
hoped I had deserved ; but the time will come when
you will do me justice. The sooner I leave you
now, I believe the better you will be satisfied ; and
far from wishing to stay three days, I do not desire to stay three minutes in your house, sir, against
your will."

Mr. Cleghorn was touched by the feeling and
honest pride with which James spoke.

" Do as I bid you, sir," said he ; " and neither
more nor less. Stay out your three days ; and
maybe, in that time, this saucy girl may come to
reason. If she does not know you love her, you
are not *so much* to blame."

The three days passed away, and the morning
came on which James was to leave his master.
The young lady persisted in her resolution not to

marry Mr. Raikes; and expressed much concern at the injustice with which James was treated, on her account. She offered to leave home, and spend some time with an aunt, who lived in the north of England. She did not deny that James appeared to her the most agreeable young man she had seen; but added, she could not possibly have any thoughts of marrying him, because he had never given her the least reason to believe that he was attached to her.

Mr. Cleghorn was agitated; yet positive in his determination that James should quit the house. James went into his master's room, to take leave of him. "So then you are really going?" said Mr. Cleghorn. "You have buckled that port-manteau of yours like a blockhead; I'll do it better; stand aside. So you are positively going? Why, this is a sad thing! But then it is a thing, as your own sense and honour tell you—it is a thing—" (Mr. Cleghorn took snuff at every pause of his speech; but even this could not carry him through it;) when he pronounced the words—" it is a thing that must be done," the tears fairly started from his eyes. " Now this is ridiculous !" resumed he. " In my days, in my younger days, I mean, a man could part with his foreman as easily as he could take off his glove. I am sure my master would as soon have thought of turning bankrupt as of shedding a tear at parting with me; and yet I was as good a foreman, in my day, as another. Not so good a one as you are, to be sure. But it is no time now to think of your goodness. Well! what do we stand here for? When a thing is to be done, the sooner it is done the better. Shake hands before you go."

Mr. Cleghorn put into James's hand a fifty-pound note, and a letter of recommendation to a Liverpool merchant. James left the house without taking leave of Miss Cleghorn, who did not think the worse of him for his want of gallantry. His master had taken care to recommend him to an excellent house in Liverpool, where his salary would be nearly double that which he had hitherto received; but James was notwithstanding very sorry to leave Monmouth, where his dear brother, sister, and father lived,—to say nothing of Miss Cleghorn.

Late at night, James was going to the inn at which the Liverpool stage sets up, where he was to sleep: as he passed through a street that leads down to the river Wye, he heard a great noise of men quarrelling violently. The moon shone bright, and he saw a party of men who appeared to be fighting in a boat that was just come to shore. He asked a person who came out of the public-house, and who seemed to have nothing to do with the fray, what was the matter. "Only some smugglers, who are quarrelling with one another about the division of their booty," said the passenger, who walked on, eager to get out of their way. James also quickened his pace, but presently heard the cry of "Murder! murder! Help! help!" and then all was silence.

A few seconds afterward he thought that he heard groans. He could not forbear going to the spot whence the groans proceeded, in hopes of being of some service to a fellow-creature. By the time he got thither, the groans had ceased : he looked about, but could only see the men in the boat, who were rowing fast down the river. As he stood on the shore listening, he for some minutes heard no sound but that of their oars; but afterward a man in the boat exclaimed, with a terrible oath, "There he is! There he is! All alive again! We have not done his business! 'D—n it, he'll do ours!" The boatmen rowed faster away, and James again heard the groans, though they were now much feebler than before. He searched, and found the wounded man; who, having been thrown

22 *

overboard, had with great difficulty swum to shore, and fainted with the exertion as soon as he reached the land. When he came to his senses, he begged James, for mercy's sake, to carry him into the next public-house, and to send for a surgeon to dress his wounds. The surgeon came, examined them, and declared his fears that the poor man could not live four-and-twenty hours. As soon as he was able to speak intelligibly, he said he had been drinking with a party of smugglers, who had just brought in some fresh brandy, and that they had quarrelled violently about a keg of contraband liquor: he said that he could swear to the man who gave him the mortal wound.

The smugglers were pursued immediately, and taken. When they were brought into the sick man's room, James beheld among them three persons whom he little expected to meet in such a situation, —Idle Isaac, Wild Will, and Bullying Bob. The wounded man swore positively to their persons. Bullying Bob was the person who gave him the fatal blow; but Wild Will began the assault, and Idle Isaac shoved him overboard; they were all implicated in the guilt; and instead of expressing any contrition for their crime, began to dispute about which was most to blame: they appealed to

James; and as he would be subpœnaed on their trial, each endeavoured to engage him in his favour. Idle Isaac took him aside, and said to him, " You have no reason to befriend my brothers. I can tell you a secret: they are the greatest enemies your family ever had. It was they who set fire to your father's hay-rick. Will was provoked by your sister Fanny's refusing him; so he determined, as he told me, to carry her off; and he meant to have done so, in the confusion that was caused by the fire; but Bob and he quarrelled the very hour that she was to have been carried off; so that part of the scheme failed. Now I had no hand in all this, being fast asleep in my bed; so I have more claim to your good word, at any rate, than my brothers can have: and so, when we come to trial, I hope you 'll speak to my character."

Wild Will next tried his eloquence. As soon as he found that his brother Isaac had betrayed the secret, he went to James, and assured him the mischief that had been done was a mere accident: that it was true he had intended, for the frolic's sake, to raise a cry of fire, in order to draw Fanny out of the house; but that he was shocked when he found how the jest ended.

As to Bullying Bob, he brazened the matter out:

declaring he had been affronted by the Franklands, and that he was glad he had taken his revenge of them; that, if the thing was to be done over again, he would do it; that James might give him what character he pleased upon trial, for that a man could be hanged but once.

Such were the absurd, bravadoing speeches he made, while he had an alehouse audience round him, to admire his spirit; but a few hours changed his tone. He and his brothers were taken before a magistrate. Till the committal was actually made out, they had hopes of being bailed: they had despatched a messenger to Admiral Tipsey, whose men they called themselves, and expected he would offer bail for them to any amount; but the bail of their friend Admiral Tipsey was not deemed sufficient by the magistrate.

" In the first place, I could not bail these men; and if I could, do you think it possible," said the magistrate, " I could take the bail of such a man as that?"

" I understood that he was worth a deal of money," whispered James.

" You are mistaken, sir," said the magistrate: " he is, what he deserves to be, a ruined man. I have good reasons for knowing this. He has a nephew, a Mr. Raikes, who is a gamester: while the uncle has been carrying on the smuggling trade here, at the hazard of his life, the nephew, who was bred up at Oxford to be a fine gentleman, has gamed away all the money his uncle has made, during twenty years, by his contraband traffic. At the long run these fellows never thrive. Tipsey is not worth a groat."

James was much surprised by this information, and resolved to return immediately to Mr. Cleghorn, to tell him what he had heard, and put him on his guard.

Early in the morning he went to his house. " You look as if you were not pleased to see me again," said he to Mr. Cleghorn ; " and perhaps you will impute what I am going to say to bad motives ; but my regard to you, sir, determines me to acquaint you with what I have heard ; you will make what use of the information you please."

James then related what had passed at the magistrate's ; and when Mr. Cleghorn had heard all that he had to say, he thanked him in the strongest manner for this instance of his regard ; and begged he would remain in Monmouth a few days longer.

Alarmed by the information he received from James, Mr. Cleghorn privately made inquiries con-

cerning young Raikes and his uncle. The distress
into which the young man had plunged himself by
gambling had been kept a profound secret from his
relations. It was easy to deceive them as to his
conduct, because his time had been spent at a distance from them: he was but just returned home,
after *completing his education.*

The magistrate from whom James first heard of
his extravagance happened to have a son at Oxford,
who gave him this intelligence: he confirmed all
he had said to Mr. Cleghorn, who trembled at the
danger to which he had exposed his daughter.
The match with young Raikes was immediately
broken off; and all connexion with Admiral Tipsey
and the smugglers was for ever dissolved by Mr.
Cleghorn.

His gratitude to James was expressed with all
the natural warmth of his character. " Come back
and live with me," said he: " you have saved me
and my daughter from ruin. You shall not be my
shopman any longer, you shall be my partner:
and, you know, when you are my partner, there
can be nothing said against your thinking of my
daughter. But all in good time. I would not have
seen the girl again, if she had married my shopman : but my partner will be quite another thing.

You have worked your way up in the world by
your own deserts, and I give you joy. I believe,
now it's over, it would have gone nigh to break
my heart to part with you; but you must be sensible I was right to keep up my authority in my
own family. Now things are changed: I give
my consent: nobody has a right to say a word.
When I am pleased with my daughter's choice,
that is enough. There's only one thing that goes
against my pride: your father—"

"Oh! sir," interrupted James, "if you are going
to say any thing disrespectful of my father, do not
say it to me; I beseech you, do not; for I cannot
bear it. Indeed I cannot, and will not. He is the
best of fathers!"

"I am sure he has the best of children; and a
greater blessing there cannot be in this world. I
was not going to say any thing disrespectful of
him: I was only going to lament that he should be
in an almshouse," said Mr. Cleghorn.

"He has determined to remain there," said
James, "till his children have earned money enough
to support him without hurting themselves. I, my
brother, and both my sisters are to meet at the
almshouse on the first day of next month, which

is my father's birthday; then we shall join all our earnings together, and see what can be done."

"Remember, you are my partner," said Mr. Cleghorn. "On that day you must take me along with you. My good-will is part of your earnings, and my good-will shall never be shown merely in words."

CHAPTER VI.

It is now time to give some account of the Bettesworth family. The history of their indolence, extravagance, quarrels, and ruin shall be given as shortly as possible.

The fortune left to them by Captain Bettesworth was nearly twenty thousand pounds. When they got possession of this sum, they thought it could never be spent: and each individual of the family had separate plans of extravagance, for which they required separate supplies. Old Bettesworth, in his youth, had seen a house of Squire Somebody's which had struck his imagination, and he resolved he would build just such another. This was his favourite scheme, and he was delighted with the thoughts that it would be realized. His wife and his sons opposed the plan merely because it was his; and consequently he became more obstinately bent upon having his own way, as he said, for once in his life. He was totally ignorant of building; and no less incapable, from his habitual indolence, of managing workmen : the house might have been finished for one thousand five hundred pounds ; it cost him two thousand pounds : and when it was done, the roof let in the rain in sundry places, the new ceilings and cornices were damaged, so that repairs and a new roof, with leaden gutters, and leaden statues, cost him some additional hundreds. The furnishing of the house Mrs. Bettesworth took upon herself; and Sally *took upon herself* to find fault with every article that her mother bought. The quarrels were loud, bitter, and at last irreconcilable. There was a looking-glass, which the mother wanted to have in one room, and the daughter insisted upon putting it into another : the looking-glass was broken between them in the heat of battle. The blame was laid on Sally, who, in a rage, declared she would not and could not live in the house with her mother. Her mother was rejoiced to get rid of her, and she went to live with a lieutenant's lady in the neighbour-

23

hood, with whom she had been acquainted three
weeks and two days. Half by scolding, half by
cajoling her father, she prevailed upon him to give
her two thousand pounds for her fortune; promising never to trouble him any more for any
thing.

As soon as she was gone, Mrs. Bettesworth gave
a house-warming, as she called it, to all her acquaintance; a dinner, a ball, and a supper, in her
new house. The house was not half-dry, and all
the company caught cold. Mrs. Bettesworth's cold
was the most severe. It happened, at this time, to
be the fashion to go almost without clothes; and
as this lady was extremely vain and fond of dress,
she would absolutely appear in the height of fashion.
The Sunday after her ball, while she had still the
remains of a bad cold, she positively would go to
church, equipped in one petticoat and a thin muslin
gown, that she might look as young as her daughter
Jessy. Everybody laughed, and Jessy laughed
more than any one else; but, in the end, it was no
laughing matter; Mrs. Bettesworth " caught her
death of cold." She was confined to her bed on
Monday, and was buried the next Sunday.

Jessy, who had a great notion that she should
marry a lord, if she could but once get into com-

pany with one, went to live with blind Mrs. Cheviott; where, according to her mother's instructions, "she laid herself out for goodness." She
also took two thousand pounds with her, upon her
promise never to trouble her father more.

Her brothers perceived how much was to be
gained by tormenting a father, who gave from
weakness, and not from a sense of justice, or a
feeling of kindness; and they soon rendered themselves so troublesome that he was obliged to buy
off their reproaches. Idle Isaac was a sportsman,
and would needs have a pack of hounds: they cost
him two hundred a year. Then he would have
race-horses; and by them he soon lost some thousands. He was arrested for the money, and his
father was forced to pay it.

Bob and Will soon afterward began to think, "it
was very hard that so much was to be done for
Isaac, and nothing for them!"

Wild Will kept a mistress; and Bullying Bob
was a cock-fighter: their demands for money were
frequent and unconscionable; and their continual
plea was, "Why, Isaac lost thousands by his race-
horses; and why should not we have our share?"

The mistress and the cockpit had their share ·
and the poor old father, at last, had only one thou

sand left. He told his sons this, with tears in his
eyes: "I shall die in a jail, after all!" said he,
They listened not to what he said; for they were
intent upon the bank-notes of this last thousand,
which were spread upon the table before him.
Will, half in jest, half in earnest, snatched up a
parcel of the notes; and Bob insisted on dividing
the treasure. Will fled out of the house; Bob pursued him, and they fought at the end of their own
avenue.

This was on the day that Frankland and his
family were returning from poor George's funeral,
and saw the battle between the brothers. They
were shamed into a temporary reconciliation, and
soon afterward united against their father, whom
they represented to all the neighbours as the most
cruel and the most avaricious of men, because he
would not part with the very means of subsistence
to supply their profligacy.

While their minds were in this state, Will happened to become acquainted with a set of smugglers, whose disorderly life struck his fancy. He
persuaded his brothers to leave home with him, and
to 'list in the service of Admiral Tipsey. Their
manners then became more brutal; and they
thought, felt, and lived like men of desperate for

tunes. The consequence we have seen. In a quarrel about a keg of brandy, at an alehouse, their passions got the better of them, and, on entering their boat, they committed the offence for which they were now imprisoned.

Mr. Barlow was the attorney to whom they applied, and they endeavoured to engage him to manage their cause on their trial, but he absolutely refused. From the moment he heard from James that Will and Bob Bettesworth were the persons who set fire to Frankland's haystack, he urged Frank to prosecute them for this crime. " When you only suspected them, my dear Frank, I strongly dissuaded you from going to law; but now you cannot fail to succeed, and you will recover ample damages."

" That is impossible, my dear sir," replied Frank; " for the Bettesworths, I understand, are ruined."

" I am sorry for that, on your account; but I still think you ought to carry on this prosecution, for the sake of public justice. Such pests of society should not go unpunished."

" They will probably be punished sufficiently for this unfortunate assault, for which they are now to stand their trial. I cannot, in their distress, revenge either my own or my father's wrongs. I am

23 *

sure he would be sorry if I did; for I have often
and often heard him say, ' Never-trample upon the
fallen.' "

" You are a good, generous young man," cried
Mr. Barlow; " and no wonder you love the father
who inspired you with such sentiments, and taught
you such principles. But what a shame it is that
such a father should be in an almshouse! You
say he will not consent to be dependent upon any
one; and that he will not accept of relief from any
but his own children. This is pride; but it is an
honourable species of pride; fit for an English yeoman. I cannot blame it. But, my dear Frank,
tell your father he must accept of your friend's
credit, as well as of yours. Your credit with me
is such, that you may draw upon me for five hundred pounds whenever you please. No thanks,
my boy: half the money I owe you for your services as my clerk; and the other half is well secured to me, by the certainty of your future diligence and success in business. You will be able
to pay me in a year or two; so I put you under no
obligation, remember. I will take your bond for
half the money, if that will satisfy you and your
proud father."

The manner in which this favour was conferred

touched Frank to the heart. He had a heart which could be strongly moved by kindness. He was beginning to express his gratitude, when Mr. Barlow interrupted him with, " Come, come! Why do we waste our time here, talking sentiment, when we ought to be writing law? Here is work to be done, which requires some expedition : a marriage settlement to be drawn. Guess for whom."

Frank guessed all the probable matches among his Monmouth acquaintance; but he was rather surprised when told that the bridegroom was to be young Mr. Folingsby; as it was scarcely two months since this gentleman was in love with Fanny Frankland. Frank proceeded to draw the settlement.

While he and Mr. Barlow were writing, they were interrupted by the entrance of Mr. Josiah Crumpe. He came to announce Mrs. Crumpe's death, and to request Mr. Barlow's attendance at the opening of her wi". This poor lady had lingered out many months longer than it was thought she could possibly live ; and during all her sufferings, Patty, with indefatigable goodness and temper, bore with the caprice and peevishness of disease. Those who thought she acted merely from interested motives expected to find she had used her

power over her mistress's mind entirely for her
own advantage: they were certain a great part of
the fortune would be left to her.   Mrs. Crumpe's
relations were so persuaded of this, that, when they
were assembled to hear her will read by Mr. Barlow, they began to say to one another in whispers,
" We'll set the will aside; we'll bring her into
the courts: Mrs. Crumpe was not in her right
senses when she made this will: she had received
two paralytic strokes; we can prove that: we can
set aside the will."

Mr. Josiah Crumpe was not one of these whis-
perers; he sat apart from them, leaning on his
oaken stick in silence.

Mr. Barlow broke the seals of the will, opened
it, and read it to the eager company.   They were
much astonished when they found that the whole
fortune was left to Mr. Josiah Crumpe.   The reason for this bequest was given in these words:

" Mr. Josiah Crumpe, being the only one of my
relations who did not torment me for my money,
even upon my death-bed, I trust that he will provide suitably for that excellent girl Patty Frankland.
On this head he knows my wishes.   By her own
desire, I have not myself left her any thing; I

have only bequeathed fifty pounds for the use of her father."

Mr. Josiah Crumpe was the only person who heard unmoved the bequest that was made to him; the rest of the relations were clamorous in their reproaches, or hypocritical in their congratulations. All thoughts of setting aside the will were, however, abandoned; every legal form had been observed, and with a technical nicety that precluded all hopes of successful litigation.

Mr. Crumpe arose as soon as the tumult of disappointment had somewhat subsided, and counted with his oaken stick the numbers that were present. "Here are ten of you, I think. Well! you every soul of you hate me; but that is nothing to the purpose. I shall keep up the notion I have of the character of a true British merchant for my own sake—not for yours. I don't want this woman's money; I have enough of my own, and of my own honest making, without legacy-hunting. Why did you torment the dying woman? You would have been better off, if you had behaved better; but that's over now. A thousand pounds apiece you shall have from me, deducting fifty pounds which you must each of you give to that excellent

girl Patty Frankland.   I am sure you must be a¹
sensible of your injustice to her."

Fully aware that it was their interest to oblige
Mr. Crumpe, they now vied with each other in doing justice to Patty. Some even declared they
had never had any suspicions of her; and others
laid the blame on the false representations and information which they said they had had from the
mischief-making Mrs. Martha. They very willingly accepted of a thousand pounds apiece; and the
fifty pounds' deduction was paid as a tax by each
to Patty's merit.

Mistress now of five hundred pounds, she exclaimed, "Oh! my dear father! You shall no
longer live in an almshouse! To-morrow will be
the happiest day of my life! I don't know how to
thank you as I ought sir," continued she turning
to her benefactor.

"You have thanked me as you ought, and as I
like best," said this plain-spoken merchant; "and
now let us say no more about it."

In obedience to Mr. Crumpe's commands, Patty
said no more to him; but she was impatient to tell
her brother Frank, and her lover, Mr. Mason, of
her good fortune: she therefore returned to Monmouth with Mr. Barlow, in hopes of seeing them

immediately; but Frank was not at work at the marriage settlement. Soon after Mr. Barlow left him he was summoned to attend the trial of the Bettesworths.

These unfortunate young men, depending on Frank's good-nature, well knowing he had refused to prosecute them for setting fire to his father's hay-rick, thought they might venture to call upon him to give them a good character. " Consider, dear Frank," said Will Bettesworth, " a good word from one of your character might do a great deal for us. You were so many years our neighbour. If you would only just say that we were never counted wild, idle, quarrelsome fellows, to your knowledge. Will you ?"

" How can I do that ?" said Frank: " or how could I be believed, if I did, when it is so well known in the country—forgive me ; at such a time as this I cannot mean to taunt you : but it is well known in the country that you were called Wild Will, Bullying Bob, and Idle Isaac."

" There 's the rub !" said the attorney who was employed for the Bettesworths. " This will come out in open court ; and the judge and jury will think a great deal of it."

" Oh ! Mr. Frank, Mr. Frank," cried old Bettesworth, " have pity upon us! Speak in favour of these boys of mine! Think what a disgrace it is to me in my old age to have my sons brought this way to a public trial! And if they should be transported! Oh! Frank, say what you can for them! You were always a good young man, and a good-natured young man."

Frank was moved by the entreaties and tears of this unhappy father; but his good-nature could not make him consent to say what he knew to be false. " Do not call me to speak to their characters upon this trial," said he, " I cannot say any thing that would serve them; I shall do them more harm than good."

Still they had hopes his good-nature would at the last moment prevail over his sense of justice, and they summoned him.

" Well, sir," said the Bettesworths' counsel, "you appear in favour of the prisoners. You have known them, I understand from their childhood; and your own character is such that whatever you say in their favour will doubtless make a weighty impression upon the jury."

The court was silent, in expectation of what Frank should say. He was so much embarrassed between his wish to serve his old neighbours and

playfellows, and his dread of saying what he knew
to be false, that he could not utter a syllable. He
burst into tears.*

"This evidence is most strongly against the
prisoners," whispered a juryman to his fellows.

The verdict was brought in at last—Guilty!
Sentence—transportation.

As the judge was pronouncing this sentence, old
Bettesworth was carried out of the court; he had
dropped senseless. Ill as his sons had behaved to
him, he could not sustain the sight of their utter
disgrace and ruin.

When he recovered his senses, he found himself
sitting on the stone bench before the court-house,
supported by Frank. Many of the townspeople
had gathered round; but regardless of every thing
but his own feelings, the wretched father exclaimed,
in a voice of despair, " I have no children left me
in my old age! My sons are gone! And where
are my daughters? At such a time as this, why
are not they near their poor old father? Have
they no touch of natural affections in them? No!
they have none. And why should they have any
for me? I took no care of them when they were

* This is drawn from real life.

24

young; no wonder they take none of me now I
am old.   Ay! neighbour Frankland was right : he
brought up his children ' in the way they should
go.'   Now he has the credit and the comfort of
them; and see what mine are come to!   They
bring their father's gray hairs with sorrow to the
grave !"

The old man wept bitterly : then looking round
him, he again asked for his daughters.   " Surely
they are in the town, and it cannot be much trouble to them to come to me !   Even these strangers,
who have never seen me before, pity me.   But *my
own* have no feeling; no, not for one another !
Do these girls know the sentence that has been
passed upon their brothers ?   Where are they ?
Where are they ?   Jessy, at least, might be near
me at such a time as this!   I was always an
indulgent father to Jessy."

There were people present who knew what was
become of Jessy ; but they would not tell the news
to her father at this terrible moment.   Two of Mrs.
Cheviott's servants were in the crowd ; and one of
them whispered to Frank, " You had best, sir, prevail on this poor old man to go to his home, and
not to ask for his daughter : he will hear the bad
news soon enough."

Frank persuaded the father to go home to his lodgings, and did every thing in his power to comfort him. But, alas! the old man said, too truly, " There is no happiness left for me in this world! What a curse it is to have bad children! My children have broken my heart! And it is all my own fault: I took no care of them when they were young; and they take no care of me now I am old. But, tell me, have you found out what is become of my daughter?"

Frank evaded the question, and begged the old man to rest in peace this night. He seemed quite exhausted by grief, and at last sank into a sort of stupefaction: it could hardly be called sleep. Frank was obliged to return home, to proceed with his business for Mr. Barlow; and he was glad to escape from the sight of misery, which, however he might pity it, he could not relieve.

It was happy indeed for Frank that he had taken his father's advice, and had early broken off all connexion with Jilting Jessy. After duping others, she at length had become a greater dupe. She had this morning gone off with a common sergeant, with whom she had fallen suddenly and desperately in love. He cared for nothing but her two thousand pounds; and to complete her misfortune, was a man of bad character, whose extravagance and profligacy had reduced him to the sad alternative of either marrying for money or going to jail.

As for Sally, she was at this instant far from all thoughts either of her father or her brothers; she was in the heat of a scolding match, which terminated rather unfortunately for her matrimonial schemes. Ensign Bloomington had reproached her with having forced him into his aunt's room, when she had absolutely refused to see him, and thus being the cause of his losing a handsome legacy. Irritated by this charge, the lady replied in no very gentle terms. Words ran high; and so high at last that the gentleman finished by swearing that he would sooner marry the devil than such a vixen!

The match was thus broken off, to the great amusement of all Saucy Sally's acquaintance. Her ill-humour had made her hated by all the neighbours; so that her disappointment at the loss of the ensign was imbittered by their malicious raillery, and by the prophecy which she heard more than whispered from all sides, that she would never have another admirer, either for " love or money."

Ensign Bloomington was deaf to all overtures of peace: he was rejoiced to escape from this virago; and as we presume that none of our readers are much interested in her fate, we shall leave her to wear the willow, without following her history further.

Let us return to Mr. Barlow, whom we left looking over Mr. Folingsby's marriage settlements. When he had seen that they were rightly drawn, he sent Frank with them to Folingsby-hall.

Mr. Folingsby was alone when Frank arrived. "Sit down, if you please, sir," said he. "Though I have never had the pleasure of seeing you before, your name is well known to me. You are a brother of Fanny Frankland's. She is a charming and excellent young woman! You have reason to be proud of your sister, and I have reason to be obliged to her."

He then adverted to what had formerly passed between them at Mrs. Hungerford's; and concluded by saying it would give him real satisfaction to do any service to him or his family. "Speak, and tell me what I can do for you."

Frank looked down, and was silent: for he thought Mr. Folingsby must recollect the injustice that he, or his agent, had shown in turning old

24 *

Frankland out of his farm. He was too proud to ask favours where he felt he had a claim to justice.

In fact, Mr. Folingsby had, as he said, " left every thing to his agent;" and so little did he know either of the affairs of his tenants, their persons, or even their names, that he had not at this moment the slightest idea that Frank was the son of one of the oldest and the best of them. He did not know that old Frankland had been reduced to take refuge in an almshouse in consequence of his agent's injustice. Surprised by Frank's cold silence, he questioned him more closely, and it was with astonishment and shame that he heard the truth.

" Good Heavens!" cried he, " has my negligence been the cause of all this misery to your father? to the father of Fanny Frankland! I remember, now that you recall it to my mind, something of an old man with fine gray hair, coming to speak to me about some business, just as I was setting off for Ascot races. Was that your father? I recollect I told him I was in a great hurry; and that Mr. Deal, my agent, would certainly do him justice. In this I was grossly mistaken; and I have suffered severely for the confidence I had in that fellow. Thank God, I shall now have my affairs in my own hands. I am determined to look into them immediately. My head is no longer full of horses and gigs, and curricles. There is a time for every thing : my giddy days are over. I only wish that my thoughtlessness had never hurt any one but myself."

" All I now can do," continued Mr. Folingsby, " is to make amends, as fast as possible, for the past. To begin with your father : most fortunately I have the means in my power. His farm is come back into my hands ; and it shall, to-morrow, be restored to him. Old Bettesworth was with me scarcely an hour ago, to surrender the farm, on which there is a prodigious arrear of rent : but I understand that he has built a good house on the farm ; and I am extremely glad of it, for your father's sake. Tell him it shall be his. Tell him I am ready, I am eager, to put him in possession of it ; and to repair the injustice I have done, or which, at least, I have permitted to be done in my name."

Frank was so overjoyed that he could scarcely utter one word of thanks. In his way home he called at Mrs. Hungerford's to tell the good news to his sister Fanny. This was the eve of their father's birthday ; and they agreed to meet at the almshouse in the morning.

The happy morning came. Old Frankland was busy in his little garden, when he heard the voices of his children, who were coming towards him. " Fanny ! Patty ! James ! Frank ! Welcome, my children ! Welcome ! I knew you would be so kind as to come to see your old father on this day ; so I was picking some of my currants for you, to make you as welcome as I can. But I wonder you are not ashamed to come to see me in an almshouse. Such gay lads and lasses ! I well know I have reason to be proud of you all. Why, I think I never saw you, one and all, look so well in my whole life !"

" Perhaps, father," said Frank, " because you never saw us, one and all, so happy ! Will you sit down, dear father, here in your arbour ; and we will all sit upon the grass, at your feet, and each tell you stories, and all the good news."

" My children," said he, " do what you will with me ! It makes my old heart swim with joy to see you all again around me looking so happy."

The father sat down in his arbour, and his children placed themselves at his feet. First his daughter Patty spoke ; and then Fanny ; then

James; and at last Frank. When they had all told the.r little histories, they offered to their father in one purse their common riches: the rewards of their own good conduct.

" My beloved children !" said Frankland, over-powered with his tears, " this is too much joy for me! this is the happiest moment of my life! None but the father of such children can know what I feel! Your success in the world delights me ten times the more, because I know it is all owing to yourselves."

" Oh! no, dear father !" cried they with one ac-cord; " no, dear, dear father, our success is all owing to you! Every thing we have is owing to you; to the care you took of us from our infancy upward. If you had not watched for our welfare, and taught us so well, we should not now all be so happy! Poor Bettesworth !"

Here they were interrupted by Hannah, the faithful maid-servant, who had always lived with old Frankland. She came running down the garden so fast that, when she reached the arbour, she was so much out of breath she could not speak. " Dear heart! God bless you all !" cried she, as soon as she recovered breath. " But it is no time to be sitting here. Come in, sir, for mercy's sake,"

said she, addressing herself to her old master.
" Come in to be ready ; come in, all of you, to be
ready !"

" Ready !   Ready for what ?"

" Oh ! ready for fine things !   Fine doings !
Only come in, and I 'll tell you as we go along.
How I have torn all my hand with this gooseberry-
bush !   But no matter for that.   So then you have
not heard a word of what is going on ?   No, how
could you ?   And you did not miss me when you
first came into the house ?"

" Forgive us for that, good Hannah : we were
in such a hurry to see my father, we thought of
nothing and nobody else."

" Very natural.   Well, Miss Fanny, I 've been
up at the great house with your lady, Mrs. Hungerford.   A better lady cannot be !   Do you know,
she sent for me on purpose to speak to me ; and I
know things that you are not to know yet.   But
this much I may tell you, there 's a carriage coming
here to carry my master away to his new house ;
and there 's horses and side-saddles besides for you,
and you, and you, and me.   And Mrs. Hungerford
is coming in her own coach ; and young Mr. Folingsby is coming in his carriage ; and Mr. Barlow
m Mr. Jos. Crumpe's carriage ; and Mr. Cleghorn

and his pretty daughter in the gig; and—and—and
—heaps of carriages besides! friends of Mrs. Hungerford's: and there's such crowds gathering in
the streets; and I'm going on to get breakfast."

"Oh! my dear father," cried Frank, "make
haste, and take off this badge-coat before they
come! We have brought proper clothes for you."

Frank pulled off the badge-coat, as he called it,
and flung it from him, saying, " My father shall
never wear you more."

Fanny had just tied on her father's clean neck-
cloth, and Patty had smoothed his reverend gray
locks, when the sound of the carriages was heard.
All that Hannah had told them was true. Mrs.
Hungerford had engaged all her friends, and all
who were acquainted with the good conduct of the
Franklands, to attend her on this joyful occasion.

" Triumphal cavalcades and processions," said
she, " are in general foolish things—mere gratifi-
cations of vanity; but this is not in honour of
vanity, but in honour of virtue. We shall do good
in the country, by showing that we respect and
admire it in whatever station it is to be found.
Here is a whole family who have conducted themselves uncommonly well; who have exerted themselves to relieve their aged father from a situation

to which he was reduced without any fault or imprudence of his own.   Their exertions have succeeded.   Let us give them what they will value
more than money, SYMPATHY."

Convinced or persuaded by what Mrs. Hungerford said, all her friends and acquaintances attended her this morning to the almshouse.   Crowds
of people followed ; and old Frankland was carried   .
in triumph by his children to his new habitation.

The happy father lived many years to enjoy the
increasing prosperity of his family.*

May every good father have as grateful children.

---

* It may be necessary to inform some readers that Patty
and Fanny were soon united to their lovers ; that James,
with Mr. Cleghorn's consent, married Miss Cleghorn ; and
that Frank did not become an old bachelor : he married
an amiable girl, who was ten times prettier than Jilting
Jessy, and of whom he was twenty times as fond.   Those
who wish to know the history of all the wedding-clothes
of the parties may have their curiosity gratified by di-
recting a line of inquiry, post paid, to the editor hereof.

May, 1801.

THE GRATEFUL NEGRO.

CHAPTER I.

In the island of Jamaica there lived two planters, whose methods of managing their slaves were as different as possible. Mr. Jefferies considered the negroes as an inferior species, incapable of gratitude, disposed to treachery, and to be roused from their natural indolence only by force; he treated his slaves, or rather suffered his overseer to treat them, with the greatest severity.

Jefferies was not a man of a cruel, but of a thoughtless and extravagant temper. He was of such a sanguine disposition that he always calculated upon having a fine season and fine crops on his plantation; and never had the prudence to make allowance for unfortunate accidents: he required, as he said, from his overseer produce and not excuses.

Durant, the overseer, did not scruple to use the

25

most cruel and barbarous methods of forcing the slaves to exertions beyond their strength.*　Complaints of his brutality, from time to time, reached his master's ears; but though Mr. Jefferies was moved to momentary compassion, he shut his heart against conviction: he hurried away to the jovial banquet, and drowned all painful reflections in wine.

He was this year much in debt; and therefore, being more than usually anxious about his crop, he pressed his overseer to exert himself to the utmost.

The wretched slaves upon his plantation thought themselves still more unfortunate when they compared their condition with that of the negroes on the estate of Mr. Edwards.　This gentleman treated his slaves with all possible humanity and kindness.　He wished that there was no such thing as slavery in the world; but he was convinced, by the arguments of those who have the best means of obtaining information, that the sudden emancipation of the negroes would rather increase than diminish

* THE NEGRO SLAVES—A fine drama, by Kotzebue. It is to be hoped that such horrible instances of cruelty are not now to be found in nature. Bryan Edwards, in his History of Jamaica, says that most of the planters are humane; but he allows that some facts can be cited in contradiction of the assertion.

their miseries. His benevolence, therefore, confined itself within the bounds of reason. He
adopted those plans for the amelioration of the state
of the slaves which appeared to him the **most likely**
to succeed without producing any violent agitation
or revolution.* For **instance, his negroes had**
reasonable and fixed daily tasks ; **and when these**
were finished, they were permitted **to employ** their
time for their own advantage or amusement. If
they chose to employ themselves longer for their
master, they were paid regular wages **for their ex-
tra work.** This reward, for as such it **was con-**
sidered, operated most powerfully upon the **slaves.**
Those who are animated by hope can **perform what**
would seem impossibilities to those who are under
the depressing influence of fear. **The wages which**
Mr. Edwards promised, he took care to see punc-
tually paid.

He had an excellent overseer, of the name of
Abraham Bayley, a man of a mild but steady temper, who was attached, not only to his master's interests, but to his virtues ; and who, therefore, **was**
more intent upon seconding his humane views than
upon squeezing from the labour of the negroes the

* History of the West Indies, from which these ideas **are
adopted—not stolen.**

utmost produce.   Each negro had, near his cottage,
a portion of land called his provision ground ; and
one day in the week was allowed for its cultivation.

It is common in Jamaica for the slaves to have
provision grounds, which they cultivate for their
own advantage ; but it too often happens that, when
a good negro has successfully improved his little
spot of ground, when he has built himself a house,
and begins to enjoy the fruits of his industry, his
acquired property is seized upon by the sheriff's officer for the payment of his master's debts ; he is
forcibly separated from his wife and children, drag-
ged to public auction, purchased by a stranger, and
perhaps sent to terminate his miserable existence
in the mines of Mexico ; excluded for ever from
the light of heaven ; and all this without any crime
or imprudence on his part, real or pretended.   He
is punished because his master is unfortunate !

To this barbarous injustice the negroes on Mr.
Edward's plantation were never exposed. He never
exceeded his income ; he engaged in no wild specu-
lations ; he contracted no debts ; and his slaves,
therefore, were in no danger of being seized by a
sheriff's officer : their property was secured to them
by the prudence as well as by the generosity of
their master.

One morning, as Mr. Edwards was walking in that part of his plantation which joined to Mr. Jefferies' estate, he thought he heard the voice of distress at some distance. The lamentations grew louder and louder as he approached a cottage which stood upon the borders of Jefferies' plantation.

This cottage belonged to a slave of the name of Cæsar, the best negro in Mr. Jefferies' possession. Such had been his industry and exertion, that notwithstanding the severe tasks imposed by Durant, the overseer, Cæsar found means to cultivate his provision ground to a degree of perfection nowhere else to be seen on this estate. Mr. Edwards had often admired this poor fellow's industry, and now hastened to inquire what misfortune had befallen him.

When he came to the cottage, he found Cæsar standing with his arms folded, and his eyes fixed upon the ground. A young and beautiful female negro was weeping bitterly, as she knelt at the feet of Durant, the overseer, who, regarding her with a sullen aspect, repeated, " He must go. I tell you, woman, he must go. What signifies all this nonsense ?"

At the sight of Mr. Edwards, the overseer's countenance suddenly changed, and assumed an
25 *

air of obsequious civility. The poor woman retired to the farther corner of the cottage, and continued to weep. Cæsar never moved. "Nothing
is the matter, sir," said Durant, "but that Cæsar is
going to be sold. That is what the woman is crying for. They were to be married; but we'll find
Clara another husband, I tell her; and she'll get
the better of her grief, you know, sir, as I tell her,
in time."

"Never! never!" said Clara.

"To whom is Cæsar going to be sold; and for
what sum?"

"For what can be got for him," replied Durant,
laughing; "and to whoever will buy him. The
sheriff's officer is here, who has seized him for
debt, and must make the most of him at market."

"Poor fellow!" said Mr. Edwards; "and must
he leave this cottage which he has built, and these
bananas which he has planted?"

Cæsar now for the first time looked up, and fixing his eyes upon Mr. Edwards for a moment, advanced with an intrepid rather than an imploring
countenance, and said, "Will you be my master?
Will you be her master? Buy both of us. You
shall not repent of it. Cæsar will serve you faithfully."

On hearing these words, Clara sprang forward, and clasping her hands together, repeated, " Cæsar will serve you faithfully."

Mr. Edwards was moved by their entreaties, but he left them without declaring his intentions. He went immediately to Mr. Jefferies, whom he found stretched on a sofa, drinking coffee. As soon as Mr. Edwards mentioned the occasion of his visit, and expressed his sorrow for Cæsar, Jefferies exclaimed, " Yes, poor devil! I pity him from the bottom of my soul. But what can I do? I leave all those things to Durant. He says the sheriff's officer has seized him; and there's an end of the matter. You know money must be had. Besides, Cæsar is not worse off than any other slave sold for debt. What signifies talking about the matter, as if it were something that never happened before! Is not it a case that occurs every day in Jamaica?"

" So much the worse," replied Mr. Edwards.

" The worse for them, to be sure," said Jefferies. "But, after all, they are slaves, and used to be treated as such; and they tell me the negroes are a thousand times happier here, with us, than they ever were in their own country."

" Did the negroes tell you so themselves?"

" No; but people better informed than negroes

have told me so; and, after all, slaves there must be; for indigo, and rum, and sugar we must have."

" Granting it to be physically impossible that the world should exist without rum, sugar, and indigo, why could they not be produced by freemen as well as by slaves? If we hired negroes for labourers, instead of purchasing them for slaves, do you think they would not work as well as they do now? Does any negro, under the fear of the overseer, work harder than a Birmingham journeyman, or a Newcastle collier, who toil for themselves and their families?"

" Of that I don't pretend to judge. All I know is, that the West India planters would be ruined if they had no slaves, and I am a West India planter."

" So am I: yet I do not think they are the only people whose interests ought to be considered in this business."

" Their interests, luckily, are protected by the laws of the land; and though they are rich men, and white men, and freemen, they have as good a claim to their rights as the poorest black slave on any of our plantations."

" The law, in our case, seems to make the right;

and the very reverse ought to be done—the right should make the law."

" Fortunately for us planters, we need not enter into such nice distinctions.   You could not, if you would, abolish the trade.   Slaves would be smuggled into the islands."

" What, if nobody would buy them !   You know that you cannot smuggle slaves into England. The instant a slave touches English ground he becomes free.   Glorious privilege !   Why should it not be extended to all her dominions ?   If the future importation of slaves into these islands were forbidden by law, the trade must cease.   No man can either sell or possess slaves without its being known: they cannot be smuggled like lace or brandy."

" Well, well !" retorted Jefferies, a little impatiently, " as yet the law is on our side.   I can do nothing in this business, nor you neither."

" Yes, we can do something ; we can endeavour to make our negroes as happy as possible."

" I leave the management of these people to Durant."

" That is the very thing of which they complain; forgive me for speaking to you with the frankness of an old acquaintance."

" Oh ! you can't oblige me more : I love frankness of all things! To tell you the truth, I have heard complaints of Durant's severity ; but I make it a principle to turn a deaf ear to them, for I know nothing can be done with these fellows without it. You are partial to negroes ; but even you must allow they are a race of beings naturally inferior to us. You may in vain think of managing a black as you would a white. Do what you please for a negro, he will cheat you the first opportunity he finds. You know what their maxim is—' God gives black men what white men forget.' "

To these common-place desultory observations Mr. Edwards made no reply ; but recurred to poor Cæsar, and offered to purchase both him and Clara, at the highest price the sheriff's officer could obtain for them at market. Mr. Jefferies, with the utmost politeness to his neighbour, but with the most perfect indifference to the happiness of those whom he considered of a different species from himself, acceded to this proposal. Nothing could be more reasonable, he said ; and he was happy to have it in his power to oblige a gentleman for whom he had such a high esteem.

The bargain was quickly concluded with the sheriff's officer ; for Mr. Edwards willingly paid several dollars more than the market price for the two slaves. When Cæsar and Clara heard that they were not to be separated, their joy and gratitude was expressed with all the ardour and tenderness peculiar to their different characters. Clara was an Eboe, Cæsar a Koromantyn negro; the Eboes are soft, languishing, and timid; the Koromantyns are frank, fearless, martial, and heroic.

Mr. Edwards carried his new slaves home with him, desired Bayley, his overseer, to mark out a provision-ground for Cæsar, and to give him a cottage which happened at this time to be vacant.

" Now, my good friend," said he to Cæsar, " you may work for yourself, without fear that what you earn may be taken from you, or that you should ever be sold to pay your master's debts. If he does not understand what I am saying," continued Mr. Edwards, turning to his overseer, " you will explain it to him."

Cæsar perfectly understood all that Mr. Edwards said; but his feelings were at this instant so strong that he could not find expression for his gratitude: he stood like one stupified! Kindness was new to him; it overpowered his manly heart; and, at hearing the words " my good friend," the tears gushed from his eyes: tears which no torture could have extorted! Gratitude swelled in his bosom; and he longed to be alone, that he might freely yield to his emotions.

He was glad when the conch-shell sounded to call the negroes to their daily labour, that he might relieve the sensations of his soul by bodily exertion. He performed his task in silence; and an inattentive observer might have thought him sullen.

In fact, he was impatient for the day to be over, that he might get rid of a heavy load which weighed upon his mind.

The cruelties practised by Durant, the overseer of Jefferies' plantation, had exasperated the slaves under his dominion.

They were all leagued together in a conspiracy, which was kept profoundly secret. Their object was to extirpate every white man, woman, and child in the island. Their plans were laid with consummate art; and the negroes were urged to execute them by all the courage of despair.

The confederacy extended to all the negroes in the island of Jamaica, excepting those on the plantation of Mr. Edwards. To them no hint of the dreadful secret had yet been given; their countrymen, knowing the attachment they felt to their master, dared not trust them with these projects of vengeance. Hector, the negro who was at the head of the conspirators, was the particular friend of Cæsar, and had imparted to him all his designs. These friends were bound to each other by the strongest ties. Their slavery and their sufferings began in the same hour : they were both brought from their own country in the same ship. This circumstance alone forms, among the negroes, a bond of connexion not easily to be dissolved. But the friendship of Cæsar and Hector commenced even before they were united by the sympathy of misfortune; they were both of the same nation, both Koromantyns; in Africa they had both been accustomed to command; for they had signalized themselves by superior fortitude and courage. They respected each other for excelling in all which they had been taught to consider as virtuous; and with them revenge was a virtue!

Revenge was the ruling passion of Hector: in Cæsar's mind it was rather a principle instilled by education. The one considered it as a duty, the other felt it as a pleasure. Hector's sense of injury was acute in the extreme; he knew not how to forgive. Cæsar's sensibility was yet more alive to kindness than to insult. Hector would sacrifice his life to extirpate an enemy. Cæsar would de-

26

vote himself for the defence of a friend; and
Cæsar now considered a white man as his friend.

He was now placed in a painful situation. All
his former friendships, all the solemn promises by
which he was bound to his companions in misfortune, forbade him to indulge that delightful feeling
of gratitude and affection, which, for the first time,
he experienced for one of that race of beings
whom he had hitherto considered as detestable
tyrants—objects of implacable and just revenge!

Cæsar was most impatient to have an interview
with Hector, that he might communicate his new
sentiments, and dissuade him from those schemes
of destruction which he meditated. At midnight,
when all the slaves except himself were asleep, he
left his cottage, and went to Jefferies' plantation, to
the hut in which Hector slept. Even in his dreams
Hector breathed vengeance. "Spare none! Sons
of Africa, spare none!" were the words he uttered
in his sleep, as Cæsar approached the mat on
which he lay. The moon shone full upon him.
Cæsar contemplated the countenance of his friend,
fierce even in sleep. "Spare none! Oh, yes!
There is one that must be spared. There is one
for whose sake all must be spared."

He wakened Hector by this exclamation. "Of what were you dreaming?" said Cæsar.

"Of that which, sleeping or waking, fills my soul—revenge! .Why did you waken me from my dream? It was delightful. The whites were weltering in their blood. But silence! we may be overheard."

"No; every one sleeps but ourselves," replied Cæsar. "I could not sleep, without speaking to you on—a subject that weighs upon my mind. You have seen Mr. Edwards?"

"Yes. He that is now your master."

"He that is now my benefactor—my friend!"

"Friend! Can you call a white man friend?" cried Hector, starting up with a look of astonishment and indignation.

"Yes," replied Cæsar, with firmness. "And you would speak, ay, and would feel, as I do, Hector, if you knew this white man. Oh, how unlike he is to all of his race, that we have ever seen! Do not turn from me with so much disdain. Hear me with patience, my friend."

"I cannot," replied Hector, "listen with patience to one who between the rising and the setting sun can forget all his resolutions, all his promises; who by a few soft words can be so wrought upon as to forget all the insults, all the injuries he has received from this accursed race; and can even call a white man friend!"

Cæsar, unmoved by Hector's anger, continued to speak of Mr. Edwards with the warmest expressions of gratitude; and finished by declaring he would sooner forfeit his life than rebel against such a master. He conjured Hector to desist from executing his designs; but all was in vain. Hector sat with his elbows fixed upon his knees, leaning his head upon his hands, in gloomy silence.

Cæsar's mind was divided between love for his friend and gratitude to his master: the conflict was violent and painful. Gratitude at last prevailed: he repeated his declaration, that he would rather die than continue in a conspiracy against his benefactor!

Hector refused to except him from the general doom. "Betray us if you will!" cried he. "Betray our secrets to him whom you call your benefactor; to him whom a few hours have made your friend! To him sacrifice the friend of your youth, the companion of your better days, of your better self! Yes, Cæsar, deliver me over to the tormentors: I can endure no more than they can inflict. I shall expire without a sigh, without a groan.

Why do you linger here, Cæsar? Why do you
hesitate? Hasten this moment to your master;
claim your reward for delivering into his power
hundreds of your countrymen! Why do you
hesitate? Away! The coward's friendship can
oe of use to none. Who can value his gratitude?
Who can fear his revenge?"

Hector raised his voice so high, as he pronounced
these words, that he wakened Durant, the overseer,
who slept in the next house. They heard him call
out suddenly, to inquire who was there: and Cæsar
had but just time to make his escape before Durant
appeared. He searched Hector's cottage; but finding no one, again retired to rest. This man's tyranny made him constantly suspicious: he dreaded
that the slaves should combine against him; and
he endeavoured to prevent them by every threat
and every stratagem he could devise, from conversing with each other.

They had, however, taken their measures hitherto so secretly, that he had not the slightest idea
of the conspiracy which was forming in the island.
Their schemes were not yet ripe for execution; but
the appointed time approached. Hector, when he
coolly reflected on what had passed between him
and Cæsar, could not help admiring the frankness

26 *

and courage with which he had avowed his change of sentiments. By this avowal, Cæsar had in fact exposed his own life to the most imminent danger, from the vengeance of the conspirators ; who might be tempted to assassinate him who had their lives in his power. Notwithstanding the contempt with which, in the first moment of passion, he had treated his friend, he was extremely anxious that he should not break off all connexion with the conspirators. He knew that Cæsar possessed both intrepidity and eloquence ; and that his opposition to their schemes would perhaps entirely frustrate their whole design. He therefore determined to use every possible means to bend him to their purposes.

He resolved to have recourse to one of those persons* who, among the negroes, are considered

---

* The enlightened inhabitants of Europe may perhaps smile at the superstitious credulity of the negroes, who regard those ignorant beings called *Obeah* people with the most profound respect and dread ; who believe that they hold in their hands the power of good and evil fortune, of health and sickness, of life and death. The instances which are related of their power over the minds of their country-men are so wonderful that none but the most unquestionable authority could make us think them credible. The following passage from Edward's History of the West Indies, is inserted, to give an idea of this strange infatuation :

" In the year 1760, when a very formidable insurrection

as sorceresses. Esther, an old Koromantyn negress, had obtained by her skill in poisonous herbs,

of the Koromantyn or Gold Coast negroes broke out, in
the parish of St. Mary, and spread through almost every
other district of the island, an old Koromantyn negro, the
chief instigator and oracle of the insurgents in that parish,
who had administered the fetish, or solemn oath, to the
conspirators, and furnished them with a magical prepara-
tion, which was to render them invulnerable, was fortunately apprehended, convicted, and hung up, with all his
feathers and trumperies about him; and his execution struck
the insurgents with a general panic, from which they never
afterward recovered. The examinations, which were taken
at that period, first opened the eyes of the public to the
very dangerous tendency of the *Obeah* practices; and gave
birth to the law which was then enacted for their suppres-
sion and punishment; but neither the terror of this law,
the strict investigation which has since been made after the
professors of *Obi*, nor the many examples of those who
from time to time have been hanged or transported, have
hitherto produced the desired effect. A gentleman, on his
returning to Jamaica, in the year 1775, found that a great
many of his negroes had died during his absence; and that,
of such as remained alive, at least one-half were debilitated,
bloated, and in a very deplorable condition. The mortality
continued after his arrival; and two or three were frequently buried in one day; others were taken ill, and began
to decline under the same symptoms. Every means were
tried, by medicine and the most careful nursing, to preserve
the lives of the feeblest; but, in spite of all his endeavours,
this depopulation went on for a twelvemonth longer, with

and her knowledge of venomous reptiles, a high reputation among her countrymen. She soon taught

more or less intermission, and without his being able to ascertain the real cause, though the *Obeah* practice was strongly suspected, as well by himself as by the doctor, and other white persons upon the plantation; as it was known to have been very common in that part of the island, and particularly among the negroes of the *Popaw* or *Popo* country. Still he was unable to verify his suspicions; because the patients constantly denied their having any thing to do with persons of that order, or any knowledge of them. At length, a negress, who had been ill for some time, came and informed him that, feeling it was impossible for her to live much longer, she thought herself bound in duty, before she died, to impart a very great secret, and acquaint him with the true cause of her disorder; in hopes that the disclosure might prove the means of stopping that mischief, which had already swept away such a number of her fellow-slaves. She proceeded to say, that her step-mother, a woman of the *Popo* country, above eighty years old, but still hale and active, had *put Obi upon her;* as she had upon those who had lately died; and that the old woman had practised *Obi* for as many years past as she could remember. The other negroes of the plantation no sooner heard of this impeachment than they ran in a body to their master, and confirmed the truth of it.**** Upon this he repaired directly, with six white servants, to the old woman's house; and, forcing open the door, observed the whole inside of the roof, which was of thatch, and every crevice of the wall, stuck with the implements of her trade, consisting of rags, feathers, bones of cats, and a thousand other arthem to believe her to be possessed of supernatural powers; and she then worked their imagination to what pitch and purpose she pleased.

She was the chief instigator of this intended rebellion. It was she who had stimulated the revengeful temper of Hector almost to phrensy. She now promised him that her arts should be exerted over his friend; and it was not long before he felt their influence. Cæsar soon perceived an extraordinary change in the countenance and manner of his beloved Clara. A melancholy hung over her, and she refused to impart to him the cause of her dejection. Cæsar was indefatigable in his exertions to cultivate and embellish the ground near his cottage, in hopes of making it an agreeable habitation for her; but she seemed to take no interest in any thing. She would stand beside him immoveable, in a deep revery; and when he in-

ticles.**** The house was instantly pulled down; and, with the whole of its contents, committed to the flames, amid the general acclamations of all his other negroes.**** From the moment of her departure, his negroes seemed all to be animated with new spirits; and the malady spread no farther among them. The title of his losses, in the course of about fifteen years preceding the discovery, and imputable solely to the *Obeah practice*, he estimates, at least, at one hundred negroes."

quired whether she was ill, she would answer no, and endeavour to assume an air of gayety: but this cheerfulness was transient; she soon relapsed into despondency. At length, she endeavoured to avoid her lover, as if she feared his further inquiries.

Unable to endure this state of suspense, he one evening resolved to bring her to an explanation. "Clara," said he, "you once loved me: I have done nothing, have I, to forfeit your confidence?"

"I once loved you!" said she, raising her languid eyes, and looking at him with reproachful tenderness; "and can you doubt my constancy? Oh, Cæsar, you little know what is passing in my heart! You are the cause of my melancholy!"

She paused, and hesitated, as if afraid that she had said too much: but Cæsar urged her with so much vehemence, and so much tenderness, to open to him her whole soul, that, at last, she could not resist his eloquence. She reluctantly revealed to him that secret of which she could not think without horror. She informed him that, unless he complied with what was required of him by the sorceress Esther, he was devoted to die. What it was that Esther required of him Clara knew not: she knew nothing of the conspiracy. The timidity of her character was ill-suited to such a project; and every thing relating to it had been concealed from her with the utmost care.

When she explained to Cæsar the cause of her dejection, his natural courage resisted these superstitious fears; and he endeavoured to raise Clara's spirits. He endeavoured in vain: she fell at his feet, and with tears, and the most tender supplications, conjured him to avert the wrath of the sorceress by obeying her commands whatever they might be.

" Clara," replied he, " you know not what you ask !"

" I ask you to save your life !" said she. " I ask you, for my sake, to save your life, while yet it is in your power !"

" But would you, to save my life, Clara, make me the worst of criminals? Would you make me the murderer of my benefactor?"

Clara started with horror.

" Do you recollect the day, the moment, when we were on the point of being separated for ever, Clara? Do you remember the white man's coming to my cottage? Do you remember his look of benevolence—his voice of compassion? Do you remember his generosity? Oh! Clara, would you make me the murderer of this man?"

"Heaven forbid!" said Clara. "This cannot be the will of the sorceress!"

"It is," said Cæsar. "But she shall not succeed, even though she speaks with the voice of Clara. Urge me no further; my resolution is fixed. I should be unworthy of your love if I were capable of treachery and ingratitude."

"But are there no means of averting the wrath of Esther?" said Clara. "Your life—"

"Think, first, of my honour," interrupted Cæsar. "Your fears deprive you of reason. Return to this sorceress, and tell her that I dread not her wrath. My hands shall never be imbrued in the blood of my benefactor. Clara! can you forget his look when he told us that we should never more be separated?"

"It went to my heart," said Clara, bursting into tears. "Cruel, cruel Esther! Why do you command us to destroy such a generous master?"

The conch sounded to summon the negroes to their morning's work. It happened this day that Mr. Edwards, who was continually intent upon increasing the comforts and happiness of his slaves, sent his carpenter, while Cæsar was absent, to fit

up the inside of his cottage; and when Cæsar returned from work, he found his master pruning
the branches of a tamarind-tree that overhung the
thatch. "How comes it, Cæsar," said he, "that
you have not pruned these branches?"

Cæsar had no knife. "Here is mine for you,"
said Mr. Edwards. "It is very sharp," added he,
smiling; "but I am not one of those masters who
are afraid to trust their negroes with sharp knives."

These words were spoken with perfect simplicity;
Mr. Edwards had no suspicion, at this time, of
what was passing in the negro's mind. Cæsar received the knife without uttering a syllable; but no
sooner was Mr. Edwards out of sight than he knelt
down, and, in a transport of gratitude, swore that,
with this knife, he would stab himself to the heart
sooner than betray his master.

The principle of gratitude conquered every other
sensation. The mind of Cæsar was not insensible
to the charms of freedom: he knew the negro
conspirators had so taken their measures, that there
was the greatest probability of their success. His
heart beat high at the idea of recovering his liberty;
but he was not to be seduced from his duty, not
even by this delightful hope; nor was he to be intimidated by the dreadful certainty that his former

27

friends and countrymen, considering him as a de-
serter from their cause, would become his bitterest
enemies.   The loss of Hector's esteem and affection was deeply felt by Cæsar.   Since the night
that the decisive conversation relative to Mr. Edwards passed, Hector and he had never exchanged
a syllable.

This visit proved the cause of much suffering to
Hector, and to several of the slaves on Jefferies'
plantation.   We mentioned that Durant had been
awakened by the raised voice of Hector.   Though
he could not find any one in the cottage, yet his
suspicions were not dissipated; and an accident
nearly brought the whole conspiracy to light.   Durant had ordered one of the negroes to watch a
boiler of sugar : the slave was overcome by the heat,
and fainted.   He had scarcely recovered his senses
when the overseer came up, and found that the
sugar had fermented, by having remained a few
minutes too long in the boiler.   He flew into a
violent passion, and ordered that the negro should
receive fifty lashes.   His victim bore them without
uttering a groan; but when his punishment was
over, and when he thought the overseer was gone,
he exclaimed, " It will soon be our turn !"

Durant was not out of hearing.   He turned sud-

denly, and observed that the negro looked at Hector when he pronounced these words, and this
confirmed the suspicion that Hector was carrying
on some conspiracy. He immediately had recourse
to that brutality which he considered as the only
means of governing black men : Hector and three
other negroes were lashed unmercifully; but no
confessions could be extorted.

Mr. Jefferies might perhaps have forbidden such
violence to be used, if he had not been at the time
carousing with a party of jovial West Indians, who
thought of nothing but indulging their appetites in
all the luxuries that art and nature could supply.
The sufferings which had been endured by many
of the wretched negroes to furnish out this magnificent entertainment were never once thought of by
these selfish epicures. Yet so false are the general
estimates of character, that all these gentlemen
passed for men of great feeling and generosity!
The human mind, in certain situations, becomes so
accustomed to ideas of tyranny and cruelty, that
they no longer appear extraordinary or detestable ;
they rather seem part of the necessary and immu-
table order of things.

Mr. Jefferies was stopped, as he passed from his
dining-room into his drawing-room, by a little

negro child, of about five years old, who was crying bitterly.   He was the son of one of the slaves
who were at this moment under the torturer's hand.
" Poor little devil !" said Mr. Jefferies, who was
more than half-intoxicated.   " Take him away:
and tell Durant, some of ye, to pardon his father—
if he can."

The child ran eagerly to announce his father's
pardon ; but he soon returned, crying more violently than before. Durant would not hear the
boy ; and it was now no longer possible to appeal
to Mr. Jefferies, for he was in the midst of an assembly of fair ladies ; and no servant belonging to
the house dared to interrupt the festivities of the
evening. The three men who were so severely
flogged to extort from them confessions were perfectly innocent : they knew nothing of the confederacy ; but the rebels seized the moment when
their minds were exasperated by this cruelty and
injustice, and they easily persuaded them to join
the league.   The hope of revenging themselves
upon the overseer was a motive sufficient to make
them brave death in any shape.

Another incident, which happened a few days
before the time destined for the revolt of the
slaves, determined numbers who had been unde-

cided. Mrs. Jefferies was a languid beauty, or
rather a languid fine lady who had been a beauty,
and who spent all that part of the day which was
not devoted to the pleasures of the table, or to re-
clining on a couch, in dress. She was one day
extended on a sofa, fanned by four slaves, two at
her head and two at her feet, when news was
brought that a large chest, directed to her, was
just arrived from London.

This chest contained various articles of dress of
the newest fashions. The Jamaica ladies carry
their ideas of magnificence to a high pitch: they
willingly give a hundred guineas for a gown,
which they perhaps wear but once or twice. In
the elegance and variety of her ornaments Mrs.
Jefferies was not exceeded by any lady in the
island, except by one who had lately received a
cargo from England. She now expected to out-
shine her competitor, and desired that the chest
should be unpacked in her presence.

In taking out one of the gowns, it caught on a
nail in the lid, and was torn. The lady, roused
from her natural indolence by this disappointment
to her vanity, instantly ordered that the unfortunate
female slave should be severely chastised. The
woman was the wife of Hector; and this fresh in-

27 *

jury worked up his temper, naturally vindictive, to the highest point. He ardently longed for the moment when he might satiate his vengeance.

The plan the negroes had laid was to set fire to the canes, at one and the same time, on every plantation; and when the white inhabitants of the island should run to put out the fire, the blacks were to seize this moment of confusion and consterna-tion to fall upon them, and make a general mas-sacre. The time when this scheme was to be carried into execution was not known to Cæsar; for the conspirators had changed their day as soon as Hector told them that his friend was no longer one of the confederacy. They dreaded he should betray them; and it was determined that he and Clara should both be destroyed, unless they could be prevailed upon to join the conspiracy.

Hector wished to save his friend; but the desire of vengeance overcame every other feeling. He resolved, however, to make an attempt, for the last time, to change Cæsar's resolution.

For this purpose, Esther was the person he em-ployed: she was to work upon his mind by means of Clara. On returning to her cottage one night, she found suspended from the thatch one of those strange fantastic charms with which the Indian

sorceresses terrify those whom they have pro-
scribed.   Clara, unable to conquer her terror,
repaired again to Esther, who received her first in
mysterious silence: but after she had implored her
forgiveness for the past, and with all possible hu-
mility conjured her to grant her future protection,
the sorceress deigned to speak.   Her commands
were that Clara should prevail upon her lover to
meet her, on this awful spot, the ensuing night.

Little suspecting what was going forward on the
plantation of Jefferies, Mr. Edwards that evening
gave his slaves a holyday.   He and his family
came out at sunset, when the fresh breeze had
sprung up, and seated themselves under a spreading palm-tree, to enjoy the pleasing spectacle of
this negro festival.   His negroes were all well clad,
and in the gayest colours, and their merry countenances suited the gayety of their dress.   While
some were dancing, and some playing on the tam-
barine, others appeared among the distant trees,
bringing baskets of avocado pears, grapes, and
pineapples, the produce of their own provision-
grounds; and others were employed in spreading
their clean trenchers, or the calabashes which
served for plates and dishes.   The negroes continued to dance and divert themselves till late in

the evening. When they separated and retired to
rest, Cæsar, recollecting his promise to Clara, repaired secretly to the habitation of the sorceress.
It was situated in the recess of a thick wood.
When he arrived there, he found the door fastened;
and he was obliged to wait some time before it was
opened by Esther.

The first object he beheld was his beloved Clara,
stretched on the ground, apparently a corpse! The
sorceress had thrown her into a trance by a prepa-
ration of deadly nightshade. The hag burst into
an infernal laugh, when she beheld the despair that
was painted in Cæsar's countenance. "Wretch!"
cried she, "you have defied my power: behold its
victim!"

Cæsar, in a transport of rage, seized her by the
throat: but his fury was soon checked.

"Destroy me," said the fiend, "and you destroy
your Clara. She is not dead; but she lies in the
sleep of death, into which she has been thrown by
magic art, and from which no power but mine can
restore her to the light of life. Yes! look at her,
pale and motionless! Never will she rise from the
earth, unless, within one hour, you obey my commands. I have administered to Hector and his
companions the solemn fetish oath, at the sound of

which every negro in Africa trembles ! You know my object ?"

" Fiend, I do !" replied Cæsar, eyeing her sternly ; " but while I have life it shall never be accomplished."

" Look yonder !" cried she, pointing to the moon : "in a few minutes that moon will set: at that hour Hector and his friends will appear. They come armed—armed with weapons which I shall steep in poison for their enemies. Themselves I will render invulnerable. Look again !" continued she : " if my dim eyes mistake not, yonder they come. Rash man, you die if they cross my threshold."

" I wish for death," said Caesar. " Clara is dead !"

" But you can restore her to life by a single word."

Cæsar, at this moment, seemed to hesitate.

"Consider ! Your heroism is vain," continued Esther. " You will have the knives of fifty of the conspirators in your bosom if you do not join them ; and, after you have fallen, the death of your master is inevitable. Here is the bowl of poison in which the negro knives are to be steeped. Your friends, your former friends, your countrymen, will be in arms in a few minutes: and they will bear down every thing before them—victory, wealth, freedom, and revenge will be theirs."

Cæsar appeared to be more and more agitated. His eyes were fixed upon Clara. The conflict in his mind was violent; but his sense of gratitude and duty could not be shaken by hope, fear, or am-bition; nor could it be vanquished by love. He determined, however, to appear to yield. As if struck with panic at the approach of the confede-rate negroes, he suddenly turned to the sorceress, and said, in a tone of feigned submission, " It is in vain to struggle with fate. Let my knife, too, be dipped in your magic poison."

The sorceress clapped her hands, with infernal joy in her countenance. She bade him instantly give her his knife, that she might plunge it to the hilt in the bowl of poison, to which she turned with savage impatience. His knife was left in his cot-tage; and, under pretence of going in search of it, he escaped. Esther promised to prepare Hector and all his companions to receive him with their ancient cordiality on his return. Cæsar ran with the utmost speed along a by-path out of the wood, met none of the rebels, reached his master's house, scaled the wall of his bedchamber, got in at the win-dow, and wakened him, exclaiming, " Arm—arm

THE GRATEFUL NEGRO

S.F.BAKER SC

yourself, my dear master! Arm all your slaves! They will fight for you, and die for you; as I will the first. The Koromantyn yell of war will be heard in Jefferies' plantation this night! Arm—arm yourself, my dear master, and let us surround the rebel leaders while it is yet time. I will lead you to the place where they are all assembled, on condition, that their chief, who is my friend, shall be pardoned."

Mr. Edwards armed himself and the negroes on his plantation, as well as the whites : they were all equally attached to him. He followed Cæsar into the recesses of the wood.

They proceeded with all possible rapidity, but in perfect silence, till they reached Esther's habitation; which they surrounded completely, before they were perceived by the conspirators.

Mr. Edwards looked through a hole in the wall; and by the blue flame of a caldron, over which the sorceress was stretching her shrivelled hands, he saw Hector and five stout negroes standing, intent upon her incantations. These negroes held their knives in their hands, ready to dip them into the bowl of poison. It was proposed by one of the whites to set fire immediately to the hut; and thus to force the rebels to surrender. The advice was followed; but Mr. Edwards charged his people to spare their prisoners. The moment the rebels saw that the thatch of the hut was in flames, they set up the Koromantyn yell of war, and rushed out with frantic desperation.

"Yield! you are pardoned Hector," cried Mr. Edwards, in a loud voice.

"You are pardoned, my friend!" repeated Cæsar.

Hector, incapable at this instant of listening to any thing but revenge, sprang forwards, and plunged his knife into the bosom of Cæsar. The faithful servant staggered back a few paces: his master caught him in his arms. "I die content," said he. "Bury me with Clara."

He swooned from loss of blood as they were carrying him home; but when his wound was examined, it was found not to be mortal. As he recovered from his swoon he stared wildly round him, trying to recollect where he was, and what had happened. He thought that he was still in a dream when he saw his beloved Clara standing beside him. The opia e which the pretended sorceress had administered to her had ceased to operate; she awaked from her trance just at the time the Koromantyn yell commenced. Cæsar's joy! We must leave that to the imagination.

In the mean time, what became of the rebel negroes and Mr. Edwards?

The taking the chief conspirators prisoners did not prevent the negroes upon Jefferies' plantation from insurrection. The moment they heard the warwhoop, the signal agreed upon, they rose in a body; and before they could be prevented, either by the whites on the estate, or by Mr. Edwards's adherents, they had set fire to the overseer's house and to the canes. The overseer was the principal object of their vengeance—he died in tortures, inflicted by the hands of those who had suffered most by his cruelties. Mr. Edwards, however, quelled the insurgents before rebellion spread to any other estates in the island. The influence of his character and the effect of his eloquence upon the minds of the people were astonishing; nothing but his interference could have prevented the total destruction of Mr. Jefferies and his family, who, as it was computed, lost this night upwards of fifty thousand pounds. He was never afterward able to recover his losses, or to shake off his constant fear of a fresh insurrection among his slaves. At length he and his lady returned to England, where they were obliged to live in obscurity and indigence. They

28

had no consolation in their misfortunes but that of railing at the treachery of the whole race of slaves. Our readers, we hope, will think that at least one exception may be made in favour of THE GRATE FUL NEGRO.

March, 1802.

TO-MORROW.

"Oh this detestable *to-morrow!*—a thing always expected, yet never found."—JOHNSON.

CHAPTER I.

IT has long been my intention to write my own
history, and I am determined to begin it to-day; for
half the good intentions of my life have been frustrated by my unfortunate habit of putting things
off till to-morrow.

When I was a young man, I used to be told
that this was my only fault: I believed it, and my
vanity or laziness persuaded me that this fault was
but small, and that I should easily cure myself of
it in time.

That time, however, has not yet arrived, and at
my advanced age I must give up all thoughts of
amendment, hoping, however, that sincere repent-
ance may stand instead of reformation.

My father was an eminent London bookseller; he happened to be looking over a new biographical dictionary on the day when I was brought into the world : and at the moment when my birth was announced to him he had his finger upon the name *Basil;* he read aloud—" *Basil,* canonized bishop of Cæsarea, a theological, controversial, and moral writer."

" My boy," continued my father, " shall be named after this great man, and I hope and believe that I shall live to see him either a celebrated theological, controversial, and moral author, or a bishop. I am not so sanguine as to expect that he should be both these good things."

I was christened Basil according to my father's wishes, and his hopes of my future celebrity and fortune were confirmed during my childhood, by instances of wit and memory which were not perhaps greater than what could have been found in my little contemporaries, but which appeared to the vanity of parental fondness extraordinary, if not supernatural. My father declared that it would be a sin not to give me a learned education, and he went even beyond his means to procure for me all the advantages of the best modes of instruction. I was stimulated, even when a boy, by the idea

that I should become a great man, and my masters
had for some time reason to be satisfied : but what
they called the *quickness of my parts* continually
retarded my progress.   The facility with which I
learned my lessons encouraged me to put off learning them till the last moment; and this habit of
procrastinating, which was begun in presumption,
ended in disgrace.

When I was sent to a public school, I found
among my companions so many temptations to
idleness, that notwithstanding the quickness of my
parts, I was generally flogged twice a week.   As
I grew older, my reason might perhaps have taught
me to correct myself, but my vanity was excited
to persist in idleness by certain imprudent sayings
or whisperings of my father.

When I came home from school at the holy-
days, and when complaints were preferred against
me in letters from my schoolmaster, my father,
even while he affected to scold me for my negligence, flattered me in the most dangerous manner by adding—*aside* to some friend of the
family—"My Basil is a strange fellow !—can do
any thing he pleases—all his masters say so—but
he is a sad idle dog—all your men of genius are
so—puts off business always to the last moment—

28 *

all your men of genius do so. For instance, there
is ——, whose third edition of odes I have just
published—what an idle dog he is! Yet who makes
such a noise in the world as he does?—puts every
thing off till *to-morrow*, like my Basil—but can do
more at the last moment than any man in England—that is, if the fit seizes him—for he does
nothing but by fits—has no application—none—
says it would ' petrify him to a dunce.' I never
knew a man of genius who was not an idle dog."

Not a syllable of such speeches was lost upon
me : the ideas of a man of genius and of an idle
dog were soon so firmly joined together in my imagination, that it was impossible to separate them,
either by my own reason or by that of my pre-
ceptors. I gloried in the very habits which my
tutors laboured to correct; and I never was seriously mortified by the consequences of my own
folly till, at a public examination at Eton I lost a
premium by putting off till it was too late the finishing a copy of verses. The lines which I had
written were said by all my young and old friends
to be beautiful. The prize was gained by one
Johnson, a heavy lad, of no sort of genius, but of
great perseverance. His verses were finished,
however, at the stated time;

"For dulness ever must be regular!"

My fragment, charming as it was, was useless, except to hand about afterward among my friends, to prove what I might have done if I had thought it worth while.

My father was extremely vexed by my missing an opportunity of distinguishing myself at this public exhibition, especially as the king had honoured the assembly with his presence; and as those who had gained premiums were presented to his majesty, it was supposed that their being thus early *marked* as lads of talents would be highly advantageous to their advancement in life. All this my father felt, and blaming himself for having encouraged me in *the indolence of genius*, he determined to counteract his former imprudence, and was resolved, he said, to cure me at once of my habit of procrastination. For this purpose he took down from his shelves Young's Night Thoughts; from which he remembered a line, which has become a *stock* line among writing-masters' copies:

"*Procrastination* is the thief of time."

He hunted the book for the words *Procrastination*, *Time*, *To-day*, and *To-morrow*, and made an extract of seven long pages on the dangers of delay.

"Now, my dear Basil," said he, "this is what
will cure you for life, and this you must get perfectly by heart, before I give you one shilling more
pocket-money."

The motive was all-powerful, and with pains,
iteration, and curses, I fixed the heterogenous quo-
tations so well in my memory that some of them
have remained there to this day. For instance—

                 " *Time* destroy'd
Is *suicide*, where more than blood is spilt.

Time flies, death urges, knells call, Heav'n invites,
Hell threatens.

We push *Time* from us, and we wish him back.

Man flies from *Time*, and Time from man too soon;
In sad divorce this double flight must end;
And then where are we?

Be wise *to-day*, 't is madness to defer, &c.
Next day the fatal precedent will plead, &c.

Lorenzo—O for *yesterdays* to come!
To-day is *yesterday* return'd; return'd,
Full power'd to cancel, expiate, raise, adorn,
And reinstate us on the rock of peace.
Let it not share its predecessor's fate,
Nor, like its elder sisters, die a fool.

Where shall I find him? Angels! tell me where:
You know him; he is near you; point him out;
Shall I see glories beaming from his brow?

Jr trace his footsteps by the rising flow'rs ?
Your golden wings *now* hov'ring o'er him shed
Protection : now are wav'ring in applause
To that blest son of foresight ! Lord of fate !
That awful independent on *to-morrow !*
Whose *work is done;* who triumphs in the past ;
Whose *yesterdays* look backward with a smile."

I spare you the rest of my task, and I earnestly
hope, my dear reader, that these citations may have
a better effect upon you than they had upon me.
With shame I confess that even with the addition
of Shakspeare's eloquent

   " To-morrow, and to-morrow, and to-morrow, &c."

which I learned by heart gratis, not a bit the better
was I for all this poetical morality. What I wanted
was, not conviction of my folly, but resolution to
amend.

When I say that I was not a bit the better for
these documentings, I must not omit to observe to
you that I was very near being four hundred pounds
a year the better for them.

Being obliged to learn so much of Young's Night
Thoughts by rote, I was rather disgusted, and my
attention was roused to criticise the lines which had
been forced upon my admiration. Afterward, when
I went to college, I delighted to maintain in oppo-

sition to some of my companions, whc were enthusiastic admirers of Young, that he was no poet.
The more I was ridiculed, the more I persisted. I
talked myself into notice; I became acquainted
with several of the literary men at Cambridge; I
wrote in defence of my opinion, or, as some called
it, my heresy. I maintained that what all the
world had mistaken for sublimity was bombast;
that the Night Thoughts were fuller of witty con-
ceits than of poetical images: I drew a parallel
between Young and Cowley; and I finished by pronouncing Young to be the Cowley of the eighteenth
century. To do myself justice, there was much
ingenuity and some truth in my essay; but it was
the declamation of a partisan who can think only
on one side of a question, and who, in the heat of
controversy, says more than he thinks, and more
than he originally intended.

It is often the fortune of literary partisans to obtain a share of temporary celebrity far beyond their
deserts, especially if they attack any writer of established reputation. The success of my essay exceeded my most sanguine expectations, and I began
to think that my father was right,—that I was born
to be a great genius, and a great man. The notice
taken of me by a learned prelate, who piqued him-

self upon being considered as the patron of young
men of talents, confirmed me at once in my self-
conceit and my hopes of preferment.

I mentioned to you that my father, in honour of
my namesake Basil, bishop of Cæsarea, and to verify his own *presentiments*, had educated me for
the church. My present patron, who seemed to like
me the better the oftener I dined with him, gave
me reason to hope that he would provide for me
handsomely. I was not yet ordained, when a
living of four hundred per annum fell into his gift:
he held it over for some months, as it was thought,
on purpose for me.

In the mean time he employed me to write a
charity sermon for him, which he was to preach,
as it was expected, to a crowded congregation.
None but those who are themselves slaves to the
habit of procrastination will believe that I could be
so foolish as to put off writing this sermon till the
Saturday evening before it was wanted. Some of
my young companions came unexpectedly to sup
with me; we sat late: in the vanity of a young
author, who glories in the rapidity of composition,
I said to myself that I could finish my sermon in
an hour's time. But, alas! when my companions
at length departed, they left me in no condition to

complete a sermon. I fell fast asleep, and was waked in the morning by the bishop's servant. The dismay I felt is indescribable; I started up—it was nine o'clock: I began to write; but my hand and my mind trembled, and my ideas were in such confusion that I could not, great genius as I was, produce a beginning sentence in a quarter of an hour.

I kept the bishop's servant forty minutes by his watch; wrote and rewrote two pages, and walked up and down the room; tore my two pages; and at last, when the footman said he could wait no longer, was obliged to let him go with an awkward note, pleading sudden sickness for my apology. It was true that I was sufficiently sick at the time when I penned this note; my head ached terribly; and I kept my room, reflecting upon my own folly, the whole of the day. I foresaw the consequences; the living was given away by my patron the next morning, and all hopes of future favour were absolutely at an end.

My father overwhelmed me with reproaches; and I might perhaps have been reformed by this disappointment; but an unexpected piece of good fortune, or what I then thought good fortune, was my ruin.

TO-MORROW.

Among the multitude of my college-friends was a young gentleman, whose father was just appointed to go out upon the *famous* embassy to China; he came to our shop to buy Du Halde; and upon hearing me express an enthusiastic desire to visit China, he undertook to apply to his father to take me in the ambassador's suite. His representation of me as a young man of talents and literature, and the view of some botanical drawings, which I executed upon the spur of the occasion with tolerable neatness, procured me the favour which I so ardently desired.

My father objected to my taking this voyage. He was vexed to see me quit the profession for which I had been educated; and he could not, without a severe struggle, relinquish his hopes of seeing me a bishop. But I argued that, as I had not yet been ordained, there could be no disgrace or impropriety in my avoiding a mode of life which was not suited to my *genius*. This word genius had now, as upon all other occasions, a mighty effect upon my father; and observing this, I declared further, in a high tone of voice, that from the experience I had already had, I was perfectly certain that the drudgery of sermon-writing would *paralyze my genius;* and that, to expand and invigorate my

29

intellectual powers, it was absolutely necessary that I should, to use a great author's expression, " view in foreign countries varied modes of existence."

My father's nopes that one-half of his prophecy would at last be accomplished, and that I should become a great author, revived ; and he consented to my going to China, upon condition that I should promise to write a history of my voyage and journey, in two volumes octavo, or one quarto, with a folio of plates. This promise was readily made ; for in the plentitude of confidence in my own powers, octavos and quartos shrank before me, and a folio appeared too small for the various information, and the useful reflections, which a voyage to China must supply.

Full of expectations and projects, I talked from morning till night of my journey : but notwith-standing my father's hourly remonstrances, I deferred my preparations till the last week. Then all was hurry and confusion ; tailors and seam-stresses, portmanteaus and trunks, portfolios and drawing-books, water-colours, crayones, and note-books wet from the stationer's, crowded my room. I had a dozen small note-books, and a huge com-monplace-book, which was to be divided and kept in the manner recommended by the judicious and immortal Locke.

In the midst of the last day's bustle, I sat down at the corner of a table with compass, ruler, and red ink, to divide and rule my best of all possible commonplace-books ; but the red ink was too thin, and the paper was not well sized, and it blotted continually, because I was obliged to turn over the pages rapidly : and ink will not dry, nor blotting-paper suck it up, more quickly for *a genius* than for any other man. Besides, my attention was much distracted by the fear that the seamstress would not send home my dozen of new shirts, and that a vile *procrastinating* boot-maker would never come with my boots. Every rap at the door I started up to inquire whether *that* was the shirts, or the boots ; thrice I overturned the red and twice the black ink bottles by these starts ; and the execrations which I bestowed upon those tradespeople who will put off every thing to the last moment were innumerable. I had orders to set off in the mail-coach for Portsmouth, to join the rest of the ambassador's suite.

The provoking watchman cried "Past eleven o'clock" before I had half-finished ruling my commonplace-book ; my shirts and my boots were not come; the mail-coach, as you may guess, set off without me. My poor father was in a terrible tremor, and walked from room to room, reproaching me and himself; but I persisted in repeating that Lord M. would not set out the day he had intended; that nobody since the creation of the world, ever set out upon a long journey the day he first appointed: besides, there were at least a hundred chances in my favour that his lordship would break down on his way to Portsmouth; that the wind would not be fair when he arrived there; that half the people in his suite would not be more punctual than myself, &c.

By these arguments, or by mere dint of assertion, I quieted my father's apprehensions and my own, and we agreed that, as it was now impossible to go to-day, it was best to stay till to-morrow.

Upon my arrival at Portsmouth, the first thing I heard was that the Lion and Hindostan had sailed, some hours before, with the embassy for China. Despair deprived me of utterance. A charitable waiter at the inn, however, seeing my consternation and absolute inability to think or act for myself, ran to make further inquiries, and brought me back the joyful tidings that the Jackal brig, which was to carry out the remainder of the ambassador's suite, was not yet under way; that a gentleman, who was to go in the Jackal, had dined at an hotel in the next street, and that he had gone to the water-side but ten minutes ago.

I hurried after him: the boat was gone. I paid another exorbitantly to take me and my goods to the brig, and reached the Jackal just as she was weighing anchor. Bad education for me! The moment I felt myself safe on board, having recovered breath to speak, I exclaimed, " Here am I, safe and sound! just as well as if I had been here yesterday; better indeed. Oh, after this, I shall always trust to my own good fortune. I knew I should not be too late."

When I came to reflect coolly, however, I was rather sorry that I had missed my passage in the Lion, with my friend and protector, and with most of the learned and ingenious men of the ambassador's suite, to whom I had been introduced, and who had seemed favourably disposed towards me. All the advantage I might have derived from their conversation, during this long voyage, was lost by my own negligence. The Jackal lost company of the Lion and Hindostan in the Channel. As my friends afterward told me, they waited for us five days in Praya Bay: but as no Jackal appeared,

29 *

they sailed again without her. At length, to our great joy, we descried on the beach of Sumatra a board nailed to a post, which our friends had set up there, with a written notice to inform us that the Lion and Hindostan had touched on this shore on such a day, and to point out to us the course that we should keep in order to join them.

At the sight of this writing my spirits revived: the wind favoured us; but, alas! in passing the Straits of Banka, we were damaged so that we were obliged to return to port to refit, and take in fresh provision. Not a soul on board but wished it had been their fate to have had a berth in the other ships; and I more loudly than any one else expressed this wish twenty times a day. When my companions heard that I was to have sailed in the ambassador's ship, if I had been time enough at Spithead, some pitied and some rallied me: but most said I deserved to be punished for my negligence. At length we joined the Lion and Hindostan at North Island. Our friends had quite given up all hopes of ever seeing us again, and had actually bought at Batavia a French brig, to supply the place of the Jackal. To my great satisfaction, I was now received on board the Lion, and had an opportunity of conversing with the men of literature and science, from whom I had been so unluckily **separated** during the former part of the voyage. **Their conversation** soon revived and increased my **regret, when** they told me of all that I had missed seeing at the various places where they **had touched ;** they talked to me with provoking **fluency of** the culture of manioc, of the root of cassada, of which tapioca is made; of **the shrub** called the cactus, on which the cochineal insect swarms and feeds; and of the ipecacuanha-plant; **all which** they had seen at Rio Janeiro, besides eight paintings representing the manner in which he diamond and gold mines in the Brazils are worked. Indeed, upon cross-examination, I found that these pictures were miserably executed, and scarcely worth seeing.

I regretted more the fine pineapples, which my companions assured me were in such abundance that they cleaned their swords in them, as being the cheapest acid that could be there procured. But, far beyond these vulgar objects of curiosity, I regretted not having learned any thing concerning the celebrated upas-tree. I was persuaded that, if I had been at Batavia, I should have extracted some information more precise than these gentlemen obtained from the keepers of the medical garden.

I confess that my mortification at this disappointment did not arise solely from the pure love of natural history : the upas-tree would have made a conspicuous figure in my quarto volume. I consoled myself, however, by the determination to omit nothing that the vast empire of China could afford to render my work entertaining, instructive, interesting, and sublime. I anticipated the pride with which I should receive the compliments of my friends and the public upon my *valuable and incomparable work;* I anticipated the pleasure with which my father would exult in the celebrity of his son, and in the accomplishment of his own prophecies ; and, with these thoughts full in my mind, we landed at Mettow, in China.

I sat up late at night writing a sketch of my preface and notes for the heads of chapters. I was tired, fell into a profound sleep, dreamed I **was** teaching the emperor of China to pronounce "chrononhotonthologos," and in the morning was waked by the sound of the gong,—the signal that the accommodation junks were ready to sail with the embassy to Pekin. I hurried on my clothes, and **was** in the junk before the gong had done beating.

I gloried in my celerity; but before we had gone two leagues up the country, I found reason to re-pent of my precipitation: I wanted to note down my first impressions on entering the Chinese ter-ritories; but, alas! I felt in vain in my pocket for my pencil and note-book: I had left them both be-hind me on my bed. Not only one note-book, but my whole dozen; which, on leaving London, I had stuffed into a bag with my night-gown. Bag, night-gown, note-books, all were forgotten!

However trifling it may appear, this loss of the little note-books was of material consequence. To be sure, it was easy to procure paper and make others; but, because it was so easy, it was delayed from hour to hour, and from day to day; and I went on writing my most important remarks on scraps of paper, which were always to be copied to-morrow into a note-book that was then to be made.

We arrived at Pekin, and were magnificently lodged in a palace in that city; but here we were so strictly guarded that we could not stir beyond the courts of the palace. You will say that in this confinement I had leisure sufficient to make a note-book, and to copy my notes: so I had, and it was my firm intention so to have done; but I put it off because I thought it would take up but a few hours' time, and it could be done any day. Besides, the weather was so excessively hot, that for the first week I could do nothing but unbutton my waist-coat and drink sherbet. Visits of ceremony from mandarins took up much of our time: they spoke and moved like machines; and it was with much difficulty that our interpreter made us understand the meaning of their formal sentences, which were seldom worth the trouble of deciphering. We saw them fan themselves, drink tea, eat sweetmeats and rice, and chew betel; but it was scarcely worth while to come all the way from Europe to see this, especially as any common Chinese paper or screen would give an adequate idea of these figures in their accustomed attitudes.

I spent another week in railing at these abomi-nably stupid or unnecessarily cautious creatures of ceremony, and made memorandums for an eloquent chapter in my work.

One morning we were agreeably surprised by a visit from a mandarin of a very different descrip-tion. We were astonished to hear a person in the habit of a Chinese, and bearing the title of a man-darin, address us in French: he informed us that he was originally a French jesuit, and came over to China with several missionaries from Paris; but as they were prohibited from promulgating their doctrines in this country, most of them had returned to France; a few remained, assumed the dress and manners of the country, and had been elevated to the rank of mandarins as a reward for their learn-ing. The conversation of our Chinese jesuit was extremely entertaining and instructive; he was de-lighted to hear news from Europe, and we were eager to obtain from him information respecting China. I paid particular attention to him, and I was so fortunate as to win his confidence, as far as the confidence of a jesuit can be won. He came fre-quently to visit me, and did me the honour to spend some hours in my apartment.

As he made it understood that these were literary visits, and as his character for propriety was well established with the government, he excited no suspicion, and we spent our time most delightfully between books and conversation. He gave me, by his anecdotes and descriptions, an insight into the characters and domestic lives of the inhabitants of Pekin, which I could not otherwise have obtained; his talent for description was admirable, and his characters were so new to me that I was in con-tinual ecstasy. I called him the Chinese La

Bruyere ; and, anticipating the figure which his portraits woud make in my future work, thought that
I could never sufficiently applaud his eloquence. He
was glad to lay aside the solemn gravity of a
Chinese mandarin, and to indulge the vivacity of a
Frenchman ; his vanity was gratified by my praises,
and he exerted himself to the utmost to enhance
my opinion of his talents.

At length we had notice that it was the emperor's pleasure to receive the embassy at his imperial residence in Tartary, at Jehol ; *the seat of
grateful coolness, the garden of innumerable trees.*
From the very name of this place I argued that it
would prove favourable to the inspirations of genius,
and determined to date at least one of the chapters
or letters of my future work from this delightful
retreat, the *Sans Souci* of China. Full of this intention, I set out upon our expedition into Tartary.

My good friend the jesuit, who had a petition to
present to the emperor relative to some Chinese
manuscripts, determined, to my infinite satisfaction,
to accompany us to Jehol ; and our conducting
mandarin, Van Tadge, arranged things so upon
our journey that I enjoyed as much of my friend's
conversation as possible. Never European travelling in these countries had such advantages as mine;

I had a companion who was able and willing to in-struct me in every minute particular of the man-ners, and every general principle of the government and policy of the people. I was in no danger of falling into the ridiculous mistakes of travellers, who, having but a partial view of things and per-sons, argue absurdly, and grossly misrepresent, while they intend to be accurate. Many people, as my French mandarin observed, reason like Vol-taire's famous traveller, who, happening to have a drunken landlord and a red-haired landlady at the first inn where he stopped in Alsace, wrote down among his memorandums, " All the men of Alsace drunkards: all the women red-haired."

When we arrived at Jehol, the hurry of prepa-ring for our presentation to the emperor, the want of a convenient writing-table, and perhaps my habit of procrastination, prevented my writing the chapter for my future work, or noting down any of the remarks which the jesuit had made upon our journey. One morning, when I collected my papers and scraps of memorandums with which the pockets of all my clothes were stuffed, I was quite terrified at the heap of confusion, and thrust all these materials for my quarto into a canvass bag, purposing to lay them smooth in a portfolio

30

the next day.   But the next day I could do nothing
of this sort, for we had the British presents to unpack, which had arrived from Pekin ; the day after
was taken up with our presentation to the emperor ;
and the day after that I had a new scheme in my
head.   The emperor, with much solemnity, presented with his own hand, to our ambassador, a
casket, which he said was the most valuable present
he could make to the King of England; it contained the miniature pictures of the emperor's an-
cestors, with a few lines of poetry annexed to each,
describing the character, and recording the principal events of each monarch's reign.   It occurred
to me that a set of similar portraits and poetical
histories of the kings of England would be a proper and agreeable offering to the Emperor of China ;
I consulted my friend the French mandarin, and
he encouraged me by assurances that, as far as he
could pretend to judge, it would be a present peculiarly suited to the emperor's taste ; and that in
all probability I should be distinguished by some
mark of his approbation, or some munificent reward.   My friend promised to have the miniatures
varnished for me in the Chinese taste ; and he undertook to present the work to the emperor when
it should be finished.   As it was supposed that the

embassy would spend the whole winter in Pekin, I
thought that I should have time enough to complete the whole series of British sovereigns. It
was not necessary to be very scrupulous as to the
resemblance of my portraits, as the Emperor of
China could not easily detect any errors of this
nature: fortunately, I had brought from London
with me striking likenesses of all the kings of
England, with the principal events of their reign,
in one large sheet of paper, which belonged to a
joining-map of one of my little cousins. In the
confusion of my packing up I had put it into my
trunk instead of a sheet almanac, which lay on the
same table. In the course of my life many lucky
accidents have happened to me even in consequence
of my own carelessness; yet that carelessness has
afterward prevented my reaping any permanent
advantage from my good fortune.

Upon this occasion I was, however, determined
that no laziness of mine should deprive me of an
opportunity of making my fortune: I set to work
immediately, and astonished my friend by the facility with which I made verses. It was my custom to retire from the noisy apartments of our
palace to a sort of alcove, at the end of a long
gallery in one of the outer courts, where our corps

of artillery used to parade. After their parade
was over, the place was perfectly quiet and solitary
for the remainder of the day and night. I used to
sit up late, writing; and one fine moonlight night
I went out of my alcove to walk in the gallery,
while I composed some lines to our great Queen
Elizabeth. I could not finish the last couplet to
my fancy: I sat down upon an artificial rock
which was in the middle of the court, leaned my
head upon my hand, and, as I was searching for
an appropriate rhyme to *glory*, fell fast asleep. A
noise like that of a most violent clap of thunder
awakened me; I was thrown with my face flat
upon the ground.

When I recovered my senses the court was
filled with persons, some Europeans, some Chinese,
seemingly just risen from their beds, with lanterns
and torches in their hands; all of them, with
faces of consternation, asking one another what
had happened? The ground was covered with
scattered fragments of wooden pillars, mats, and
bamboo cane-work; I looked and saw that one end
of the gallery in which I had been walking and
the alcove were in ruins. There was a strong
smell of gunpowder. I now recollected that I had
borrowed a powder-horn from one of the soldiers

in the morning; and that I had intended to load my pistols, but I delayed doing so. The horn, full of gunpowder, lay upon the table in the alcove all day, and the pistols, out of which I had shaken the old priming. When I went out to walk in the gallery I left the candle burning; and I suppose during my sleep a spark fell upon the loose gunpowder, set fire to that in the horn, and blew up the alcove. It was built of light wood and cane, and communicated only with a cane-work gallery, otherwise the mischief would have been more serious. As it was, the explosion had alarmed, not only all the ambassador's suit who lodged in the palace, but many of the Chinese in the neighbourhood, who could not be made to comprehend how the accident had happened.

Reproaches from all our own people were poured upon me without mercy; and in the midst of my contrition I had not for some time leisure to lament the loss of all my kings of England: no vestige of them remained; and all the labour that I had bestowed upon their portraits and their poetical histories was lost to the Emperor of China and to myself. What was still worse, I could not even utter a syllable of complaint, for nobody would sympathize with me, all my companions were so much

30 *

provoked by my negligence, and so apprehensive of the bad consequences which might ensue from this accident. The Chinese, who had been alarmed, and who departed evidently dissatisfied, would certainly mention what had happened to the mandarins of the city; and they would report it to the emperor.

I resolved to apply for advice to my friend the jesuit; but he increased instead of diminishing our apprehensions: he said that the affair was much talked of and misrepresented at Jehol; and that the Chinese, naturally timid, and suspicious of strangers, could not believe that no injury was intended to them, and that the explosion was accidental. A child had been wounded by the fall of some of the ruins of the alcove, which were thrown with great violence into a neighbouring house: the butt-end of one of my pistols was found in the street, and had been carried to the magistrate by the enraged populace, as evidence of our evil designs. My jesuit observed to me that there was no possibility of reasoning with the prejudices of any nation; and he confessed he expected that this unlucky accident would have the most serious consequences. He had told me in confidence a circumstance that tended much to confirm this opinion :

a few days before, when the emperor went to examine the British presents of artillery, and when
the brass mortars were tried, though he admired
the ingenuity of these instruments of destruction,
yet he said that he deprecated the spirit of the
people who employed them; and could not re-
concile their improvements in the arts of war with
the mild precepts of the religion which they professed.

My friend the mandarin promised he would do
all in his power to make the exact truth known to
the emperor; and to prevent the evil impressions
which the prejudices of the populace, and perhaps
the designing misrepresentations of the city mandarins, might tend to create. I must suppose that
the good offices of my jesuit were ineffectual, and
that he either received a positive order to interfere
no more in our affairs, or that he was afraid of
being implicated in our disgrace if he continued his
intimacy with me, for this was the last visit I ever
received from him.

CHAPTER II.

In a few days the embassy had orders to return to Pekin. The ambassador's palace was fitted up for his winter's residence; and after our arrival he was arranging his establishment, when, by a fresh mandate from the emperor, we were required to prepare with all possible expedition for our departure from the Chinese dominions. On Monday we received an order to leave Pekin the ensuing Wednesday; and all our remonstrances could procure only a delay of two days. Various causes were assigned for this peremptory order, and among the rest my unlucky accident was mentioned. However improbable it might seem that such a trifle could have had so great an effect, the idea was credited by many of my companions; and I saw that I was looked upon with an evil eye.

I suffered extremely. I have often observed, that even remorse for my past negligence has tended to increase the original defect of my character. During our whole journey from Pekin to Cantòn, my sorrow for the late accident was an excuse to myself for neglecting to make either notes or observations. When we arrived at Canton my time was taken up with certain commissions for my friends at home, which I had delayed to execute while at Pekin, from the idea that we should spend the whole winter there. The trunks were on board before all my commissions were ready, and I was obliged to pack up several toys and other articles in a basket. As to my papers, they still remained in the canvass bag into which I had stuffed them at Jehol: but I was certain of having leisure during our voyage home to arrange them, and to post my notes into Locke's commonplace-book.

At the beginning of the voyage, however, I suffered much from sea-sickness : towards the middle of the time I grew better, and indulged myself in the amusement of fishing, while the weather was fine : when the weather was not inviting, in idleness. Innumerable other petty causes of delay occurred: there was so much eating and drinking, so much singing and laughing, and such frequent card-playing in the cabin, that though I produced my canvass bag above a hundred times, I never could accomplish sorting its contents : indeed, I seldom proceeded further than to untie the strings.

One day I had the state cabin fairly to myself, and

had really begun my work, when the steward came
to let me know that my Chinese basket was just
washed overboard. In this basket were all the
presents and commissions which I had bought at
Canton for my friends at home. I ran to the cabin
window, and had the mortification to see all my
beautiful scarlet calabash boxes, the fan for my
cousin Lucy, and the variety of toys which I had
bought for my little cousins, all floating on the sea
far out of my reach. I had been warned before
that the basket would be washed overboard, and
had intended to put it into a safe place; but unluckily I delayed to do so.

I was so much vexed with this accident that I
could not go on with my writing: if it had not been
for this interruption, I do believe I should that day
have accomplished my long-postponed task. I
will not, indeed I cannot, record all the minute
causes which afterward prevented my executing
my intentions. The papers were still in the same
disorder, stuffed into the canvass bag, when I arrived in England. I promised myself that I
would sort them the very day after I got home:
but visits of congratulation from my friends upon
my return induced me to delay doing any thing for
the first week. The succeeding week I had a mul-

tiplicity of engagements : all my acquaintance,
curious to hear a man converse who was fresh from
China, invited me to dinner and tea parties ; and I
could not possibly refuse these kind invitations,
and shut myself up in my room, like a hackney
author, to write.   My father often urged me to
begin my quarto ; for he knew that other gentlemen
who went out with the embassy designed to write
the history of the voyage ; and he, being a bookseller, and used to the ways of authors, foresaw
what would happen.   A fortnight after we came
home the following advertisement appeared in the
papers :—" Now in the press, and speedily will be
published, a Narrative of the British Embassy to
China, containing the various Circumstances of the
Embassy ; with Accounts of the Customs and Manners of the Chinese ; and a Description of the
Country, Towns, Cities, &c."

I never saw my poor father turn so pale or look
so angry as when he saw this advertisement : he
handed it across the breakfast-table to me.

" There, Basil," cried he, " I told you what
would happen, and you would not believe me.   But
this is the way you have served me all your life,
and this is the way you will go on to the day of
your death, putting things off till to-morrow.   This

is the way you have lost every opportunity of distinguishing yourself; every chance, and you have
had many, of advancing yourself in the world!
What signifies all I have done for you, or all you
can do for yourself? Your genius and education
are of no manner of use. Why, there is that heavy
dog, as you used to call him at Eton, Johnson;
look how he is getting on in the world, by mere
dint of application and sticking steadily to his profession. He will beat you at every thing, as he
beat you at Eton in writing verses."

"Only in copying them, sir. My verses, everybody said, were far better than his; only, unluckily, I had not mine finished and copied out in
time."

"Well, sir, and that is the very thing I complain
of. I suppose you will tell me that your Voyage
to China will be far better than this which is advertised this morning."

"To be sure it will, father; for I have had opportunities, and collected materials, which this man,
whoever he is, cannot possibly have obtained. I
have had such assistance, such information from
my friend the missionary—"

"But what signifies your missionary, your information, your abilities, and your materials?" cried

my father, raising his voice. " Your book is not out, your book will never be finished ; or it will be done too late, and nobody will read t; and then you may throw it into the fire. Here you have an opportunity of establishing your fame, and making yourself a great author at once ; and if you throw it away, Basil, I give you fair notice, I never will pardon you."

I promised my father that I would set about my work *to-morrow ;* and pacified him by repeating that this hasty publication, which had just been advertised, must be a catchpenny, and that it would serve only to stimulate instead of satisfying the public curiosity. My quarto, I said, would appear afterward with a much better grace, and would be sought for by every person of science, taste, and literature.

Soothed by these assurances, my father recovered his good-humour, and trusted to my promise that I would commence my great work the ensuing day. I was fully in earnest. I went to my canvass bag to prepare my materials. Alas, I found them in a terrible condition ! The seawater somehow or other, had got to them during the voyage ; and many of my most precious documents were absolutely illegible. The notes, written in pencil,

31

were almost effaced, and, when I had smoothed the crumpled scraps, I could make nothing of them. It was with the utmost difficulty I could read even those that were written in ink; they were so villanously scrawled and so terribly blotted. When I had made out the words, I was often at a loss for the sense; because I had trusted so much to the excellence of my memory, that my notes were never sufficiently full or accurate. Ideas which I had thought could never be effaced from my mind were now totally forgotten, and I could not comprehend my own mysterious elliptical hints and memorandums. I remember spending two hours in trying to make out what the following words could mean: *Hoy—alla—hoya;—hoya, hoya,—hoy—waudihoya.*

At last, I recollected that they were merely the sounds of the words used by the Chinese sailors in towing the junks, and I was much provoked at having wasted my time in trying to remember what was not worth recording. Another day I was puzzled by the following memorandum: " W : C : 30. f. h.—24 b.—120 m—l—mandarin—C. tradition—2000—200 before J. C."—which, after three-quarters of an hour's study, I discovered to mean that the wall of China is 30 feet high, 24 feet broad, and 120 miles long ; and that a mandarin told me, that, according to Chinese tradition, this wall had been built above 2000 years, that is, 200 before the birth of our Saviour.

On another scrap of paper, at the very bottom of the bag, I found the words, " Wheazou—Chan-chin--Cuaboocow--Caungchumfoa–Callachottueng Quanshanglin— Callachotre shansu," &c. ; all which I found to be a list of towns and villages through which we had passed, or places that we had seen ; but how to distinguish these asunder I knew not, for all recollection of them was obliterated from my mind, and no further notes respecting them were to be found.

After many days tiresome attempts, I was obliged to give up all hopes of deciphering the most impor-tant of my notes,—those which I had made from the information of the French missionary. Most of what I had trusted so securely to my memory was defective in some slight circumstances, which rendered the whole useless. My materials for my quarto shrank into a very small compass. I flat-tered myself, however, that the elegance of my composition, and the moral and political reflections with which I intended to intersperse the work, would compensate for the paucity of facts in my narrative.

That I might devote my whole attention to the business of writing, I determined to leave London, where I met with so many temptations to idleness, and set off to pay a visit to my uncle Lowe, who lived in the country, in a retired part of England. He was a farmer, a plain, sensible, affectionate man; and as he had often invited me to come and see him, I made no doubt that I should be an agreeable guest. I had intended to write a few lines the week before I set out, to say that I was coming; but I put it off till at last I thought that it would be useless, because I should get there as soon as my letter.

I had soon reason to regret that I had been so negligent: for my appearance at my uncle's, instead of creating that general joy which I had expected, threw the whole house into confusion. It happened that there was company in the house, and all the beds were occupied: while I was taking off my boots, I had the mortification to hear my aunt Lowe say, in a voice of mingled distress and reproach. "Come! is he?—My goodness! What shall we do for a bed?—How could he think of coming without writing a line beforehand? My goodness! I wish he was a hundred miles off, I'm sure."

My uncle shook hands with me, and welcomed

me to old England again, and to his house; which, he said, should always be open to all his relations. ʹ I saw that he was not pleased: and, as he was a man who, according to the English phrase, scorned *to keep a thing long upon his mind*, he let me know, before he had finished his first glass of ale to my good health, that he was *inclinable to take it very unkind indeed* that, after all he had said about my writing a letter now and then, just to say how I did, and how I was going on, I had never put pen to paper to answer one of his letters since the day I first promised to write, which was the day I went to Eton school, till this present time of speaking. I had no good apology to make for myself, but I attempted all manner of excuses; that I had put off writing from day to day, and from year to year, till I was ashamed to write at all; that it was not from want of affection, &c.

My uncle took up his pipe and puffed away while I spoke: and when I had said all that I could devise, I sat silent; for I saw by the looks of all present that I had not mended the matter. My aunt pursed up her mouth, and " wondered, if she must tell the plain truth, that so great a scholar as Mr. Basil could not, when it must give him so little trouble to indite a letter, write a few lines to an

31 *

uncle who had· begged it so often, and who had ever been a good friend."

"Say nothing of that," said my uncle; "I scorn to have that put into account. I loved the boy, and all I could do was done of course; that's no-thing to the purpose; but the longest day I have to live I'll never trouble him with begging a letter from him no more. For now I see he does not care a fig for me; and of course I do not care a fig for he. Lucy, hold up your head, girl; and don't look as if you were going to be hanged."

My cousin Lucy was the only person present who seemed to have any compassion for me; and, as I lifted up my eyes to look at her when her father spoke, she appeared to me quite beautiful. I had always thought her a pretty girl, but she never struck me as any thing very extraordinary till this moment. I was very sorry that I had offended my uncle: I saw he was seriously dis-pleased, and that his pride, of which he had a large portion, had conquered his affection for me.

"'Tis easier to lose a friend than gain one, young man," said he; "and take my word for it, as this world goes, 'tis a foolish thing to lose a friend for want of writing a letter or so. Here's seven years I have been begging a letter now and

then, and could not get one. Never wrote a line
to me before you went to China, should not have
known a word about it but for my wife who met
you by mere chance in London, and gave you
some little commissions for the children, which it
seems you forgot till it was too late. Then, after
you came back, never wrote to me."

"And even not to write a line to give one notice
of his coming here to-night," added my aunt.

"Oh, as to that," replied my uncle, "he can
never find our larder at a nonplus: we have no
dishes for him dressed Chinese fashion; but as to
roast-beef of old England, which, I take it, is
worth all the foreign meats in the world, he is welcome to it, and to as much of it as he pleases. I
shall always be glad to see him as a relation, and
so forth, as a good Christian ought, but not as the
favourite he used to be—that is out of the question;
for things cannot be done and undone, and time
that's past cannot come back again, that is clear;
and cold water thrown on a warm heart puts it
out; and there's an end of the matter. Lucy,
bring me my nightcap.".

Lucy, I think, sighed once; and I am sure I
sighed above a dozen times; but my uncle put on
his red nightcap, and heeded us not. I was in

hopes that the next morning he would have been better disposed towards me after having slept off his anger. The moment that I appeared in the morning, the children, who had been in bed when I arrived the preceding night, crowded round me, and one cried, "Cousin Basil, have you brought me the tumbler you promised me from China?"

"Cousin Basil, where's my boat?"

"O Basil, did you bring me the calabash box that you promised me?"

"And pray," cried my aunt, "did you bring my Lucy the fan that she commissioned you to get?"

"No, I'll warrant," said my uncle. "He that cannot bring himself to write a letter in the course of seven years to his friends will not be apt to trouble his head about their foolish commissions when he is in foreign parts."

Though I was abashed and vexed, I summoned sufficient courage to reply that I had not neglected to execute the commissions of any of my friends; but that by an unlucky accident, the basket into which I had packed all their things was washed overboard.

"Hum!" said my uncle.

"And pray," said my aunt, "why were they all packed in a basket? Why were not they put

into your trunks, where they might have been
safe ?"

I was obliged to confess that I had delayed to
purchase them till after we left Pekin; and that the
trunks were put on board before they were all procured at Canton.   My vile habit of procrastination!
How did I suffer for it at this moment!   Lucy
began to make excuses for me, which made me
blame myself the more: she said that, as to her
fan, it would have been of little or no use to her;
that she was sure she would have broken it before
it had been a week in her possession; and that,
therefore, she was glad that she had it not.   The
children were clamorous in their grief for the loss
of the boat, the tumbler, and the calabash boxes;
but Lucy contrived to quiet them, and to make my
peace with all the younger part of the family.   To
reinstate me in my uncle's good graces was impossible; he would only repeat to her, " The
young man has lost my good opinion; he will
never do any good.   From a child upward he has
always put off doing every thing he ought to do.
He will never do any good; he will never be any
thing."

My aunt was not my friend, because she suspected that Lucy liked me; and she thought her

daughter might do much better than marry a man who had quitted the profession to which he was bred, and was, as it seemed, little likely to settle to any other. My pretensions to genius and my literary qualifications were of no advantage to me, either with my uncle or my aunt; the one being *only* a good farmer, and the other *only* a good housewife. They contented themselves with asking me, coolly, what I had ever made by being an author? And when I was forced to answer *nothing*, they smiled upon me in scorn. My pride was roused, and I boasted that I expected to receive at least 600*l.* for my Voyage to China, which I hoped to complete in a few weeks. My aunt looked at me with astonishment; and, to prove to her that I was not passing the bounds of truth, I added that one of my travelling companions had, as I was credibly informed, received a thousand pounds for his narrative, to which mine would certainly be far superior.

"When it is done, and when you have the money in your hand to show us, I shall believe you," said my aunt; "and then, and not till then, you may begin to think of my Lucy."

"He shall never have her," said my uncle;

'he will never come to good. He shall never
nave her."

The time which I ought to have spent in composing my quarto I now wasted in fruitless endeavours to recover the good graces of my uncle.
Love, assisted as usual by the spirit of opposition,
took possession of my heart ; and how can a man
in love write quartos ? I became more indolent
than ever, for I persuaded myself that no exertions
could overcome my uncle's prejudice against me ;
and, without his approbation, I despaired of ever
obtaining Lucy's hand.

During my stay at my uncle's, I received several
letters from my father, inquiring how my work
went on, and urging me to proceed as rapidly as
possible, lest another Voyage to China, which it
was reported was now composing by a gentleman
of high reputation, should come out, and preclude
mine for ever. I cannot account for my folly :
the power of habit is imperceptible to those who
submit passively to its tyranny. From day to day
I continued procrastinating and sighing, till at last
the fatal news came that Sir George Staunton's
History of the Embassy to China, in two volumes
quarto, was actually published.

There was an end to all my hopes. I left my

uncle's house in despair: I dreaded to see my
father.   He overwhelmed me with well-merited reproaches.   All his expectations of my success in
life were disappointed ; he was now convinced that
I should never make my talents useful to myself
or to my family.   A settled melancholy appeared
in his countenance : he soon ceased to urge me to
any exertion, I idled away my time, deploring that
I could not marry my Lucy, and resolving upon a
thousand schemes for advancing myself, but always
delaying their execution till to-morrow.

CHAPTER III.

Two years passed away in this manner; about
the end of which time my poor father died.   I cannot describe the mixed sensations of grief and self-
reproach which I felt at his death.   I knew that I
had never fulfilled his sanguine prophecies, and that
disappointment had long preyed upon his spirits.
This was a severe shock to me : I was roused from
a state of stupefaction by the necessity of acting as
my father's executor.

Among his bequests was one which touched me particularly, because I was sensible that it was made from kindness to me. " I give and bequeath the full-length picture of my son Basil, taken when a boy (a very promising boy) at Eton school, to my brother Lowe. I should say to my sweet niece Lucy Lowe, but am afraid of giving offence."

I sent the picture to my uncle Lowe, with a copy of the words of the will, and a letter written in the bitterness of grief. My uncle, who was of an affectionate though positive temper, returned me the following answer:

" **DEAR NEPHEW BASIL,**

" Taking it for granted you feel as much as I do, it being natural you should, and even more, I shall not refuse to let my Lucy have the picture bequeathed to me by my good brother, who could not offend me dying, never having done so living. As to you, Basil, this is no time for reproaches, which would be cruel ; but, without meaning to look back to the past, I must add that I mean nothing by giving the picture to Lucy but respect for my poor brother's memory. My opinions remaining as heretofore, I think it a duty to my girl to be steady in my determination; convinced that no

32

man (not meaning you in particular) of what I call
a *putting-off* temper could make her happy, she
being too mild to scold and bustle, and do the man's
business in a family. This is the whole of my
mind, without malice ; for how could I, if I were
malicious, which I am not, bear malice, and at such
a time as this, against my own nephew? and as to
anger, that is soon over with me; and though I
said I never would forgive you, Basil, for not
writing to me for seven years, I do now forgive you
with all my heart. So let that be off your conscience. And now I hope we shall be very good
friends all the rest of our lives ; that is to say, putting Lucy out of the question ; for, in my opinion,
it is a disagreeable thing to have any bickerings
between near relations. So, my dear nephew,
wishing you all health and happiness, I hope you
will now settle to business. My wife tells me she
hears you are left in a good way by my poor
brother's care and industry ; and she sends her
love to you, is which all the family unite, and
hoping you will write from time to time, I remain,

    " My dear nephew Basil,

     " Your affectionate uncle,

      " THOMAS LOWE."

My aunt Lowe added a postscript, inquiring more particularly into the state of my affairs. I answered, by return of post, that my good father had left me much richer than I either expected or deserved: his credit in the booksellers' line was extensive and well established; his shop was well furnished, and he had a considerable sum of money in bank; besides many *good* debts due from authors, to whom he had advanced cash.

My aunt Lowe was governed by her interest as decidedly as my uncle was swayed by his humour and affection; and, of course, became more favourable towards me when she found that my fortune was better than she had expected. She wrote to exhort me to attend to my business, and to prove to my uncle that I could cure myself of my negligent habits. She promised to befriend me, and to do every thing to obtain my uncle's consent to my union with Lucy, upon condition that I would for six months steadily persevere, or, as she expressed herself, *show that I could come to good.*

The motive was powerful, sufficiently powerful to conquer the force of inveterate habit. I applied resolutely to business, and supported the credit which my father's punctuality had obtained from his customers. During the course of six entire months, I am not conscious of having neglected or delayed to do any thing of consequence that I ought to have done, except whetting my razor. My aunt **Lowe** faithfully kept her word with me, and **took** every opportunity of representing, in the most favourable manner to my uncle, the reformation that love had wrought in my character.

I went to the country, full of hope, at end of my six probationary months. My uncle, however, with a mixture of obstinacy and good sense, replied to my aunt in my presence, " This reformation that you talk of, wife, won't last. 'T was begun by love, as *you* say ; and will end with love, as *I* say. You and I know, my dear, love lasts little longer than the honeymoon ; and Lucy is not, or ought not to be, such a simpleton as to look only to what a husband will be for one short month of his life, when she is to live with him for twenty, thirty, maybe forty long years ; and no help for it, let him turn out what he will. I beg your pardon, nephew Basil ; but where my Lucy's happiness is at stake, I must speak my mind as a father should. My opinion, Lucy, is, that he is not a whit changed ; and so I now let you understand, if you marry the man, it must be without my consent."

Lucy turned exceedingly pale, and I grew extremely angry. My uncle had, as usual, recourse to his pipe ; and to all the eloquence which love and indignation could inspire, he would only answer, between the whiffs of his smoking, " If my girl marries you, nephew Basil, I say she must do so without my consent."

Lucy's affection for me struggled for some time with her sense of duty to her father ; her mother supported my cause with much warmth ; having once declared in my favour, she considered herself as bound to maintain her side of the question. It became a trial of power between my uncle and aunt ; and their passions rose so high in the conflict, that Lucy trembled for the consequences.

One day she took an opportunity of speaking to me in private. " My dear Basil," said she, " we must part. You see that I can never be yours with my father's consent ; and without it I could never be happy, even in being united to you. I will not be the cause of misery to all those whom I love best in the world. I will not set my father and mother at variance. I cannot bear to hear the altercations, which rise higher and higher between them every day Let us part, and all will be right again."

It was in vain that I combated her resolution ; I

32 *

alternately resented and deplored the weakness which induced Lucy to sacrifice her own happiness and mine to the obstinate prejudices of a father; yet I could not avoid respecting her the more for her adhering to what she believed to be her duty. The sweetness of temper, gentleness of disposition, and filial piety which she showed on this trying occasion endeared her to me beyond expression.

Her father, notwithstanding his determination to be as immoveable as a rock, began to manifest symptoms of internal agitation; and one night after breaking his pipe, and throwing down the tongs and poker twice, which Lucy twice replaced, he exclaimed, " Lucy, girl, you are a fool! and what is worse, you are grown into a mere shadow. You are breaking my heart. Why, I know this man, this Basil, this cursed nephew of mine, will never come to good. But cannot you marry him without my consent?"

Upon this hint Lucy's scruples vanished; and a few days afterward we were married. Prudence, virtue, pride, love, every strong motive which can act upon the human mind, stimulated me to exert myself to prove that I was worthy of this most amiable woman. A year passed away, and my Lucy said that she had no reason to repent of her choice. She took the most affectionate pains to convince her father that she was perfectly happy, and that he had judged of me too harshly. His delight at seeing his daughter happy vanquished his reluctance to acknowledge that he had changed his opinion. I never shall forget the pleasure I felt at hearing him confess that he had been too positive, and that his Lucy had made a good match for herself.

Alas! when I had obtained this testimony in my favour, when I had established a character for exertion and punctuality, I began to relax in my efforts to deserve it: I indulged myself in my old habits of procrastination. My customers and country correspondents began to complain that their letters were unanswered, and that their orders were neglected. Their remonstrances became more and more urgent in process of time; and nothing but actually seeing the dates of their letters could convince me that they were in the right, and that I was in the wrong. An old friend of my father's, a rich gentleman, who loved books, and bought all that were worth buying, sent me, in March, an order for books to a considerable amount. In April he wrote to remind me of his first letter.

" MY DEAR SIR,   " April 3.

" Last month I wrote to request that you would
send me the following books :—I have been much
disappointed by not receiving them; and I request
you will be so good as to forward them *immediately.*   I am, my dear sir,
                    " Yours sincerely,
                         " J. C."

In May he wrote to me again :

" DEAR SIR,

" I am much surprised at not having yet received the books I wrote for last March—beg to
know the cause of this delay; and am,
                    " Dear sir,
                         " Yours, &c.
                         " J. C."

A fortnight afterward, as I was packing up the
books for this gentleman, I received the following :

" SIR,

" As it is now above a quarter of a year since I
wrote to you for books, which you have not yet
sent to me, I have been obliged to apply to another
bookseller.

" I am much concerned at being compelled to

this : I had a great regard for your father, and would not willingly break off my connexion with his son ; but really you have tried my patience too far. Last year I never had from you any one new publication until it was in the hands of all my neighbours ; and I have often been under the necessity of borrowing books which I had bespoken from you months before. I hope you will take this as a warning, and that you will not use any of your other friends as you have used,

"Sir,

"Your humble servant,

"J. C."

This reprimand had little effect upon me, because, at the time when I received it, I was intent upon an object in comparison with which the trade of a bookseller appeared absolutely below my consideration. I was inventing a set of new taxes for the minister, for which I expected to be liberally rewarded. I was ever searching for some *short cut* to the temple of Fame, instead of following the beaten road.

I was much encouraged by persons intimately connected with those high in power to hope that my new taxes would be adopted ; and I spent my

time in attendance upon my patrons, leaving the
care of my business to my foreman, a young man
whose head the whole week was intent upon riding
out on Sunday.   With such a master and such a
foreman affairs could not go on well.

My Lucy, notwithstanding her great respect for
my abilities, and her confidence in my promises,
often hinted that she feared ministers might not at
last make me amends for the time I devoted to my
system of taxation; but I persisted.   The file of
unanswered letters was filled even to the top of the
wire; the drawer of unsettled accounts made me
sigh profoundly, whenever it was accidentally
opened.   I soon acquired a horror of business, and
practised all the arts of apology, evasion, and in-
visibility, to which procrastinators must sooner or
later be reduced.   My conscience gradually became callous: and I could, without compunction,
promise, with a face of truth, to settle an account
to-morrow, without having the slightest hope of
keeping my word.

I was a publisher as well as a bookseller, and
was assailed by a tribe of rich and poor authors.
The rich complained continually of delays that
affected their fame; the poor of delays that concerned their interest, and sometimes their very ex-

istence. I was cursed with a compassionate as well as with a procrastinating temper; and I frequently advanced money to my poor authors, to compensate for my neglect to settle their accounts, and to free myself from the torment of their reproaches.

They soon learned to take a double advantage of my virtues and my vices. The list of my poor authors increased, for I was an encourager of genius. I trusted to my own judgment concerning every performance that was offered to me; and I was often obliged to pay for having neglected to read, or to send to press, these multifarious manuscripts. After having kept a poor devil of an author upon the tenterhooks of expectation for an unconscionable time, I could not say to him, " Sir, I have never opened your manuscript; there it is, in that heap of rubbish: take it away for heaven's sake." No, hardened as I was, I never failed to make some compliment, or some retribution; and my compliments were often in the end the most expensive species of retribution.

My rich authors soon deserted me, and hurt my credit in the circles of literary fashion by their clamours. I had ample experience, yet I had never been able to decide whether I would rather meet the "desperate misery" of a famishing pamphleteer, or the exasperated vanity of a rich *amateur*. Every one of my authors seemed convinced that the fate of Europe or the salvation of the world depended upon the publication of their book on some particular day; while I all the time was equally persuaded that their works were mere trash in comparison with my new system of taxation: consequently I postponed their business, and pursued my favourite tax-scheme.

I have the pride and pleasure to say that all my taxes were approved and adopted, and brought in an immense increase of revenue to the state; but I have the mortification to be obliged to add, that I never, directly or indirectly, received the slightest pecuniary reward; and the credit of all I had proposed was snatched from me by a rogue, who had no other merit than that of being shaved sooner than I was one frosty morning. If I had not put off whetting my razor the preceding day, this would not have happened. To such a trifling instance of my unfortunate habit of procrastination must I attribute one of the most severe disappointments of my life. A rival financier, who laid claim to the prior invention and suggestion of my principal taxes was appointed to meet me at the house of my great man at ten o'clock in the morning. My opponent was punctual; I was half an hour too late; his claims were established; mine were rejected, because I was not present to produce my proofs. When I arrived at my patron's the insolent porter shut the door in my face; and so ended all hopes from my grand system of taxation.

I went home and shut myself up in my room, to give vent to my grief at leisure : but I was not permitted to indulge my sorrow long in peace. I was summoned by my foreman to come down stairs to one of my enraged authors, who positively refused to quit the shop without seeing me. Of the whole irritable race, the man who was now waiting to see me was the most violent. He was a man of some genius and learning, with great pretensions and a vindictive spirit. He was poor, yet lived among the rich ; and his arrogance could be equalled only by his susceptibility. He was known in our house by the name of *Thaumaturgos, the retailer of wonders*, because he had sent me a manuscript with this title: and once or twice a week we received a letter or message from him, to inquire when it would be published. I had unfortunately mislaid this precious manuscript. Under

33

this circumstance, to meet the author was almost as dreadful as to stand the shot of a pistol. Down stairs I went, unprovided with any apology.

"Sir," cried my angry man, suppressing his passion, "as you do not find it worth your while to publish *Thaumaturgos*, you will be so obliging as to let me have my manuscript."

"Pardon me, my dear sir," interrupted I; "it shall certainly appear this spring."

"Spring! Zounds, sir, don't talk to me of spring. Why you told me it should be out at Christmas; you said it should be out last June; you promised to send it to press before last Easter. Is this the way I am to be treated?"

"Pardon me, my dear sir. I confess I have used you and the world very ill; but the pressure of business must plead my apology."

"Look you, Mr. Basil Lowe, I am not come here to listen to commonplace excuses. I have been ill used, and know it; and the world shall know it. I am not ignorant of the designs of my enemies; but no cabal shall succeed against me. Thaumaturgos shall not be suppressed! Thaumaturgos shall see the light! Thaumaturgos shall have justice in spite of all the machinations of malice. Sir, I demand my manuscript."

" Sir, it shall be sent to you to-morrow."

" To-morrow, **sir**, will not do **for** me. I have heard of to-morrow from you this twelvemonth past. I will have my manuscript to-day. I do not leave this spot without Thaumaturgos."

Thus driven to extremities, I was compelled to confess that I could not immediately lay my hand upon it; but I added that the whole house should be searched for it instantly. It is impossible to describe the indignation which my author expressed. I ran away to search the house. He followed me, and stood by while I rummaged in drawers and boxes full of papers, and tossed over heaps of manuscripts. No Thaumaturgos could be found. The author declared that he had no copy of the manuscript; that he had been offered 500*l.* for it by another bookseller; and that, for his own part, he would not lose it for twice that sum. Lost, however, it evidently was. He stalked out of my house, bidding me prepare to abide by the consequences. I racked my memory in vain to discover what I had done with this bundle of wonders. I could recollect only that I carried it a week in my great-coat pocket, resolving every day to lock it up; and that I went to the Mount coffee-

house in this coat several times. These recollec-
tions were of little use.

A suit was instituted against me for the value of
Thaumaturgos : and the damages were modestly
laid by the author at eight hundred guineas. The
cause was highly interesting to all the tribe of London
booksellers and authors. The court was crowded at
an early hour ; several people of fashion, who were
partisans of the plaintiff, appeared in the gallery ;
many more, who were his enemies, attended on
purpose to hear my counsel ridicule and abuse the
pompous *Thaumaturgos.* I had great hopes myself
that we might win the day ; especially as the lawyer
on the opposite side was my old competitor at Eton,
that Johnson whom I had always considered as a
mere laborious drudge, and a very heavy fellow.
How this heavy fellow got up in the world, and how
he contrived to supply by dint of study the want
of natural talents, I cannot tell ; but this I know to
my cost, that he managed his client's cause so ably,
and made a speech so full of sound law and clear
sense, as effectually to decide the cause against me.
I was condemned to pay 500*l.* damages and costs
of suit. Five hundred pounds lost by delaying to
lock up a bundle of papers ! Everybody pitied me,
because the punishment seemed so disproportioned

to the offence. The pity of everybody, however, did not console me for the loss of my money.

CHAPTER IV.

The trial was published in the papers: my uncle Lowe read it, and all my credit with him was lost for ever. Lucy did not utter a syllable of reproach or complaint; but she used all her gentle influence to prevail upon me to lay aside the various schemes which I had formed for making a rapid fortune, and urged me to devote my whole attention to my business.

The loss which I had sustained, though great, was not irremediable. I was moved more by my wife's kindness than I could have been by the most outrageous invective. But what is kindness, what is affection, what are the best resolutions, opposed to all-powerful habit? I put off settling my affairs till I had finished a pamphlet against government, which my friends and the critics assured me would make my fortune, by attaching to my shop all the opposition members.

My pamphlet succeeded, was highly praised, and loudly abused: answers appeared, and I was called

33 *

upon to provide rejoiners. Time thus passed away, and while I was gaining fame, I every hour lost money. I was threatened with bankruptcy. I threw aside my pamphlets, and, in the utmost terror and confusion, began, too late, to look into my affairs. I now attempted too much : I expected to repair by bustle the effects of procrastination. The nervous anxiety of my mind prevented me from doing any thing well; whatever I was employed about appeared to me of less consequence than a hundred other things which ought to be done. The letter that I was writing, or the account that I was settling, was but one of a multitude; which had all equal claims to be expedited immediately. My courage failed; I abandoned my business in despair. A commission of bankruptcy was taken out against me; all my goods were seized, and I became a prisoner in the King's Bench.

My wife's relations refused to give me any assistance; but her father offered to receive her and her little boy, on condition that she would part from me, and spend the remainder of her days with them. This she positively refused; and I never shall forget the manner of her refusal. Her character rose in adversity. With the utmost feminine gentleness and delicacy, she had a degree of courage and fortitude which I have seldom seen equalled in any of my own sex. She followed me to prison, and supported my spirits by a thousand daily instances of kindness. During eighteen months that she passed with me in a prison, which we then thought must be my abode for life, she never, by word or look, reminded me that I was the cause of our misfortunes; on the contrary she drove this idea from my thoughts with all the address of female affection. I cannot, even at this distance of time, recall these things to memory without tears.

What a woman, what a wife had I reduced to distress! I never saw her, even in the first months of our marriage, so cheerful and so tender as at this period. She seemed to have no existence but in me and in our little boy, of whom she was dotingly fond. He was at this time just able to run about and talk; his playful caresses, his thoughtless gayety, and at times a certain tone of compassion for *poor papa*, were very touching Alas! he little foresaw . . . . But let me go on with my history, if I can, without anticipation.

Among my creditors was a Mr. Nun, a papermaker, who from his frequent dealings with me, had occasion to see something of my character and of my wife's: he admired her and pitied me. He was in easy circumstances, and delighted in doing all the good in his power. One morning my Lucy came into my room with a face radiant with joy.

"My love," said she, "here is Mr. Nun below, waiting to see you : but he says he will not see you till I have told you the good news. He has got all our creditors to enter into a compromise, and to set you at liberty."

I was transported with joy and gratitude; our benevolent friend was waiting in a hackney-coach to carry us away from prison. When I began to thank him, he stopped me with a blunt declaration that I was not a bit obliged to him; for that, if I had been a man of straw, he would have done just the same for the sake of my wife, whom he looked upon to be one or other the best woman he had ever seen, Mrs. Nun always excepted.

He proceeded to inform me how he had settled my affairs, and how he had obtained from my creditors a small allowance for the immediate support of myself and family. He had given up the third part of a considerable sum due to himself. As my own house was shut up, he insisted upon taking us home with him: "Mrs. Nun," he said, "had provided a good dinner; and he must not have her ducks and green pease upon the table, and no friends to eat them."

Never were ducks and green pease more acceptable; never was a dinner eaten with more appetite, or given with more good-will. I have often thought of this dinner, and compared the hospitality of this simple-hearted man with the ostentation of great folks, who give splendid entertainments to those who do not want them. In trifles and in matters of consequence this Mr. Nun was one of the most liberal and unaffectedly generous men I ever knew; but the generous actions of men in middle life are lost in obscurity. No matter: they do not act from a love of fame; they act from a better motive, and they have their reward in their own hearts.

As I was passing through Mr. Nun's warehouse, I was thinking of writing something on this subject; but whether it should be a poetic effusion, in the form of "An Ode to him who least expects it," or a prose work, under the title of "Modern Parallels," in the manner of Plutarch, I had not decided, when I was roused from my revery by my wife, who, pointing to a large bale of paper that was directed to "Ezekiel Croft, merchant, Philadelphia," asked me if I knew that this gentleman was a very near relation of her mother ? "Is he, indeed ?" said Mr. Nun. "Then I can assure you that you have a relation of whom you have nc occasion to be ashamed : he is one of the most respectable merchants in Philadelphia."

"He was not very rich when he left this country about six years ago," said Lucy.

"He has a very good fortune now," answered Mr. Nun.

"And has he made this very good fortune in six years ?" cried I. "My dear Lucy, I did not know that you had any relations in America. I have a great mind to go over there myself."

"Away from all our friends ?" said Lucy.

"I shall be ashamed," replied I, "to see them after all that has happened. A bankrupt cannot have many friends. The best thing that I can possibly do is to go over to a new world, where I may establish a new character, and make a new fortune."

"But we must not forget," said Mr. Nun, "that in the new world, as in the old one, a character and a fortune must be made by much the same means ; and forgive me if I add, the same bad habits that are against a man in one country will be as much against him in another."

"True," thought I, as I recollected at this instant my unfortunate voyage to China. But now that the idea of going to America had come into my mind, I saw so many chances of success in my favour, and I felt so much convinced I should not relapse into my former faults, that I could not abandon the scheme. My Lucy consented to accompany me. She spent a week in the country with her father and friends, by my particular desire; and they did all they could to prevail upon her to stay with them, promising to take the best possible care of her and her little boy during my absence; but she steadily persisted in her determination to accompany her husband. I was not too late in going on shipboard this time; and, during the whole voyage, I did not lose any of my goods; for, in the first place, I had very few goods to lose, and, in the next, my wife took the entire charge of those few.

And now behold me safely landed at Philadelphia, with one hundred pounds in my pocket—a small sum of money; but many, from yet more trifling beginnings, had grown rich in America. My wife's relation, Mr. Croft, had not so much, as I was told, when he left England. Many passengers who came over in the same ship with me had

not half so much. Several of them were indeed
wretchedly poor.

Among others there was an Irishman who was
known by the name of Barny, a contraction, I believe, for Barnaby. As to his surname he could
not undertake to spell it ; but he assured me there
was no better. This man, with many of his rela-
tives, had come to England, according to their
custom, during harvest-time, to assist in reaping,
because they gain higher wages than in their own
country. Barny heard that he should get still
higher wages for labour in America, and accordingly he and his two sons, lads of eighteen and
twenty, took their passage for Philadelphia. A
merrier mortal I never saw. We used to hear him
upon deck, continually singing or whistling his Irish
tunes ; and I should never have guessed that this
man's life had been a series of hardships and misfortunes.

When we were leaving the ship, I saw him, to
my great surprise, crying bitterly ; and upon inquiring what was the matter, he answered that it
was not for himself, but for his sons, he was griev-
ing, because they were to be made *redemption men ;*
that is, they were to be bound to work, during a
certain time, for the captain, or for whomever he

pleased, till the money due for their passage should be paid. Though I was somewhat surprised at any one's thinking of coming on board a vessel without having one farthing in his pocket, yet I could not forbear paying the money for this poor fellow. He dropped down on the deck upon both his knees, as suddenly as if he had been shot, and, holding up his hands to heaven, prayed, first in Irish, and then in English, with fervent fluency, that " I and mine might never want ; that I might live long to reign over him; that success might attend my honour wherever I went ; and that I might enjoy for ever-more all sorts of blessings and crowns of glory." As I had an English prejudice in favour of silent gratitude, I was rather disgusted by all this eloquence ; I turned away abruptly, and got into the boat which waited to carry me to shore.

As we rowed away I looked at my wife and child, and reproached myself with having indulged in the luxury of generosity, perhaps at their ex-pense.

My wife's relation, Mr. Croft, received us better than she expected, and worse than I hoped. He had the face of an acute money-making man ; his manners were methodical ; caution was in his eye, and prudence in all his motions. In our first half-

34

hour's conversation he convinced me that he deserved the character he had obtained, of being upright and exact in all his dealings.   His ideas were
just and **clear,** but confined to the objects immediately relating to his business ; as to his heart, he
seemed to have no notion of general philanthropy,
but to have perfectly learned by rote his duty to his
neighbour.   He appeared disposed to do charitable
and good-natured actions from reason, and not
from feeling ; because they were proper, not merely
because they were agreeable.   I felt that I should
respect, **but** never love him ; and that he would
never either love or respect me, because the
virtue which he held in the highest veneration was
that in which I was most deficient—punctuality.

   But I will give, as nearly as I can, my first con-
versation with him ; and from that a better idea of
his character may be formed than I can afford by
any description.

   I presented to him Mr. Nun's letter of introduction, **and mentioned** that my wife had the honour of being related to him.   He perused Mr.
Nun's letter very slowly.   I was determined not to
leave him in any doubt respecting who and what I
was ; and I briefly told him the particulars of my
history.   He listened with immoveable attention ;

and when I had finished he said, " You have not yet told me what your views are in coming to America."

I replied, " that my plans were not yet fixed."

" But of course," said he, " you cannot have left home without forming some plan for the future. May I ask what line of life you mean to pursue?"

I answered, " that I was undetermined, and meant to be guided by circumstances."

" Circumstances!" said he. " May I request you to explain yourself more fully? for I do not precisely understand to what circumstances you allude."

I was provoked with the man for being so slow of apprehension; but, when driven to the necessity of explaining, I found that I did not myself understand what I meant.

I changed my ground; and lowering my tone of confidence, said, that as I was totally ignorant of the country, I should wish to be guided by the advice of better informed persons; and that I begged leave to address myself to him, as having had the most successful experience.

After a considerable pause he replied, it was a hazardous thing to give advice; but that as my wife was his relation, and as he held it a duty to assist his relations, he should not decline giving me—all the advice in his power.

I bowed and felt chilled all over by his manner.

" And not only my advice," continued he, ' but my assistance—in reason."

I said, " I was much obliged to him."

" Not in the least, young man ; you are not in the least obliged to me yet, for I have done nothing for you."

This was true, and not knowing what to say, I was silent.

" And that which I may be able to do for you in future must depend as much upon yourself as upon me. In the first place, before I can give any advice I must know what you are worth in the world."

My worth in money, I told him with a forced smile, was but very trifling indeed. With some hesitation I named the sum.

" And you have a wife and child to support !" said he, shaking his head. " And your child is too young and your wife too delicate to work. They will be sad burdens upon your hands ; these are not the things for America. Why did you bring them with you ? But, as that is done, and cannot be mended," continued he, " we must make the

best of it, and support them. You say you are ignorant of the country. I must explain to you then
how money is to be made here, and by whom.
The class of labourers make money readily, if
they are industrious, because they have high wages
and constant employment; artificers and mechan-
ics, carpenters, shipwrights, wheelwrights, smiths,
bricklayers, masons, get rich here without difficulty, from the same causes : but all these things
are out of the question for you. You have head,
not hands, I perceive. Now mere head, in the
line of bookmaking or bookselling, brings in but
poor profit in this country. The sale for imported
books is extensive; and our printers are doing
something by subscription here, in Philadelphia,
and in New York, they tell me. But London is
the place for a good bookseller to thrive; and you
come from London, where you tell me you were a
bankrupt. I would not advise you to have any
thing more to do with bookselling or bookmaking.
Then as to becoming a planter: our planters, if
they are skilful and laborious, thrive well; but you
have not capital sufficient to clear land and build a
house; or hire servants to do the work, for which
you are not yourself sufficiently robust. Besides,
I do not imagine you know how much of agricul-

34*

tural concerns, or country business; and even to
oversee and guide others, experience is necessary.
The life of a back settler I do not advise, because
you and your wife are not equal to it.   You are
not accustomed to live in a log-house, or to feed
upon racoons and squirrels: not to omit the constant dread, if not imminent danger, of being
burnt in your beds, or scalped by the Indians with
whom you would be surrounded.   Upon the whole,
I see no line of life that promises well for you but
that of a merchant: and I see no means of your
getting into this line, without property and without
credit, except by going into some established house
as a clerk.   You are a good penman and ready
accountant, I think you tell me; and I presume
you have a sufficient knowledge of book-keeping.
With sobriety, diligence, and honesty, you may do
well in this way; and may look forward to being
a partner, and in a lucrative situation, some years
hence.   This is the way I managed, and rose myself by degrees to what you see.   It is true, I was
not at first encumbered with a wife and young
child.   In due time I married my master's daughter,
which was a great furtherance to me; but then,
on the other hand, your wife is my relation; and
to be married to the relation of a rich merchant is

next best to not being married at all, in your situation. I told you I thought it my duty to proffer assistance as well as advice : so take up your abode with me for a fortnight : in that time I shall be able to judge whether you are capable of being a clerk ; and if you and I should suit, we will talk further. You understand that I enter into no engagement, and make no promise ; but shall be glad to lodge you and your wife, and little boy, for a fortnight ; and it will be your own fault, and must be your own loss, if the visit turns out waste of time—I cannot stay to talk to you any longer at present," added he, pulling out his watch, " for I have business, and business waits for no man. Go back to your inn for my relation and her little one. We dine at two, precisely."

I left Mr. Croft's house with a vague, indescribable feeling of dissatisfaction and disappointment ; but when I arrived at my inn, and repeated all that had passed to my wife, she seemed quite surprised and delighted by the civil and friendly manner in which this gentleman had behaved. She tried to reason the matter with me ; but there is no reasoning with imagination.

The fact was, Mr. Croft had destroyed certain vague and visionary ideas that I had indulged, of making, by some unknown means, a rapid fortune in America; and to be reduced to real life, and sink into a clerk in a merchant's counting-house, was mortification and misery. Lucy in vain dwelt upon the advantage of having found, immediately upon my arrival in Philadelphia, a certain mode of employment; and a probability of rising to be a partner in one of the first mercantile houses, if I went on steadily for a few years. I was forced to acknowledge that her relation was very good; that I was certainly very fortunate; and that I ought to think myself very much obliged to Mr. Croft. But after avowing all this, I walked up and down the room in melancholy revery for a considerable length of time. My wife reminded me repeatedly that Mr. Croft said he dined precisely at two o'clock; that he was a very punctual man; that it was a long walk, as I had found it, from the inn to his house; that I had better dress myself for dinner; and that my clean shirt and cravat were ready for me. I still walked up and down the room in revery till my wife was completely ready, had dressed the child, and held up my watch before my eyes to show me that it wanted but ten minutes of two. I then began to dress in the greatest hurry imaginable: and unluckily, as I was pulling on my silk stocking, I tore a hole in the leg, or, as my wife expressed it, a stitch dropped, and I was forced to wait while she repaired the evil. Certainly this operation of *taking up a stitch*, as I am instructed to call it, is one of the slowest operations in nature; or rather, one of the most tedious and teasing manœuvres of art. Though the most willing and the most dexterous fingers that ever touched a needle were employed in my service, I thought the work would never be finished.

At last I was *hosed* and shod, and out we set. It struck a quarter past two as we left the house; we came to Mr. Croft's in the middle of dinner. He had a large company at table; everybody was disturbed; my Lucy was a stranger to Mrs. Croft, and was to be introduced; and nothing could be more awkward and embarrassing than our *entree* and introduction. There were such compliments and apologies, such changing of places, such shuf-fling of chairs, and running about of servants, that I thought we never should be seated.

In the midst of the bustle my little chap began to roar most horribly, and to struggle to get away from a black servant, who was helping him up on his chair. The child's terror at the sudden ap-proach of the negro could not be conquered, nor could he by any means be quieted. Mrs. Croft at last ordered the negro out of the room, the roaring ceased, and nothing but the child's sobs were heard for some instants.

The guests were all silent, and had ceased eating; Mrs. Croft was vexed because *every thing was cold;* Mr. Croft looked much discomfited, and said not a syllable more than was absolutely necessary, as master of the house. I never ate, or rather I was never at, a more disagreeable dinner. I was in pain for Lucy as well as for myself; her colour rose up to her temples. I cursed myself a hundred times for not having gone to dress in time.

At length, to my great relief, the cloth was taken away; but even when we came to the wine after dinner, the cold formality of my host continued unabated, and I began to fear that he had taken an insurmountable dislike to me, and that I should lose all the advantages of his protection and assistance : advantages which rose considerably in my estimation, when I apprehended I was upon the point of losing them.

Soon after dinner, a young gentleman of the name of Hudson joined the company; his manners and appearance were prepossessing; he was frank and well-bred; and the effect of his politeness was

soon felt, as if by magic, for everybody became at
their ease; his countenance was full of life and
fire; and though he said nothing that showed remarkable abilities, every thing he said pleased.
As soon as he found that I was a stranger, he addressed his conversation principally to me. I recovered my spirits, exerted myself to entertain him,
and succeeded. He was delighted to hear news
from England, and especially from London, a city
which he said he had an ardent desire to visit.
When he took leave of me in the evening, he expressed very warmly the wish to cultivate my acquaintance; and I was the more flattered and
obliged by this civility, because I was certain that
he knew exactly my situation and circumstances,
Mrs. Croft having explained them to him very fully,
even in my hearing.

CHAPTER V.

In the course of the ensuing week, young Mr.
Hudson and I saw one another almost every day,
and our mutual liking for each other's company
increased. He introduced me to his father, who
had been a planter, and having made a large for-

tune, came to reside at Philadelphia, to enjoy himself, as he said, for the remainder of his days.
He lived in what the sober Americans called a
most luxurious and magnificent style. The best
company in Philadelphia met at his house; and he
delighted particularly in seeing those who had convivial talents, and who would supply him with wit
and gayety, in which he was naturally rather deficient.

On my first visit, I perceived that his son had
boasted of me as one of the best companions in the
world; and I determined to support the character
that had been given of me; I told two or three
good stories, and sang two or three good songs.
The company were charmed with me; old Mr.
Hudson was particularly delighted; he gave me a
pressing general invitation to his house, and most
of the principal guests followed his example. I
was not a little elated with this success. Mr. Croft
was with me at this entertainment; and I own I
was peculiarly gratified by feeling that I at once
became conspicuous, by my talents, in a company
where he was apparently of no consequence, notwithstanding all his wealth and prudence.

As we went home together, he said to me, very
gravely, " I would not advise you, Mr. Basil Lowe,

to accept of all these invitations; nor to connect yourself intimately with young Hudson. The society at Mr. Hudson's is very well for those who have made a fortune, and want to spend it; but for those who have a fortune to make, in my opinion, it is not only useless but dangerous."

I was in no humour at this moment to profit by this sober advice; especially as I fancied it might be dictated, in some degree, by envy of my superior talents and accomplishments. My wife, however, supported his advice by many excellent and kind arguments. She observed that these people, who invited me to their houses as a good companion, followed merely their own pleasure, and would **never be of any real advantage to** me; that Mr. Croft, on the contrary, showed, from the first hour when I applied to him, a desire to serve me; that he had pointed out the means of establishing myself; and that, in the advice he gave me, he could be actuated only by a wish to be of use to me; that it was more reasonable to suspect him of despising than of envying talents which were not directed to the grand object of gaining money.

Good sense from the lips of a woman whom a man loves has a mighty effect upon his understanding, especially if he sincerely believe that the wo-

35

man has no desire to rule.   This was my singular
case.   I promised Lucy I would refuse all invitations for the ensuing fortnight, and devote myself
to whatever business Mr. Croft might devise.   No
one could be more assiduous than I was for ten
days ; and I perceived that Mr. Croft, though it was
not his custom to praise, was well satisfied with my
diligence.   Unluckily, on the eleventh day, I put
off in the morning making out an invoice, which he
left for me to do, and I was persuaded in the evening to go out with young Mr. Hudson.   I had expressed, in conversation with him, some curiosity
about the American *frog-concerts*, of which I had
read, in modern books of travels, extraordinary
accounts.

   Mr. Hudson persuaded me to accompany him to
a swamp, at some miles' distance from Philadelphia,
to hear one of these concerts.   The performance
lasted some time, and it was late before we returned
to town : I went to bed tired, and waked in the
morning with a cold, which I had caught by standing so long in the swamp.   I lay an hour after I
was called, in hopes of getting rid of my cold :
when I was at last up and dressed, I recollected my
invoice, and resolved to do it the first thing after
breakfast ; but, unluckily, I put it off till I had look-

ed for some lines in Homer's "Battle of the Frogs
and Mice." There was no Homer, as you may
guess, in Mr. Croft's house, and I went to a bookseller's to borrow one: he had Pope's Iliad and
Odyssey, but no Battle of the Frogs and Mice. I
walked over half the town in search of it; at length
I found it, and was returning in triumph, with Homer in each pocket, when at the door of Mr. Croft's
house I found half a dozen porters, with heavy
loads upon their backs.

"Where are you going, my good fellows?" said I.

"To the quay, sir, with the cargo for the Betsy."

"My God!" cried I, "Stop. Can't you stop a
minute? I thought the Betsy was not to sail till to-
morrow. Stop one minute."

"No, sir," said they, "that we can't; for the
captain bade us make what haste we could to the
quay to load her."

I ran into the house; the captain of the Betsy
was bawling in the hall, with his hat on the back
of his head; Mr. Croft on the landing-place of the
warehouse-stairs, with open letters in his hand, and
two or three of the under-clerks were running different ways with pens in their mouths.

"Mr. Basil! the invoice!" exclaimed all the
clerks at once, the moment I made my appearance.

"Mr. Basil Lowe, the invoice and the copy, if you please," repeated Mr. Croft. "We have sent three messengers after you. Very extraordinary to go out at this time of day, and not even to leave word where you are to be found. Here's the captain of the Betsy has been waiting this half-hour for the invoice. Well, sir! Will you go for it now? And at the same time bring me the copy, to enclose in this letter to our correspondent by post."

I stood petrified. "Sir, the invoice, sir!—Good heavens! I forgot it entirely,"

"You remember it now, sir, I suppose. Keep your apologies till we have leisure. The invoices, if you please."

"The invoices! My God, sir! I beg ten thousand pardons! They are not drawn out."

"Not drawn out. Impossible!" said Mr. Croft.

"Then I'm off," cried the captain, with a tremendous oath. "I can't wait another tide for any clerk breathing."

"Send back the porters, captain, if you please," said Mr. Croft, coolly. "The whole cargo must be unpacked. I took it for granted, Mr. Basil, that you had drawn the invoice, according to order, yesterday morning; and of course the goods were packed in the evening. I was certainly wrong in

taking it for granted that you would be punctual.
A man of business should take nothing for granted.
This is a thing that will not occur to me again as
long as I live."

I poured forth expressions of contrition ; but apparently unmoved by them, and without anger or
impatience in his manner, he turned from me as
soon as the porters came back with the goods, and
ordered them all to be unpacked and replaced in
the warehouse. I was truly concerned.

" I believe you spent your evening yesterday
with young Mr. Hudson ?" said he, returning to
me.

" Yes, sir,—I am sincerely sorry—"

" Sorrow, in these cases, does no good, sir," interrupted he. " I thought I had sufficiently
warned you of the danger of forming that intimacy.
Midnight carousing wil' not do for men of business."

" Carousing, sir !" said I. " Give me leave to
assure you that we were not carousing. We were
only at a *frog-concert.*"

Mr. Croft, who had at least suppressed his displeasure till now, looked absolutely angry ; he
thought I was making a joke of him. When I convinced him that I was in earnest, he changed from

35 *

anger to astonishment, with a large mixture of contempt in his nasal muscles.

" A frog-concert," repeated he. " And is it
possible that any man could neglect an invoice
merely to go to hear a parcel of frogs croaking in
a swamp? Sir, you will never do in a mercantile house." He walked off to the warehouse, and
left me half-mortified and half-provoked.

From this time forward all hopes from Mr.
Croft's friendship were at an end. He was coldly
civil to me during the few remaining days of the
fortnight that we staid at his house. He took the
trouble, however, of looking out for a cheap and
tolerably comfortable lodging for my wife and boy;
the rent of which he desired to pay for his relation,
he said, as long as I should remain in Philadelphia,
or till I should find myself in some eligible situation.
He seemed pleased with Lucy, and said she was a
very properly conducted, well disposed, prudent
young woman, whom he was not ashamed to own
for a cousin. He repeated, at parting, that he
should be happy to afford me every assistance *in
reason*, towards pursuing any feasible plan of advancing myself; but it was his decided opinion that
I could never succeed in a mercantile line.

I never liked Mr. Croft; he was much too

punctual, too much of an automaton, for me ; but
I should have felt more regret at leaving him, and
losing his friendship, and should have expressed
more gratitude for his kindness to Lucy and my
boy, if my head had not at the time been full of
young Hudson.   He professed the warmest regard
for me, congratulated me on getting free from old
Croft's mercantile clutches, and assured me that
such a man as I was could not fail to succeed in
the world by my own talents and the assistance of
friends and good connexions.

I was now almost every day at his father's house,
in company with numbers of rich and gay people,
who were all *my friends.*   I was the life of society,
was invited everywhere, and accepted every invitation, because I could not offend Mr. Hudson's intimate acquaintance.

From day to day, from week to week, from month
to month, I went on in this style.   I was old Hudson's grand favourite, and everybody told me he
could do any thing he pleased for me.   I had formed
a scheme, a bold scheme, of obtaining from government a large tract of territory in the ceded lands
of Louisiana, and of collecting a subscription in
Philadelphia, among *my friends*, to make a settlement there : the subscribers to be paid by instal-

ments, so much the first year, so much the second, and so onward, till the whole should be liquidated. I was to collect hands from the next ships, which were expected to be full of emigrants from Ireland and Scotland. I had soon a long list of subscribers, who gave me their names always after dinner, or after supper. Old Hudson wrote his name at the head of the list, with an ostentatiously large sum opposite to it.

As nothing could be done till the ensuing spring. when the ships were expected, I spent my time in the same convivial manner. The spring came, but there was no answer obtained from government respecting the ceded territory ; and a delay of a few months was necessary. Mr. Hudson, the father, was the person who had undertaken to apply for the grant ; and he spoke always of the scheme, and of his own powers of carrying it into effect, in the most confident manner. From his conversation anybody would have supposed that the mines of Peru were upon his plantation ; and that in comparison with his, the influence of the President of the United States was nothing. I was a full twelvemonth before I was convinced that he was a boaster and a *fabulist ;* and I was another twelvemonth before I could persuade myself that

ne was one of the most selfish, indolent, and obstinate of human beings. He was delighted to have
me always at his table to entertain him and his
guests, but he had not the slightest real regard for
me, or care for my interests. He would talk to
me as long as I pleased of his possessions, and his
improvements, and his wonderful crops ; but the
moment I touched upon any of my own affairs, he
would begin to yawn, throw himself on a sofa,
and seem going to sleep. Whenever I mentioned
his subscription, he would say with a frown, " We
will talk of that, Basil, *to-morrow*."

Of my whole list of subscribers not above four
ever paid a shilling into my hands : their excuse
always was, " When government has given an
answer about the ceded territory, we will pay the
subscriptions ;" and the answer of government
always was, " When the subscriptions are paid,
we will make out a grant of the land." I was disgusted, and out of spirits ; but I thought all my
chance was to preserve, and to keep *my friends* in
good-humour : so that I was continually under the
necessity of appearing the same jovial companion,
laughing, singing, and drinking, when Heaven
knows, my heart was heavy enough.

At the end of the second year of promises, delays, and disappointments, my Lucy, who had always foretold how things would turn out, urged me to withdraw myself from this idle society, to give up my scheme, and to take the management of a small plantation in conjunction with the brother of Mr. Croft. His regard for my wife, who had won much upon this family by her excellent conduct, induced him to make me this offer; but I considered so long, and hesitated so much, whether I should accept of this proposal, that the time for accepting it passed away.

I had still hopes that my friend young Hudson would enable me to carry my grand project into execution; he had a considerable plantation in Jamaica, left to him by his grandfather on the mother's side; he was to be of age, and to take possession of it the ensuing year, and he proposed to sell it, and to apply some of the purchase-money to our scheme, of the success of which he had as sanguine expectations as I had myself. He was of a most enthusiastic, generous temper. I had obtained the greatest influence over him, and I am convinced, at this time, there was nothing in the world he would not have sacrificed for my sake. All that he required from me was to be his constant companion. He was extravagantly fond of field sports; and, though a Londoner, I was a good shot, and a good angler: for, during the time I was courting Lucy, I found it necessary to make myself a sportsman to win the favour of her brothers. With these accomplishments, my hold upon the esteem and affections of my friend was all-powerful. Every day in the season we went out shooting or fishing together: then, in the winter-time, we had various employments, I mean various excuses for idleness. Hudson was a great skater, and he had infinite diversion in teaching me to skate at the hazard of my scull. He was also to initiate me in the American pastime of *sleighing*, or sleding. Many a desperately cold winter's day I have submitted to be driven in his sled, when I would much rather, I own, have been safe and snug by my own fireside, with my wife.

Poor Lucy spent her time in a disagreeable and melancholy way during these three years: for, while I was out almost every day and all day long, she was alone in her lodging for numberless hours. She never repined, but always received me with a good-humoured countenance when I came home, even after sitting up half the night to wait for my return from Hudson's suppers. It grieved me to the heart to see her thus seemingly deserted, but I comforted myself with the reflection that this way of life would last but for a short time; that my friend would soon be of age, and able to fulfil all his promises; and that we should then all live together in happiness. I assured Lucy that the present idle, if not dissipated, manner in which I spent my days was not agreeable to my taste; that I was often extremely melancholy, even when I was forced to appear in the highest spirits; and that I often longed to be quietly with her, when I was obliged to sacrifice my time to friendship.

It would have been impossible that she and my child could have subsisted all this time independently, but for her steadiness and exertions. She would not accept of any pecuniary assistance except from her relation, Mr. Croft, who regularly paid the rent of her lodgings. She undertook to teach some young ladies whom Mrs. Croft introduced to her various kinds of fine needle work, in which she excelled; and for this she was well paid. I know that she never cost me one farthing during the three years and three months that we lived in Philadelphia. But even for this I do not give her so much credit as for her sweet temper during these trials, and her great forbearance in never reproaching or disputing with me. Many wives, who are called excellent managers, make their husbands pay tenfold in suffering what they save in money. This was not my Lucy's way; and therefore, with my esteem and respect, she ever had my fondest affections. I was in hopes the hour was just coming when I should be able to prove this to her, and when we should no longer be doomed to spend our days asunder. But, alas! her judgment was better than mine.

My friend Hudson was now within six weeks of being of age, when, unfortunately, there arrived in Philadelphia a company of players from England. Hudson, who was eager for every thing that had the name of pleasure, insisted upon my going with him to their first representation. Among the actresses there was a girl of the name of Marion, who seemed to be ordinary enough, just fit for a company of strolling players, but she danced passably well, and danced a great deal between the acts that night. Hudson clapped his hands till I was quite out of patience. He was in raptures, and the more I depreciated, the more he extolled the girl. I wished her in Nova Zembla, for I saw that he was falling in love with her, and had a kind of presentiment of all that was to follow. To tell the matter briefly, for what signifies dwelling upon past

36

misfortunes, the more young Hudson's passion increased for this dancing girl, the more his friendship for me declined; for I had frequent arguments with him upon the subject, and did all I could to open his eyes. I saw that the damsel had art, that she knew the extent of her power, and that she would draw her infatuated lover in to marry her. He was headstrong and violent in all his passions; he quarrelled with me, carried the girl off to Jamaica, married her the day he was of age, and settled upon his plantation. There was an end to all my hopes about the ceded territory.

Lucy, who was always my recourse in misfortune, comforted me by saying I had done my duty in combating my friend's folly at the expense of my own interest; and that, though he had quarrelled with me, she loved me the better for it.

Reflecting upon my own history and character, I have often thought it a pity that, with certain good qualities, and I will add talents, which deserve a better fate, I should have never succeeded in any thing I attempted, because I could not conquer one seemingly slight defect in my disposition, which had grown into a habit. Thoroughly determined, by Lucy's advice, to write to Mr. Croft, to request he would give me another trial, I put off sending

the letter till the next day : and that very morning
Mr. Croft set off on a journey to a distant part of
the country, to see a daughter that was newly married.

I was vexed, and from a want of something better to do, went out a-shooting to get rid of disagreeable thoughts. I shot several pheasants, and when
I came home carried them, as was my custom, to
old Mr. Hudson's kitchen, and gave them to the
cook. I happened to stay in the kitchen to feed
a favourite dog, while the cook was *preparing* the
birds I had brought. I observed in the crop of one
of the pheasants, some bright green leaves, and
some buds, which I suspected to be the leaves and
buds of the *kalmia latifolia*, a poisonous shrub.
I was not quite certain, for I had almost forgotten
the little botany which I knew before I went to
China. I took the leaves home with me, to examine
them at leisure, and to compare them with the botanical description ; and I begged that the cook
would not dress the birds till she saw or heard from
me again. I promised to see her or send to her,
the next day. But the next day, when I went to
the library, to look in a book of botany, my attention was caught by some new reviews, which were
just arrived from London. I put off the examina-

tion of the *kalmia latifolia,* till the day after.   To-
morrow, said I, will do just as well, for I know the
cook will not dress the pheasants to-day ; old Hudson does not like them till they have been kept *a
day or two.*

To-morrow came, and the leaves were forgotten
till evening, when I saw them lying on my table,
and put them out of the way, lest my little boy
should find and eat them.   I was sorry that I had
not examined them this day, but I satisfied myself
in the same way as I had done before : to-morrow
will do as well : the cook will not dress the pheasants to-day : old Mr. Hudson thinks them the better for being kept *two or three days.*

To-morrow came ; but, as the leaves of the
kalmia latifolia were out of my sight, they went
out of my mind.   I was invited to an entertainment this day at the mayor's : there was a large
company, and after dinner I was called upon, as
usual, for a song ; the favourite song of

> " Dance and sing, Time 's on the wing,
>   Life never knows return of spring ;"

when a gentleman came in, pale and breathless, to
tell us that Mr. Hudson and three gentlemen who
had been dining with him, were suddenly seized

with convulsions after eating of a pheasant, and
that they were not expected to live. My blood ran
cold; I exclaimed, "My God! I am answerable
for this." On my making this exclamation there
was immediate silence in the room; and every eye
turned upon me with astonishment and horror. I
fell back in my chair, and what passed afterward
I know not; but when I came to myself, I found
two men in the room with me, who were set to
guard me. The bottles and glasses were still upon
the table, but the company had all dispersed; and
the mayor, as my guards informed me, was gone
to Mr. Hudson's to take his dying deposition.

In this instance, as in all cases of sudden alarm,
report had exaggerated the evil: Mr. Hudson, though
extremely ill, was not dying; his three guests, after
some hours' illness, were perfectly recovered. Mr.
Hudson, who had eaten the most plentifully of the
pheasant, was not *himself*, as he said, for two days;
the third day he was able to see company at dinner
as usual, and my mind was relieved from an insupportable state of anxiety.

Upon examination, the mayor was convinced that
I was perfectly innocent: the cook told the exact
truth, blamed herself for not sending to me before
she dressed the birds: but said that she concluded

36 *

I had found the leaves I took home were harmless, as I never came to tell her the contrary.

I was liberated, and went home to my wife. She clasped me in her arms, but could not articulate a syllable. By her joy at seeing me again, she left me to judge of what she must have suffered during this terrible interval.

For some time after this unfortunate accident happened it continued to be the subject of general conversation in Philadelphia. The story was told a thousand different ways, and the comments upon it were in various ways injurious to me. Some blamed me, for what indeed I deserved to be most severely blamed, my delaying one hour to examine the leaves found in the crop of the pheasant; others affected to think it absolutely impossible that any human being could be so dilatory and negligent, where the lives of fellow-creatures and *friends*, and friends by whom I had been treated with the utmost hospitality for years, were concerned. Others, still more malicious, hinted that, though I had been favoured by the mayor, and perhaps by the goodness of poor Mr. Hudson, there must be something more than had come to light in the business; and some boldly pronounced that the story of the leaves of the *kalmia latifolia* was a mere blind, for that the pheasant could not have been rendered poisonous by such means.*

That a motive might not be wanting for the crime, it was whispered that old Mr. Hudson had talked of leaving me a considerable legacy, which I was impatient to touch, that I might carry my adventuring schemes into execution. I was astonished as much as shocked at the sudden alterations in the manners of all my acquaintance. The tide of popularity changed, and I was deserted. That those who had lived with me so long in convivial intimacy, that those who had courted, admired, flattered me, those who had so often professed themselves my friends, could suddenly, without the slightest probability, believe me capable of the most horrible crime, appeared to me scarcely credible.

* " In the severe winter of the years 1790 and 1791, there appeared to be such unequivocal reasons for believing that several persons in Philadelphia had died in consequence of their eating pheasants, in whose crops the leaves and buds of the *kalmia latifolia* were found, that the mayor of the city thought it prudent and his duty to warn the people against the use of this bird, by a public proclamation. I know that by many persons, especially by some lovers of pheasants' flesh, the circumstance just mentioned was supposed to be destitute of foundation : but the foundation was a solid one."—*Vide* a paper by B. Smith Barton, M.D. American Transactions, vol. 51.

In reality, many would not give themselves the trouble to *think* about the matter, but were glad of a pretence to shake off the acquaintance of a man of whose stories and songs they began to be weary, and who had put their names to a subscription which they did not wish to be called upon to pay. Such is the world! Such is the fate of all *good fellows* and excellent bottle companions! Certain to be deserted by their dear friends at the least reverse of fortune.

CHAPTER VI.

My situation in Philadelphia was now so disagreeable, and my disgust and indignation were so great, that I determined to quit the country. My real friend Mr. Croft was absent all this time from town. I am sure, if he had been at home, he would have done me justice; for, though he never liked me, he was a just, slow-judging man, who would not have been run away with by the hurry of popular prejudice. I had other reasons for regretting his absence: I could not conveniently quit America without money, and he was the only person to whom I could or would apply for assistance.

We had not many debts, for which I must thank my excellent wife: but, when every thing to the last farthing was paid, I was obliged to sell my watch and some trinkets, to get money for our voyage. I was not accustomed to such things, and I was ashamed to go to the pawnbroker's, lest I should be met and recognised by some of my friends. I wrapped myself up in an old surtout, and slouched my hat over my face.

As I was crossing the quay, I met a party of gentlemen walking arm-in-arm. I squeezed past them, but one stopped to look after me; and, though I turned down another street to escape him, he dogged me unperceived. Just as I came out of the pawnbroker's shop, I saw him posted opposite to me: I brushed by; I could with pleasure have knocked him down for his impertinence. By the time that I had reached the corner of the street, I heard a child calling after me. I stopped, and a little boy put into my hands my watch, saying, " Sir, the gentleman says you left your watch and these thingumbobs by mistake."

" What gentleman ?"

" I don't know, but he was one that said I looked like an honest chap, and he'd trust me to run and

give you the watch. He is dressed in a blue coat.
He went towards the quay. That's all I know."

On opening the paper of trinkets I found a card
with these words:

"*Barny*—with kind thanks."

Barny! Poor Barny! The Irishman whose
passage I paid coming to America three years ago.
Is it possible?

I ran after him the way which the child directed,
and was so fortunate as just to catch a glimpse of
the skirt of his coat, as he went into a neat, good-
looking house. I walked up and down some time,
expecting him to come out again; for I could not
suppose that it belonged to Barny. I asked a
grocer, who was leaning over his hatch door, if he
knew who lived in the next house.

"An Irish gentleman, of the name of O'Grady."

"And his Christian-name?"

"Here it is in my books, sir—Barnaby O'Grady."

I knocked at Mr. O'Grady's door, and made my
way into the parlour; where I found him, his two
sons, and his wife, sitting very sociably at tea. He
and the two young men rose immediately to set me
a chair.

"You are welcome, kindly welcome, sir," said
he. "This is an honour I never expected, any way.

Be pleased to take the seat near the fire. 'T would
be hard indeed if you *would** not have the best
seat that's to be had in this house, where we none
of us never should have sat, nor had seats to sit
upon, but for you."

The sons pulled off my shabby great-coat, and
took away my hat, and the wife made up the fire.
There was something in their manner altogether
which touched me so much that it was with difficulty I could keep myself from bursting into tears.
They saw this, and Barny (for I shall never call
him any thing else,) as he thought that I should
like better to hear of public affairs than to speak
of my own, began to ask his sons if they had *seen
the day's* papers, and what news there were?

As soon as I could command my voice, I congratulated this family upon the happy situation in
which I found them ; and asked by what lucky accidents they had succeeded so well.

" The luckiest accident ever *happened me* before
or since I came to America," said Barny, " was
being on board the same vessel with such a man
as you. If you had not given me the first lift, I
had been down for good and all and trampled under

* Should.

foot long and long ago. But, after that first lift,
all was as easy as life. My two sons here were
not taken from me—God bless you! for I never
can bless you enough for that. The lads were left
to work for me and with me ; and we never parted,
hand or heart, but just kept working on together,
and put all our earnings, as fast as we got them,
into the hands of that good woman, and lived hard
at first, as we were bred and born to do, thanks
be to Heaven! Then we swore against drink of
all sorts entirely. And, as I had occasionally
served the masons, when I lived a labouring man
in the county of Dublin, and knew something of
that business, why, whatever I knew I made the
most of, and a trowel felt no ways strange to me ;
so I went to work, and had higher wages at first
than I deserved. The same with the two boys :
one was as much of a blacksmith as would shoe a
horse ; and t'other a bit of a carpenter ; and the
one got plenty of work in the forges, and t'other in
the dockyards, as a ship-carpenter. So, early and
late, morning and evening, we were all at the
work, and just went this way struggling on even
for a twelvemonth, and found, with the high
wages and constant employ we had met, that we
were getting greatly better in the world. Besides,

the wife was not idle. When a girl, she had seen baking, and had always a good notion of it, and just tried her hand upon it now, and found the loaves went down with the customers, and the customers coming faster and faster for them; and this was a great help. Then I grew master-mason, and had my men under me, and took a house to build by the job, and that did; and then on to another and another; and after building many for the neighbours, 'twas fit and my turn, I thought, to build one for myself, which I did out of theirs, without wronging them of a penny. And the boys grew master-men, in their line; and when they got good coats, nobody could say against them, for they had come fairly by them, and became them well perhaps for that *rason*. So, not to be tiring you too much, we went on from good to better, and better to best; and if it pleased God to question me how it was we got on so well in the world, I should answer, Upon my conscience, myself does not know; except it be that we never made Saint Monday,* nor never put off till the morrow what we could do the day."

* *Saint Monday,* or St. Crispin. It is a custom in Ireland, among shoemakers, if they intoxicate themselves on Sunday, to do no work on Monday; and this they call

I believe I sighed deeply at this observation, not-withstanding the comic phraseology in which it was expressed.

" But all this is no rule for a gentleman born," pursued the good-natured Barny, in answer, I sup-pose, to the sigh which I uttered ; " nor is it any disparagement to him if he has not done as well in a place like America, where he had not the means ; not being used to bricklaying and slaving with his hands, and striving as we did. Would it be too much liberty to ask you to drink a cup of tea, and to taste a slice of my good woman's bread and but-ter ? And happy the day we see you eating it, and only wish we could serve you in any way what-soever."

I verily believe the generous fellow forgot, at this instant, that he had redeemed my watch and wife's trinkets. He would not let me thank him as much as I wished, but kept pressing upon me fresh offers of service. When he found I was going to leave America, he asked what vessel we should go in. I was really afraid to tell him, lest he should attempt to pay for my passage. But for

making a St. Monday, or keeping Saint Crispin's day. Many have adopted this good custom from the example of the shoemakers.

this he had, as I afterwards found, too much deli
cacy of sentiment. He discovered, by questioning
the captains, in what ship we were to sail; and
when we went on board, we found him and his sons
there to take leave of us, which they did in the
most affectionate manner; and, after they were
gone, we found in the state cabin, directed to me,
everything that could be useful or agreeable to us,
as sea-stores for a long voyage.

How I wronged this man when I thought his expressions of gratitude were not sincere, because they
were not made exactly in the mode and with the
accent of my own countrymen! I little thought
that Barny and his sons would be the only persons
who would bid us a friendly adieu when we were
to leave America.

We had not exhausted our bountiful provision of
sea-stores when we were set ashore in England.
We landed at Liverpool; and I cannot describe the
melancholy feelings with which I sat down, in the
little back parlour of the inn, to count my money,
and to calculate whether we had enough to carry
us to London. Is this, thought I, as I looked at
the few guineas and shillings spread on the table,
is this all I have in this world? I, my wife, and
child! And is this the end of three years' absence

from my native country ? As the negroes say of a fool who takes a voyage in vain, I am come back, *"with little more than the hair upon my head."* Is this the end of all my hopes, and all my talents ? What will become of my wife and child ? I ought to insist upon her going home to her friends, that she may at least have the necessaries and comforts of life, till I am able to maintain her.

The tears started from my eyes; they fell upon an old newspaper, which lay upon the table under my elbow. I took it up to hide my face from Lucy and my child, who just then came into the room ; and, as I read without well knowing what, I came among the advertisements to my own name.

" If Mr. Basil Lowe, or his heir, will apply to Mr. Gregory, attorney, No. 34 Cecil-street, he will hear of something to his advantage."

I started up with an exclamation of joy, wiped my tears from the newspaper, put it into Lucy's hand, pointed to the advertisement, and ran to take places in the London coach for the next morning. Upon this occasion I certainly did not delay. Nor did I, when we arrived in London, put off one moment going to Mr. Gregory's, No. 34 Cecil-street.

Upon application to him I was informed that a very distant relation of mine, a rich miser, had just died, and had left his accumulated treasures to me, " because I was the only one of his relations who had never cost him a single farthing." Other men have to complain of their ill fortune, perhaps with justice ; and this is a great satisfaction which I have never enjoyed; for I must acknowledge that all my disasters have arisen from my own folly. Fortune has been uncommonly favourable to me. Without any merit of my own, or rather, as it appeared, in consequence of my negligent habits, which prevented me from visiting a rich relation, I was suddenly raised from the lowest state of pecuniary distress to the height of affluent prosperity.

I took possession of a handsome house in an agreeable part of the town, and enjoyed the delight of sharing all the comforts and luxuries which wealth could procure with the excellent woman who had been my support in adversity. I must do myself the justice to observe that I did not become dissipated or extravagant; affection and gratitude to my Lucy filled my whole mind, and preserved me from the faults incident to those who rise suddenly from poverty to wealth. I did not forget my good friend Mr. Nun, who had relieved me formerly from prison; of course I paid the debt which he

37 *

had forgiven, and lost no opportunity of showing him kindness and gratitude.

I was now placed in a situation where the best parts of my character appeared to advantage, and where the grand defect of my disposition was not apparently of any consequence. I was not now obliged like a man of business, to be punctual; and delay in mere engagements of pleasure was a trifling offence, and a matter of raillery among my acquaintances. My talents in conversation were admired; and if I postponed letter-writing, my correspondents only tormented me a little with polite remonstrances. I was conscious that I was not cured of my faults; but I rejoiced that I was not now obliged to reform, or in any danger of involving those I loved in distress by my negligence.

For one year I was happy, and flattered myself that I did not waste my time; for, at my leisure, I read with attention all the ancient and modern works upon education. I resolved to select from them what appeared most judicious and practicable; and so to form from the beauties of each a perfect system for the advantage of my son. He was my only child; he was the darling of his mother, whom I adored, and he was thought to be in mind and person a striking resemblance of myself. How

many reasons had I to love him! I doted upon
the child. He certainly showed great quickness
of intellect, and gave as fair a promise of talents
as could be expected at his age. I formed hopes
of his future excellence and success in the world
as sanguine as those which my poor father had
early formed of mine. I determined to watch
carefully over his temper, and to guard him particularly against that habit of procrastination which
had been the bane of my life.

One day, while I was alone in my study, leaning on my elbow, and meditating upon the system
of education which I designed for my son, my
wife came to me and said, " My dear, I have just
heard from our friend Mr. Nun a circumstance
that alarms me a good deal. You know little
Harry Nun was inoculated at the same time with
our Basil, and by the same person. Mrs. Nun
and all the family thought he had several spots,
just as much as our boy had, and that was enough ;
but two years afterward, while we were in America,
Harry Nun caught the small-pox in the natural
way, and died. Now it seems the man who inoculated him was quite ignorant, for two or three
other children, whom he attended, have caught the
disease since, though he was positive that they

were safe. Don't you think we had better have our boy inoculated again immediately by some proper person?"

"Undoubtedly, my dear; undoubtedly. But I think we had better have him vaccined. I am not sure, however; but I will ask Dr. ——'s opinion this day, and be guided by that: I shall see him at dinner: he has promised to dine with us."

Some accident prevented him from coming, and I thought of writing to him the next day, but afterward put it off. Lucy came again into my study, where she was sure to find me in the morning. "My dear," said she, "do you recollect that you desired me to defer inoculating our little boy till you could decide whether it be best to inoculate him in the common way or the vaccine?"

"Yes, my dear, I recollect it perfectly well. I am much inclined to the vaccine. My friend Mr. L—— has had all his children vaccined, and I just wait to see the effect."

"Oh, my love!" said Lucy, "do not wait any longer; for you know we run a terrible risk of his catching the small-pox every day, every hour."

"We have run that risk, and escaped for these three years past," said I; "and in my opinion, the boy has had the small-pox."

" So Mr. and Mrs. Nun thought, and you see what has happened. Remember, our boy was inoculated by the same man. I am sure, ever since Mr. Nun mentioned this, I never take little Basil out to walk, I never see him in a shop, I never have him in the carriage with me without being in terror. Yesterday a woman came to the coach-door with a child in her arms, who had a breaking out on his face. I thought it was the small-pox, and was so terrified that I had scarcely strength or presence of mind enough to draw up the glass. Our little boy was leaning out of the door to give a halfpenny to the child. My God! if that child had the small-pox !"

" My love," said I, " do not alarm yourself so terribly; the boy shall be inoculated to-morrow."

" To-morrow! Oh, my dearest love, do not put it off till to-morrow," said Lucy ; " let him be inoculated to-day."

" Well, my dear, only keep your mind easy, and he shall be inoculated to-day, if possible; surely you must know I love the boy as well as you do, and am as anxious about him as you can be."

" I am sure of it, my love," said Lucy ; " I meant no reproach. But since you have decided that the boy shall be vaccined, let us send directly for the surgeon, and have it done, and then we will be safe."

She caught hold of the bell-cord to ring for a servant : I stopped her.

" No my, dear, don't ring," said I ; " for the men are both out. I have sent one to the library for the new Letters on Education, and the other to the rational toyshop for some things I want for the child."

" Then, if the servants are out, I had better walk to the surgeon's, and bring him back with me."

" No, my dear," said I ; " I must see Mr. I——'s children first. I am going out immediately ; I will call upon them : they are healthy children ; we can have the vaccine infection from them, and I will inoculate the boy myself."

Lucy submitted. I take a melancholy pleasure in doing her justice, by recording every argument that she used, and every persuasive word that she said to me upon this occasion. I am anxious to show that she was not in the least to blame. I alone am guilty ! I alone ought to have been the sufferer ! · It will scarcely be believed—I can hardly believe it myself, that, after all Lucy said to me, I delayed, two hours, and staid to finish making an extract from Rousseau's Emilius before I set out. When I arrived at Mr. L——'s, the children were just gone out to take an airing, and I could not see them. A few hours may sometimes make all the difference between health and sickness, happiness and misery : I put off till the next day the inoculation of my child.

In the meantime a coachman came to me to be hired: my boy was playing about the room, and, as I afterward recollected, went close up to the man, and, while I was talking, stood examining a greyhound upon his buttons. I asked the coachman many questions, and kept him for some time in the room. Just as I agreed to take him into my service, he said he could not come to live with me till the next week, because *one of his children was ill of the small-pox.*

These words struck me to the heart. I had a dreadful presentiment of what was to follow. I remember starting from my seat, and driving the man out of the house with violent menaces. My boy, poor innocent victim! followed, trying to pacify me, and holding me back by the skirts of my coat. I caught him up in my arms. I could not kiss him; I felt as if I was his murderer. I set him down again: indeed I trembled so violently that I could not hold him. The child ran for his mother.

I cannot dwell on these things. Our boy sickened the next week; and the week afterward died in his mother's arms!

Her health had suffered much by the trials which she had gone through since our marriage. The disapprobation of her father, the separation from all her friends, who were at variance with me, my imprisonment, and then the death of her only child, were too much for her fortitude. She endeavoured to conceal this from me; but I saw that her health was rapidly declining. She was always fond of the country; and, as my sole object now in life was to do whatsoever I could to console and please her, I proposed to sell our house in town, and to settle somewhere in the country. In the neighbourhood of her father and mother there was a pretty place to be let, which I had often heard her mention with delight; I determined to take it: I had secret hopes that her friends would be gratified by this measure, and that they would live upon good terms with us. Her mother had seemed by her letters to be better disposed towards me since my rich relation had left me his fortune. Lucy expressed great pleasure at the idea of going to live in the country, near her parents; and I was rejoiced to see her smile once more. · Being naturally of a sanguine disposition, hope revived in my heart; I flattered myself that we might yet be happy, that my Lucy would recover her peace of mind and her health, and that perhaps Heaven might bless us with another child.

I lost no time in entering into treaty for the estate in the country, and I soon found a purchaser for my excellent house in town. But my' evil genius prevailed. I had neglected to renew the insurance of my house; the policy was out but nine days,* when a fire broke out in one of my servants' rooms at midnight, and, in spite of all the assistance we could procure, the house was burnt to the ground. I carried my wife out senseless in my arms; and when I had deposited her in a place of safety, returned to search for a portfolio, in which was the purchase-money of the country estate, all in bank-notes. But whether this portfolio was carried off by some of the crowd which had assembled round the ruins of my house, or whether it was consumed in the flames, I cannot determine. A more mise-

* Founded on fact.

38

rable wretch than I was could now scarcely be found in the world; and, to complete my misfor‐ tunes, I felt the consciousness that they were all occasioned by my own folly.

I am now coming to the most extraordinary and the most interesting part of my history. A new and surprising accident happened.

* * * * * *

* * * * * *

Note by the Editor.—What this accident was can never now be known; for Basil put off finishing his history till TO-MORROW.

This fragment was found in an old escritoir, in an obscure lodging in Swallow-street.

August, 1803.

THE END.